The Other Way Home series:

A Journey by Chance

"Everybody knows everything in tiny Valley Oaks. That puts Gina Philips at a distinct disadvantage when she arrives from California for a family wedding. Had she really thought four weeks in the Midwest would help her recover from a failed relationship, a lost job, and a serious injury? Now, Gina can't shake off Brady Olafsson, a successful Christian author who annoys her with hints of family mysteries. When Gina's mom reveals a long-kept secret, it forever changes how Gina views her family, her future, and her relationship to Brady. First impressions need second looks as Gina witnesses faith in action."
—*Inspirational Market News*

After All These Years

"At the center of The Other Way Home series is a group of warm and loving women, a medley of personalities and lifestyles bound together by their faith. Isabel Mendoza's past is just a faded memory...until Tony Ward arrives in Valley Oaks. *After All These Years,* a novel of old love reunited and new love discovered, demonstrates how the redeeming grace of God can touch the past and bring healing and mercy into present-day life."
—*Inspirational Market News*

Just to See You Smile

"These are the most compelling books that I have read in a long time. The average woman, such as myself, can easily relate to the characters. They are all fresh and unique, yet they are still everyday people. The plot lines run current with today's issues, so a reader does not feel that the story is too 'way out.' Aside from those basics, Ms. John's style made *Just to See You Smile,* as well as the others, a

pure joy to read. I felt great disappointment when the book came to an end. I just hate to let go of the characters, as well as the story."
—*Deborah Piccurelli, author*

The Winding Road Home

"Having just finished reading *The Winding Road Home,* I'm not only pleased to offer this endorsement, but I also want to rush out and buy the rest of the series! Sally John creates unique, endearing characters and makes them live on the page. Their struggles, hurts, and triumphs become as real as those of family or close friends. You'll relish every moment you spend with them."
—*Janelle Schneider, author*

In a Heartbeat series:

In a Heartbeat

WOW! I feel as though I have been away for a while and I didn't want to come back. *In a Heartbeat* was incredible, wonderful, heartwarming, heartaching, loving—I absolutely loved it. We have to stop and remember that we do not always know what is going on in someone else's life and why they are the way they are. We never know the whole story, and that is what I learned from this book.
—*Patti John*

I just finished *In a Heartbeat,* and it was fabulous! I cried for Rachel because I could relate in some ways about wanting a child so very badly and not being able to have one of my own. I dealt with not wanting to go to showers, not wanting to hear about another friend being pregnant, being asked when my husband and I would be having a child, etc. Now I am an adopted aunt and grandma to several young children and babies. Thank you for writing a book on a subject that DOES NOT get talked about even in this day and age. Rachel and Vic's story will always have a special place in my reading life.
—*Carol Hoefs*

FLASH *Point*

SALLY JOHN

HARVEST HOUSE PUBLISHERS
EUGENE, OREGON

Scripture quotations are taken from the New American Standard Bible®, © 1960, 1962, 1963, 1968, 1971, 1972, 1973, 1975, 1977, 1995 by The Lockman Foundation. Used by permission. (www.Lockman.org); from The Jerusalem Bible, Copyright © 1966 by Darton, Longman & Todd, Ltd. and Doubleday & Company, Inc., all rights reserved; from The New English Bible, copyright © Oxford University Press and Cambridge University Press 1961, 1970. All rights reserved; and from The Message. Copyright © by Eugene H. Peterson 1993, 1994, 1995, 1996, 2000, 2001, 2002. Used by permission of NavPress Publishing Group.

Cover by Garborg Design Works, Minneapolis, Minnesota

Published in association with the literary agency of Alive Communications, Inc., 7680 Goddard Street, Ste #200, Colorado Springs, CO 80920.

FLASH POINT
Copyright © 2004 by Sally John
Published by Harvest House Publishers
Eugene, Oregon 97402
www.harvesthousepublishers.com

Library of Congress Cataloging-in-Publication Data

John, Sally, 1951–
 Flash point / Sally John.
  p. cm.—(In a heartbeat series)
 ISBN 0-7369-1314-9 (pbk.)
 1. Emergency medical technicians—Fiction. 2. Chicago (Ill.)—Fiction.
 3. Fire fighters—Fiction. I. Title. II. Series.
 PS3560.O323F55 2004
 813'.54—dc22   2004002780

Printed in the United States of America

05 06 07 08 09 10 11 /BC-MS/ 10 9 8 7 6 5 4

For the Birthday Girls,
Sharon Helms
Vicky Miller
Sally Weckel

Acknowledgments

Many thanks to my "technical support team," who rose graciously to the challenge of explaining emergency medicine to someone who didn't have a clue. While I strove to realistically depict characters and events, the story is purely a figment of my imagination—which has been known to confuse the facts. Misrepresentations are mine and should in no way reflect on the caliber of these professionals. I hold these three in the highest esteem for their unselfish service in the emergency field. My thanks go to:

Matt Shoemaker, graphic designer with Harvest House Publishers and EMT with the Monroe, Oregon, Fire Department.

Nancy Teerlinck, flight paramedic, serving on special assignment as "pig doulah."

Jason Durbin, paramedic with the Chicago Fire Department.

And my thanks go to those who helped with so many details along the way:

Jo Ann Hull, for the connection.

Shana Smith, project editor with Harvest House Publishers, for the *español*.

Cindi Cox, Elizabeth John, Michael Skelton, and Sally Weckel, for eliminating my research time in various ways.

Sandy Carlson, for taking on the role of personal assistant.

My mother, Mary Carlson; Patti John; and Janet Fyfe, for the timely encouragement after they cried through *In a Heartbeat*.

Kim Moore, my editor, for being the world's best. Her wise and gracious fingerprints are on every page.

My "other family" at Harvest House, which includes *everyone* there.

Tim, for loving me no matter what.

I will not wish thee riches nor the glow of greatness,
but that wherever thou go
some weary heart shall gladden at thy smile,
or shadowed life know sunshine for a while.
And so thy path shall be a track of light,
like angels' footsteps passing through the night.

Words on a church wall
in Upwaltham, England

> *There is therefore now no condemnation*
> *for those who are in Christ Jesus.*
> ROMANS 8:1

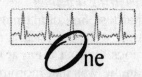

One

Paramedic Terri Schuman leaned against the side of her ambulance, raised her foot, and swung it backward. It hit the vehicle with a resounding thwack.

"Ter!" Kai Rushman, her partner, called from the interior of the rig. He was in the process of disinfecting it, and his voice carried through the open doors. "I could do without the thuds!"

She set her foot on the pavement and left it there. They were both on edge. If Kai's bravado failed, for certain her macho mask wasn't about to stay in place.

The ambulance sat in a parking area near Cutler-Barr Hospital's emergency room entrance. Muggy Chicago heat bounced off the pavement, yet Terri felt chilled to the bone. Huddled in an oversized white cardigan sweatshirt she'd borrowed from a nurse, she closed her eyes and turned her face upward to catch the full effect of the midmorning sun. She tried to blot the emergency run from her short-term memory. It wasn't happening. The aftermath of the call swamped her emotions like a reservoir bursting through a broken dam.

Lord, help him. Help him. Fix his leg. Fix his leg. Oh, God, fix his leg.

She didn't know how else to pray other than in those repetitive phrases. Her friend Rachel would say to just let it all out. It wasn't as if God didn't know what she was thinking anyway. Terri was good at letting it all out no matter who was within hearing distance. Except God. God was...God.

Didn't He want her on her best behavior in His presence? Shouldn't she be respectful? Shouldn't she act like a Christian? After all, she'd been referring to herself as such for months now.

At least he was wearing a helmet.

Kids were the hardest. She didn't have any or want any, probably because they were the hardest. All that helpless vulnerability. It did things like put them at the mercy of idiotic adults. A prime example was that morning's driver. The man had been drunk or high on something, she'd bet her life on it. Friday morning, broad daylight, flying around a quiet neighborhood corner at 40 miles per hour. Not a scratch on him. Walked away. *Walked* away.

God, he's only eight years old!

She squeezed her eyes shut more tightly, as if the motion would wipe clear the images flashing across her mind.

Herself in the ambulance, responding to the dispatcher, acknowledging a Code 3, flipping on lights and sirens, unnecessarily urging Kai to step on it, reading the map with one eye, watching traffic with the other.

On scene. Mass confusion, not all that organized at first. Too many bystanders closing in, some hysterical. Kids viewing the unspeakable.

A car, a grotesque anomaly parked randomly on a terraced front yard, its windshield a spider web of cracks.

The small body and shiny bicycle, twisted into one obscene pretzel.

Blood. Everywhere.

Coworkers, paramedics as well as firefighters, working closely with her and Kai. Working feverishly: stabilize, stabilize, stop the hemorrhage, check his vitals, cut apart the pretzel, start an IV, log roll him onto the board. Gently, gently. *Gently!*

Other firefighters taking care of everything else: carry equipment, keep the crowd at bay, assess the driver's condition, hand him off to the police as soon as possible...remain at the scene, gather wrappings the medics had torn from sterile equipment, hose the street and sidewalk, wash away gas, oil, other fluids....

Terri shook her head. The boy was still in surgery. The boy... Austin. Austin. She didn't want to give him a name. That always made it worse.

Going into surgery, his vitals had been weak but okay. She had lingered outside the operating room. After a while she found an empty desk and wrote her report. She called Susie at dispatch for the log of departure and arrival times. She filled in blanks. She rehashed every action and second-guessed every decision. The exercise was a tangible, final touch that always brought final order to the chaos. Usually a sense of closure followed.

At last, satisfied there was nothing they could have done better or differently, she turned her attention to the inevitable meeting with the parents. She could have skipped it, not thought of it as the inevitable. No one was holding a gun to her head. She could have remained nameless, faceless. The world of those strangers had been ripped apart when they met her. They'd never be able to identify her in a lineup.

But no. That was not Terri's way.

She found the boy's parents in the waiting room and, quite literally, she held their hands. She explained medically as best she could what had happened, what was going on, what the positive signs were. If only she could stick a bandage on their knee or finger, make the hurt go away with an "all-better" kiss! But how did one kiss a heart breaking in two?

She combed her fingers through her short black hair and swung another backward kick against the ambulance.

"Ter!" Kai yelled once more. "Do you mind?"

She blew out a breath.

"Socorro!" a voice shrieked. *"Socorro!"*

At the Spanish cry for help, Terri opened her eyes and looked over her shoulder. Another ambulance occupied the covered drive adjacent to the ER entrance, a short distance from hers. A man and woman stood beside a stretcher and were evidently in the middle of an altercation.

"Socorro!" the female wailed again, flapping her arms about as if to hold the man at bay.

He replied in a loud but calm voice, using the worst rendition of Spanish Terri had ever heard. His vocabulary and phrasing were not even a close cousin to the language.

Without hesitation, Terri walked in their direction. "Help" in any language immediately clamped a lid on all her other thoughts.

The woman was quite short and pleasantly plump, all rounded curves and no angles. Her hair was dark and wavy. She wore a loose-fitting, brightly colored housecoat.

The man's navy blue pants and short-sleeved shirt duplicated Terri's own uniform now covered with the sweatshirt. Even from a distance she recognized his shoulder patches. The bright red-and-white one on the left was a circle surrounded by four tabs. Stitched on it was "Chicago Fire Dept." with a fire hydrant on one side, a pike pole and ladder on the other. At the bottom was a fifth tab, curved like the profile of a rocking chair's foot. Identical to Terri's, it displayed the word "Paramedic."

Quickly crossing the area, she reached them and didn't bother with introductions. She spoke in Spanish directly to the five-foot, dark-eyed woman, asking if she might be of assistance.

Relief soon smoothed the flushed, glowering, late-thirties face. Her eyebrows went up, her voice down, and she succinctly expressed her opinion of the guy standing within arm's reach.

He huffed. "What did she just call me?"

Terri turned to the scowling man and hedged. "Uh, I think 'nincompoop' is about as close as English gets to it."

Now his brows shot up and his jaw muscles grew visible. At least he didn't respond vocally. She guessed him to be a few years older than herself and just under six feet tall. He typified California cute more than Midwest hardy. His hair was short, a shade past dark blond, almost a deep, burnished gold. His tanned complexion reddened. He needed defusing.

She asked politely, "What's the problem?"

He blinked twice before unclenching his jaw. "Twenty minutes ago she was in excruciating abdominal pain, begging to come to the ER. Now she says she's fine and wants to go home." Though his tone remained calm, he raised his arms and let them fall heavily at his side, a gesture of annoyance. Then he faced the Hispanic woman. As he addressed her, his voice rose in that comical way, as if increased volume would shed light on his indecipherable Spanish. He said something about *pushing blood*.

Terri couldn't mask her own annoyance and shouted, "What?"

"I need to check her BP again! What's so hard to understand?" The calm tone was gone. "I told her earlier it was 180 over 95!"

Terri doubted that. Not the numbers, just his translation from English to the woman's native tongue. She changed the subject. "Any family or friends with her?"

"No. She said they all went fishing."

Wasting no more time on him, Terri spoke quietly to the woman. She learned her name was Neva and verified most of the medic's story. He'd missed a few details, such as the friends and family were at *church* and Neva was *pregnant*. Last year she'd lost a baby, which was why she panicked and called 911 when the pains began to strike at six-minute intervals.

Neva agreed to let the "nice lady paramedic" take her blood pressure. As Terri helped her sit on the stretcher, the woman moaned. In one continuous, automatic action, Terri glanced at her watch, lifted the woman's legs onto the stretcher, urged her to lie on her side, felt the tightened abdominal muscles, explained a shallow breathing technique, and then breathed it with her, their eyes locked and hands held.

When the pain subsided, Terri ordered, "Let's get her inside. I'm pretty sure we're in labor here."

"Labor?" The guy stared at her in disbelief. "Why would she be in labor?"

"Only one reason I can think of."

"She doesn't *look*—"

"She doesn't *look?*" She straightened and her voice almost squeaked. "She doesn't *look* pregnant?"

All the anger and fear she hadn't wanted to unleash on God burned in her throat, a torrent of volcanic lava hurtling upward along the path of least resistance. The unsuspecting stranger stood at the receiving end.

"Since when do we assume because of *looks?* Who said you could wear that paramedic patch anyway? Who lets you ride in this ambulance? And who on earth allowed you to step foot anywhere near this woman without some semblance of a working knowledge of Spanish?"

"I speak the language fine! Just because I don't know the vulgar—"

"You don't know vulgar or otherwise. A first-year high school student would have picked up more vocabulary than you did on this run! She's only seven months along but she lost one at this stage. And her family is at church! Where they can probably be reached! Can I have a little help here?"

She kicked off the gurney brakes and pulled, rolling it toward the doors behind her. When she felt the weight lessen, she knew he was pushing from the other end. Too distraught to play nice, she ignored him and focused on Neva's face.

Her eyes expressed fear, but she smiled softly and repeated her earlier assessment of the other paramedic. The phrase encompassed a little more than "nincompoop."

Drawing on her last ounce of willpower, Terri managed not to wink in silent agreement. She'd deal with Mr. Cool Surfer Dude later.

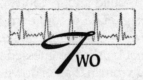

$\mathcal{T}$WO

By late that afternoon, little Austin, pregnant Neva, and Surfer Dude had all faded like yesterday's news from Terri's awareness. Her focus had been jerked in a myriad of directions, feeding her addiction to adrenaline. Typical of days she was on duty, it was fed more regularly than her stomach.

As the siren whooed and Kai expertly guided their ambulance through traffic, he complained. "After this one, Terri, we are unavailable until I eat. No negotiating."

"You are such a weakling, Rushman." She grinned, never taking her eyes from the road. "Watch that guy up there in the white Nissan, on the left. He's in la-la land, changing lanes willy-nilly."

"I'm serious about food."

"Got it, big guy. Don't go passing out on me now."

Terri considered teasing her partner one of the perks of the job. He took it and gave it amiably. Nine years her junior, he was serious about his work. Being tall, broad-shouldered, and blue-eyed with a model's chiseled jaw hadn't spoiled him in the least, and he remained surprisingly unaware of his impact on women. Watching female patients interact with him was worth the price of admission. At times he even blushed to the roots of his buzz-cut dark brown hair.

He usually drew more attention than she did. Her nondescript appearance contributed to that factor. She wore her coal black hair short. Two swipes with a brush secured it behind

15

her ears. Another one across her mop of unruly bangs completed her grooming protocol. Why buy a hair dryer or curling iron? Her eyes were the color of burnt coffee. Why highlight them with makeup? A runner and not a stranger to weights, she was of medium build and in good shape. Still, she found it necessary to exaggerate a confident image. Despite that patch on her sleeve, the public in general did not automatically trust her at first blush. She guessed their hesitancy came because she was a woman, hands down the minority gender in the field.

She and Kai reached the scene. Emergency vehicles lined the four-lane road, strobe lights flashing more brilliantly than the sun from its cloudless sky. Police stood on the highway and rerouted traffic that slowed more from "Looky Lou" drivers than the accident itself. Bystanders clustered here and there. The instant Kai braked, Terri was out the door.

An elongated cry pierced the sweltry afternoon. "Help!"

Fifty yards from its source, Terri discerned sheer terror in the feminine voice that rose above the clamor of traffic and wailing sirens. Conditioned to disregard heat and noise as well as heartrending screams, she stepped over a low guardrail and scuttled down a grassy embankment, her paramedic's drug box bouncing at her side.

"Oh! Oh!" Nonverbal screeches punctuated the words. "Help!"

Terri noted automatically that the patient was, at the very least, breathing. Always a good sign.

The scene imprinted itself on her mind, an intuitive response that bypassed rational thought. As always, the first impression was one of absolute chaos.

The woman's cries emanated from a monstrosity that resembled a car-sized accordion. Front and back ends were scrunched toward the middle. The driver's side abutted a thick tree trunk, making it inaccessible. A policeman bent over the passenger side. That anyone remained within and capable of shrieking was almost incomprehensible. *Almost.* In Terri's 11 years as a firefighter and medic, the paradoxical had become the familiar.

The wreckage sat in a field between the busy four-lane and a wooded area. Another crinkled automobile lay in the distance to its right.

A fire truck's wailing siren tapered off. Medics from a second ambulance now scrambled down the same embankment Terri had just scaled. They headed toward the other car. She knew without turning that Kai was on her heels, bringing oxygen and the backboard. On his heels were firefighters, carrying extrication tools.

Chaos? Yes. But organized chaos. Controlled chaos. Every one of the gathered emergency workers had a well-rehearsed role to play.

"Get me out!" Again the distinct, overriding tone of fear. More fear than pain?

Terri hurried through the thick, calf-high prairie grasses, resisting the urge to sprint. Onlookers would wonder why she didn't race like the wind. She had been asked the question often and always replied she wouldn't be much help with a sprained ankle.

When the scream diminished, another sound assaulted her. To some it would be inaudible. Terri didn't know if she were cursed or blessed with the ability to hear it. Like white noise it blended in with other sound: traffic, sirens, humans shouting, radios blaring, birds singing. Still, it was there. A perceptible *silence*. An overlay of eerie quiet. An absence of breath. An announcement that life was exiting the area.

From the corner of her eye Terri spotted a policeman and two firefighters huddled over a figure on the ground near the other car. *Thrown from the vehicle?*

"No man is an island...any man's death diminishes me..."

The impression registered itself, again an intuitive response that she shoved aside. It would be processed later. Not now, not when a millisecond lost or won could determine the fate of a human being.

Her own task at hand came into sharp focus. Adrenaline had jumped into high gear the instant she'd heard the call four minutes ago. It surged now, blocking all unrelated feelings and thoughts.

Chaos. Organized chaos.

⁓

Terri reached the car, a late-model sport utility vehicle. One of the big ones. An Expedition. Twenty seconds had ticked by since she passed the guardrail.

"Help!" A bloodcurdling scream. "Help!"

"Lady!" The hefty officer kneeling before the passenger door was clearly at the end of his polite rope. "I said calm down!"

In one fluid motion, Terri set the medical box at her feet, pulled on a pair of latex gloves, and nudged the cop's arm.

He turned and heaved a quick sigh of relief. "We'll have to cut her out."

No kidding.

The accordion-like vehicle must have hit everything on its journey from highway to field. Hairline cracks veined the rear and side windows as well as the front windshield, but they all remained intact. The passenger door frame, like the roof and front end, was squished beyond recognition. Prying it open would be impossible. Its window opening was clear, though narrower than its normal width. It was plausibly large enough to accommodate a small dog. Maybe a pug.

"I can't get her to calm down."

"Mmm." On the other hand, a dalmatian could probably squeeze through. "Just the driver inside?" She stepped onto the running board and leaned against the car.

"Yeah— Hey! Be careful. There's glass—"

"Don't mind me. You just stand there and twiddle your thumbs now." She punctuated the impudent remark with a brief smirk.

She hadn't seen any glass. The window must have popped clean out at the time of impact. Tuning out his voice, she inserted her right arm through the narrow opening, wriggled in half a shoulder, and dipped her head.

"Schuman!" That would be Kai wanting to appraise the situation ad nauseam before she proceeded. In her opinion the kid was a first-class paramedic and an expert driver. She seldom questioned his opinion. However, every now and then his response time made the average snail look like Speedy Gonzales.

Terri maneuvered her head into the car, wishing for earplugs. "Miss!"

The woman's eyes were closed, her face a flushed mask of hysteria; tears flowed steadily. Her right hand clutched at the side of her head. She sat in the driver's seat, safety belt still strapped across her shoulder. The airbag drooped, a punctured balloon over the steering wheel. There were minor burns on her forearms, most likely from the bag's escaping hot air. Her legs were out of sight due to numerous odd-shaped protrusions of door, roof, dashboard, and console between the bucket seats.

The whole scene was like a cave of vehicular stalactites and stalagmites. They hemmed the woman in, but miraculously they did not appear to even be touching her.

But then, miracles were known to happen in the midst of chaos.

Terri smelled heat, like steaming metal. There was another scent...not alcohol. A pervading subtle fragrance. Perfume, sweet and pungent. Department store smell. Something designer.

Though the woman sat mere inches from Terri's outstretched hand, she couldn't reach her. Things were in the way, everything crumpled out of place. She elongated her arm until her shoulder blade protested. Sensing movement all around the exterior of the car, she knew the guys were preparing to cut away a section. Their first priority was to give her access to her patient.

As the woman paused to take a breath, Terri said loudly, "Miss! It's okay! It's okay!"

She screamed in reply.

Terri continued to reassure the woman in a firm, calm tone while noting details. The patient was young, mid-twenties, dressed in black slacks and a snug V-necked burgundy knit shirt. Despite tears and the violent impact she'd experienced, her makeup remained in decent shape, as did her short hair, a blonde-streaked brown worn swept up in one of those gravity-defying styles that always mystified Terri. She had the unmistakable appearance of a well put-together cosmetologist. On a better day she was probably perky.

"You're all right! Come on, hon. Come on. Relax now. Just relax."

At last, during time out for another breath, she seemed to hear. Her eyelids fluttered partially open. She turned her head slightly.

"Hi! How you doing?"

The next scream sank a decibel. "Help!"

Terri locked eyes with her and smiled. "That a girl. Keep looking at me. You're going to be just fine. We'll get you out of here in two shakes of a lamb's tail."

The wide eyes were a deep blue, pupil dilation normal. Blood trickled from her forehead along her left temple. A minor cut.

"Oh, please!" Down another decibel.

"My name's Terri, and I'm a paramedic. Here, take my hand."

Trembling uncontrollably, the poor woman had trouble coordinating her movements. At last her hand came near enough for Terri to clasp.

"All right! Contact! Can you take a deep breath for me?" She slid her fingers down to the woman's wrist, reaching for a pulse, and took a deep breath of her own. "That a girl. Do it again. That's it. Nice deep breaths. I need to ask you some questions, but don't shake your head. Okay?"

She lifted her chin.

"No!" Terri didn't want her aggravating any neck injury. "Just say okay."

"O-okay."

"What's your name?"

"Air." Her voice shook. "Air." She swallowed.

"Air!"

"Erin," she blurted the name in one quick gasp. Her face had grown pale. Not a good sign.

"Erin!" *Okay!* Erin, not air. The girl could breathe. "Hi, Erin."

"I'm—I'm claustrophobic."

"Hey, you and me both." She methodically rubbed her thumb on the girl's hand. Latex glove notwithstanding, the touch was still human. "But the rescue guys are here with their handy-dandy tools. They'll get us out in no time. Can you tell me what day it is?"

"Friday."

"And where are you?"

"Chicago."

"Can you tell me what happened? No, don't shake your head."

"I—I don't know. I was driving. I don't know!"

"That's all right. We'll figure it out. The guys are going to do some cutting here. It'll be noisy, and I'll put a blanket over us—"

"My car!" she wailed.

"Cars are replaceable."

Not daring to break eye contact, Terri continued chatting. There was precious little else she could do for the woman except keep her company. She hadn't yet mastered the art of taking blood pressure or inserting an IV with one hand tied behind her back which was, essentially, what the situation felt like.

Come on, guys!

"Erin, do you hurt anywhere?"

Except for her gasping breaths, she was quiet for a moment. "No." Evidently the burns on her forearms were too minor to notice yet. "My left arm's stuck."

Not a surprise. The tree had pressed the door all the way in to her shoulder. "Does it hurt?"

"N-not bad."

"How about your legs?"

"Stuck, but they don't hurt."

Maybe nothing was broken. Maybe there was no internal bleeding. Maybe she wouldn't go into shock. Even if she did have a mild concussion, she was oriented and responsive. Still, Terri felt anxiety bubble within her. Nothing was for certain until she could examine the woman. Two minutes had passed since she'd poked her head through the window. Two minutes! *Now, guys!*

She felt a hand on her shoulder, a blanket brushed against her arm, Kai's communication they were about ready.

"Okay, Erin. The guys are ready to cut. I'm going to get the blanket here—"

"Don't go!"

"I'm not leaving, I promise." Terri squeezed her hand and smiled again. "I'll be right here the whole time. Don't *you* go anywhere."

Erin smiled tentatively.

Now *that* was always a good sign.

Three

Terri and Kai missed the six o'clock dinner hour at the station. The day was a blur of activity, fuller than the average for their 24-hour shift. They rummaged through the refrigerator and pulled together a hasty meal of leftovers.

While on duty in her busy district, Terri measured time in nanoseconds. On a scene, each one was priceless. At the station, each one was to be savored. There might not be enough strung together to finish a meal, a conversation, a nap, or a housekeeping chore.

Kai stood beside the microwave, his nose wrinkled in a look of disgust. "Terri, I'll never understand how you can eat this stuff cold."

She smiled from the nearby table. "I keep telling you it's an acquired taste. Takes years of missed and interrupted meals."

"Well, I can understand eating pizza cold. Maybe." He carried his steaming plate over and sat across from her. "Even macaroni and cheese. *Maybe*. In a pinch. But mashed potatoes? Not on your life."

"But they're *Teague's* garlic mashed potatoes. A classic dish. I'd rather eat a few mouthfuls than get called out while they're heating in the microwave."

He shook his head, disagreeing. "And yet here I am, eating hot ones."

"No, you're not. They're too hot to take a bite. Meanwhile," she pointed her fork at her own plate, "I'm half finished. Mmmm. Kai, you've got to learn to savor the nanoseconds."

He lowered his head and blew a cooling breath across his food.

The kitchen was quiet, much like in a home when the family kicked back after a full day, intent on relaxing. Generally speaking, as calls allowed, the firefighters spent mornings doing household chores, the afternoons practicing drills. Evenings, like now, were for hanging out. They watched television, read, played cards. Terri thought of how friends or relatives would stop by at just such a time and voice disbelief that the group was prepared to respond to any sort of emergency.

Kai glanced at her over his forkful of roast beef. "So, Ter, what do you think my chances are with her?"

She glanced at him. Of course she knew he referred to someone they had treated that day. And the someone would mostly likely be Erin Morgan. The woman was attractive, single, and 25, a year younger than Kai.

Still, Terri feigned puzzlement. "Who in the world are you talking about?"

"How could you not know?" The lanky medic slapped a hand to his chest and his voice rose in dismay. "I transport the love of my life to the hospital in our rig and you don't even notice?"

His melodramatic tendencies could still throw her off guard at times, but she managed to keep a straight face. To grin would give him points in their round-the-clock teasing war. He was not winning this battle.

She scooped a forkful of potatoes and continued to play along. "Okay, give me a minute. Um, would that be the six-year-old who slipped on the pool deck? Hey, she was a cutie. Or maybe the eighty-two-year-old complaining of chest pain? Or the mom with six wild kids who twisted her ankle chasing one of them? No, wait, her husband came home and chased us out. Surely it wasn't the woman who fell down the staircase? She seemed nice enough, but get real, Rushman. She was stoned! You don't want to get involved with that."

He shut his eyes and whispered, "Erin Morgan."

"Oh! Of course! How could I forget Erin Morgan? Well, she definitely wins the 'Miracle of the Week' award." From the condition of the woman's car, she should have been DOA. Her life had been preserved by God long before emergency workers got there. It didn't matter. She would credit the crew for saving her life.

"So." He looked at her. "What are my chances?"

Thinking the question part of his melodramatic playfulness, she continued in like manner. "You know she'll give you the 'Miracle Worker of Her Life' award. That increases your chances at least a hundredfold."

"Do you really think so?"

Oh, no! He was serious?

She stifled a weary sigh by taking a bite of roast beef. *Men.* Developing a crush in the time it took to insert an IV was such a guy thing. Especially when they were in between girlfriends as Kai was.

"I mean," he went on, "she was the naturally grateful type and kept thanking all of us. But it seemed like she was flirting with me while you put the splint on her arm. Do you really think she noticed me in particular?"

She should not add fuel to his fire by pointing out that he attracted female attention no matter what the circumstances. With his good looks, he was a magnet. Though he could be goofy and slow-paced, he was an excellent paramedic. She had seen him under the worst of circumstances and knew she could trust him with her own life. Somehow he exuded that abstract quality of being fundamentally capable. Of course Erin Morgan had noticed him in particular.

"Oh, horsefeathers, Kai. Are you out of practice or what?"

He shook his head. "I don't know."

His forlorn expression toppled her better judgment to *not* encourage his brand-new crush. A few months ago his girl-friend had told him to take a hike. Though Kai hadn't divulged all the sordid details, Terri sensed he'd been deeply hurt.

"Vanessa did a number on you, didn't she?"

He shrugged.

Terri groaned to herself. She shouldn't. She really shouldn't. But she was a paramedic, in the business of helping those who suffered. He clearly needed a shot of emotional morphine. How could she turn her back on him?

"Kai, remember the PEA phenomenon."

"PEA? Uh...give me a hint?"

She wadded up her napkin and threw it at him.

"Just tell me what textbook it's in."

"Rushman!" She clenched her jaw. "Get a grip!"

"What? What'd I do?"

In response she glared. Kai had interned with her. He knew, when he was thinking clearly anyway, that she took it personally if he could not recall information.

"Okay, okay." He held up a hand as if in defense. "I know this. PEA. PEA. Pulseless electrical activity!"

"Yeah, yeah, but we're not talking heart rhythm here."

"Speak for yourself."

"Ha, ha. Come on. Think chemical." She took another bite.

"Chemical? I know! Phenyl something! Right? That would be in chapter— No! It's not in a textbook! It's from Schuman 101. It's, um, phenyl, phenyl—" He snapped his fingers. "Phenylethylamine!"

Still chewing, she rotated her hand, gesturing for more details.

"Phenylethylamine. Um...it's a chemical in the body. Which...which gives an amphetamine-like high during certain life experiences. Such as being newly in love or going through danger!"

"Application?"

He grinned. "Erin Morgan was in danger. I was there. She experienced this chemical response. *Voilá!* She falls in love with me."

"Gold star."

"I better strike while the iron is hot. If we get back to Cutler-Barr tonight—"

"If?" Their 24-hour shift officially started at 8:00 A.M, though they always arrived by 7:00. The real fun didn't begin until after 10:00 P.M., especially on hot, humid Friday nights. Gun shootings, knifings, domestic violence, bar brawls... Terri and Kai would be back at Cutler-Barr Hospital, no ifs about it.

"Right," he said. "While we're there, give me a few minutes to track her down?"

"What makes you think she'll still be there? Broken arms usually go home."

"I overheard her tell the nurse she lives alone. I think she had a concussion. They'll keep her overnight for observation. Wake her up every so often. *I* could wake her up."

"And get her phone number."

He nodded. "I could always just lift it from the report, but I think the personal touch would be better, don't you?"

"I think somebody might have a problem with either approach. Erin, for starters."

"Why would she? She's got that PEA thing working for her. For me. Come on, Ter. She might be long gone by the time I get off tomorrow. We stop in and see patients all the time."

"Not to get their phone number! We are not having this discussion."

Six firemen had walked in. Four joined them at the table.

One of them, named Harlan, asked, "What discussion aren't you having?"

Kai's furrowed brow relaxed. Terri knew what he was thinking: Reinforcements had arrived.

He said, "I want to ask a patient for her phone number."

Harlan replied, "This afternoon's MVA." Motor vehicle accident. "Good-looking chick."

Kai smiled, one bundle of testosterone to another. "Thought I'd look her up at the hospital, get her number. Straitlaced Schuman here doesn't think it's such a hot idea."

Terri kept her face impassive and continued eating. For 11 years, first as firefighter in a downstate unit and then as paramedic with this Chicago unit, she had served as the lone female in all-male companies. Sometimes it was best to simply ignore the conversation.

Harlan grinned now. "Terri's right. I mean, you'll just get your heart broken, kid. The woman was checking *me* out."

"But you're married!"

Duke set a half-gallon carton of Mississippi Mud ice cream on the table. "Not only that, he's bald and ugly."

Harlan laughed. "I didn't say I wanted her phone number. It just goes to show she prefers mature men."

"Bald and ugly," Duke reiterated.

"Right. So, Kai, you don't stand a chance."

The guys hooted. Marty dropped a handful of spoons on the table. No need for bowls. They would all simply dig out of the community carton.

When the laughter died, Marty held out a dark glass bottle. Taped across it was a piece of paper which displayed "Kai" in large block letters.

Marty said, "Hey, Kai, what do you use this for? Is it any good on ice cream?"

"That's not mine. What is it?"

"I don't know. Let's see. The label says 'Molasses.' Hmm. Mo-lass-es." He drew the word out.

Terri bit her lip, delighted that it had been quick-witted Marty to discover the bottle she'd placed in the cupboard that morning.

He went on. "Isn't there some old saying about molasses? Slow as—"

"Schuman!" Kai yelled above the laughter, his face reddening.

The joke was not lost on anyone. Kai's methodical, deliberate pace was well on its way to becoming legendary. That his last name was Rushman didn't help matters. Even if he were the speediest thing on two feet, his name alone would beg for teasing.

Terri laughed loudest of all. "Call me straitlaced, will you?" Kai sputtered.

The alert sounded, a series of electronic tones. All laughter and movement stopped. The dispatcher's voice came over the loudspeaker, directing the engine and ambulance to go. "Respond to Fifty-seventh and Hickory."

Everyone moved now. Terri's personal life went on hold. Would she complete the round of laughter her molasses joke so richly deserved? Savor the nanosecond of one-upmanship over Kai? Enjoy one more bite of nutty chocolate ice cream? Grab a cup of coffee? Brush her teeth? Use the washroom?

Forget it.

Before any more information was relayed, Terri had pulled open the ambulance door. Kai was already behind the wheel starting the engine, not living up to his reputation in the least.

～

Midnight quiet had settled over the firehouse. Most of the guys were asleep. A late-night television talk show could be heard from the adjacent room. Terri sat alone at the long picnic-style table in the fire station's kitchen, newspaper in one hand, coffee mug in the other.

"Hi, Schuman." Lieutenant Walt Kemper strode across the room. "Got a minute?"

"Sure. There's fresh coffee in the pot."

"Great. Need some?"

"No, thanks."

Terri studied his white shirt from the back as he poured himself a cup and thought, not for the first time, that he was rather nondescript. A nice enough guy, fiftyish, hair going to silver, of medium build, in fairly good shape. He knew his stuff. Still, he was no Vic Koski, the man whose shoes he had been trying to fill for a year.

He slid onto the bench across the table from her. "How you doing?"

"Fine." That wasn't true.

There had been a Critical Incident Stress Debriefing after the little boy's accident. A CISD was normal procedure to give any emergency worker involved the opportunity to uncork heavy emotions. She had attended and decompressed to a certain extent. Connecting with her coworkers on a deep level helped, but the camaraderie helped only so far. She needed to vent full force, preferably with her friend Rachel, or her sister Shelley, or Nan, the medic who relieved her tomorrow. A woman. Not the man across the table. She still shied away from revealing any weakness in front of Walt. Something in his tone, something she couldn't put her finger on, always prompted her to keep the macho mask in place.

"Just fine," she repeated.

"Hmm." His eyes shifted away briefly. Clearly he wasn't buying into what she said, but he didn't challenge her. Vic would have expressed his doubt, and she would have said exactly what she was thinking, that she wasn't fine. Perhaps that was the problem with Walt. He never challenged her as he would a man.

Walt cleared his throat. "Um, we had one minor complaint. Cooper asked me to pass it along."

Oh, horsefeathers. He referred to Dwight Cooper, the chief paramedic. What had she done now that reached his ears? An image of herself fussing at Mr. Cool Surfer Dude came to mind. She should have listened to her conscience and apologized on the spot. Now it was too late. None of the medics wore name tags; to advertise their names in public was too dangerous. She felt the tips of her ears grow warm with a guilty flush.

He went on, "About this afternoon's car accident."

Ahh. Not that guy. It was the Erin Morgan incident. She held up a palm. "Oh, let me guess. Our rig wasn't needed because even though we didn't let her, the girl could have walked away."

His smile was polite. "Actually, protocol won out on that one. No complaints about you giving her a ride to the hospital."

"It can't be that we took too long. We got there in two and a half, the engine crew was thirty seconds behind—"

"No, it was more like we didn't take long enough." He shrugged. "The cop you met there said you were out of line to go crawling through the car window."

She laughed at the absurdity of the complaint. "My head and one arm was crawling through the car window?"

"Terri, he's serious. Said you're obviously not a team player, going ahead before the others got there."

"Like I'm going to stand there within reach while the subject freaks out."

"He said you endangered yourself."

"And how did I do that? The car was on solid ground. There was a clear opening. The guys needed a minute to get there and figure things out."

"And they were behind you because you heard the call en route, nearer the scene. The dispatcher understood it to be a multiple-vehicle crash with serious injuries and gave you the nod to go."

"Exactly. Walt, you know what happened."

"I'm just clarifying in case the battalion chief gets wind of it. Turns out the cop is his nephew."

A shirttail relation to big brass. Not too serious. Terri tilted her head toward one shoulder and then the other, stretching tense neck muscles. "And then there's my reputation."

"Yes, there is that."

"Pure gossip. My middle name is *not* Lone Ranger." She suspected the nickname grew from her fierce resistance to condescension toward female paramedics and firefighters. In

the early years, she had an attitude along with a mouth that
tended to freely reveal it. Well, she still had remnants of those
things, but nothing like back then.

"How about Hot Dog?"

She winced. "I don't like that one at all."

"Johnny on the Spot?"

She laughed. "Now, that one's kind of cute. Where did
you hear it?"

"I promised not to tell." Another little smile. "Terri, I've
seen nothing but teamwork from you. And you are the most
exacting stickler for protocol I've ever met."

She cleared her throat, buying time to let his words register. They sure sounded like a major compliment. "Well,
thank you."

"I'm trying to figure out that cop's problem."

"Maybe he just felt silly for not at least poking his head
inside the car. He could have offered her some comfort. I
think his head would have fit."

"Did you snub him?"

"I didn't waste any words on him, which is different from
snubbing. Normal procedure under the circumstances. And I
didn't yell at him either."

Walt sipped his coffee. "I wouldn't worry about it. The guy
probably just wants to ask you out."

She laughed with him, but wondered if the complaint
would be formalized and end up on her record. If push came
to shove, would the lieutenant vouch for her? In spite of his
supportive words, the truth was he'd only known her a year.
Besides that, she hadn't yet reached the point of total trust in
him. Or, for that matter, most of the male species.

Four

Five minutes after eight the next morning, Terri shut the rear ambulance doors with relief and gratitude. Her shift was over, and 72 free hours awaited. She and Kai had even managed to restock their vehicle with medical supplies that were kept at the station before signing off to the next shift. In the past 24 hours they hadn't lost a patient. There was only one wild goose chase: a shooting turned out to be kids, firecrackers, and no injuries. They had helped a lot of people, had probably literally saved one life during a cardiac arrest. They had even slept between 1:30 and 3:17 A.M. During one run to Cutler-Barr she learned Neva the pregnant Hispanic had given birth to a healthy baby girl, her sweet husband at her side, and Austin, the eight-year-old boy, was not going to lose his leg. *Thank You, Lord.*

She spun around to face Kai. "Smile, partner! We're going home! And right on schedule!"

He leaned against the wall, his face not as jubilant as it should have been given the circumstances. Terri placed her hands on her hips. Kai had been her partner for two years. Before that he had served as an intern with her. He didn't need to say a word. She knew what was bugging him.

"Kai, she'll show up with a cake or something."

His mouth grew lopsided with the familiar smile that conveyed he wasn't totally buying into the premise. "PEA guarantees it." He raised a hand for a halfhearted high five.

She slapped it. "Absolutely. Erin Morgan can easily find what firehouse you're from. You can wipe that pitiful lovesick teenager expression off your face."

"The hospital sent her home last night! Do you believe that? I still can't believe that."

"And I can't believe you're thinking about this now." She grabbed her backpack from a nearby bench with one hand and his elbow with the other. "Come on. You're giving me a ride home, remember?"

"Why am I doing that?"

"Because my car is at my brother's shop being repaired." She pulled him around to the front of the rig and out the large opened garage door into the morning sunshine.

"Ter, did I bring you here yesterday?"

"Yes."

"Hmm. I don't remember that."

"Did I ever tell you about the time I ended a shift and couldn't remember where I parked? The lot had been full, so I parked on a side street. It took me an hour to find my car."

He laughed. "We're like zombies every fourth day."

"Would you trust this person with your life?" She mimicked a bowlegged sailor, hand on brow, worriedly scanning the horizon. "I see smoke, but where's the fire?"

His laughter grew into a slaphappy rumble. "Don't you just love it?"

She did. She totally loved it, despite the fact that she had been squeezed through the wringer both professionally and personally over the past year. Maybe it was still fallout from all the changes. Normal procedure. Whatever.

She and Kai walked along the sidewalk around the brick firehouse. It resembled a family's yard. Colorful summer flowers bloomed profusely at the base of the building, their fragrance billowing across the well-manicured lawn. Even now at 8:15 in the morning—when sandpaper had replaced her eyelids, when her neck and shoulder muscles felt like twisted rope, when her stomach churned from what had indiscriminately been added to it—even now she loved it.

"So, Ter, I guess you owe me. You know, for the rides."

She peered up at him. The forlorn expression was back. "Uh-uh. No way. Patient records are confidential. I will not look the other way while you copy down Erin Morgan's phone number."

"Then maybe I won't give you a ride home."

"Maybe she's in the phone book!"

"Hey, isn't that your dog?"

Terri looked toward the parking lot. A haze of strawberry blonde fur streaked across her vision.

"Zoë!" She locked her knees, spread her arms wide, and received the full force of the 100-pound golden retriever's love attack. "Hi, girl! Hi!"

Terri knelt and hugged; Zoë slobbered dog smooches and pranced, nearly losing her balance from the fierce wagging of her tail. Relishing the expression of wild joy, Terri kept her eyes lowered, delaying the inevitable.

There was only one reason Zoë greeted her in the parking lot. His name was Lee Reynolds.

Lee.

The ex-boyfriend.

The proverbial thorn.

⌒

"Lee, I can't keep her today!" Frustration punched Terri's voice up into whine stratosphere. She hated the sound. Hated the evidence that he still tripped her trigger.

"She's your dog!" Lee's voice had risen to the level of a disappointed football coach in the locker room at halftime with a team down by three. He was capable of making himself heard across the field in the middle of a game with a stand full of vociferous, disgruntled parents.

They still had a ways to go before somebody called the cops on them for disturbing the peace. Standing nearly toe-to-toe with him, she didn't back down. She no longer noticed his dark wavy hair or muscular physique.

She continued. "I haven't slept in twenty-four hours!" Those 40 winks at two in the morning did not count. "I have training this afternoon. I don't have my car!" She didn't mention the obvious, which he already knew: Pets were not allowed in her apartment building. The last time she'd kept Zoë for a few days, someone had complained.

"And you *know* my August schedule! Double practices. School starts next week."

"It's Saturday!"

"What's your point? We still practice and I happen to have plans for later! *Your* dog has been cooped up for days on end." He pressed his lips together, and his nostrils flared.

She knew he had more to say, but the words had already been said at least once within the past six months. Clenching her own jaw to prevent spewing forth more unnecessary verbiage, she glanced away. Kai wrestled with Zoë on the lawn, two innocent bystanders frolicking in the sunshine until the coast was clear.

How had she gotten herself into such a mess? She shook her head. That was the easy question.

Part one: Four years ago her little brother Jimmy lay on the 30-yard line, not moving after two punk football players from a rival high school team tackled him. It didn't matter that two EMTs sat at the end of the field in an ambulance. She made it onto the field three steps behind the coaches and trainers. After all, Jimmy was *her* brother and she'd had more training than any of those guys, say by about a few hundred hours or so. Of course the head coach wasn't aware of either of those facts. He blew his stack; she ignored him and maintained her professional cool.

Later at the hospital, when she fell apart, Coach Lee Reynolds apologized and offered a shoulder just the right height for crying on. Jimmy was fine. Lee invited her to dinner the next evening.

He epitomized everything she thought she wanted in a man. He was aggressive, passionate about his work as a high school coach and biology teacher, and an adrenaline junkie like herself. Tall, dark, nearing 40 but still in excellent physical shape. Love at first sight.

Integrity issues didn't surface until much later.

Part two: Zoë had been a gift from the grateful parents of a little boy whom Terri spotted across a restaurant, choking to death. She cleared his airway and administered CPR. A few months later they presented her with a purebred golden retriever with papers, named the Greek word for "life" in tribute to what she had done. Zoë bumbled into the firehouse, covered in beautiful reddish-gold silken fur, uncoordinated on paws huge enough for a dog three times her size. Love at first sight. Again.

Part three: The breakup with Lee six months ago. She moved from the home they shared, one side of a duplex where pets were allowed. The only place she could afford on her own was a dinky studio apartment, no animals whatsoever permitted. Lee agreed to keep Zoë. He was crazy about the dog—when it was convenient to be so.

How she had entangled herself in the mess was clear-cut. The tough question was how to get out of it.

"Terri?" Lee's hands were still on his hips. Zoë's leash dangled at his side.

A word popped into her head. It was a vulgar word, used by people of limited vocabulary or those who enjoyed the punch of profanity. Until recently, she had been one of the latter.

Lee snickered. "God must be proud of that."

Evidently the word had popped right on out with her exasperated breath. "Lee, just go. Give me the leash."

He handed it to her, turned on his heel, and walked away. "Bring her by tomorrow afternoon." With that he was gone.

No apologies for his mockery of her faith. Not that she expected one.

Kai appeared at her side. "Why do you let that doofus walk all over you?"

"Well, he was right about Zoë. She is my dog."

He took the leash from her and knelt to hook it onto Zoë's collar.

"Kai, I have a big favor to ask. Will you take me to my parents' house instead?" Her apartment was on his way home. Her parents' house with its fenced-in backyard and spare bedroom was most definitely not.

"Oh, I don't know. I'm pretty tired to be driving miles out of my way. And the price of gas these days... Of course we could probably strike a bargain. Let's see, what could you do for me?"

She grabbed the leash from him. "If Erin Morgan comes in, I will ask her for her phone number."

"Not good enough. If she comes in, I'll ask her myself."

"Kai!" She stomped to the parking lot, Zoë bounding alongside.

He followed. "Think of how you're depriving this woman of my company. Trust me. Someday she will thank you for getting us together."

"You certainly don't have any ego problems." She reached Kai's small-sized pickup and released the rear gate. "Up, Zoë."

"Down, Zoë!" He grabbed the dog's collar. "No helpee, no ridee, Schuman. Pity. I was really looking forward to cruising along and watching Zoë's mandibles flap in the wind back here."

She couldn't help but laugh. "Okay, okay! I'll do what I can. She's probably in the phone book." There couldn't be that many Morgans in Chicago, could there?

Terri was able to sleep anywhere at any time of the day or night, especially after a busy 24-hour shift. Sunshine? No problem. Not at home? No problem. Run-in with Lee?

Problem. Apparently a huge problem.

She flipped onto her stomach, shoved aside the pillow, and buried her face against the mattress. The crisp sheets smelled of fresh air. Her mother was a laundry fanatic. During summers when she was off from her job as teacher's aide, Maria Schuman wore a path in the lawn between the back door and the clothesline. Terri heard her out there now, even through windows shut because the air conditioner ran. Maria shooed Zoë to the other side of the yard, her stern tone a slim disguise for her real feelings. Like everyone in the family, she loved the dog. She just didn't want the animal living at her house.

Terri wriggled around to her back and groaned. Her nerves felt like a glob of electrical wires twisted together.

Maybe she'd ask her parents again to take Zoë. Maybe now they would agree and thereby eliminate the sole reason for her to communicate with Lee.

Is that why you don't find a place for Zoë? So you have an excuse to keep talking to him?

Her good friend Rachel had asked that. It was a fair question, though it rankled Terri because it was true. But that was three months ago. Somewhere along the way she had lost all desire to talk to him. *Yes, I have. I really have!*

A sense of peacefulness nuzzled the edges of her discomfort.

Thank You, Lord.

Serenity flowed now, pushing aside anger and self-pity.

Why did it surprise her? Every time? Just the simple recognition of God's presence... Even after she had more or less ignored Him for days on end.

She rolled, hung over the side of the bed, reached into her backpack on the floor, and pulled out her cell phone. A minute later Rachel Koski answered on the other end, from the middle of nowhere in Iowa.

Terri cut short the exchange of pleasantries with a rendition of the morning's main event. "And just now, this very minute, I realized I don't care if I talk to Lee anymore. I simply don't need to go there!"

Rachel whooped and laughed. "Oh, Terri! Hallelujah."

Terri loved her friend's deep, rich laugh. She had heard it rarely over the past year. In her mind's eye, she saw Rachel, wide mouth smiling, eyes lit up. Like Terri, she was practical and despised wasting time. She was probably cleaning her kitchen and writing a to-do list while they spoke.

"Okay, so now what?"

"First I'll ask my parents to keep Zoë. Again. She's the only reason our paths have to cross. If Mom and Dad say no, I'll start apartment hunting. Again."

The line was silent for a moment. "How about praying?"

Terri blew out a breath. "Guess that's why I called you, to remind me. Rache, when does it become automatically my first response?"

"Nobody gets totally there. But it increases with time. You've told me about some situations when you've been at a scene and it's on your mind."

That was true. At emergencies she sensed she prayed, not consciously and not at the time things were happening, but later. There was an awareness that subconsciously, as if from some level of her mind or heart that had never before existed, she prayed for the injured people, for their families, for the crews.

She said, "Yeah. Can I tell you about this little boy? Do you have time?"

"Of course."

Terri proceeded to describe the emergency and her feelings.

"See, Terri? You prayed for his leg and God answered."

"Really?"

"Yes, really. And I know it's a two-way street. You hear God communicate things to you."

"Yeah."

There'd been subtle nudges. Like some undiagnosed infection, they took hold of her and she couldn't shake them. She didn't understand the whys and wherefores, only that if she didn't live by them, she would no longer be able to look at herself in the mirror.

One nudge convinced her that living with Lee was, quite simply, wrong. That was when she had given him the ultimatum: If they didn't marry, she was moving out. The decision went against every pragmatic bone in her body. Her down-to-earth attitude bit the dust. What had happened to the facts? She and Lee cared for each other, got along well, shared similar goals, could stretch their dollars much further by combining households. Why not live together? She didn't know, couldn't explain it coherently. Lee thought she'd lost touch with reality.

On the contrary, a dimension was added to reality. Ending their relationship paralleled jumping from a nine-story building and remaining conscious. Every part of her being cried out in pain. She still loved him. She missed him. To top it all off, she missed her dog. But...she felt an unfamiliar, undeniable sense of well-being overwhelm her at odd moments. Hints that she was on the right track.

"Terri, are you praying every day? Reading the Bible somewhat regularly?"

"N-no."

"Those are the basics, hon. The line gets clogged between us and Him if we don't use it regularly. The world's dingy perspective gums it all up."

With anyone else, Terri would have recited a host of reasons why the word "regular" was not in her frame of reference. She had moved from Lee's to her sister's to the dumpy apartment, all within a matter of months. She was adjusting to her new home and neighborhood. Her schedule was always changing. Yada, yada, yada. But Rachel was hard-nosed. She crumbled rationalizations with a look. No way would she buy into an excuse.

Rachel murmured, almost as if to herself, "Maybe it's time."

"For what?"

"Church."

In the six years since they'd first met, Rachel had never condemned Terri's behavior or attitude or lack of faith. She never dogmatically dictated what she should or shouldn't do. She simply loved her unconditionally. Her gentle suggestions pulverized all defenses.

Terri took a deep breath. "Church?"

"Mm-hmm."

She had a hundred and one biases against church. They were all imbedded in two childhood memories. When she was four years old, Grandma Delgado took her to church to be baptized. Terri vaguely recalled a crowd of people standing around while water dripped down her face. What happened later at home she remembered clearly. Her parents and grandparents argued loudly over the event, which her father learned of after the fact. Terri had become hysterical.

Her second encounter with church occurred soon after Grandpa Delgado's death, when Terri was nine. Her mother and grandmother thought it was time the five Schuman children—the youngest two hadn't yet been born—go to Sunday school. Her father ignored the entire discussion and their subsequent Sunday morning trip. His wife and mother-in-law must have nagged the fight out of him by then.

Terri found the experience mortifying. She wore the wrong clothes, sang off-key, had never heard of Jonah, Jacob's ladder, or that queen who wasn't allowed to talk to her husband. Even at that age she'd adopted Scarlett O'Hara's attitude of not thinking about uncomfortable subjects. She sloughed off the experience. That worked until the following Sunday when her mother told her to get ready for church. She became hysterical—again. Her dad intervened and the subject was dropped. Humiliation at the hands of adults and children alike had carved a deep wound. Now, a lifetime later, the scar tissue still itched.

"Terri, you were nine years old." Rachel read her mind. "You are beyond letting the opinions of others define you."

"They don't. I really don't care about opinions. However, I do care about sticking out like a sore thumb. You told me people at your old church here huddle in groups and pray out loud. I'm just getting the hang of praying by myself. Sometimes. I'd stick out like—"

"Go to Bryan's church."

Reverend Bryan O'Shaugnessy was a mutual friend, an Episcopal priest, a part-time chaplain for her battalion.

"What difference—"

"You know him, and the entire service is printed on a cheat sheet."

"And why..." She took another breath. They trod groundbreaking territory. "Why is it I should go?"

"Hon, you need others. We all do."

No man is an island?

Maybe Lone Ranger was her middle name after all.

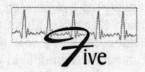

Five

Not yet fatigued after her conversation with Rachel, Terri lay in the bed at her parents' house and watched the mid-morning sunlight dance on the white plaster ceiling. Her friend's words tumbled about in her head until their main thrust rose to the top. *Pray. Read. Those are the basics.*

She sat up and fished her Bible from her backpack. Although she hadn't opened it in a couple of weeks, it always traveled with her in the bag.

"Okay, Lord. Here I am, asking for help. First off, thank You for curing me of Lee."

She smiled. She *was* cured. Gone was that clinging, unhealthy, woe-is-me-I'm-lonely nonsense she'd interpreted as love. How pathetic! She'd longed for him when he mocked her faith and even when he latched onto a new girlfriend only weeks after the separation. At least the pain had dwindled. She searched for it now and found only a vague hope that he would change. For his own sake, not hers.

"So why is it I got upset with him today?" She closed her eyes. "Lord, I am obviously not there yet, not where Rachel says You can take me. Please show me the way?"

She opened the Bible to the bookmark where she'd left off reading. A word jumped out at her. *Wrangling.*

"Wrangling. That about sums up our encounters." She read more. "'*What I fed you with was milk, not solid food, for you were not ready for it; and indeed, you are still not ready for it*

44

since you are still unspiritual.' Okay, yeah. We agree. I am unspiritual. Moving right along... *Isn't that obvious from all the jealousy and wrangling that there is among you, from the way that you go on behaving like ordinary people?'* Yep, that's me, unspiritual and ordinary. Jealous of his girlfriends, jealous that he got to stay in the duplex and keep my dog. Wrangling every chance I get at cops and cool surfer dudes."

She slid back down into a prone position and whispered, "Unspiritual, ordinary, jealous. Floundering at work and at that crummy studio apartment. Pretending that driver's death yesterday didn't affect me." She yawned. "I'm not exactly church material, am I?"

Whatever.

"Scarlett and I will think about it tomorrow. Or the next day."

~

In the end, Rachel's words drowned out Scarlett's. They grew too weighty to ignore. Terri borrowed her mother's car and drove to St. James Episcopal Church on Ashland, Bryan O'Shaugnessy's church.

She hesitated on the steps leading up to a pair of tall red doors. According to the year carved into a cornerstone, they were the entrance to a large stone building 175 years old. The edifice intimidated her beyond measure.

Ridiculous. Over the course of her career she had entered countless structures, never deterred by their size, age, or sheer unfamiliarity. But then, those buildings were either on fire or housed someone in dire need of medical attention.

In her mind she saw two little girls wearing party dresses and ribbons in their long hair. They whispered, snickered, and pointed at her, specifically at her shoes. The memory dimmed and she saw the black oxfords on her feet. Her childhood shoes would have been similar: casual, practical, comfortable. They were probably the once-white canvas tennies she wore all the time unless there was enough snow on the ground to require wearing her brother's hand-me-down boots. And, like today, she would have worn slacks, not a party dress.

Lord, could we do something about this old tape? Like yank it out of the tape deck! I'm a grown woman and I want to go inside this church.

She eyed the tall doors again. *I think I do.*

Something told her she did. At the stress debriefing session, she had aired emotions of anxiety and helplessness. She was angry at the driver who had hit the boy. She felt empathy in the extreme for Austin's parents. The word "empathy" resounded in her own ear. What did she know about empathy? She wasn't a parent.

Shawn Leonard, a young firemen, latched onto the word. He had three little ones at home. On the scene he was Terri's right-hand man until she left in the ambulance. Of course, he would feel a bone-deep empathy. He said he was going to church to be quiet, pray for the family, and let God heal the horror that lingered.

It was a new thought. Not so much the praying for the family and letting God heal. Those things she had experienced to some degree. She would never doubt God's reality again, of that she was sure. But Rachel's suggestion on the heels of Shawn's idea nagged. Was there some added dimension to be experienced within the walls of a church building? Something the hospital chapel didn't offer?

She chose St. James because Rachel had recommended the place and Bryan was an acquaintance. While she trusted Kai with her physical life, she trusted every other part of herself to those two.

Bryan was known around the department. He was a regular sort of guy who had counseled her in the past. She remembered the first time she met him. If not for his clerical collar, she would have guessed he was a lumberjack. He was a big man with an Irishman's curly red hair, clear green eyes, and friendly manner.

She had sought him out after one of her early experiences with death as a Chicago paramedic. The situation hadn't been all that traumatic, comparatively speaking. A simple cardiac arrest involving an 82-year-old was more or less over by the time she arrived. Only she and her partner had been present. She already knew how to wear the macho mask from having to prove her mettle as a firefighter with another all-male company, but a code in the back of her ambulance threw her for a loop. Bryan let her unravel without losing face.

Kai and others still had the ability to "stuff" the fallout from regular encounters with battered babies, drug overdoses, and death. But some of the men opened up more at the CISD sessions than in previous years. Sensitivity was an acceptable form of behavior. The ironic thing was she held back, struggling to maintain a tough exterior, still feeling the need to prove herself in a male-dominated environment.

Or still battling to be accepted, period.

She pulled open the heavy red door and stepped inside. Though she had been in Bryan's office twice, she had never even seen the church proper. She found herself in a tiny foyer, facing another set of double doors and inhaling the stuffy scent of aged wood. With a deep breath, she pulled open a smaller, creaky door.

The scene before her was like something out of a movie. A grouping of votive candles, some of them lit, were on a stand at the back wall near the door. The ceiling was vaulted with wooden cross beams. The wood floor shone. As she entered, it creaked like the door. An expanse of pews filled most of the area. Stained-glass windows lined both side walls, colorful depictions of what she assumed were Biblical scenes. The only light came from the late afternoon sun filtering through them. At the front she glimpsed a pulpit off to the side and, in the center, a rectangular table covered in a white cloth. Behind that the area narrowed. A large cabinet-like structure dominated the space. Made of carved wood, it went from floor to ceiling, side wall to side wall, like an old-fashioned, ornate wardrobe. Flowers and tall, unlit candles adorned it.

Her eyes feasted on the unfamiliar surroundings, but there was something else, something not visible.

She needed to sit down. Her footsteps echoed as she made her way to the last row of pews.

Perhaps it was the quiet, a total absence of human sound in the midst of the city, a distinct hush quieting even her own mental voice. Perhaps it was the simple beauty of wood and of sunlight sparkling in a stained-glass window. Perhaps it was the layers and layers of prayers spoken within these walls, 175 years worth of accumulated thanksgiving, requests, and sins confessed, of thanks received, needs answered, and wrongs forgiven.

Whatever it was, that something else immediately relieved Terri of her macho mask. She noticed an odd contraption at her feet, like a miniature padded bench with upended legs. Leaning over, she pulled gently and it went down, a perfect accommodation for bent knees.

She slipped onto it, rested her arms on the pew in front of her, and let that something else do its work.

A summer thunderstorm raged outdoors, but Terri's own storm had receded to a significant degree. The time spent crying on her knees the previous day had been a cathartic experience she didn't want to spend much time analyzing for fear it would disintegrate. Instead she faced the one cloud remaining on her horizon.

"Lois, I have to apologize to Mr. Surfer." Terri addressed the woman who sat across the hospital cafeteria table.

"Agreed." Lois Quayle fingered the short pearl-white curlicues that covered her head. "Since you didn't do it when you were *with* him. I can't believe you didn't even introduce yourself. You're a professional, for goodness' sake."

"All right already, *Mom!*" The woman was like a second mother to her. Terri had known Lois forever, as far back as she could remember. She was short and attractive, always somewhat formal in appearance and demeanor, wearing tailored clothes that accentuated her still feminine shape.

"That tone will get you nowhere fast, young lady."

Terri sat on her hands, stifling the urge to fling her coffee cup across the large cafeteria. "Okay, okay. I was unkind and contentious. Satisfied?"

Lois smiled in that enigmatic way of hers.

"Please, Lois. You're on a first-name basis with every medic who walks through the ER door. Who is he?"

"Eat up, punkin." Her voice was low and even with a not-so-subtle hint of unflappable authority, ideal for her position as admitting clerk in the ER at Cutler-Barr. "You look like an undernourished raccoon with those dark circles around your eyes."

She dutifully removed one hand from under her thigh, picked up the turkey salad sandwich in front of her, and took a bite.

"You're getting too old to mainline junk food."

In hopes of forestalling a familiar dietary lecture, Terri nodded and quickly took another bite.

"His name is Gabe Andrews. *Gabriel* Andrews. *Angel* of a guy. And for the record, you had no business chewing him out."

Of course Lois had waited until Terri was literally chewing food before unleashing her own reprimand.

"I don't care how bad his Spanish is!" The authoritative quality in her voice mushroomed. "He's a good one. Wouldn't harm a fly if his life depended on it. You've come a long way, Miss Sassy, but that quick tongue of yours has annihilated your better judgment once again."

"I said I'm sorry! And I will tell him that! It was just bad timing, what with the apartment and missing Zoë and—"

"And life is difficult."

Terri frowned. "How come you never let me whine or make excuses?"

Lois allowed herself a brief smile. "Gabe's with Engine Company Eighty-Nine."

"What was he doing on the ambulance?"

"He subs now and then."

Another adrenaline junkie. Not enough fires to feed his habit. Nothing like a good cardiac arrest to get one's own heart pumping. She smiled to herself, remembering how a little Hispanic woman had set him off.

"Terri, how's your father?"

"What do you mean how's my father? You see him more than I do." Bob Schuman Sr. was as much a fixture at Cutler-Barr as was Lois. He'd worked in the area of food service since long before his third child was born.

"Exactly." Lois shifted her powder blue eyes toward the table and fiddled with her coffee cup.

Was she laying a guilt trip on Terri? Unlikely. The woman could maintain order in an emergency room full of disgruntled, combative, not-so emergency patients. That authoritative tone of hers melded together with an indiscriminate compassion. Like some grandmother-slash-Army general in a field full of hurting soldiers, she packed a powerful punch. She wouldn't waste time creating a guilt trip.

"Lois, is there something I should know about Dad?"

"It's not my place."

Her throat went dry. *Dear God.*

"Just ask him. Ask your mom. And keep asking. It's nothing definitive. They're not going to mention it unless you hound them because they don't want to needlessly alarm any of their children. But you didn't hear it from me, okay?"

"'Nothing definitive.' He had a test. All the results aren't in yet."

Her friend glanced away.

Terri knew she had guessed correctly.

"You didn't hear it from me," Lois repeated.

"Okay." Her dad was in pretty good shape for 62. He watched his diet, walked nightly. It would be the smoking. All those years of a pack and a half a day. It would be his lungs. A tumor—

"Terri." Lois reached over and placed a hand atop hers. "Don't diagnose. Just ask them."

The brief thunderstorm had given way to sunshine and dense humidity by the time Terri arrived at Gabe Andrews' fire station. She walked up to a few guys who were washing a truck on the driveway and asked for him.

A young fireman grinned and gave her a sweeping head-to-toe once-over. "Andrews? Where's he been hiding you?"

"*Excuse* me?"

The grin faded. "Uh, I meant, uh—" A large wet sponge smacked the side of his red face. "Hey!"

There was laughter from the other guys working around the truck. One of them approached her with his hand extended. He wore the light blue shirt of an engineer, the firefighter who drove the truck and ran the pump. "Hank Stockwell."

She accepted his handshake. "Terri Schuman."

"Please ignore Ben here. It's just that we're not sure how to act. A woman hasn't come looking for Andrews since 1954."

She laughed. "He's not that old."

Hank smiled. He was a big man with sandy hair and a grandfatherly personality. "Gabe's off today. Can I help you with something?"

"No, thanks. We sort of worked together at the hospital the other day. I was going to let him know what happened to the woman." That was the truth, as far as it went. "No big deal."

"Well, he's just down the street."

"Oh?"

"Weekend soccer tournament. He's coaching some of the neighborhood kids." He pointed to the right. "Three blocks, hang a left, and you'll see a school. Field's behind it."

"Okay, thanks."

Terri walked in the direction he indicated. Her old Blazer sat half a block away, between her and the new destination. Once again she felt the impulse to chuck the whole idea, hop in the car, and head on home. And then introspection took over. It gave her the sense of a brick wall rising up within her. The impulse to bolt rushed headlong into the wall. *Kersplat.* Obviously the impulse was an idiot. She should keep going.

The solid wall came, she knew, from her disregard to the subtle nudge to apologize to Gabe Andrews after they'd wheeled Neva into the ER and handed her off to a doctor. Instead she had turned on her heel and flippantly called over her shoulder, "Your run sheet." At least she hadn't voiced her other thought: *And don't forget to write into the report that she's pregnant!*

She'd blown the perfect moment when she should have apologized. The guy had made a mistake, true. He couldn't speak Spanish, true. But those facts gave her no right to treat him with such blatant disrespect. Now she had a brick wall to contend with. No getting over it, around it, or through it. She had to annihilate it. Fortunately, she had the ammunition.

A year ago introspection had begun to open her mind to the concept of the Holy Spirit. Up to that point, she had never considered that God would bother to communicate with her. The nudges began then, nudges to do the decent thing—even if it made her look like a weirdo. The thought of using love and forgiveness as weapons of mass destruction took hold. She felt gratitude flow through her like a burst of endorphins.

"Thank You, Lord," she whispered, "for not giving up on me."

⌣

Terri scanned the soccer field. It was a makeshift affair with one rickety goal net propped on the infield of a baseball diamond that had seen better days 30 years ago. Gabe Andrews was easy to spot. His golden hair shone like a beacon amid darker shades of brown and black.

She had walked through a neighborhood full of colorful storefronts, some boarded up. Many of their signs were written in Spanish only. Run-down apartment buildings were plentiful. There were yards full of late-summer flowers, but the houses were old and in need of repair. She had noted the narrow firehouse scrunched between a small market and beauty shop, with no green space beside it.

The low-income status of the area was obvious. Gangs, drug dealers, and violence would be part of everyday life. Behind the accoutrements of poverty, though, was a solid core that refused to succumb. The baseball-turned-soccer field before Terri overflowed with families. Noisy, laughing people of all ages, were picnicking on blankets and lawn chairs or watching the game in progress and cheering.

Terri wove her way through the crowd to where Gabe Andrews crouched now, his back to her. He was surrounded by a dozen little boys about ten or eleven years old. From their somber expressions, she guessed they weren't winning the tournament.

They wore black shorts and emerald green T-shirts, on the backs of which numbers had been written with a marker pen. She thought of her nephew. All the kids in his league wore shiny uniforms with numbers professionally appliquéd and knee-high matching socks. She glanced down at the scrawny legs before her. Well, the socks didn't match the shirts, and they didn't look official, but at least shin guards were in place.

The coach stood. His green T-shirt was drenched in sweat. He wasn't a big man. His arms were sinewy, lean yet muscular. A biker probably.

"Five minutes!" he shouted, and the boys scattered.

She stepped toward him. "Mr. Andrews," she said, trying not to wince.

He turned, scowling as he had at the hospital. Some angel.

"What?" he asked curtly.

"Uh, we met—"

"Manny!" he yelled over her head and waved an arm. "Not there! Over *there!*"

At the ER she hadn't noticed the color of his eyes and brows. They were unusual, almost matching the deep gold of his hair. A taffy color. Or caramel. The lighter candies, not the darker—

"You're that loudmouthed EMT."

"Paramedic. Look, I'm sorry. I was out of line."

He shrugged. "Feel better now?"

"Yes."

"Good for you." He strode past her. "Manny!"

She tilted her head forward and moved it around in a slow circle over her shoulders. The kinks straightened and the hackles went back down.

Angel? *I don't think so.*

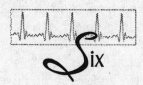

Six

At 7:00 on Tuesday morning, Terri parked in the lot at the fire station and gathered her things, listening to the DJ's weather forecast. A silly habit. What could they say in August except that it was going to be another scorcher?

The car door opened and Kai stuck his head inside. "Did you get Erin Morgan's phone number?"

She laughed and pushed him out of the way. "Good morning to you too."

"I'm serious."

She climbed out and slung her backpack over her shoulder. "Uh-uh."

He fell into step beside her as they headed toward the fire station. "I suppose you think you're off the hook now that you've got your wheels back and don't have to ask me for a ride."

"I checked the phone book. Do you have any idea how many Morgans live in Chicagoland?"

"Do I care?"

"No *Erin* Morgans, by the way. But she'll show up. Ask me how my weekend was."

"Do I care?"

"Come on, Kai! It was a good one."

He jutted his chin, ignoring her.

"I found a home for Zoë! There I was, eating lunch with Mom and Dad, begging them for a month—"

"Promising them all kinds of things you've no intention of delivering. Oh, Mom!" He curled his lip and spoke in a falsetto. "I'll scrub the kitchen. And Dad, let me mow the lawn! Clean out the garage."

Now she ignored him. "And in walks my older brother Bobby and his two kids. Guess who starts begging? Turns out their cat just died!"

"You'll never get her back."

Terri halted in the middle of the driveway. "What do you mean?"

He continued on and through the open garage door and spoke over his shoulder. "Zoë and a couple of little kids? You'd break three hearts."

Break three hearts? She hadn't thought of that. No. That wouldn't happen. It couldn't! She called out to Kai's receding back. "But their dad will never allow—"

"Yoo-hoo!" The voice came from behind her.

She turned. A young woman with a cast on her left arm stood across the street. A round plastic cake carrier dangled from her right hand. Smiling, she waited for a car to pass, and then she strode toward the drive. She wore black slacks and a V-necked burgundy polo shirt with a day spa logo on it.

Even without the uniform, Terri would have recognized her. "Erin. Hi."

She stopped in front of her. "You remembered my name!"

How could she not? Kai had repeated it often enough. *Speaking of Kai…* She glanced over her shoulder. Nowhere to be seen.

"And your name is Terri. It was easy to remember that! How could I forget the name of the woman who saved my life?"

Accustomed to such exaggeration, Terri smiled graciously. "How are you?"

"Great. Well, except for this cast. But I can still work."

Terri recognized the day spa logo on her shirt. Nice place.

"I came by yesterday to thank you. They said you'd be in today about seven." The girl most definitely possessed one of those chirpy demeanors. Her hair and makeup were just so, even at seven in the morning. "I baked you a cake. It's chocolate. I hope you like chocolate."

"Love chocolate. So do most of the guys. Kai does. Remember Kai? He helped take care of you."

"Was he the balding one?"

Terri held her grin in check. "No. The tall lanky one. Buzz cut."

"Oh."

"Let me get him. He'll want to thank you for the cake too." *And get your phone number.*

She batted heavily mascaraed eyes and handed her the carrier. "I'm late for work. I've got to go. Can I stop by again?"

"Sure. You'll want to pick up this cake carrier. We're usually done around eight in the morning."

"You're here all night?"

"Yeah."

"Wow. Gotta run." She turned and scurried down the drive, shouting over her shoulder, "Oh! Thanks for saving my life!"

"You're welcome!"

"Toodles!" She ran across the street.

"Toodles," Terri murmured.

Horsefeathers. Was Kai ever going to be ticked!

⌒

By midafternoon, Terri's fuel tank of good graces had hit empty. Kai's running dialogue of complaints at her failure to get Erin's number had ceased to be amusing.

"What did you want me to do? Grab her good arm and drag her inside? To tell the truth, Rushman, when I mentioned you she described Harlan!"

"Just totally break my heart, why don't you?"

"Let's drop the subject, all right?"

"Fine with me!"

"Fine."

"I ask you to do one simple thing—"

"Kai!"

Every now and then he truly got on her nerves. She knew the feeling was mutual. Close proximity at work and off-the-chart stress exacted a toll. On the other hand, that same trying nature of their work also paid enormous dividends. They unequivocally supported each other.

By midnight, after 16 hours of exchanging only emergency-related words, she needed to talk. In the darkened cab of the rig, on a return trip from the hospital to the station, she turned down the blaring music from his portable CD player. It had served as a buffer between them when they weren't on their way to a scene.

"Kai, is my middle name Hot Dog?"

"Only on Tuesdays and Thursdays."

She frowned at him.

"Left yourself wide open with that one, Schuman." He chuckled.

"Ha, ha."

"Okay, seriously, no. Six months ago I would have said yes. Three months ago, occasionally. What brought this up? Does this have something to do with your little tête-à-tête tonight with the lieutenant?"

Walt had called her into his office after dinner. "Yes. I told you about that cop at the MVA scene being the chief's nephew?"

"And he complained about you. Like I do when you won't let me be the hero. We're just jealous. Don't tell me he filed a formal grievance?"

"No, though there's probably a note in my records by now. Walt said in a *half*-formal way that the chief told him to keep an eye on me."

"All us guys like to keep an eye on you." He turned and made a show of winking.

"You're going to get sued some day." She shook her head in exasperation. "You really do drive me crazy at times."

"I'm sure that's what the chief says about you. The lieutenant probably does too."

"Back to seriously. The next time I even look like I want to show off, shoot me with a megadose of morphine. Enough to knock me on my backside."

"My pleasure. I hardly ever get to give the drugs."

"I'm serious!"

"Hey, don't sweat it, Ter. You didn't do anything wrong the other day, and you're—I don't know. You're different somehow."

"What do you mean?"

He shrugged. "I can't put my finger on it. It's like you don't seem so concerned anymore with proving you're every bit as macho as the next guy."

"Oh, the concern is still there."

"But mostly it's not there, not like it was a year ago. The change has been subtle, but I think it started after you told me you believe in God."

"Really?" She hesitated saying too much about her newfound faith. Her actions were nothing to brag about. She still occasionally swore, especially if Lee was in the vicinity. She still had a beer now and then with the guys after a softball game. Yesterday she laughed at a raunchy joke. Her checking account was overdrawn. She didn't read the Bible every day. Her prayers were made on the run. Unspiritual, ordinary, and wrangling. That was her. Why would she embarrass the Lord by telling people He made a difference in her life?

"Really, Schuman. Lee sure missed the boat when he let you go, but then he's an idiot as well as a doofus. You can count on me though. I know where we keep the morphine."

～

The next morning Terri and Kai rounded the corner of the firehouse on their way to the parking lot.

"Déjà vu!" Kai exclaimed. "Look who's here!"

Zoë streaked across the lawn, her tail wagging and ears flapping. Terri braced herself for the impact, surprised to see the dog. "Hi, girl! Okay, okay." She giggled and pushed aside Zoë's head. "No more kisses. Calm down."

Her brother approached. He wore his CPA uniform, which consisted of a gray suit, power tie, and apologetic expression.

Terri's heart sank.

"I'm sorry."

"Bobby." She was instantly seven years old, and he was twelve and refusing to let her play basketball on the driveway with his friends.

Kai said, "Hi, Bob."

"Hi, Kai." He shook his hand. "How are you doing?"

She interrupted. "What happened?"

He rocked on his heels and blew out a noisy breath. His black hair was cut in a short professional style. Resembling her other two brothers, he had a stocky build. "Well, a few things happened. Your dog sailed through a porch screen. Dug up Colleen's tomato plants. Tracked mud onto the beige living room carpet when we thought she was tied up in the backyard. She crashed into Megan's doll display case, which crashed to the floor. Marcus cut his hand picking up glass. No stitches. And that was just Sunday."

Her shoulders slumped, and she plopped onto the grass alongside the culprit.

"It's not going to work."

She nodded, scratching behind Zoë's ear.

"I'm sorry, sis."

"I know. I appreciate you trying. I'll buy Megan a new doll case."

"Don't worry about it. No glass on the doors will serve as a reminder of why we don't want a big dog. I have to get to the office." He dropped the leash in her lap and ruffled her hair. "Bye. See you, Kai."

"See you."

Bobby hurried to his car.

"Well, Ter, at least you don't have to worry about breaking the kids' hearts."

"Yeah." She wrapped her arms around the dog and buried her face in Zoë's furry neck. "Only Megan's doll case, Marcus's hand, and their mother's prize tomato plants."

"Wish I could help you out—Whoa! Is that who I think it is? Be still, my beating heart!"

Terri looked up. "What?"

"Behind you!" His voice actually squeaked.

Erin Morgan emerged from a car parked curbside. She walked in a distinctive clipped style that matched her perkiness. "Yoo-hoo!"

Kai waved. "Yoo-hoo!"

Perhaps the day wasn't a complete loss. If balding Harlan didn't show up in the next few minutes, she was at least out of the doghouse with Kai. That left making amends with her sister-in-law. Right after she found a new home for Zoë.

~

Twenty minutes later Terri sat beside Kai in a booth at The Stackhouse, a pancake restaurant. She had left her dog back at the station under the watchful eye of a dozen firefighters. Across the table Erin tearfully expressed her gratitude.

She was a sweet girl, attractive in a doe-eyed, vulnerable sort of way. The cast on her arm enhanced the image. Tears glistened in her deep blue eyes; now and then one slid down a cheek without spoiling her makeup. She sniffed delicately, though her nose didn't leak. Terri had never mastered the art of crying without sacrificing half a box of tissues or both shirt sleeves. It mystified her as much as the upswept hair with its evenly distributed blonde streaks.

At such a sight, Kai's inclination to help others must have burst into flame. Surely his heart was melting. He would get Erin's phone number or die trying.

"I owe you guys *everything!*" the girl said for the umpteenth time.

Kai's grin came and went, a definite sign his thoughts were scrambled. "It's what we do."

"But how can I thank you? I can never thank you enough! What can I do for you?"

Terri pressed her foot on top of Kai's. The question wasn't a green light to ask for her number. She said, "You brought us cake. You're buying us breakfast. That's more than enough."

"But that's hardly— I know! I could keep Zoë for you until you find her another home."

Terri laughed. "I told you what happened at my brother's, and he's related to me. He's obligated to dog sit. It would be sheer torture for a stranger. I couldn't ask—"

"But we're not *exactly* strangers. We shared a pretty special moment. Didn't we, Kai?"

His grin twisted more askew, giving him a decidedly sophomoric expression. "I'll say."

I'll say? The guy was tongue-tied. Terri crossed her legs, kicking his shin in the process. *She tossed you the ball! Get in the game!* Buying time for her friend, she said, "Erin, you're right. Nothing compares to the kind of moment we experience on an emergency scene. Right, Kai?"

"Uh, right." His Adam's apple bobbed, and the grin rearranged itself into an adult smile. He cleared his throat twice. "We see it all the time. That split second when life kicks death in the teeth and laughs and shouts, *Not today, bud!*"

A few people from nearby tables turned at his loud command. Erin sat unblinking as a statue, adoration in her gaze.

He went on in a low, intimate tone. "When you share a moment like that with someone, you're friends for life. What else could matter? You've been through the deepest horror and scaled the highest mountain together. All the rest is just details. Are pets allowed where you live?"

Smooth, Rushman. Very smooth.

Erin blinked. "Oh, Kai! That's exactly how I feel! Friends for life." She dug in her purse and presented a business card to each of them. "Here are my work and home phone numbers."

He hadn't even asked! Terri pressed her lips together to keep from laughing.

Erin said, "And yes, pets are allowed. The backyard is even fenced in. I live in a house left to me by my parents. They're both dead. I was their only child."

They murmured condolences.

"It happened a long time ago. What do you say, Terri? Let me take care of Zoë?"

The waitress arrived at the table with their breakfast, pancakes and sausages for Terri and Kai, a vegetable omelet for Erin. While the others were distracted, Terri considered her options. Of course, like everyone, Erin had immediately fallen in love with Zoë. Not so common was the dog's response: She accepted Erin without hesitation. The girl seemed grounded enough, more optimistic than plain ditzy. Still, she was a stranger.

After the waitress refilled their coffee cups, Terri said, "Erin, I really appreciate your offer, but I'd like to think about it."

"What will you do with her in the meantime?"

"I'll just keep her in my apartment until the manager threatens to kick me out. I can probably get by with it for a couple of weeks if the one neighbor doesn't see or hear her. Another neighbor doesn't care, and she'll walk Zoë when I'm at work."

"Well, the offer stands."

"Thank you."

"So, I was wondering." She smiled shyly. "Are you two dating?"

Kai glanced at Terri. "Each other?"

"Yeah. You seem like a perfect couple."

They laughed. Kai said, "She's *nine* years older. Not to mention— But we won't go there. No. Ter and I only save lives together."

"Kai!" Terri breathed out the syllable with an exasperated sigh. "You are such a braggart. Look, Erin, we truly don't save all that many lives. Mostly we get patients ready and transport them to the ER in time for doctors to do their thing."

"Don't believe her, Erin. I've seen her save plenty of lives."

"I bet you've saved plenty of lives too."

"Oh, sure. But she's been at it longer. And she's the PIC."

"What's that?" The girl was hooked.

"Paramedic in charge. She goes in first, calls the shots, does the glamorous stuff like stop gushing arteries and restart hearts."

"Wow. That is so cool. And you help?"

"Yeah. But sometimes all I get to do is hold hands and kiss owies."

Erin smiled. "You kiss owies?"

"Yes. It says right on my certificate that I'm *required* to kiss owies." He grinned.

Terri figured that was her cue to leave.

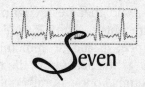

Seven

The following week, Kai slid the newspaper across the kitchen table in the fire station. "Ter, you're being way too picky. I see possibilities in these ads. There's even one that says 'pets allowed.'"

"I don't want to drive thirty miles to work."

"Picky, picky, picky. Your apartment manager won't be half so picky when he dumps your belongings on the front lawn. Hey, I'm not finished with the ham yet." He lightly swatted her hand away from the food in the center of the table. "And leave the bread."

"You're making another sandwich?" The amount of food Kai could eat in one sitting still amazed her.

"Of course I'm making another sandwich. As long as we're here, I'm eating. We might miss dinner."

That was true enough. At two o'clock in the afternoon, the meal they'd just eaten qualified for coffee break and lunch. Back-to-back calls had kept them occupied since eight that morning. She carried her dishes to the sink and turned on the faucet.

"Excuse me."

Terri peered over her shoulder to see Gabe Andrews entering the kitchen. Mr. Cool Surfer Dude himself in blue jeans and a white polo shirt.

"Hi," he said to Kai. "Gabe Andrews." They shook hands.

"Kai Rushman." He kinked his mouth. One corner went down, the other tucked itself inward.

Terri turned back to her dishes and cringed. Kai's facial twitch was an unconscious movement, brief and subtle, but it spoke volumes. It said that he recognized Gabe from her encounter with him outside the ER, which he had watched from a short distance. It said he remembered the less than complimentary things she said about the man, those momentary disgruntled thoughts one naturally unloaded upon a close coworker, words that should never be repeated. Kai's expression said her rendition of the soccer field apology was at the forefront of his mind. And it said he remembered the jar of molasses on which she had written his name.

Behind her, Kai chuckled. "I'm the loudmouth's partner."

"Is that right?"

She heard the grin in Gabe's voice. *I don't even know the guy, have never seen him smile, and I hear a grin?*

"Actually," Gabe went on, "I'm looking for the Lone Ranger."

"You're in luck. She's one and the same!"

"No kidding. Any chance I can find Johnny on the Spot here too?"

"Not sure about that one, but Hot Dog is here. As a matter of fact, she's doing the dishes."

"Pretending like she doesn't know me."

Now she heard the pleasant rise and fall in his pitch. He had an easy-listening, songs-through-the-night radio disc jockey voice. Like velvet.

There was the sound of hands smacking. They were doing a high five.

She picked up a towel and turned around, drying her hands. "Are you two finished?"

Kai stood, a sandwich in his hand. "Yes, ma'am. I'm outta here. No offense, Andrews, but I'd like to get clear of the area before she says another word."

"Understandable. No offense taken."

Laughing, Kai sauntered off.

Gabe turned to her. His smile put a dimple in his left cheek and took ten years off his face. Or more. Except for the receding hairline, he probably hadn't changed much since he was 16 years old. Above the square jaw there was a hint of youthfulness.

"Terri Schuman, right?"

"I prefer that to the other three names."

"I apologize for the teasing."

She nodded her acceptance. "How did you find me?"

"Same as you. I asked Lois. She knew right away who I was describing."

"The loudmouthed one who speaks Spanish?"

"Well, those weren't my exact words. If you don't mind, I have one more apology."

"Okay." She crossed her arms, fully admitting to herself that her attitude stunk. But the guy had totally missed a pregnancy, not to mention the woman was in labor! What if it had been a life-threatening condition?

"I'm sorry for brushing you off at the soccer field. I was, uh, preoccupied."

"Okay."

"Do you mind if we sit down? It might feel less like a face-off this time."

"We have more to talk about? We've both given offense and both apologized. What else could there possibly be?"

"Please?" He gestured at the bench seat and sat.

She followed suit across the table. "So how badly did your team lose?"

He smiled sheepishly. "It showed?"

"Yes, it showed."

"Last place. No, below last place."

"Do the boys speak English?"

His smile froze in place.

"I'm sorry."

"I seriously doubt that." The smile faded.

"I am! I mean, there's got to be a nicer way to express my opinion that you're like a duck out of water in that environment."

"The kids speak English."

"Great. How about the parent who tells you her son fell *veinte* feet out of a tree?"

He held up a hand. "Message received, okay? Back off a little. I'm here because I know my neighborhood has a problem. There aren't that many medics and firefighters who speak fluent Spanish on every shift working out of my station. We need people like you who know the language."

"You sure do!"

"How did you learn to speak it so well?"

She uncrossed her arms and gave herself a moment to let the adrenaline dissipate. "Home and school. My mother's parents came to the states from Mexico eons ago. Mom was born here, but English was a second language for her. Once she worked her way out of the neighborhood and married a gringo, she stopped speaking it."

"She didn't teach you?"

"No, to her it was a stigma. Grandma lived with us the last ten years of her life. I was eight when she moved in." She shrugged. "We bonded. I took classes later in high school and junior college."

"Terri, would you consider transferring?"

"Transferring? To where?"

"My station."

"No."

He waited a beat. "You gave that a lot of thought."

"I'm perfectly content here. Wouldn't change a thing."

"We have a problem and you could be part of the solution. I have a medic leaving at Christmas. And besides." An unmistakable twinkle in the caramel eyes reflected his smile. Two dimples appeared this time, one in each cheek. "The good rumors about you surpass those nicknames. All I'm asking is that you think about it."

"Well, I'll probably think about it because you've put the thought in my head, but my answer won't change."

He extended his hand across the table and shook hers. "No problem. The answer doesn't matter today. Just listen to the thought, and whatever happens, happens."

She might hear the thought, but she certainly wasn't going to listen to an idea that would place her in a working situation with Gabe Andrews. She wasn't even sure she liked the guy.

Except for his eyes. He did have nice eyes. And voice. There was that too. His voice was exactly what anyone in trouble would welcome hearing.

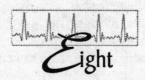

Eight

A few weeks later, at the end of a shift, Terri sat yawning in the captain's office, legs outstretched, and kneaded her aching lower back. She craved sleep, but her stomach refused to unknot itself, and her heartbeat thumped like an internal yo-yo spinning out of control.

Across the cramped space, Kai slumped against a wall. His puffy eyes and pale face probably mirrored her own. Four runs between 10:00 P.M. and 5:00 A.M. meant they hadn't slept last night. Their adrenaline had pumped without a break. One shooting, two drug overdoses, one cardiac arrest. It was now 8:00. Technically they were off duty. The next shift was already out on a call.

"I'll never understand it," she said. "How can I be so exhausted and so wound up at the same time?"

Kai rubbed his eyes. "The real mystery is why a cop wants to talk to us about some car accident that happened a month ago." His voice, like hers, sounded of vocal cords scraped raw.

"Which we assume from the timing was Erin's."

Kai glanced at her long enough to convey discomfort.

The subject of Erin Morgan was a sore spot between them. As it turned out, she wasn't the love of Kai's life. Before realizing that, however, he had talked Terri into accepting Erin's offer to care for Zoë. With the manager breathing down her neck and her apartment search yielding zilch, she had no other choice. Now, three weeks later, they both realized the young woman was a bit of a pest. On good days they teased each other about the awkward relationship. Today was not a good one.

"Simple solution, Terri. Swallow your pride and call what's-his-name."

"Over my dead body. I'm not about to depend on Lee Reynolds for anything ever again."

There was a knock on the open door and a woman stepped inside. "Hi. Terri Schuman and Kai Rushman?" She shook their hands. "I'm Detective Cara Fleming. Thanks for seeing me. I'm sure you're ready to go home. Please, sit down." Closing the door, she glanced around the closet-sized office. "Hmm. Two seats and three people. Oh well, at least we've got privacy."

Kai said, "Take the chair behind the desk. If I sit I'll fall asleep."

"That makes two of us." The policewoman leaned against the desk and pulled a notepad from her shoulder bag.

Terri guessed her to be around her own age, mid-thirties. Also similar to Terri, she seemed unconcerned about appearance. She wore no makeup and her light brown hair hung straight, almost to her shoulders. Her white blouse, dark brown pants, and jacket were as wrinkled as if she'd slept in them.

"This shouldn't take long," she muttered, flipping through the pad. "Soon as I find…" Her voice trailed off. She exuded an air of familiarity, as if she were an absentminded old friend. All she needed was a baggy raincoat, and she'd make a perfect female Columbo.

Terri asked, "Would you like some coffee, Detective?"

"Call me Cara. No thanks. I drank a pot— Ah, here we go." She smiled at them. Her eyes were wide set, above a narrow nose. "Erin Morgan. Remember the incident?"

Terri nodded along with Kai.

"Tell me about the scene. You were the first paramedic to reach her, Ms. Schuman?"

"Terri." She told her about the condition of the car, of being able to put her head and one arm inside, of Erin's screaming and eventual calming, of the extrication and her condition.

The detective jotted notes. "Sounds fairly straightforward. Tell me about the window you poked your head through. Was there broken glass around the opening's edges?"

"No. It was a tight squeeze."

"To quote Winnie-the-Pooh."

Terri smiled. "Yeah. I couldn't have gone in if there'd been any sign of glass. There wasn't enough space. I assumed the window must have been pressed clean out at the time of impact. Or else it was open." She shrugged. "Which seems unlikely for such a hot day. The driver's window and the back windows were all cracked. They'd been shut, as if the air conditioning were on."

"Mm-hmm. Mr. Rushman." She turned to him.

"Kai."

"All right. Do you have anything to add?"

"Only that Terri called things correctly. Can we ask why this is being investigated now? We were told that the cause of the accident was that Erin must have blacked out. She'd been having dizzy spells out in the heat that week."

"Who told you that?"

"Erin."

"You follow up on all your victims?" She grinned. "Or just the cute ones?"

Kai blushed.

Terri laughed. "Just the cute ones, if they're female and over eighteen."

Kai said, "Ha, ha. So, Detective, why are you looking into this now?"

"Some new information just came up."

"What sort of information?"

Cara stared at him, a look of concern replacing the nonchalant expression. "I'm not at liberty— Just how well do you know Erin Morgan?"

"I took her out a few times before I realized she's one of those flypaper types. You know, wanting to stick together, day and night. She's dog sitting for Terri."

"Are you both in frequent contact with her?"

They groaned simultaneously. Kai said, "She keeps showing up."

Terri added, "She's probably outside the fire station right now. Sometimes she meets us when we get off duty. She brings my dog, Zoë. She begs me to do things, and I keep turning her down."

"What sort of things?"

"*Girl* things. Lunch, shopping. She offers to give me a facial and style my hair." Terri ran her fingers through her floppy bangs. "Like I care."

"Why do you have her dog sitting?"

"It's a long story. I don't have another place for Zoë at this time. She offered. I'm paying her."

"She offered. And as far as you're concerned, it's a business relationship."

"Yeah, I guess so."

"Do either of you find any of this odd, the phone calls, the waiting for you to get off work?"

"She's a flibbertigibbet."

Kai added, "And we think she'll outgrow the infatuation. She still has the cast on her arm, a reminder that, in her words, we 'saved' her life. Which, of course, we didn't literally do."

"A kind of hero worship?"

"I suppose. She's a groupie."

Cara tapped her pad with a pencil. Except for a faraway look in her eyes, her expression remained passive.

Terri reviewed the last few weeks. Erin's numerous calls usually resulted in perky messages on the answering machine.

Terri wasn't all that available between work, apartment hunting, and teaching a CPR class. Then there were her parents. They had come clean when she confronted them. Her dad had a tumor; the tests were incomplete.

Cara cleared her throat. Her eyes were refocused. "Well, I wouldn't trust Erin Morgan as far as I could throw her." She smiled. "Maybe I'll take that coffee now."

⌒

Ten minutes later, the three of them reconvened in the office. Kai had carried in another chair for himself. Cara sat behind the desk. Terri poured coffee into three mugs, her hand shaking. Caffeine overload, lack of sleep, or a creeping uneasiness? Probably all three.

Cara sipped from her cup. "I can't tell you about the ongoing investigation, but since you know Erin, I want to tell you the facts. Though I have to ask you not to mention any of this to her."

They nodded in agreement.

"Thanks. Okay. Let's start with what else you know about her."

Kai replied, "She's an orphan, an only child, lives in her parents' house, works as a makeup artist. That's about it."

"The first part is true. The rest— She hasn't worked since April. She'd only been at that job three months. Her parents died in a plane accident several years ago; she received a hefty insurance settlement. Probably doesn't need to work."

Terri exchanged a look with Kai. His face mirrored her own confusion.

"And." She paused. "Erin knew the other driver. Melanie Lareau."

Terri started and felt Kai do the same.

"From your reaction, I take it she hasn't mentioned this to you?"

Kai answered, "No. She told me she felt guilty. I said that was natural, but maybe she should see a therapist to work through it. She said she went to the visitation and apologized to the family. They didn't blame her. That was all she needed."

"Melanie Lareau's family say they've never met her. A close friend, Melanie's assistant, came to us with this information. She'd been out of the country for six weeks and just recently returned. Melanie was a city councilwoman, a high-profile type. According to the friend, Erin introduced herself at a grocery store, expressed gratitude for the councilwoman's work, offered to volunteer on some project. She began to call Melanie at all hours of the day and night. She'd show up at her condo, outside the office. In general, she made herself a nuisance."

Terri's throat had gone dry. "She's a stalker?"

"Do you feel that you're being stalked?"

"I don't exactly know what that feels like."

"Has she threatened you in any way?"

"No. Did she threaten Melanie Lareau?"

"The friend says no. Not as far as she knows anyway."

Kai said, "Erin is just a ditz who's desperate for a friend."

"Kai!" Terri set down her mug. Coffee sloshed over its rim. "Don't you find it the least bit bizarre that this woman dies in an accident Erin probably caused?"

"Come on. How could she cause something like that? She could have been killed herself."

"Think of the vehicles! Her huge SUV against a small Toyota. The other woman didn't stand a chance."

"Terri," Cara interrupted, pressing tissues around the spilled coffee. "Are you all right?"

"She has my dog!"

"You might want to consider another option."

"You think?"

"Ter." Kai came over to her chair and knelt, placing an arm around her shoulders. "Hey, don't overreact. We'll just arrange to pick up Zoë and then not take her back. Okay? We'll do it this morning, before sleep. Take a deep breath."

She followed his advice and looked at Cara. "I'm sorry."

"No problem. I suggest you get your dog as soon as possible and cut all ties with her. Both of you. There's a real possibility that she worships you, Terri. You're an attractive woman with an exciting career."

Kai said, "Then there's the PEA factor."

"The what?"

He explained the chemical reaction one experienced in a dangerous situation, how it gave an amphetamine-like high. They had never considered linking it to someone of the same gender. Given the circumstances, though, with Terri first on the scene, Erin was more likely to connect the response to her.

The detective cocked a brow. "If you say so. The point is, Terri, if I'm reading the tea leaves correctly, she admires you. She wants to be just like you, with your dog, your car, your career, your partner, your boyfriend, your apartment. She'll mimic as much as possible, believing that she is you. And we'll all pray nothing bursts her bubble."

Kai whistled softly. "I guess we're not talking simple airhead here?"

"No, we're not."

He squeezed Terri's shoulders and grinned. "Hey, Ter, I got it. Offer her a trade. Zoë for Lee." He said to Cara, "The boyfriend."

"Ex." Terri took another shaky breath and frowned at him. His face was inches from hers. She saw the dark circles under his blue eyes, the dark stubble that lined his jaw. More than anything he needed to go home, eat, and sleep, but there he was, taking care of her, cheering her up.

She smiled. "I'd throw in my dumpy studio apartment too. Make it an even trade."

They laughed. Cara Fleming only cocked her brow again.

"Cara, hi." Terri held the cordless phone between her chin and shoulder while she spread peanut butter on a piece of toast. "It's Terri Schuman."

"Hey, I'm glad you called. How did it go?"

"Well, Erin refused to take Lee. She wasn't interested in the apartment either."

"Sorry to hear that." She chuckled softly. "At least you're joking. Does that mean things went well?"

Terri poured a large glass of milk. "To be honest, I wish I'd snagged some Valium from work."

"Oh?" There was an obvious nuance in her tone, a law enforcement officer probing. Did the paramedic filch prescription drugs?

"I'm joking. If I don't, I'm going to burst into tears." She gulped the milk.

"I'd bet you don't do that too often."

"Just did. Last month. In church. At least the place was empty." The words tumbled, uncontrollable nervous chatter. "Time before that was..." At the hospital. All kinds of people were there, all of them in tears. "A fireman...he..." She took another drink of milk. *He died.*

"Terri, just tell me what happened. Did Kai go with you?"

"He stayed out of sight, like you suggested." She had called Erin and said she wanted to pick up Zoë and take her for the day. "I went inside Erin's house. She had made me breakfast." Terri shuddered, recalling the young woman's cloying attitude, the smells of bacon and eggs and that sweet perfume.

"Cara, that was the eeriest situation I've ever been in, and you know how weird things can get on my job. I made excuses. Got Zoë on her leash and out the door as fast as I could. Then I told Erin thanks, but I didn't need her help any more. *She* burst into tears. There I am, apologizing to this stalking murderer!"

"We don't know either of those things for a fact."

"Whatever. I drove past Kai, gave him a thumbs-up, and then I went out to the kennel." Forty-five miles away, in the suburbs, budget-breaking. Her last resort. "Erin followed."

Cara was silent.

"Followed me *forty-five miles*. In a brand new *Blazer*. And guess what? It's black. Mine's black! Is it my imagination or is this getting downright bizarre?"

"It's not your imagination. Does she know where you live?"

"She does now."

"Do you have somewhere else you can stay? Some place she wouldn't know about?"

Terri wiped at her eyes. Tears of exhaustion spilled. "I don't know. I can't think straight. I haven't slept since the night before last. I've just spent two hours on the road and promised to pay two hundred and fifty dollars a month more than exists in my checking account."

"Okay. Give me your address. I'll send a patrol car by. Get some rest and then get out."

"It's that serious?"

"I may be wrong. I hope I'm wrong."

"Are you ever wrong?"

Again she was silent. Unlike Terri, Cara Fleming certainly knew how to measure her words. "Last month. In church. Stood up when I was supposed to stay seated."

"Is that supposed to make me feel better?"

She chuckled, a short, whispery expression of mirth. "It's supposed to remind you to be careful and keep me posted."

Like she had a choice.

Nine

Terri spent three weeks in a whirlwind. She never had liked the studio apartment, but the thought of Erin Morgan lurking outside made it completely unlivable. She slept at her sister Shelley's condominium downtown and ignored the disapproval of Shelley's significant other, Dave, who paid half the rent. They'd been down that road before. She had stayed with them during the initial breakup with Lee.

She investigated every plausible apartment for rent within a 40-mile radius, taught another series of CPR classes, and worked part-time for a private ambulance company transferring patients between hospitals and nursing homes to make money for Zoë's board and keep.

She screened every call. Erin left three friendly voice mail messages before Terri changed her cell phone number. She spent every waking moment looking over her shoulder.

And, sometimes, Erin was there. Across the street from the station, around the corner from the ER entrance, outside a restaurant. She either waved or drove by in her car. Not close enough to disrupt or to appear a threat, but within sight. At least she had not surfaced near Shelley's place.

Cara regularly checked in with Terri. They even met twice for coffee. Under different circumstances, they might have become friends, but the mere fact that a cop was a necessary fixture in her life unnerved her. That Cara gave her tips on how to spot and evade a tail totally rocked her equilibrium.

Her fears and anger spilled over into their conversations. Unruffled, Cara listened without comment.

Kai, on the other hand, always had a comment. He berated himself for acting like an idiot by falling for a pretty face. Breaking into a cold sweat, he expressed gratitude to his lucky stars that the relationship had not progressed. He swore off women. He discussed the merits of a restraining order against Erin for both of them.

In short, he did not have a calming effect. His efforts to empathize with Terri only added layers to the tension that already clung about her like a thick fog. She felt as though she were an explosion waiting to happen. All she needed was a detonator.

There hadn't been much occasion to laugh, but the night she and Kai caught the six o'clock dinner hour at the station offered a reprieve. With all 15 of the crew sitting around the table at the same time, laughing was as inescapable a pleasure as Teague's garlic mashed potatoes.

Until Gabe Andrews walked through the door. His grin widened as she felt her own dissolve.

He spread his arms wide. "Terri Schuman, come on down! I've got a deal you can't resist."

The alarm sounded then, and the dispatcher called out the ambulance.

She hurried past him, grinning again. "Saved by the bell."

"That's what you think."

There was no time to protest. Gabe knew his way around a fire station. He was in the back of the rig before Kai had started the engine.

Terri went into emergency mode. Her brief history of conflict with Gabe Andrews would not play a role in the coming moments. Reaching for the radio, she murmured a quick "Thank You, Lord," for the extra pair of hands on board. *Even if he can't speak Spanish.*

Like an animal handler stepping into the tiger's cage, Terri entered the old tavern, her senses on full alert. Cigarette smoke floated, a gauzy blue stinging veil. The sour odor of liquor permeated the air, as solid a presence as was the bar that ran down one side of the long narrow room. Dark wooden booths lined the other wall. Her rubber soles stuck to the checkerboard-patterned linoleum. The place was crowded, wall-to-wall people, all eerily silent.

She fought back a rush of sheer panic. Were they in the right place? Where were the cops? Was the place secured? Dispatch said yes, but she didn't spot a uniform.

Her mental stopwatch ticked loudly. In saner moments, she visualized the phenomenon as a miniature referee standing in a corner of her mind, wearing black pants and a black-and-white striped shirt. His sternly set mouth clamped around a whistle. He held an oversized stopwatch. The split moment she heard her ambulance called out, her adrenaline pumped straight to his thumb, which depressed the timer. Seconds began resounding in elongated ticktocks. At some unconscious level she counted them...added them into minutes...subtracted them from the total time required to preserve a life. Total times varied, of course. So many factors entered in. A shooting meant, more often than not, that the patient needed to have been in surgery before they even reached the scene.

Kai bumped her from behind.

She grabbed the nearest elbow. "Where's the guy who got shot?"

Before the man could answer, someone pulled on her other arm. "At the back!"

Of course it would be at the back. Maybe there was a back room. With a back door.

She let Kai go first, his height and shoulders a plus as they forged their way through the sea of people. Gabe followed, wheeling the stretcher. At last she spotted a policeman, a tearful woman, and a man crumpled on the floor. There was no back room or back door in sight. Just a tiny, dark, filthy space cramped between a booth and a bar stool.

They had to get him out of there.

Terri knelt beside the injured man. He was in a fetal position, staring at her. She wasn't sure if he saw or heard her, but she introduced herself anyway.

"Sir, my name's Terri. I'm a paramedic, and I'm here to take care of you."

The cop knelt near her and pointed. "Looks like an in and out, on his side there. Bullet's in the wall—"

"Save the diagnosis! Just get these people out of here!" Examining the patient, she didn't mince words or make eye contact with the officer.

A large hand gently squeezed her shoulder, Kai's subtle suggestion she calm down. He'd been doing that a lot in the past three weeks.

Three weeks? In truth, more like three months. Or six. Or more? A coworker's death last year, Lieutenant Walt Kemper's semi-support and weak leadership, Chief Paramedic Cooper breathing down her neck at every turn, Rachel's move, Lee's estrangement, Zoë issues, a putrid apartment and no other prospects, her dad's illness. Exactly what was her newfound faith supposed to do for her?

As the stopwatch in the referee's hand ticked away the seconds, she assessed the situation. Short of breath. Drenched in perspiration. Bleeding wound, but he would not bleed to death before they got to the ER. Shock would complicate things as his body reacted to the invasion of a bullet.

Stench from a nearby washroom fused now with the smoke and liquor. They had to get him out of there.

She pulled the bag-valve-mask resuscitator from her kit and placed the mask on him to help him breathe. Gabe applied pressure to the bleeding wound. Within moments they had him packed on the stretcher. By then backup had arrived. Firefighters and police cleared a path, physically holding people out of the way. Other firefighters helped them wheel the man outside to the rig.

With Terri giving orders, they worked on him quickly. They cut away clothing, checked blood pressure, inserted an IV, listened to his lungs, hooked him to the EKG. His eyes closed.

Gabe continued tending to the wound while Kai climbed into the driver's seat and patched into the hospital, describing the situation. He relayed vitals and Terri's summation. She crouched behind the patient's tilted head, a laryngoscope in her hand. The lighted instrument allowed her to look into his larynx. She needed to see the vocal cords before she could intubate. To slip the breathing tube down into his trachea was essential. They had to keep him breathing and get him as ready as possible for surgery. For a trained professional, the procedure was a routine connect-the-dots. She had performed it countless times, performed it regularly. She proceeded as usual.

And then it happened. The inconceivable.

"I can't see his cords!"

Being unable to view them was not the inconceivable. That had happened. Sometimes they were difficult to find or keep in sight. Frustrating, yes, but there were ways around that. Kai would apply pressure on a particular spot of the patient's neck and—*voilà*—vocal cords. If they still slipped from view and the situation was desperate, she ditched the scope and felt her way in with her fingers. She *knew* what to do. She knew *how* to do it. She had *done* it.

Gabe's fingers were on the man's neck.

"No!" she cried. "It's me! *I* can't see!"

That was the inconceivable. Her vision had blurred. No amount of blinking or shaking her head cleared it. Her hands shook. Nausea enveloped her. There was a shrilling sound in her ears, as if the referee blew with all his might on that whistle fixed between his scrunched lips. Time's up!

Gabe took the scope from her hands. "Trade places!"

She scrambled around him. The whistle still blew and at some level she knew her innate sense of timing was gone. The stopwatch had been blown to pieces.

Gabe shouted, "Go, Kai, go!" A stranger, the surfer dude who couldn't speak Spanish, was in charge.

An explosion waiting to happen? She'd just hit the detonator.

～

Meltdown.

Naturally. It would come after an explosion, wouldn't it? First a kaboom shattered the eardrums. Intense heat followed, melting everything in its path, reducing all thought, action, and emotion into liquid tears.

It wasn't pretty. Terri used both sleeves as well as a roll of toilet tissue in the hospital's ladies' room. She wouldn't swear to it, but now, in the middle of the night, she vaguely recalled sobbing against someone's shoulder. She hoped it was Kai's and not the stranger's who couldn't speak Spanish.

Introspection kicked into high gear. Her vision lost its off-kilter angle and straightened. At last she saw clearly what had been waiting out there just beyond her range of vision for months now. It was herself, of course. Her soul, the real Terri Schuman, whatever name she wanted to give it. And it was…burned out. All the signals had been there to read, in big print and capital letters, but she had refused to acknowledge them.

Now she sat in a recliner in the stranger's condominium, bundled in a silky, billowing comforter and sipping warm milk. Warm milk! Without chocolate! She couldn't remember ever drinking warm milk without plenty of chocolate and marshmallows added.

Gabe entered the softly lit room. "How are you doing?" he asked in a quiet voice and sat gingerly on the edge of the couch, leaning forward, elbows on knees, lacing his fingers together. Either the demeanor was his paramedic's bedside manner or else a cautious stance against another explosion from her.

"I'm better. Thanks. You can breathe now and I won't crack, I promise."

He smiled. It was a nice smile, no teeth showing, folds pressed into his cheeks but not deeply enough for the dimples to appear. Self-deprecating. "If you want to sleep, the room's ready."

"My dad has cancer."

"I'm sorry. How bad is it?"

"We don't know yet. He just found out."

"I'll pray for him."

It was what Rachel had said when she told her on the phone. It was what Vic would have said. She couldn't think of many other people she knew who would respond that way, and now a guy she'd just met said the most comforting words imaginable. Her throat constricted and fresh tears stung, dangerously close to spilling. She would make a mess of the silky duvet that didn't even belong to her.

"What's his name?"

"Bob," she whispered and pulled the comforter more tightly about her shoulders. Between her shot nerves and the cool air-conditioned home, she was freezing.

"Bob," he repeated, and she nodded.

They sat in silence for a long moment. It was a comfortable enough silence, the kind that allowed her to chase rabbit trail thoughts until at last two of them collided.

"Bob," she said, "would not be proud of his third child tonight."

"These things happen. Anybody could understand."

She gave her head half a shake.

"Do you want to talk about it?"

"No. Yes."

"Typical woman."

"You think riling my dander will help?"

"Well, let's see. You talked a blue streak outside the ER when your dander was all riled up. You yammered away with no problem when I dropped in at the firehouse. Yeah, I'd say it would help."

"I don't yammer." She squirmed in the chair.

"Terri." He'd dropped the teasing tone. "Why do you think tonight happened?"

"You know, if you really want to rile my dander, keep using euphemisms like 'tonight.' Let's call a spade a spade. I blew it. I mean, I've made mistakes through the years, but this time I lost total control of the situation, of *myself*. I put a patient at risk by my own incompetency."

"It wasn't incompetency."

"Please, no more euphemisms."

"In the first place, he wasn't at great risk at that point. Secondly, you didn't lose total control because, like a professional, you called it when your vision blurred. If I hadn't been there, Kai could have done it. We reached the hospital in plenty of time. Thirdly, you know how to tube, you've done it innumerable times under all kinds of circumstances, upside down and in the dark. I doubt this has happened before."

"It hasn't."

"It wasn't incompetency."

"Then what?"

He paused and took a deep breath. "What I saw was burnout."

His words vocalized her thoughts. She closed her eyes.

"When was the last time you took two weeks off? A week? A day?"

Time off? Ten months ago, Christmastime...three days skiing. July...two days to visit Rachel. "My job is my life. There's nothing else I'd rather be doing."

"Admit it. You've seen the symptoms."

She squirmed again, reluctant to follow the trail he was taking her on. "Like what?"

"Like yelling at me. Granted, you had a good point, and in the long run you saved my neck. Like yelling at that cop on the scene tonight. Kai says you can be somewhat of a loose cannon, but he's never heard you quite so—"

"I've had a lot on my mind lately!"

"Understandably. There's your dad. And your dog. Then there's the boyfriend rebound thing. Not to mention the wacko woman following you around, which is why you don't want to go home and you've ended up here at my place."

"Well, you and Kai certainly had some conversation!"

"You were in the ladies' room a long time. He's concerned."

The wind of indignation stopped puffing in her chest. Yes, Kai would be concerned. He would be crazy with worry. What Gabe said was true. She had never been quite so overdone. And Kai had never seen her lose control of a situation the way she had tonight.

"Terri, the job is stressful enough without real-life issues. When those start to interfere with the job, you need a vacation. You've probably got time coming."

Yes, but it wouldn't cover the fortune she was spending on her dog and empty apartment.

"Think about it?"

"Okay." She yawned, her eyelids suddenly heavy.

"You should sleep."

"Yeah. Where's the phone? I'll call a cab."

"Where would you take it?" He stood. "Your sister's place is way downtown. Kai said your apartment is off limits until the wacko woman leaves you alone. His place is a pigsty. Your best friend moved out of town. You wouldn't want to go to your parents' in the middle of the night. It's three o'clock in the morning. I'm leaving."

"Leaving?"

He swept his arm in a half circle. "*Mi casa es su casa.* Stay as long as you like. Kai and one of the guys will bring your car here when they get off."

"Gabe, this is too much to ask."

He laughed. "*This* is too much? I bail you out of an emergency, hang around the hospital until you're done boohooing, and cart you off to my condo because you're too incoherent to tell us where you want to go. I make you warm milk and then sit up half the night talking with you. Leaving to sleep in my under-construction house for what few hours remain of the night is not too much to ask. I planned to work there tomorrow anyway. Uh, make that today."

"You don't have to go!"

"I've just rescued you. It's my bounden duty as a hero not to sully your reputation by sleeping in the same house."

"Trust me, it's been sullied. Beyond repair. Please don't go on my account."

"Nothing's beyond repair." He smiled and his voice softened. "Do you need anything? Kai found your backpack. I put it in the guest room. Is there anything else?"

She shook her head.

"Okay. Sleep well then. My cell number's on the fridge. See you."

He left the room.

"Gabe!" She clambered from the recliner. The comforter entangled her feet and she fell on her knees to the floor with a thud. "Ouch."

"You okay?"

She sat up and saw him grinning in the doorway. "No, not really, but then I think that's what we've been discussing." She rubbed her shin. "Why did you come to the station tonight? I mean last night. You said you have a deal for me?"

"It'll keep." He waved and disappeared again into the kitchen.

"Gabe!"

She heard his retreating footsteps stop. After a moment they grew loud again. This was one patient man. He filled the doorway once more, a questioning expression on his tired face.

"I just wanted to say thanks."

"You're welcome." He smiled.

And she smiled back.

Ten

Terri stood in Gabe Andrews' kitchen, a compact galley affair with the back door at the far end. Parallel counters ran along the side walls, white cabinets above and below. And there was a coffeemaker. A yellow sticky note was attached to the carafe. "Ready to go. Help yourself."

He'd made coffee for her.

Still groggy after a deep, nine-hour sleep, she rubbed her eyes. The note displayed the same message she'd read the first time.

He'd made coffee for her.

Imagine that.

He must want something. What could he want from her? What did she have that he didn't? Put a man with a woman and there was the obvious. Last night would have been his perfect opportunity to come on to her. Instead he refused to even sleep under the same roof. Apparently chivalry still lived.

There was a knock on the door. Through the thin yellow curtain she saw the outline of broad shoulders.

She flipped on the coffeemaker and went to the door. "Morning, Kai. You're just in time for coffee."

"It's after twelve, Schuman." He grinned and stepped inside, shutting the door behind himself.

"It is? Wow. I was dead to the world."

He dropped a set of keys on the counter. "Here are your keys. Hey, what's this note? He made coffee for you?"

She nodded. "Go figure."

He whistled. "What do you think he wants?"

"That was exactly my first response. Rushman, we've been together too long. I'm feeling like a clone. Have a seat."

"How are you?" He sat at a small table.

Terri busied herself opening and closing cupboard doors, searching for coffee mugs. "Gabe doesn't seem like an odd-ball, but his condo looks a little unbalanced. Bookshelves are empty. The walls are empty. No knickknacks. Not even a photo. Four plates and bowls up here. Two mugs. But I guess that's all we need."

"He's moving. Built himself a house out in the 'burbs somewhere. He's a carpenter too."

"I guess he did say something about going to sleep at his under-construction house."

"He didn't sleep here then?"

"Nope."

He smiled. "How about that. He told me he wouldn't. I think what we have here is an old-fashioned gentleman."

"That's much nicer than calling him a weird duck."

"I wouldn't let a weird duck whisk you away. He seemed like a decent guy. And Jim talked with him at the station. They know each other from church. Shawn knows him too. He lives just down the street. His wife had taken him to work yesterday, so he drove your car here and walked home. I hope you didn't mind. I didn't know what else to do..." His voice faded.

She stared at him. She hadn't thanked him because that would mean going there, and she did not want to go there, did not want to rehash last night.

"Ter, you okay?"

"I'm sorry," she whispered and turned to pour coffee.

"Hey, it happens. And I know the strain you've—"

"Kai, can we not discuss it?" She set mugs on the table and sat across from him. "Thank you for taking care of me. You did good, kid. I will forever be indebted to you for not calling my parents or sister. They would have been upset beyond measure. And that only would have made things worse. So thank you. Gabe was a complete gentleman. I was totally comfortable sleeping in my clothes on a bunk bed in the guest room."

She remembered finding a lamp left burning in the sparsely furnished room. The bottom bunk's covers were turned down. She half-expected to find a pair of pajamas laid out for her and a piece of chocolate on the pillow.

"Terri, I think you should take some time off. You've got vacation—"

"I don't want to talk about it! Good grief, I haven't even finished my first cup of coffee. What are you doing here anyway? You should be at home."

"Well, excuse me for checking in on you and making sure Shawn left the keys under the mat. I didn't have the luxury of sleeping until all hours, and I want to talk. You know, you left us in a major mess last night."

"I know that! You think I need a guilt trip?"

"I think you need to quit pretending that everything is all right. It's not, and last night's stunt jerked around the entire company as well as dispatch."

"Go home."

"I'm not done talking."

"Then just say what you have to say, all right?"

"You lost your edge last night."

"I know! I fouled up! I apologize. What—"

"It wasn't just a momentary glitch. I've seen it coming for months. It's been like a flash point."

"Flash point? What's that supposed to mean? The brink of a crisis? We're on the brink of a crisis every time we hop in the rig."

"It's more than that. It's like you're this combustible liquid. Everything that's been happening ever since Vic died last year has been affecting the temperature around you, pushing it down until last night it got low enough. Ignition. Kapow."

She stared at him. He'd just reiterated her own thoughts of feeling like an explosion waiting to happen.

"Terri." His tone was urgent, but he paused before continuing. "I'm transferring. I got on with Thirteen."

She blinked. "What?"

"Next month. They need a PIC. You know I'm eligible. My name's been on the list—"

"You're just walking out? We haven't even talked about it!"

"For crying out loud, Schuman, we're not married! You know I've been wanting to join them since the first day I interned with you. That crew is in the thick of things. Twenty runs a shift. I got in. I got in! What's to talk about?" He stood, his face red, and marched toward the door. "Well, congratulations, Kai." His voice was a falsetto. "I knew you could do it."

"I didn't even know you were trying to do it! Some friend you are! Get out!"

He yanked open the door. "Yeah, well, you said it yourself. We've been together too long."

The door slammed behind him, its window rattling. She winced.

First Vic. Then Rachel. Lee... her dad... now Kai.

Abandonment issues? *Oh, grow up, Schuman. You're thirty-five years old.*

She carried her mug to the sink and slammed it on the countertop. Slammed it firmly and forcefully. Against the solid, concrete-hard ceramic tile.

Gabe Andrews was down to one mug.

~

Terri glanced around Reverend Bryan O'Shaugnessy's comfortable office. Like the church, it was full of richly grained wood. Green plants sat on the sill of a tall, mullioned window. Important-looking books lined the many shelves. There was a faint scent of Bryan's cherry pipe tobacco. She sat in a creased leather winged-back chair. Decades ago some wealthy congregation had cared generously for their pastor.

She said, "Do you know what I kept telling Rachel when she was going through her nightmare?" Terri snorted at the ridiculous implication. "Not to say that I'm experiencing to *any* degree her kind of nightmare. By comparison, I'm just having an uncomfortable dream."

Across his polished oak desk, Bryan said, "That doesn't diminish the intensity of what you're feeling."

Her half nod was noncommital. Rachel had been through a hell, the likes of which Terri could not begin to fathom.

"What was it you kept telling Rachel?" Bryan refocused her wandering thoughts once again. Unmitigated compassion shone in the clear green eyes of the redheaded lumberjack who wore a clerical collar.

His demeanor resembled Cara Fleming's in a way. The policewoman's compassion didn't shine quite so tenderly, though, probably for the same reason Terri held her own in check. A woman working in a man's world sometimes masked her purely feminine side in order to prove herself. But Cara, like Bryan now, listened quietly, without judging. Which was why Terri had called him right after dumping the broken mug pieces into the trash can.

"I kept telling Rachel that she didn't need to be anxious about tomorrow. That she didn't have to be afraid of anything. I quoted *Scripture* to *her*. Of all the nerve. The woman knew more about the Bible when she was a *nine*-year-old than I'll ever comprehend."

He smiled knowingly. Rachel was his good friend too. "What do you think about applying your excellent counsel to your own situation?"

"In my dreams."

He waited. He was very good about not commenting on her flippant retorts. He let them whiz on by, giving her time to reconsider. She fiddled with her bangs, twisting a strand of hair.

"Scripture is Scripture," she concluded. "It's true."

He nodded. "Yet there's a 'but' in your tone."

Her throat constricted. She had never been much of a tear shedder. She must be making up for all those dry years. Her voice could only whisper, but she blurted, "I don't deserve it."

"None of us do." He slid a box of tissues nearer her side of the desk.

She grabbed a tissue and blew her nose.

"Why don't you tell me about your dad?"

She had already told him about the cancer diagnosis. He had responded as she knew he would, repeating Gabe's words: *I'll pray for him.* Which was another reason she had decided to see him. "What do you want to know?"

"How did he handle raising seven kids?"

She smiled. "He'd been a sergeant in the Army. Need I say more?"

"So there was order in your home?"

"Oh, yeah. Big time. Most of my growing up years he worked second shift at the hospital. I was the squeaky wheel, so I got the attention, good and bad. I'm sure I hold the record for most spankings received because it was my loud mouth that woke him up summer mornings. The good side was he often took me to work with him. I begged him to and Mom was glad to be rid of me. I spent many afternoons and evenings hanging around the ER. That's how I came to know Lois. It's where I met all the doctors and nurses, firefighters and medics."

"And dreamt of becoming one of them."

She smiled. "Lois encouraged it."

"What did your dad think of that dream?"

Her smile faded and she shrugged. "I'm a girl. It didn't seem to matter what I did, so long as I didn't come home pregnant."

"Do you think your dad loves you?"

"Sure. He doesn't accept me, but he loves me. He even took care of my dog."

"Why wouldn't he accept you?"

She thought about the question, not sure she wanted to pursue the light glimmering on the horizon.

"Terri, do you feel unworthy of his acceptance? That you're not good enough because you're a woman? Or because a paramedic isn't, say for example, a doctor?"

That was what she didn't want to pursue. "Probably. To all of the above."

"Are you still trying to gain his acceptance?"

"No, I gave that up long ago."

"Do you think God accepts you?"

"You're linking my feelings toward my dad with how I feel about God."

"I find they often intersect. God is our heavenly Father. Earthly fathers can be poor substitutes."

"And what's your point?"

He grinned. "I always did like your pragmatism. What do you think the point is?"

She toyed with her bangs again. "My dad's rejection does not mean God rejects me. I should remember that because Jesus died on the cross, God accepts me."

"God not only accepts you, Terri, He accepts you just as you are. He even *likes* you just as you are. He is your holy Father."

"No matter what I've done?"

"No matter what you've done or will do in the future. It's a tough concept to grasp, especially when we've spent years trying to earn a parent's love. Once we forgive a parent, we're free to move on."

"There's nothing to forgive. He did the best he could raising me."

"Terri, we humans are imperfect. Your dad let you down simply by being imperfectly human. That left a wound within you. Only God can heal it and give you the ability to forgive."

"Bryan, all I wanted to know was what I'm supposed to do about the mess I'm in with Kai and work and Erin Morgan and my dog and my apartment!"

His burst of laughter mellowed into a deep rumble. "One thing at a time, Terri. One thing at a time."

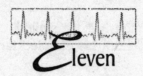

Eleven

After her three days off duty, Terri arrived at the firehouse earlier than usual for work. No big deal. Fall off a bicycle? Get back on and pedal. Fall off a horse? Climb right back into that saddle. Giddyup. She would schedule vacation time just as soon as she slapped on a pair of latex gloves and delivered a patient she herself had stabilized to the ER.

Offending a friend and coworker was a different story. The fact that she and Kai occasionally got on each other's nerves was unavoidable. Abrasive words flew between them like a shuttlecock in a game of badminton. No matter. It came with the territory. Days later, by their next shift, all would be forgotten.

Not so this time. She knew that. The exchange had been intense and personal. And true. Oh, so true! She owed him an apology, but she did not want to give it over the telephone. Besides that, he needed plenty of time to cool off. If he wasn't ready to accept her apology—

There was that word again. Acceptance. Okay, she hadn't worked through things yet. But what was the point of sticking out her neck if Kai was just going to wring it? So she waited until their next shift. By then he would be feeling bad enough to forgive her.

She talked with the medic going off duty and learned what supplies were needed on the ambulance. While she was restocking, Shawn Leonard appeared, the young firefighter and father of three. He had white blond hair and a thousand-watt smile.

"Shawn. Hey, thanks for delivering my car the other day."

"You're welcome. How are you doing?"

"Not bad."

"Kai's not coming in." He smiled, and an all-American freshness beamed from his dimpled face. "Guess who you get."

She swallowed her disappointment. The rehearsed apology would have to wait. "Is he sick?" Kai hadn't been sick a day in his life.

He shrugged. "They didn't tell me. What can I do?"

"You can help me restock. We'll wait until after roll call to do the detailed check." The check was a daily chore that took about an hour. They had to determine that everything on the ambulance was in working order and that they were prepared for every conceivable and inconceivable emergency under the sun.

"Yeah, right. And maybe nobody will call 911 first thing."

She gave him a brief smile. They usually ended up doing the check at the hospital because more often than not they were called out immediately. "Yeah, maybe."

Maybe. If only. Oh, please.

Perspiration collected on her upper lip. She felt it under her arms. The weather was cool, clear, and crisp, an exquisite mid-October morn. She wasn't the least bit warm even in the long-sleeved shirt.

Why Shawn Leonard?

She needed Kai today. She had counted on Kai's backup. Why Shawn? He was a firefighter and paramedic. He was a good guy, young, energetic, friendly, able, and willing. He volunteered for all the extra duty he could. But on the ambulance with her? Over six hundred medics with CFD and he gets called?

Kai understood her nuances. If she blanked again, he would know it the moment she did, if not before. He would be that steady hand on the bicycle as she pedaled. He would grasp the horse's reins as she accustomed herself again to the saddle and stirrups. A seasoned paramedic might have a clue. But Shawn?

As she joined the firefighters for roll call, the answer came to her. She thought a couple of the guys gave her sidelong glances. Greetings from others were...stilted. Or was it only her imagination? Even though they weren't the same group on duty three nights ago, they would have heard about her flaking out. Sure they worked together as a team. In ways they were closer even than a family, interdependent in emergencies, entrusting one another with their lives. Though the situation hadn't threatened her coworkers, she had sent a ripple through that circle of trust.

A little over a year ago Shawn had drawn sidelong glances and stilted greetings from the group. For the most part, the coworkers' response to his presence was not malicious or even intentional. She knew that for a fact because she herself had done it to him.

She hadn't meant to treat Shawn differently or to hold him responsible for the tragedy, but she did. Human nature said someone had to be blamed for the death of her friend. The details didn't matter. There was a fire. Shawn's breathing apparatus didn't work. He got lost, was overcome with smoke. The other firefighter went in to save him. He succeeded. He got Shawn out in time. But not himself.

For a while, Shawn was somewhat of a pariah. She was surprised he didn't quit or at least put in for a transfer, but he didn't. That and his giving attitude said something for his mettle.

She too had let down the brotherhood, and she couldn't even blame a piece of malfunctioning equipment. Sure, no one had died, but she'd endangered others by ignoring signs of burnout and then falling apart at the seams while on the job. And now there she was, back in her Lone Ranger's saddle that should have been a seat on a bus, a seat she should have let someone else use for awhile.

So God must have dialed Shawn's number today. Who better to provide backup for a shaky outcast? The guy was a role model for losers like herself.

"Terri."

She blinked. Shawn's face was inches from hers.

"You'll be fine."

At 8:30 the next morning, Terri placed her thumb on the doorbell and leaned against it with all her weight. There came a deeply satisfying long discordant buzz from within.

Kai opened his apartment door. "All right, already!" He wore jeans and a plaid flannel shirt as if dressed for the day, but his eyes were at half mast and stubble covered his jaw.

"Rushman, if you think I've come to apologize, you're wrong."

He backed away, letting her walk inside. "Fine."

"Fine. Twenty-four hours ago an apology was on the tip of my tongue. A profuse apology, but not now. No, sirree."

He shut the door. "Do you want some coffee?"

"Sure." She followed him across the living room to the counter that divided it from the kitchen, pulled out a stool, and sat down. "I was on my way home from work and couldn't remember where it is I'm living today. So I thought I'd stop by and ask you in person why you left me in the lurch."

His back to her, he poured coffee into two mugs and didn't reply.

"Rushman, it was the hardest thing I've ever done. Climb back in the rig and face that first patient after what happened."

"Then why did you do it?" He set the mugs on the counter between them and sat down on his side. "Hmm?"

She wrapped her hands around a cup and avoided his eyes. "To prove to myself I could."

"You're a hot dog."

She winced. "I know." Bryan's words of affirmation came to mind. God loved and accepted her, hot dog though she was. She didn't have to prove her worth to anyone. "Kai, I'm sorry. Everything you said was true. I'm sorry for allowing things to get to this point."

"Was that the profuse apology?" He crossed his arms on the countertop, rested his chin on them, and studied her face. "Kind of short for a profuse one."

"I'm sure more will come out as we move along."

"You did fine, didn't you?"

"Shawn Leonard filled in. He's the calmest medic I've ever met." He'd kept her centered. They found a common denominator in their faith and spent time in between runs discussing Jesus. She felt as if she'd been nourished at some deep, unknowable level.

"And you did fine," Kai repeated. "Right?"

She lifted a hand and dropped it on the counter. "Home free until six-seventeen this morning."

"What was it?"

"The woman who called in said she thought her husband had suffered a heart attack. She was this little bird of a thing flitting around. Not hysterical, just concerned. 'I didn't know what to do. He won't wake up.' She takes us into the bedroom where the seventy-year-old is in bed, flat on his back, not a muscle moving. I'm thinking, 'oh man, he must have just gone peacefully in his sleep, in the blink of an eye.'" She snapped her fingers. "I touch his neck, and the guy sits up!"

"No! He sits up?"

"Boing!" She slapped her hands together. "Straight up. 'What's going on?' he shouts. 'Who are you? Woman,' he actually called his wife that, 'who are these people?' She says, 'The paramedics, dear. You wouldn't wake up.' 'Of course not. I was asleep!'"

Kai laughed.

"Shawn almost burst a blood vessel trying to keep a straight face. The wife offered us coffee and coffee cake. If the husband hadn't been fussing so much, we would have accepted."

"Sorry I missed that one."

"It was pretty good." She smiled. "But it was a gift. I can go out smiling. What do you think? Two weeks off?"

"Minimum."

She nodded. "Wait and see. I just need to get away. Find a place to live. Maybe go to church."

"Sounds like a good plan." He rubbed his eyes with a fist.

"Kai, you don't look so good. Are you really sick?"

He shrugged. "You hungry?"

"No. We didn't take the coffee cake but Shawn's wife brought in homemade cinnamon rolls. Mmm."

"You didn't bring me any."

"You think there was one available after the guys got to them? You changed the subject. What's wrong?"

"I have to tell you something. Promise not to go ballistic."

"You already told me about your new job." She reached over and punched his arm. "Congratulations. I am mad and heartbroken, but very proud of you and happy for you. If you're sure it's what you really want."

He gave her a half smile. "It is what I really want. Thanks. Anyway, you promise?"

"Okay, okay."

He sat up straighter and took a swig of coffee. "Night before last, I went over to Erin's."

"What!"

"You promised. Look, I blame her, and myself for getting snookered in by her, for your situation."

"Kai, that's not true. This burnout or whatever was coming anyway, just like you said."

"All that aside, it would help if she stopped bugging you."

"You went to her house? I can't believe it. You didn't tell her what Cara said!"

He glared at her.

Of course he wouldn't repeat that information. "Sorry."

"It was late, but she let me in. Ever the gushing flirt, you know. Showed me her dog. Golden retriever, same as Zoë. Looked the same age. Even had that little bump on her head. Purebred. And her name was Zoë."

Terri shuddered.

"Yeah, weirded me out too. Erin kept talking about how she knew I'd come back to her. Finally I got a chance to tell her to stay away from you. It was as if I hadn't said a word. That's when I started to get the drift that you can't talk sanely to an insane person. Gets you nowhere fast. I got out of there."

"Thanks for trying."

"Well, that's not the end of the story. And Cara Fleming thinks I could have made matters worse, but things turned out all right."

"You called Cara?"

"Later. First I called the kennel."

Terri stared at him.

"I couldn't sleep. I spent most of the night calling them. Nobody answered until five. It's okay, Ter. It's okay! Breathe, girl." He reached over and squeezed her hand. "Zoë is safe and sound at the kennel. Now."

"Now? Kai!"

"She wasn't there when I first talked to them. That's when I called Cara. She met me at Erin's. Nobody home. No dog barking. She called the kennel and learned that Zoë had just been dropped off. They found her tied to a fence. We went out there. Zoë's fine. She's—"

"Erin *took* her?"

"That's my guess. 'Course, there's no way of proving it. Cara interviewed employees. They don't know how it happened.

There was a note that your sister Shelley Schuman picked her up."

Terri covered her mouth with her hands, the horror sinking in.

"Cara sent a uniformed officer to Erin's house. She denied ever having a dog, said I was mistaken. Invited him inside. He couldn't find any evidence of a dog ever having been there."

"Oh, Kai! What if you hadn't gone to her house? I have got to find a place to live and get Zoë back with me!"

"You've got to do more than that. Cara and I started tailing Erin yesterday morning. And she was tailing you."

"Me? While I was on duty?"

He nodded. "She didn't keep up with you on every run, but she'd catch up either at the hospital or back at the station. This is getting way too weird, Ter. Cara thinks it's time for a restraining order."

∿

Later that afternoon Terri sat in a downtown restaurant in Chicago's Loop district sipping coffee, her first cup since the one at Kai's that morning. From her seat at the window she watched congested traffic stop and go. Pedestrians hurried along the sidewalk, probably heading home after the workday. Shadows filled Wabash Avenue, but then they always did. Elevated train tracks formed a canopy above it, casting shade even on the brightest of days. Now the sun was already setting behind skyscrapers.

Gabe Andrews was late.

She took a swig of coffee. Why hadn't she listened to her own voice instead of Kai's? Her partner reached her on the cell phone a short while after she left his apartment. They talked as she drove to her sister's place. Gabe had called Kai, asking for her number.

"Kai, I don't want to talk to him. I've got enough on my mind as it is without him complicating things by rehashing last

Friday night. He saw me at my worst. I'd rather put that behind me. Besides...I broke his mug."

"You broke his mug?"

"Yeah. A special one. It said something about best dad in the world."

"How did—"

"Don't ask."

"Okay. Well, be that as it may, I think you should talk to him. He's got an idea that might help you out. I gave him your cell and pager numbers."

Thank you, Kai, she thought sarcastically. The pager she used exclusively for work-related matters. The new cell number she treated as an ultra private one, giving it out at work and to parents, siblings, and the closest of friends only after they swore not to give it out even to other closest of friends. Now a complete stranger had both of them.

Complete stranger except for the fact she'd slept in his condo.

Gabe approached. She spotted him through a break in traffic, across the street waiting for the light to change. Even in the shadows his hair gleamed. He wasn't brawny like Lee, but the breadth of his shoulders left no doubt that things like firefighting gear were borne regularly by them. He wore jeans and a tweedy sport jacket over a dark, open-collared shirt.

She wondered why he wanted to talk in person rather than over the phone. When she explained that she was living downtown, he didn't hesitate offering to make the 30-minute drive. If she pushed aside that business about him working in a largely Hispanic neighborhood and not speaking Spanish, she figured he was a nice enough guy.

"Hi." He pulled out a chair opposite her and sat, a friendly smile on his face.

"Hi."

"Sorry I'm late. Traffic. I tried to call and page you."

"I'm electronically unplugged. Somebody said I was on vacation. Would you like some coffee?" She lifted the carafe the waitress had left on the table with an extra cup.

"Sure. Thanks. So you're on vacation?" He smiled again. It wasn't only his hair that gleamed. His caramel eyes and tanned face joined in on the act.

"Something like that."

The smile dwindled, but his eyes still radiated...pity? He'd seen her at her absolute worst. "Kai told me about Zoë."

Gabe Andrews knew way too much about her. "You guys are getting awfully chummy."

"I'd rather be chummy with you, but you're kind of tough to get a hold of."

"I'll kill him."

"What?"

"Kai gave you my number so you could make a pass at me?"

"Huh? I made a pass?"

"You want to be *chummy* with me?"

"That was your word."

"You used it!"

"Are you flirting with me?" He raised his brows as if appalled at the thought. "I'm sorry to disappoint you, but I'm already involved."

The tips of her ears warmed. "I am not flirting with you."

"Well, good, because I have a business proposition, and it won't work if you're flirting with me."

"Excuse me. I'm just a little on the defensive side these days, okay?"

"I'd say it's more like the offensive side."

"That is the best defense." Her entire face felt hot now. "The rug keeps getting pulled out from under me."

"So I hear. You know how *chummy* I am with Kai."

His grin was like a dash of water on her flaming embarrassment. Her mounting tension released itself in a chuckle. "Yeah, yeah. I know. All right, business proposition. It must have to do with working in your district, to which I already said—"

"Can we save this?" He checked his watch. "How about a movie first? There's one I want to see down at that place on State Street. Kind of artsy. No subtitles, though. It was made in Australia."

"What's a movie got to do with anything?"

"I want to talk to you as soon as possible and I want to see this movie that starts in fifteen minutes. Therefore, I'm asking you to go with me. And this is not a pass."

The thought struck her that conversing with Gabe had eclipsed her worries. Zoë, Erin, and apartment hunting had faded to the back burner. She thought of her sister's dinner party, which would probably last until at least ten. She had no desire to mingle with Shelley's friends. A movie would certainly help while away the hours. After all, she was supposed to be relaxing on vacation.

He said, "What do you say?"

"Do you always get your cake and eat it too?"

"No, not usually."

"It's your lucky day then." She stood up, pulled some money from her jacket pocket, and dropped it on the table. "Let's go."

Twelve

"Are you going to tell me about your business proposition tonight or what?" Terri chased a scoop of melting cinnamon ice cream across a piece of hot apple pie with her fork.

"A spoon works better." Gabe, who'd ordered the same dessert, neatly slipped a spoonful of it into his mouth.

"But this is more fun." She laughed and smeared the ice cream around her plate.

They were back at the same restaurant where they'd met before the movie. He'd suggested dinner since he hadn't had a chance yet to tell her what he wanted to tell her. And besides, how could he come all the way downtown and not eat world-famous baby back ribs? They'd eaten the ribs while totally engaged in a discussion of the movie.

He said, "You look like a kid playing in the mud."

"Now I know I'm on vacation. So, do you really have a business proposition or not?"

His mouth slid into a contorted half smile, causing only one dimple to appear. The left one. "I just wanted to make sure you felt comfortable with me."

"I shared my popcorn with you. And told you Dave thinks I'm a substandard creep." Dave was her sister's live-in boyfriend, a prosecuting attorney with the DA's office.

He smiled. "Which is why you went to the movie and are now playing with your food, to postpone going home."

"Home. We use *that* term loosely."

"Yes, we do. Have you ever told Dave he'd better hope you're around when some truly substandard creep he sent to prison gets out and comes after him with a gun?"

"I can't even joke with the guy. Though I discussed a particularly nasty gunshot wound in gory detail once at dinner, solely for his benefit. He did not appreciate my humor."

He laughed. "I'd say it's time to move out. Why don't you move into my condo?"

"Now you are making a pass at me." She took a bite of pie. Sweet warm bits of apple and brown sugary crumble topping created an ambrosial sensation in her mouth. "Mmmm."

"There you go, flirting with me again, batting those long thick eyelashes."

She recognized the bait and ignored it. "I could live in the bunk bed room. Who uses those bunk beds, by the way?"

"My kids. Every other weekend. *If* I'm not working. Some holidays. *If* I'm not working." He shrugged.

"Oh." He had kids. That meant there must be a wife somewhere in the picture. He carried baggage that didn't show in his laid-back personality. "How old are they?"

"Jordan is fifteen, and she's not too crazy about sharing the room with Spencer anymore. He's ten. I thought it was about time I offered them a little more. I built a house out a ways. Three bedrooms, trees in the yard."

She set down her spoon. "Oh my gosh! You're moving. You are moving! Are you serious about the condo?"

He grinned. "Yes. The place is yours if you want it. Zoë is more than welcome too."

"But...but..." There were so many buts, she didn't know where to begin.

"I'll explain. The new house is finished sooner than I'd hoped. Finished enough for me to live in, anyway. I'm keeping the condo and renting it out. I didn't bother advertising; people have already inquired about it. Seeing that you need a place ASAP, I'm offering it first to you. I'll be completely moved out on Saturday."

"But...but... It's a nice place. A really, really nice place."
As in sky-high rent district.

He contemplated her face for a moment. The glow shone
in his eyes. She'd begun to suspect it was more compassion
than pity. He flashed that half smile again.

"Rent's not out of sight. My second job is working construction with a friend who owns the company."

That explained the shoulders and perpetual tan.

"We built this condominium complex fifteen years ago,
and that's when I bought my unit, as an investment property.
I rented it out until, uh, until my wife left me and I needed a
place of my own."

"When was that?"

"Eight years ago. She didn't like firefighting. She met an
older guy who wasn't married to his job. Actually he had
been, but his wife left him while he was. So he'd made his
millions and was ready to settle down by the time Paula came
along. End of story."

"I'm sorry."

"Thanks." He smiled softly. "You want to move in this
weekend?"

"How much?"

He quoted her an unbelievably reasonable figure.

To her chagrin, tears sprang in her eyes. She looked down
at her plate.

"Terri, we can negotiate."

She quietly sniffed and cut another bite. "If I paid less, I'd
feel like a thief."

"Okay, it's a deal then."

She looked at him. "Okay. Thanks. Does this sweetheart of
a deal come with strings?"

"Absolutely not."

She lowered her voice, mimicking him the night he'd
shown up at the station, "Terri Schuman, come on down!
Have I got a deal for you!"

He laughed.

"What was that all about? You didn't know I needed a place to live that night."

"No, but I knew you could speak Spanish."

"Gabe, I'd already told you I wasn't interested in transferring."

"But I had a new idea. Come ride with the guy who's quitting and informally check things out. Maybe whet your appetite for serving in a different way. Fall in love with working in your grandmother's native tongue. Things like that."

She watched his face. It wasn't just his golden hair or his tan or his melting caramel eyes. The man gleamed most of the time with...what? Passion. Passion for his work, for making his condo available to her, for his children, for the movie discussion. Even for the world-famous baby back ribs. For life itself. She'd only seen such fervency in one other male.

Vic Koski had embodied a love of life, all of life. She'd been attracted to him, as were most people. Not in a romantic sense, but in the sense that he was unequivocally trustworthy. In time she came to understand that his faith in Christ had made him so.

"Gabe, are you a Christian?"

He looked surprised. "Yeah."

"It shows. Me too." She hadn't admitted *that* to many people. "It doesn't show."

He grinned. "We're all different."

"Mm-hmm."

"Terri, the idea to ride is not a string. It's a chance for an adventure. I won't say anything more."

There was much more he could say. Kai was leaving. Vic's departure had created a giant void at the firehouse and within herself. A strange woman was following her. Even before that development she had avoided the wretched studio apartment. Yes, she was ripe for a change.

Gabe laid a pair of keys beside her plate on the table.

She looked at him.

"Front and back doors. Think about the other?"

Her stomach fluttered as if she stood on the brink of a cliff, toes dangling, a strong steady breeze pressing against her back. Letting go of control was still a new concept to her. To even consider letting go caused extreme discomfort. What was that Bible verse? Something about the God of all comfort. What did that mean?

"Tell you what, Gabe. I'll pray about it."

He smiled and gave her a thumbs-up.

~

Standing on a sidewalk, Terri held a lunch-sized brown paper bag in one hand and Zoë's leash in the other. Unfettered, her dog frolicked about in a crisscross pattern in the grass. The ride had been a long one from the kennel, extra so considering the circuitous route she'd driven with her right eye practically glued to the rearview mirror.

The grassy area where Zoë ran was enclosed on three sides by two-story condominiums. Although in general the buildings' style reflected an English chateau, the individual units were distinctive in their colors and roof lines. The contrasting landscapes along their front exteriors made them appear almost like a group of separate houses without side yards.

Gabe's condo was on the right-hand side, fifth down from the drive, flanked by two taller units. Gray siding. Creeping juniper beneath a picture window. It lacked the personal touches of the door wreaths or potted mums that graced some of the neighbors' homes. Although there were no second-story windows, she remembered a staircase in the living room. She also recalled leaving through the back door and finding a fenced-in patio, a gate, and a carport.

Odd. Beyond the address, she didn't know a whole lot about what she was moving into. Two facts were clear though. One, at least 15 minutes had been added to her commute.

And two, the first month's rent would deplete her checking account because she owed another month on the studio's lease.

She reminded herself to inhale deeply. Since owning up to a state of burnout and a need for time off, she had noticed a curious urge to stop and smell the roses. Or burning leaves. The scent hovered. Fall was winding down. The sky was overcast, the temperature chilly. Zoë raced between a smattering of small trees on which shriveled yellow leaves clung.

She took another breath.

What do You think, Lord?

She watched the dog now chasing her own tail, revelling in pure, unadulterated joy. Terri smiled. *This is the moment of a new beginning. Zoë's with me and Erin isn't. What more do I need?*

"Thanks, Lord."

⁓

Before Terri had a chance to ring the bell, a towheaded boy opened the door, his face a miniature of Gabe's in full grin. Two dimples accented his round cheeks. "Is that your dog?"

She laughed. "Yes, this is Zoë." The dog sat obediently beside her on a short leash, panting from her playtime. "You must be Spencer. I'm Terri. Did your dad tell you I was coming?"

He nodded and shook her outstretched hand, but he had eyes only for the dog.

"You can play with her. May we come in?"

He moved aside.

An overwhelming pine scent greeted her as she walked into the living room. The dull roar of a vacuum cleaner could be heard coming from the back of the condo. The staircase just inside the door suggested a loft area. Nice.

Terri knelt beside her dog. "Zoë, this is Spencer."

He also knelt, which put him below Zoë's eye level.

"She likes her neck rubbed. Right there. That's it."

"Terri. Hi."

She looked up to see that Gabe had entered the living room. "Hi. I hope you don't mind that I brought Zoë along."

"Of course not." He leaned over and scratched the dog's ear. "Hey, Zoë." He laughed at her thumping tail. "Look, Spence, I think she's grinning."

The boy laughed with his dad.

"Do you want to take her out back?" He glanced at Terri. "It's fenced in."

"Sure." She unhooked the leash and stood.

Spencer's big caramel eyes glowed. "Thanks! Come on, girl." He slapped his small thigh and the dog followed as quickly as she could, slowed by the frenzied wagging of her tail.

Gabe moaned. "He's going to want one. She is beautiful."

"Thanks. Uh, here." She handed him the small brown paper bag. "Housewarming gift."

"You didn't have to—" He pulled out a coffee mug. "What's this? Number One Dad?"

She scrunched her nose. "I broke your other one. I'm sorry. It was probably a really special one from your kids. I feel awful. This is the closest thing I could find to best dad in the world or whatever—"

He burst into laughter.

"What?"

Wiping the corners of his eyes, he said, "I'm sorry. I don't mean to laugh at you. Thank you. This is a nice gesture. And please don't feel bad. I hadn't really noticed the message on the other one for years. It was just a mug. From Paula, not the kids."

"Ah."

"The gift was given out of guilt and didn't mean anything." There was no bitterness in his tone, leading her to believe that he'd come to terms with whatever had happened eight years ago.

He held up the mug, inspecting it. "This one is much nicer and given with a purer motive."

"Not exactly. Only a boatload of guilt would get me inside a gift shop."

He smiled. "Let me show you around. This is the living room."

The rectangular room was bare except for the freshly vacuumed beige carpet. "You really didn't have to clean."

A teenage girl entered from the kitchen doorway. "See, Dad. I told you we didn't have to." The pout on her face indicated she wasn't joking.

In spite of the pout, she was drop-dead gorgeous. Terri tried not to stare. In her opinion, 15-year-olds should not be drop-dead gorgeous. Flawless skin. Delicate nose. Bright baby blues emphasized by eyeliner above and below. Perfectly arched eyebrows. A model's shape flaunted by hip-hugging blue jeans and cropped white sweater. Except for the straight, shoulder-length hair the color of burnished gold, she did not look like Gabe. The ex-wife must be a knockout.

"Jordan," he said, "this is Terri Schuman."

"Hi, Jordan." Terri offered her hand.

The girl limply shook it. "Hi." Evidently the pout was a permanent fixture.

Terri smiled, fighting the impulse to respond in like manner. "It's a hazard of the trade, you know, all that cleaning. Firefighters are endlessly cleaning apparatus and the firehouse."

There was a slight fluttering of her eyelids, a "give me a break" expression. "I thought he was a Marine Corps drill sergeant."

Like she knew anything about the Marines.

"Jordan." A muscle in Gabe's jaw twitched.

"What?" Exasperation underscored the word. The eyelids did their thing again.

He crossed his arms. The jaw was definitely clenched now. Perhaps there was a slight resemblance to a Marine Corps drill sergeant.

Jordan's pout deepened. "I finished all the vacuuming. May I be excused?"

"Yes."

"I'll be outside." She flounced from the room. A moment later there was the double click of the back door opening and closing.

Gabe stared at the space she'd vacated, immobile.

Terri tapped his arm. "What's upstairs?"

"Hmm? Oh, the master bedroom. Look, I'm sorry. She's a snob."

"Gabe, she's fifteen. Fifteen-year-olds are supposed to be snobs."

"Her demeanor is the spitting image of her mother's, and that woman is thirty-nine."

"Some of us take a while to outgrow it."

He shook his head but smiled.

"Anything you want to show me up there?"

"Yeah. There's a great balcony off the room. It overlooks the carports, but you can't see the neighbors."

He showed her everything from the balcony to closets to light switches to the laundry room in the basement to the idiosyncrasies of faucets, front door latch, and a temperamental window. He took her and Zoë next door to meet the twin teenage boy and girl who said dog sitting was their forte. The tour ended in the kitchen.

Terri pulled her checkbook from the back pocket of her jeans. "First and last months' rent plus how much for deposit?"

"First month will cover everything."

"No way."

"I don't need any more. And we can sign a lease later for whatever time period you prefer."

"Gabe, you don't even know me."

"I know enough."

"Strings," she muttered.

He grinned. "Wouldn't think of it. Do you need any help moving in?"

"Enough already! The strings are choking me as it is. No, I don't need help!" She bent over the counter, talking as she wrote the check. "Actually, Zoë and I are moving in tonight. I promised her no more kennel. I brought a sleeping bag and coffeepot. Kai and a couple of the other guys will move the big stuff tomorrow."

She tried to ignore a fizzy sensation in her chest. Her good fortune was difficult to process. The condo was larger and in better shape than the duplex she'd shared with Lee. With only a month's rent to subtract, the bite out of her checking account would be a mere nibble. Gabe Andrews was a genuinely nice guy. Words she didn't want to say danced on the frothy bubbles, making their way to her tongue.

She handed him the check. "How about if I ride some time this week with your medic?"

His mouth eased into his crooked half smile. "You don't owe me."

"Yes, I do. One ride anyway."

The smile spread into a two-dimpled grin. He shook her hand. "Okay. One ride, even steven."

There was something about his bright eyes and dimpled cheeks that made her think he'd just offered her a dare. What was she getting herself into?

Thirteen

Late the next afternoon, Terri shut the kitchen door and leaned against it, smiling. The countertops were hidden beneath empty pizza boxes and soda cans. A plate overflowed with chocolate chip cookies on the dinette table. *Her* table. In *her* kitchen. Her very nice galley kitchen with white cabinets that widened into a square area with pale yellow walls and doorways leading to the living room and hall, just large enough for four chairs and the table. *Her* table.

Cara Fleming entered from the living room followed by Kai.

He grinned. "Schuman, as I live and breathe, you're sighing."

"I am?"

Cara said, "I never would have pegged you to be the sighing type."

Terri let out an exaggerated sigh complete with a soprano accompaniment. "It just feels so good to be home again!"

Kai laughed. "It has been a while for you. Well, I'm taking off. Thanks for the backup, Cara."

"You're welcome."

Earlier, while others loaded Terri's furniture into pickup trucks, the detective had followed Erin Morgan around a shopping mall. Knowing her whereabouts had relieved Terri. Though she hadn't run into Erin for a while, the fact that the girl would have no clue about the move filled her with a new peace of mind.

Kai, Shawn Leonard, and Kevin Gray had made quick work of transferring her things. Other guys from the station had offered to help, though with her few possessions it wasn't needed. Terri felt the pariah's hat had been removed. Maybe it was, after all, her imagination.

Jody Leonard and Jessie Gray, the men's wives, joined the party. They brought homemade cookies, unpacked the kitchen, and ordered pizzas. Thankfully they left the six kids they had between them at home with sitters. Last year Terri had been in a Bible study with them, something she had urged Rachel to create. Since Rachel had moved away, the group had grown but the dynamics had changed. Young mothers became the majority and most of them were not married to firefighters. Terri lost interest in the meetings.

Still, the bond was there today, that mysterious connection she sometimes felt with fellow Christians. Perhaps that's what it was with Gabe. Perhaps it wasn't strings. Perhaps it was anything but what jumped into her head as she drifted off to sleep last night on the floor beside Zoë. The guy fascinated her. She'd never met such a genuinely nice guy.

"Terri." Kai approached. "Take care."

Impulsively she wrapped her arms around his neck. "Thank you, Kai. For everything."

The two of them weren't often physically demonstrative, but he hugged her. "Sure."

"I can't believe you won't be there when I get back."

He let go and looked down at her, a sober expression on his face. "Maybe you should consider the transfer. Get a fresh start. Not that my absence will be a big deal for a hot dog like you."

She grinned and smacked his arm. His absence would be a big deal but, not wanting to lay a guilt trip on him, she remained quiet.

"You've had a lot of upheaval, things piling up on each other. Now might be the right time."

She shrugged. "I don't know."

"I hear you're taking a ride this week."

Her jaw dropped. "What is this? Are you and Gabe like best friends now?"

He grinned and walked past her to the door. "Don't be a stranger."

Before she could respond, he was gone.

"Do you mind if I ask something?"

Terri turned.

Cara was sitting at the table, half a cookie in her hand.

She joined her. "Ask away."

"What transfer?"

Terri helped herself to a cookie. "Gabe Andrews, the guy who owns this place, is a fireman. He wants me to transfer to his district because I speak Spanish. They could use the help and one of their medics is leaving."

"What are you thinking?"

Suddenly overcome with a feeling of loneliness, she lowered her eyes and broke apart the cookie.

"Maybe you don't want to talk about it."

"Actually…" Her voice trailed off as she studied the policewoman for a moment.

On an otherwise unremarkable face, Cara's eyes were extraordinary. They were hazel, a changing mixture of brown, yellow, green, and gray. They were unusually wide set. In general, her disposition was one of aloofness. It probably served her well in her frequent encounters with society's criminal element. On the other hand, she had the endearing quality of a scatterbrain. She would search every pocket for the pen that was behind her ear. She often didn't finish one sentence before starting another. Either she was greatly incompetent or else her mind was simply too concerned with the matter at hand to bother with mundane details. Terri was betting on the latter cause. Since the first day they met, she felt it gave her permission to speak freely.

"Actually," Terri repeated, "I'm about ready to explode. No one has asked me what I'm thinking for a long, *long* time."

Cara smiled. "Why don't you put on another pot of coffee?"

∽

"Things started to fall apart almost a year ago." Terri set down her coffee mug and carefully considered her next words. It didn't help. There wasn't any other way to say it. "About the same time I started believing and trusting in God. I mean, as in talking to Him and studying the Bible."

The corners of Cara's mouth twitched.

"Go ahead and say it. You think I'm looney."

She smiled. "If I do, that makes two of us. No, I'm smiling because I know what you mean about how giving Him control seems tantamount to signing up for disaster."

"Really?"

"Mm-hmm."

Terri sat back in her chair, momentarily overcome with an odd sense of awareness. Something unseen within her had just connected with something unseen in Cara. Was that the Holy Spirit?

Cara said, "Tell me how things fell apart."

She listened patiently to Terri's litany of woes: Vic's death, Lee, Erin, a policeman complaining about her, yelling at Gabe, her dad's cancer, living out of a suitcase, freezing up during a simple procedure in the back of the ambulance, Kai's transfer.

When she had finished, Cara said, "I think I have to agree with your assessment. Things are falling apart. But I imagine you know as well as I do that such circumstances are the springboard for new insight. Let's go back to the original question: What are you thinking?"

"I'm thinking I don't know what to think."

"Then that's why you're taking some time off. Give it a rest. It'll become clear."

"I hate waiting."

Cara smiled. "You know, something changes in your demeanor when you talk about Gabe."

"What do you mean something changes?" She felt a tickle in her throat.

"Like that. A subtle shift in pitch. Your head tilts a bit. Whoops. Now your neck has stiffened. You don't want to go where this is leading, do you?"

"No."

"Here's my theory."

Terri felt her eyelids flutter. They probably resembled Jordan's.

Cara ignored her. "I thought about that hormone you and Kai discussed. The one that kicks in when we're stressed out and produces a high. I'm just trying to see here if I understand it correctly." She grew animated, her voice urgent. "Now, you're totally stressed out with this Erin thing. You miss your dog. And you lose focus on the job. Then shazam! Along comes the hero."

"I don't want to go there."

Cara went there. "Gabe rescues you! He tubes the guy and offers you a way out of your situation. New home and new job. Bingo. Hormone does its thing."

"Hey, I'm just under your everyday, garden-variety kind of stress. It has to be an all-out, life-threatening situation for the hormone to work."

"The body differentiates between stresses?" Suddenly she grinned. "Tell me to back off if I'm annoying you."

"Back off."

"Okay."

"I mean, Gabe Andrews? I don't think so."

Cara shrugged. "Consider this your first alert. You can thank me later."

"Why don't we change the subject? What do you think I should do?"

"About Gabe?"

Terri groaned and laid her forehead on the table.

"Sorry. I couldn't resist."

"This is not a laughing matter."

"Love never is."

Terri burst into frustrated laughter and straightened. "Cara! I was talking about my life!"

"Okay. Seriously, I think you should relax. Right after we go to the courthouse tomorrow and get a restraining order against Erin."

"How does that work?"

"First, you need to fill out a petition for an emergency order of protection. If you don't want to hire an attorney, I can walk you through it. Then you give it to the clerk, who gives it to the judge, who will probably want to ask you questions. On paper Erin's description may come across as you and Kai describe her, a harmless 'groupie.' I can talk to the judge too and explain the investigation. Then hopefully he'll grant the order. A law enforcement officer then serves Erin with it."

"So she'll know to stay away from me?"

"She'll know. Initially the order lasts up to twenty-one days. We'll reassess things then and decide if we need to ask for more time."

"Is there anything new on the investigation?"

"No. We've put out the word for anyone who witnessed the collision to call us. That stretch of road is never without traffic. Someone had to have seen it happen. Now we wait."

"Meanwhile, she follows me. At least she doesn't know where I live. When I go back to work though, won't I still have to keep looking over my shoulder, even with a restraining order?"

"Yes, but if she comes anywhere near you, call the cops. They will arrest her."

"That sounds so cold and heartless."

"It's for her own good as well as yours. She needs boundaries and consequences, Terri."

"She needs help."

"Exactly. So who says you can't pray for her *and* get an order?"

That sounded like something Rachel would say. Pragmatic without losing sight of an otherworldly perspective. Maybe there was a silver lining in the mess of her life after all. It came in the form of a police detective.

∽

Later that week, on Friday morning, Terri studied her reflection in the medicine cabinet mirror.

"Gabe."

Involuntarily her chin tucked itself downward, causing her head to tilt slightly to the right.

She shook her head, straightened her shoulders, inhaled, and exhaled.

"Gabe."

The same thing happened.

"Oh, horsefeathers!" She shook her head violently and repeated the process.

"Gabe."

It happened again.

She flipped off the light, stomped down the short hall to the kitchen, and thought about calling Cara Fleming to gripe. There should be a law against implanting suggestions into the subconscious mind of an unwitting friend. Instead, she made coffee and washed her cereal bowl. Gabe was due to arrive at any moment. He had just gotten off duty and phoned, asking if he could stop by with the lease.

In synchronized fashion, the last drop of coffee plunked into the carafe as Zoë yipped a hello bark from the patio.

Terri opened the back door. Gabe shut the tall privacy fence gate and stooped to roughhouse with the dog.

Okay, so the guy was cute. Albeit in a California surfer sort of way.

He was under six feet tall, lean, and— Well, there was no other word for it. He was nice. Incredibly so. Any male with at least one of those three traits had never ever drawn a second glance from her.

He said he was already involved. That translated into romantically with someone.

He had kids.

What was it her niece used to say? *Gag me with a spoon.*

She wasn't about to let a crazy hormone dictate her emotions. Fascinated by him? *Give me a break.*

"Hi, Terri."

"Hi, Gabe."

He followed her into the house. "Are you okay?"

"I'm fine!" Her alto voice jumped into soprano range.

"You look like you've got a crick in your neck, like you slept on it wrong."

"No, it's fine." She tilted her head from side to side to demonstrate flexibility. "Would you like some coffee?"

"Yes, thanks. Any problems with the place?"

"Nope. It's great." She poured two cups of coffee and joined him at the table.

They went over the lease. Again, he was generous in his terms, not requiring her promise to a year's commitment. Month-by-month worked for him.

She said, "At this point, I would agree to five years. Maybe the rest of my life."

"You like it?"

"I like it. A lot. I've got my own home, my dog, my job, and a restraining order. What more could I possibly want?"

He laughed. "Does the order mean that strange woman can't come near you?"

"Yeah. I couldn't prove that she took Zoë, but her apparent stalking convinced the judge there was enough of a threat to put this temporary thing in place. I really don't want to use it, though, but I guess I will have to if I think she's following me."

"Maybe if you never leave this area, you can avoid her altogether."

"Never leave? You mean live and *work* over here."

He smiled.

She shook her head. The man's tenacity was exasperating. "You heard."

"I heard. You're riding out of my station tomorrow."

"Yes, but I'm not making any promises."

"None expected."

"I'm on vacation. I didn't have anything better to do."

"The experience may leave you totally unaffected." The laughter in his eyes said he didn't think so.

"I'm happy where I am."

"Except for Kai's leaving, Erin's presence, the long drive—"

"Gabe!"

He held his hands up in surrender.

"Do you want some more coffee?" She stood abruptly and stepped over to the counter.

"Sure."

Carafe in hand, she returned to the table and filled their mugs, aware of him watching her. Men had surrounded her for years. More often than not the lone woman in the group, she was accustomed to being the object of their attention when they weren't in crisis mode. It didn't necessarily mean anything; she took it in stride. Now, however, Gabe's attention unsettled her. At the counter with her back to him, she widened her eyes and blew out a silent breath.

He said, "How did you happen to end up in the EMS business?"

Feigning confidence, she straightened her shoulders and turned with a smile. "I fell in love with a fireman." Overly conscious of placing one foot in front of the other, she walked to the table and sat. "I was eight and Harry was, oh, forty-five or fifty."

Gabe laughed. His laughter was an extension of that easy-listening radio station announcer's voice, low and velvet smooth. Mesmerizing. "How did you meet Harry?"

"Huh? Oh, through my dad. He's worked for years in the food service at Cutler-Barr."

"I know who he is. When you told me his name was Bob, I didn't connect it with Schuman."

"We don't look anything alike. He's super tall and skinny with brownish-gray hair that used to be all brown. Blue eyes." She pointed to her own black hair and dark eyes. "Maria Delgado Schuman." She pronounced her mother's name with a Spanish accent.

"He's a great guy."

That was the public's general consensus about her dad. She never rebutted it. "Mm-hmm. Anyway, I hung out at the hospital a lot while he worked. Lois took me under her wing. The ER was like my second home. It was a madhouse the day Harry came in with an ambulance. There had been an apartment house fire, a lot of injuries. Of course, right off he got my attention. Big guy. Soot all over his face. Still wearing his turnouts, big coat, helmet, and boots. He was comforting someone on a stretcher. I was in awe. The next day his picture was in the newspaper for rescuing a family of six. Wow. I wanted to be a hero like Harry."

"Did you get to meet him?"

She nodded, smiling. "Whenever I'd see him, he always gave me a handful of butterscotch candies and told me yes, girls could be firefighters too. He moved to Florida when I was in high school. That's how the dream got started. I became a firefighter."

"Really?"

"Yeah, really. Girls can be firefighters too, you know."

He grinned. "I knew that."

"I started down in Bloomington as a firefighter and EMT. Finally, at twenty-nine, I was a paramedic and made it to my dream job in Chicago."

"Why did you stop firefighting?"

"Kept breaking my nails lugging around those heavy hoses."

He laughed.

She debated with herself about whether or not to go into the story. It wasn't exactly her favorite topic.

Gabe was watching her expectantly, as if he cared.

A shiver rolled through her, and then the words tumbled out. "I had a friend named Sunni. Sunni ending in an 'i' just like my name. Best friends from kindergarten until eighth grade. We were on a school bus, heading back after a field trip to the Shedd Aquarium. Some driver on the expressway braked, and then a semi driver behind him braked and swerved into us. It could have been worse. Sunni was the only one who died."

"I'm so sorry."

She nodded, taken aback at the tenderness in his expression. She always made fun of sensitive males, but no automatic flippant remark came to mind. Maybe because for the first time she was the recipient of a man's sensitivity.

"You saw the emergency workers on the scene at the bus." It was a statement. He intuited where she was going.

She nodded again. "Lois used to let me do homework in the back of the ER. All the doctors and nurses there knew me. I became almost like a fixture. When patients were brought in, nobody paid any attention to me. I saw everything. Blood and gore never bothered me. I was enthralled with the stitching-up process. But that day..."

She was on the bus again, the enormous vehicle nearly severed in half. She heard the cries of her classmates...the sirens...but louder than all, the eerie silence surrounding Sunni that nearly shattered her eardrums. Her friend lay in her arms.

She went on. "That day I was on the real scene. The most vivid thing…" Most vivid except for that silence. "What my fourteen-year-old mind saw was a medic glance at Sunni. Another one yelled to him, 'Too late there; I need your help here.' And they took care of Todd, the class jerk."

She rubbed her eyes, pressing the scene back into its hole. "I blamed myself. Sunni and I had just changed seats. I couldn't live with that, so I blamed the medics that she died. I pushed the whole incident aside as best I could. It was gone until I started EMT training. Then I remembered how much I liked the stitching-up part." She gave him a sad smile. "If I couldn't save Sunni, I was going to save the rest of the world."

"Naturally." He reached over and put his hand on her left one that clutched the mug. "What an awful thing for a teen to carry around."

Oh, she did not want to go into *that*. The years following Sunni's death were a yawning chasm.

But the touch of human compassion melted her resistance and pulled the memories from her. "I only went to the hospital when I needed to talk to Lois. High school was basically one long party." She shrugged. "Then I woke up about a week after graduation and decided it was time to get on with my life."

"And you became a firefighter." He squeezed her hand and let go.

"Yep. And in my spare time I got my associate's degree and took some Spanish courses." What was this compulsion to explain her life to him?

"It's a good ending to a tragic story. Thank you for telling me."

"Thank you for listening."

They stared at one another, long past when propriety would suggest eyes be averted. She felt a distinct sense of incompleteness, as if there was much more to be said.

He cleared his throat. "Uh."

She blinked. "What?"

"Uh, nothing."

If he were Kai or one of her brothers, she would have called him on his bald-faced lie. Nothing? He wanted to say *something*, something like "Busy tonight?" But she didn't want to hear it because her subconscious would reply. That errant part of her mind responsible for tilting her head and doing strange things to the pitch of her voice would reply, "No I'm not busy. What do you have in mind?"

His shoulders heaved and he began to talk about drippy faucets.

Fourteen

Terri sat on the edge of a padded burgundy vinyl recliner kitty-corner from an identical one occupied by her father. She watched as a talkative nurse in white pants and a floral smock inspected the underside of his forearm, searching in vain for a vein.

Terri kept her mouth shut and grasped her knees tightly.

Bob Schuman's 6'4" frame extended beyond the recliner's raised footrest. He appeared healthy as ever, no potbelly or excess fat at 62. His posture was unbowed. He had a full head of hair, thick and, as always, buzzed in an Army-style cut. If the chemotherapy followed its normal pattern, he would turn gaunt and bald in a short period of time.

"Teresa, you don't have to stay." He spoke in a friendly but clipped manner, the voice of a man who'd spent most of his life supervising others. "This is a six-hour ordeal. Come back at three."

It's going to take Andrea here until three just to insert the IV. "I'm staying."

"You just want to make sure they do things right. They're professionals. They know what they're doing." He looked at the nurse. "My daughter is a—" His pause would be imperceptible to the uninitiated ear. "Paramedic."

The statement was not that of a proud papa. It was not a smiling "My daughter is a paramedic. Isn't that great?" No, it was more like, "She's *only* a paramedic, nowhere near trained to the extent of a doctor. Or even a nurse, for that matter. You work with doctors and in hospitals."

He had never said those exact words, but the implication hovered. When Terri learned to tie her shoes, he asked if she knew how to make a double knot. When she brought home straight A's in fourth grade, he discussed the deportment comments. In middle school she ran track and made it to the state finals. As an eighth grader, before the bus accident, she took first place in the 220-yard dash. He said if she could do that in high school, some college might offer her a scholarship. In high school she kept running, though more for sanity's sake than for trophies. She stopped looking to him for approval and, as she'd told Bryan, acceptance.

Andrea the nurse, a 20-something with pale complexion and long blonde hair, smiled, her eyes never leaving his arm as she removed the needle again from another hapless insertion. "I'm sure she could do this faster than I'm doing it."

Two points for Andrea.

"Ma'am," she addressed Terri, "you really don't have to stay. We'll take good care of him. There's television, newspapers, and magazines. There'll be other patients to visit with. He may want to nap."

"I'm staying." *My dad has cancer, and this is his introduction to chemo, which may in the end kill him before the cancer does. And besides that, I would have had that IV in yesterday!*

When at last the process was underway, Andrea left and Terri settled back in her chair. Though her dad ran a tight ship at home and on the job, his style wasn't heavy-handed. Talkers by nature, they conversed freely now as they had throughout her life. With nine Schumans in the family plus in-laws, significant others, and four grandchildren, there was always some gossip to share. Eventually their conversation turned to Terri. She told him about Gabe Andrews.

"So I spent Saturday riding with Bill Sanchez. He's moving soon to Arizona."

"Why would you want to transfer? You knew Kai wouldn't stay forever. The cops can take care of the weirdo."

"I suppose."

"And it's only a lateral move."

She chose to ignore that comment. They'd covered the territory often enough. There were no vertical moves she was interested in pursuing. If the day came when she quit treating patients in emergency situations, she would teach others how.

She shrugged. "It's the Spanish dimension. Remember Grandma and how we had to call 911 once for her when she had the heart attack? She knew English, but those guys never heard a word of it."

"Yeah. That drove me crazy about her. Whenever she got upset, her English flew right out the window. Shelley always had to interpret."

Shelley this and Shelley that. Her older sister, the apple of his eye right after Bobby Jr. and before little Jimmy. With seven offspring, he was bound to miss some details—like the existence of his four middle kids.

"Dad, Shelley wasn't there that day. I was."

"Yeah? Yeah, that's right. You picked up some of the language too."

"Anyway, three-fourths of the calls Saturday were to treat Hispanics. And most of them were like Grandma. That district only has one other medic besides Bill and a handful of firefighters who are really fluent in Spanish." She shrugged. "I don't know. I felt like I could help. Which is why I'm a paramedic in the first place, to help people. This would be an added dimension. A new challenge."

"Well, it'd look good on your resume. But there's all the red tape of transferring. You'd have to be replaced right on the heels of Kai. Then, if they okay it, you have to get to know a whole new batch of coworkers. That area is rougher than the one you're in. It's not like you've been speaking Spanish on a daily basis. Maybe someone else will apply for the job."

Her dad droned on as her stomach muscles tightened in a familiar way. His negativism had never succeeded in quashing her ideas. On the contrary, it energized her determination to prove to him she could do it. She was capable and therefore acceptable, deserving of his stamp of approval, which, of course, had never come wholeheartedly. Suddenly she was struck with the thought that stomach aches shouldn't be part of her relationship with him.

"Dad," she interrupted him, "why is it I've never done the right thing or the best thing in your opinion?"

He stared at her. "What are you talking about?"

"I always feel like you don't accept me for who I am."

"Teresa, if you want to transfer, go ahead. You're grown up. You know better than I do what works for you." His complexion had turned ashen gray.

"I think I'll get some coffee." She left the room without a backward glance.

What was it Bryan had said? *God not only accepts you, Terri, He accepts you just as you are. He even likes you just as you are. He is your holy Father.*

"Sorry, Lord. The Father image just doesn't click."

~

"Peace be with you," Reverend Bryan O'Shaugnessy spoke to the congregation, his voice deep and rich, carrying easily across the expanse of the church now filled to capacity on Sunday morning.

"And also with you," the assembly replied as one.

Terri sensed movement all around her. She rose from the kneeling bench alongside Rachel Koski.

Her friend embraced her. "Peace be with you."

Terri whispered, "Now what are we doing?"

Rachel backed away, her brown spice eyes twinkling, and murmured, "Just say 'peace be with you' and shake people's hands." She turned to greet the woman on her other side.

Terri followed suit, as she had been doing since they set foot inside the church. It wasn't the sort of church Rachel attended, but she had visited often enough with her in-laws that she was somewhat familiar with things. She informed Terri she could do whatever she felt comfortable doing, but nothing was mandatory. No one would frown if she didn't go through all the customized motions. Nor would anyone laugh.

But, like the time she had prayed alone in the place, kneeling when no one told her to do so, she felt no reservations giving physical expression to her worship. And so she mimicked most of what she observed. She went down briefly on the right knee before entering the pew in recognition of Christ's presence. She stood, sat, knelt, and sang. She used the liturgy cheat sheet and added her voice to the responsive readings.

"Peace be with you."

As more people shook her hand and smiled, the easier it became to say the unfamiliar phrase. Peace felt like a tangible entity, passing swiftly through the church, side to side, front to back, back to front. A magnetic field, its forces enlivened as palm clasped palm.

"Terri."

She turned to the velvet smooth voice behind her.

Gabe Andrews smiled his full smile, the one that highlighted his dimples and squished crow's feet around his eyes. He took her hand in both of his. "Peace be with you."

"Peace be with you."

The magnetic energy soared.

~

Terri watched her new friend and her old friend talk about her as if she weren't present. They all stood in something called the parish hall, a good-sized room with some round tables and folding chairs set about here and there. People had gathered to drink coffee and visit after the service.

Rachel looked great. There was a new softness in her face. Grandmotherhood agreed with her, as did the wavy, reddish brown hair worn at a longer length than in the past.

"Gabe," Rachel said. Unlike Terri, she wore a dress, hose, and heels that lifted her to only a couple of inches below his eyes. "I drove three and a half hours, one way, because I've been so concerned about her. She hasn't been herself for months. I've never known her to shout at a stranger. Not unnecessarily anyway."

"Well, I came under the category of necessary. If she hadn't shouted, I might not have paid her any attention."

"Don't be too sure. Normally she has this perfect paramedic's voice. Even and soothing and yet commanding."

"I've heard it. Low. She would probably sing alto in the choir."

"Yes. As her friend, I just want to thank you for letting her rent your condo."

Rachel sometimes resembled her late grandmother Ruth Goldberg, an effusive Jewish woman. Ruth never hid the fact that the well-being of her family was a priority. The only thing missing from Rachel was the German accent.

Gabe smiled. "My pleasure."

"I think another change would work wonders for her, something like a job transfer."

He grinned now.

"She loved riding with your guys last week."

"Really?"

"She didn't tell you?" A sidelong glance at Terri. "Well, it's true. The thought of helping with the Spanish-speaking community resonated with her. You knew it would, didn't you?"

"Let's say I had hoped it would. We need her desperately."

"She needs you desperately. I mean, she needs to get into a totally new environment. Away from some old ghosts and away from that strange woman."

As if on cue, they both took a sip of coffee and turned, eyeing her over their cups.

"Okay, okay. You two win. I'll put in for a transfer tomorrow."

Rachel hadn't needed to go to so much trouble. Terri had made up her mind during a handshake in church.

∽

The bounce was restored to Terri's step after her two weeks of vacation. Or was it Rachel's visit? Or church? Or the prospect of a new start? Or...Gabe? She didn't linger on analyzing the reasons.

Not that she had time. Her request for a transfer was granted almost immediately after she returned to work. With Kai's move, word had gotten out of an opening, and so a shuffling of medics had already been set in motion. Her spot was filled, and, simultaneously, an opening became available for her at the other station, six weeks before Bill Sanchez was to leave. Which meant she would have the privilege of working with the older man, something she hadn't dared hope for.

Of course that other thing she hadn't dared hope for came true also. That other thing she didn't put into words...that fleeting sensation, an impression that never made it from her heart to her head because it reeked of hormones gone amuck, and she never ever credited hormones for her behavior. Only once in her life had she felt like this. It was Christmas morning, the year her parents gave her the exact bicycle she wanted, the one she hadn't asked for because of its prohibitive cost. Unbelievable. There it stood beside the Christmas tree. The joy she felt was boundless. Kind of like what bubbled in her at the thought of working with Gabe Andrews.

She reported early for duty, fighting the urge to giggle at 6:45 on a dark, late fall morning.

"Welcome aboard, Terri." He smiled as he shook her hand beside the ambulance.

"Thank you, Mr. Andrews." She engaged her most professional demeanor, shoving aside berserk hormones. "And thank you for not saying 'I told you so.'"

"Why would I say that?"

"Because you knew I couldn't take just one ride over here."

He shrugged. "Lucky shot in the dark. You wouldn't have yelled at me if you didn't care. I figured if you saw an entire district full of Nevas and guys like me who aren't exactly fluent, there was a good chance you'd be hooked."

"You remembered her name?"

"I'm not totally hopeless." The left dimple appeared. "How are you?"

"I'm great. Saying goodbye was hard, but...okay." In fact the goodbyes were more painful than she'd imagined. She had worked with most of those firemen for over six years. "I'm ready. I won't let you down."

"I know. So, have you gone back to the church? I've worked the past two Sundays."

"Yes, I have. All by myself even." Rachel's advice over the telephone that she give St. James a try had gone unheeded. It had taken the force of her friend's physical presence to dislodge Terri like some stubborn donkey and get her to that first service. Like Gabe, Rachel seemed to know that one visit would get her hooked.

Now that was a scary thought, that he would understand her in the way her closest friend did.

He asked, "What do you think of it?"

"At first I thought there was an awful lot of pomp and circumstance and rigamarole going on."

He laughed. "That's what I thought too. At first."

At first. He echoed her sentiments. Although the possibility of seeing Gabe at church colored her initial decision to return, something at a deeper level was at work that drew her back again. She was at a loss to explain it in words and wondered if he could.

She said, "At first. But now?"

"It's a mystery, not of this seen world, that's for sure. Something happens there. I think it's related to all the Scriptures and words spoken about Jesus. The entire morning's focus is on Him alone."

"That's it! And then there's all the prayers and the kneeling."

"Exactly. And receiving communion. It's like a fresh beginning every time."

"Yeah!" The connection she felt with him leapt into another level. Goose bumps prickled on her arms, and she redirected the conversation. "How long have you been going there?"

"About seven years. It's a long, typical story. The wife leaves, the husband hits bottom, someone grabs his hand and pulls him up." He gave her his half smile. "Father Bryan."

She nodded. "I've been pulled up by him a couple of times myself."

"Really? We'll have to compare stories sometime."

"Sure." She almost added, *It's a date*. No, it wasn't a date. It was common ground with a coworker, thoughts to be explored, fellowship to be shared.

He was involved with someone. He had an ex-wife and kids. Big-time baggage.

She was going to have to get over this snowballing infatuation with Gabe Andrews.

~

Despite the feeling that she'd jumped from the frying pan into the fire, Terri soon remembered why it was she had changed job locations. The first run of the day with Bill Sanchez brought it back to mind. As with her decision to attend St. James, Gabe played a role, but he wasn't the main reason.

Bill was a small Hispanic man, shorter than Terri. His dark hair was brushed back, and he sported a pencil-thin moustache. His English carried the musical undertone of a Spanish accent.

She had hoped to work with him because he was a rare find. He was in his late forties, older than any medic she knew, and a treasure chest of experience. He exuded a confidence that spilled over onto those around him. Two minutes after they'd met, she put to rest her hard-boiled persona that easily rose to the surface when working with a male for the first time. She wouldn't have to prove to Bill that she, as a woman, could handle whatever came their way. She sensed he already believed that was the case.

The run was to an apartment building. A ten-year-old asthmatic boy was having trouble breathing. Fortunately, the mother had called in time. He only required oxygen and a ride to the hospital.

As Terri drove the ambulance back to the firehouse, she thanked Bill.

"*En español, por favor.*"

She grinned. "*Gracias.*"

He was a gentle taskmaster. Except for when he gave her directions, he refused to dialogue with her in English. As they spoke in his native tongue, she listened intently to his inflections. And to think that she was getting paid for such a learning situation!

Bill asked, "Thanks for what?"

Where to begin? "For improving my Spanish."

He nodded.

"And for…" She gestured with her hand, as if scooping the words from air. "For back there. For everything."

Bill had stepped aside, allowing her to take the lead. While placing the oxygen mask on the boy, she talked soothingly to him and communicated with the mother. All in Spanish. The three of them rode in the back of the ambulance to the hospital, giving Terri the opportunity to get to know the woman.

First-day jitters flowed away. A desire to ease the fears of patients who did not speak English, already burning in her heart, now felt like a crackling wildfire.

Bill smiled. "I like your style, Schuman. You're going to be just fine here. Just fine."

~

Terri held Bill's "just fine" comment like a talisman in her heart at six o'clock that evening. Feeling like a new kid at school, she sat down to dinner with 13 firemen who didn't know her. The situation called for a defense mechanism. It beckoned her tough-as-nails demeanor to make an appearance. Macho mask time.

From the group she knew Gabe. She knew Bill. She had met the engine guys she'd worked with that day. Their assistance had been needed at a drug overdose and a stabbing. Other than that, she was a complete stranger to the crew.

She was only halfway through her first shift, not enough time yet to have proven her mettle. Trepidation filled her.

Bill stood and clinked his spoon against his water glass. "Attention, everyone! We need to welcome our newcomer."

Across the table, Gabe smiled at her. That smile didn't help matters.

As the room quieted, Bill turned to her. "Terri, we have a special dinner prepared just for you."

The guy sitting on her left whipped away her plate. Behind her someone said, "Ta da," and slid another plate before her.

On it was a lone hot dog in a bun.

Apparently the nickname had preceded her. She burst into laughter.

ifteen

Falling in love with Gabe Andrews was as easy as hoisting the backboard occupied by a 90-pound, 90-year-old wisp of a woman who smiled behind the oxygen mask.

Terri knew it the moment she said, "On three!"

Kneeling on the floor, she grasped her corner of the backboard and locked eyes with those of the firefighter directly across from her. Gabe's. He shouldn't have even been there. The 911 caller, a neighbor, indicated a major predicament, leading dispatch to believe backup was needed. And so there he was, and there she was, wanting desperately to know what thoughts he held behind those caramel-colored eyes.

"*Unos, dos, tres.*"

Like a synchronized dance movement, they rose as one.

She helped him and others carry the little lady through the tiny apartment and out to the ambulance through mid-December snow flurries. Her thoughts never strayed from the emergency. The woman complained almost apologetically that her chest felt as if an elephant sat on it. She was having a heart attack. Terri was fully engaged with every fiber of her being.

But beneath the awareness of the medical emergency was another...awakening. Like silent electrical impulses gliding effortlessly and with lightening speed, the process escaped her notice until the transmission was complete. The connection made, Terri felt an undertone of satisfaction as if something had been accomplished.

Absurd.

There was no time to analyze it. The referee had returned to duty in her mind, his hand on the stopwatch, his eye on the fleeing seconds.

Gabe climbed into the ambulance behind her. They worked together to stabilize and comfort the patient while Bill drove them to the hospital. Six minutes later they wheeled her into the ER and handed her off to a doctor and team of nurses. In the blink of an eye, the flurry of activity ceased.

She and Gabe stood in a wide, brightly lit hall and watched a pair of doors swish quietly together. He wore his turnout coat with the yellow stripes, she a dark blue jacket. The familiar antiseptic scent saturated the hospital air.

He raised his hand for a high five. "Good work."

"Thanks." Smiling, she slapped his hand. "A little different from the last time." She referred to the situation with the shooting victim, when Gabe had to take over for her in the ambulance.

"A little." He grinned. "I knew that was a momentary glitch. You're fine."

Of course she was fine. Falling in love tended to make one feel no pain whatsoever. "Um, time off and job transfers work wonders." Not to mention that wildcard of a hormone, PEA. "I'd better go write my report."

"Yeah."

Neither one of them moved. His eyes were focused on her face. She had the sneaky suspicion that she'd follow those eyes anywhere.

"Terri."

"Yeah?"

"I have a rule against dating coworkers."

"Okay."

They stared at each other for another long moment.

"But," he said, "I think I made it up because I've only worked with men and married women."

"Okay."

"And even if a single woman were available, the teasing from the guys would become unbearable. Or they might even ostracize me and her. I've seen it happen. Reasons enough not to even start."

"Okay."

"Will you have dinner with me tomorrow night?"

"Um, maybe you'd better back up. I missed the transition. You don't date coworkers but you're asking me— Oh. Maybe you're not asking me on a date. It's more like we both have to eat so let's share a meal because we happen to work together and get along well?"

"Do you always need things spelled out in detail?"

"No. I'm just a little gun-shy."

"Hesitant to trust men?"

"You could say that."

He crossed his arms and cocked his head to one side. "I'm asking you out on a date. Date, as in boy wants to get to know girl. As in he can't stop thinking about her. As in this will mostly likely be the first of an indefinite number of dates even if the other guys get wind of it. Did I scare you away yet?"

"No."

"Will you have dinner with me?"

"Yes."

He grinned. "Okay then."

"Okay."

"Guess we'd better head back."

"Okay." Evidently PEA robbed one of a decent vocabulary.

"Lois, he told me he's involved with someone," Terri whispered, leaning across the high counter toward her friend on the other side.

"Punkin." Lois stilled the pen in her hand and looked over the top of her half-glasses. "I don't know about his personal life except he was divorced years ago and he's a genuinely nice guy."

Terri exhaled loudly. How could she have been so agog that she'd forgotten his statement about being involved? The context had been teasing at that restaurant downtown, but he wouldn't say something like *that* if it weren't true! A guy in a relationship was synonymous with one married. It was a slam dunk, over and done with, decision made. She didn't get within ten feet of those situations. Until now. Man, she was within *three* feet—

"Terri, he can't be too serious if he invited you out on a date."

"Uh-huh. That's probably what Lee's girlfriends thought too. That he wasn't serious about me." Her chuckle was self-derisive. "Which was true. I just didn't know it at the time. I don't want to get in the middle of something like that. I wouldn't do that to another woman. Guys like that are major jack—"

"Gabe's a genuinely nice guy."

She heard her friend's unspoken words: Lee was not a genuinely nice guy. Lois had never been too fond of him. Upon hearing about the breakup, she had uncharacteristically clenched her fists and danced around in a little circle whispering "Yes! Yes!"

Terri changed the subject. "He's got kids."

"One dinner doesn't mean you're signing up for life."

"I should back out now."

"You could always change your position on kids."

"No. I promised myself not to end up like three of my friends, all that his, hers, ours, and theirs confusion."

"Theirs?"

"The remarried ex who has her own set of his, hers, and ours. You've always got to factor in the 'theirs.'"

Lois shook her head of white curls. "You know, this is the real world, Scarlett. Blended families all over the place. And besides, you don't have kids of your own, and as far as I know, his ex doesn't have any with her second husband. Which brings you down to his two and your future 'ours.'"

A noise of disgust puffed out Terri's lips. "No way. Nieces and nephews are plenty enough for me. I'll tell him I'm not interested."

"That'd be an out-and-out lie." She went back to her writing. "Like I've said a number of times, he's genuinely nice."

"And that's exactly why I'm backing back out." One date with Gabe Andrews would be like that one ambulance ride.

⌐

Feeling punch-drunk after a busy night, Terri ambled down the street to the municipal lot where she parked. The sky was clear and a brisk wind blew out of the north. Conditions were ripe for keeping temperatures miserably low. She squinted against the bright sunshine and breeze.

"Morning, Terri." Gabe called out. He stood near her car, smiling, bundled in a pine green down parka with the hood up, hands in pockets.

At the sight of him, that sense of deep satisfaction rolled through her like a river, carrying with it the resolve to end things before they began. It floated on by. She stopped in front of him. "Morning."

"I thought I'd pick you up at seven tonight. Is that all right with you?"

The entire scene felt so natural, as if they'd already lived it. Him waiting for her by the car, discussing evening plans, his nose red from the cold, his eyes half shut against the brilliant sunlight. Their breath made small puffs of vapor between them. The way he looked at her, the way she knew she was looking at him. It was what people did when they were falling in love.

But... Self-preservation flung a life jacket out to her resolve almost buried now beneath that rushing current of sweet contentment.

"No." She looked down at her black oxfords and toed a loose piece of concrete.

"No what?"

"No, I can't go. I'm sorry, Gabe, but you told me you're involved with someone."

"When did I say that?"

"At the rib place. Before the movie."

"Terri, I didn't say *with someone*. I just said I'm involved, period. There are a couple of women at church."

He was, as Lois kept saying, genuinely nice. He was also attractive in that healthy California surfer way. He carried himself with confidence. His lean physique was strong, though in a subtle way. No bulging muscles. He looked youthful with a hint of maturity in the receding hairline. Aside from the fact that Spanish eluded him, his mind was sharp, his ability to think clearly in emergency situations evident. Last but not least was his voice. That voice of all voices. Yes, there would be at the very least two women.

He hunched his shoulders. "How do I put it? They've been chasing me." His shoulders went down. "And friends are always trying to set me up. So I say I'm involved. With two kids, two jobs, and church activities I don't have time to be chased."

"I wasn't chasing you."

He blew out a breath. "I know. But I was chasing you."

She felt her eyebrows go up.

"I gave you my standard line, trying to convince myself I wasn't interested."

"Why did you feel the need to convince yourself?"

"Because I knew from the time you showed up at the soccer field that you were going to complicate my life."

She turned her head aside for a moment while his words sank into her heart. He was dead serious. He still had kids. But...he wasn't involved with someone else.

She looked at him. "I'll be ready at five."

His smile spread until both dimples appeared.

Fresh-faced, golden-haired men with dimples and under six feet tall never used to make her feel as though she'd just jumped off a cliff and was soaring beneath the wings of a hang glider.

~

That night he chased her—literally. On ice skates. They were at a festive outdoor rink where thousands of strands of lights nearly obliterated the stars peeking from behind skyscrapers. Holiday music blared from loudspeakers. Bales of hay and brightly lit evergreen trees surrounded the area. At one end, hot chocolate was served from a shed. Despite the polar temperatures, the place was crowded with skaters of every age.

Terri easily out-distanced Gabe as she zipped in and out of the throng. He followed gamely and, when she lost control rounding a curve, he caught up. She went down as elegantly as possible, sliding like a softball runner stealing base, grateful to avoid wiping out a family of four.

"Home run!" Gabe knelt beside her, out of breath. "You okay?"

"Ow!" She rolled to her back and laid her head on the ice. "Call 911."

"Seriously?" He tore off his gloves and began probing her jeans-covered left leg, a medic searching for broken bones.

She laughed. "Andrews, your flirting is getting seriously out of control."

He sat back on his haunches and laughed with her. "You're not hurt."

"No, but we both will be if we don't get out of the way." Skaters swirled around them, the swish of blades against ice too near for comfort.

Still laughing, they clung to each other and somehow managed to stand up, wobbling. As Terri leaned against his strong arms, a sense of joy and freedom shot through her. It was like nothing she'd ever felt before. She wondered if it were addictive.

∽

Later that night Terri and Gabe sipped hot cider in a restaurant. Seated at a candlelit table, they also stuffed themselves with steak and baked potatoes. Artificial logs glowed in a nearby fireplace, emitting real heat and a cozy ambience. Terri's senses were saturated, but overriding everything was a tingling sensation in her hand from when Gabe held it as they had skated round and round.

"Gabe, do you realize we haven't stopped talking in over four hours?"

"Yeah." He grinned. "I think it's got something to do with being in the same line of work. Have you ever dated anyone in emergency services?"

"No. The firefighters and medics I've known were either married, or, like Kai, much younger. Or else it was like they wore this neon sign across their forehead." She brought the tips of her forefingers and thumbs together and held the oval shape against her bangs. "Warning: I am obnoxious and no woman in her right mind would have anything to do with me."

He laughed. "I suppose you saw one of those on me."

"Oh, yeah. But it was definitely gone by the time you offered me your condo. Okay, your turn."

"The dating or the obnoxious sign?"

She grinned. "I already know about the obnoxious part. You called me a loudmouth."

"A clear signal of how, um, unpleasant I can be. You should have run."

"But it was the truth, which greatly reduces your obnoxious charge against me."

"As my mother used to warn me, if I can't say anything nice, keep quiet." His smile lessened, and the firelight reflected in his eyes. "About the dating. I haven't. Period. Well, except for a few dinners with one of those women I mentioned earlier. In recent years I truly haven't been interested. Life is full. And before that, when we first split..." He shrugged. "There was no interest, only hurt. And anger. A lot of anger. At Paula. At women period." He tapped his forehead. "The warning sign flashed in huge capital letters: I am obnoxious."

Compared to some men she had met, he was a far cry from the true sense of that word. "You've changed then."

"Only by God's remarkable grace and power."

"You said she didn't like firefighting. Why did you get married in the first place?" The personal question spun off her tongue before she considered asking it. Gabe's mellow attitude invited such familiarity. Or maybe it was something to do with that falling in love business.

He didn't hesitate in answering. "I wasn't a firefighter in the first place. We met down at Western Illinois University, two college kids crazy about each other, following the usual agenda. She majored in elementary education, I was in business. We graduated, got jobs, got married, set up house. She became a teacher. Jordan was born two years later. I sat in an office and pushed paper around for four years. I was twenty-six and already looked like my dad, who was fifty-three and all dried up from spending a lifetime at a job he'd always hated. He wasn't meant to be a sales rep. I wasn't meant to sit at a desk, even if it was the respectable, responsible thing to do."

Terri thought of her friend Jessie who had married Kevin when he was a teacher. His transition to firefighting nearly split them apart. She knew Gabe's ex-wife's side of the story.

He went on. "I might still be in that office if there hadn't been a window. A fire engine went screaming by one summer afternoon and stopped down the block. Instantly I was a kid again, playing with my fire trucks in my special patch of dirt in the backyard. It was like a taste of heaven, you know? Every concern pales when you're there."

She nodded, understanding. The connection she felt with Gabe was unlike anything she could have experienced with Lee. As a coach, he lived and breathed his work as she did, but their work was as different as night from day. Discussing the events from her shift, either horrors or euphoria, tended to frustrate them both. Why was it people said opposites attracted?

He said, "I put in my two-weeks' notice that day. Paula hit the roof, of course. What wife wouldn't? I'd just cut our income by more than half. We depleted our savings while I went to firefighting school. I got on with the department right away, but you know those salaries. She hated everything about my job. The crazy schedule, which actually gave me more time at home, but she didn't see it that way. The potential for injury. Mostly, though, I think it was the money. Or lack thereof. So when she and Mr. Millionaire Moneybags struck up a conversation in a toy store one Christmas, she found a way out."

"I'm sorry."

"Spencer was only two. Just a little guy." He gazed at the fire for a long moment. "Father Bryan tells me there's no condemnation for those who are in Christ."

"The book of Romans."

He gave her a brief smile. "You know your Bible."

"I'm familiar with parts. Not that I understand the parts."

"Most days I have a handle on the reality of that particular verse. It's the only thing that empties this boatload of guilt I have about the kids. If I'd lived up to Paula's expectations, she wouldn't have run off and I'd have a full-time relationship with them. I think Jordan wouldn't be a snob and Spence would enjoy hammering nails with me instead of playing computer games. Maybe they'd want to give me a coffee mug that says best dad in the world."

"And maybe none of the above."

"Maybe not. Sorry you asked why we got married in the first place?"

"Yes and no."

He smiled. "Care to explain?"

"Well." She hesitated.

"I'm almost forty. I've got emotional baggage as well as two kids. Which should make a single, independent woman like you want to run in the opposite direction as fast as you can."

"It does, which is why I'm sorry I asked."

"So why am I still looking at your mesmerizing deep brown eyes with those incredibly thick eyelashes instead of at the back of your head?"

She smiled. "You think flattery will keep me in this seat?"

"I'm willing to try whatever it takes."

"I've never dated a guy who cares about what God thinks. Just keep quoting Scripture, Gabe. That's why I'm not sorry I asked. That's why I'm still sitting here."

He slid his hand across the table, palm up. The tenderness in his expression was unlike anything she'd ever witnessed on the face of a man looking at her.

She laid her hand in his, and ever so slowly, ever so gently, he curled his fingers around it.

⌒

At times Terri felt as if she and Gabe had simply jumped into the middle of a friendship that already existed. It both exhilarated and frightened her. She held back and sensed that he did likewise.

Not that they had too much of a choice. Their shifts intersected only three times in December. Their church attendance coincided just once, on Christmas Eve. He had the children with him, who did not yet know about the new woman in their dad's life. Days off were packed with her teaching, ongoing training for both of them, his construction work, her time with her dad. Such constantly fluctuating schedules limited dating opportunities. They fit in only one dinner, one lunch, and one afternoon of Christmas shopping.

Christmas night she made dinner for him.

"I thought you didn't cook." He sat across the candlelit table from her.

"I don't." She smiled and resisted the urge to reveal that he brought out a nesting instinct she never would have guessed existed within herself.

"This is delicious."

"Lasagna is my one and only recipe."

As always, they laughed and talked about everything under the sun. And, as often happened, he took her emotional temperature.

"Are you ready?" he asked, standing beside her at the sink.

She knew he referred to the fact she had worked her last day with Bill Sanchez. Tomorrow a new partner would join her, an unknown in the district and one who did not speak Spanish.

"Gabe." She handed him a dish towel and began washing the dishes. "Isn't my probationary period over yet?"

"You haven't been on proba—"

"Andrews!" Frowning, she grabbed his ear with a soapy hand and pulled his face down.

"Ouch!" He grinned.

"Stop grinning."

He held up his hands in self-defense. "Okay, okay. I'm not grinning." That wasn't true. "I am not grinning," he repeated and once again tucked his smile away. This time it remained hidden, but then he winked.

She ignored that and tried to ignore the pleasure of his face mere centimeters from hers. With a slight tilt of her head she could brush her lips against his or feel his rough jaw against her cheek. But she had other things on her mind. "I am not some delicate hothouse orchid that has to be fussed over every time there's a change in the temperature. Please tell me you know this."

"I know this. I swear!"

She let go of his ear, but neither of them moved.

"Terri Schuman, you're flirting with me."

"So what if I am?" she taunted, wiping her damp hands against her jeans.

"Well, you're changing the temperature. It's definitely going up."

She smiled. "About time."

"I think so too," he murmured, his eyes at half mast.

The moment he kissed her, she knew it was exactly what she'd wanted for Christmas. Just one kiss from Gabe Andrews, her gentle hero who couldn't speak Spanish. She wondered if one kiss was like one ambulance ride...or like one dinner.

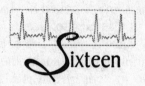

Sixteen

When Erin Morgan walked into the hospital classroom in early January, Terri stopped talking in the middle of a sentence. Her throat felt as though she were being strangled. The handful of EMT candidates already seated exchanged puzzled glances.

"Terri! Hi! Are *you* teaching this class?" She turned her perky face toward the young women and men gathered and announced, "She saved my life!"

"Cool!" someone responded.

Another asked for details, and Erin began describing the car accident. With her shapely figure clothed in black spandex, her makeup colorful and thick as war paint, she easily held their attention. When the scent of her sweet perfume registered, Terri nearly gagged. Anger washed over her as she thought of Zoë and of Erin's disruptive manipulations.

"Erin!" she impolitely interrupted the conversation. "We need to talk." She turned on her heel and walked out the door.

Not bothering to see if she followed her, Terri continued a short distance down the hall to a vacant corner. She was at Cutler-Barr, the resource hospital for the area. EMTs and paramedics were certified there under the jurisdiction of one of its physicians. Terri taught different training sessions, from CPR to first aid to the introductory basics of emergency medicine. Her new class that night was on stabilization. Her thoughts should have been there. They weren't.

She faced the wall, her arms crossed, terrified at what was going through her mind. How long had it been since she kicked a girl in the shins or pulled her hair? She and her sister Shelley had gone at it as preadolescents, sometimes punching hard enough to raise bruises on each other's arms. As teenagers they simply ignored each other, but by then Terri's propensity to live in overdrive was fueled by alcohol and sheer hatred at the world for taking her young friend Sunni. Physical run-ins with other girls were not uncommon.

She did the math. Math calmed her brain. Next month, February, she turned thirty-six. Thirty-six minus seventeen equaled nineteen. Nineteen years! Nineteen years and now out of the blue she wanted to swing a punch at another human being.

"Oh, Lord," she whispered to the wall, "I'm sorry. This is new. No, it's old. So old. Am I still that person? Rachel said I'm not. Just take it away. Please take it away."

Gabe was teaching her about talking to God often, whenever, wherever, and about whatever. He said that was how to practice God's presence, and that the more she turned her mind to His presence, the easier it was to let Him live through her.

"Terri?"

Please take it away. Amen. So be it. She turned, inhaling deeply.

Erin wore a concerned expression. "What's wrong?"

"I'm supposed to call the cops if you come near me."

"Why? Oh, yeah. That restraining doohickey thingamajig. But it's out of date."

That was true. The order's 21 days had elapsed. Cara recommended she pursue getting a longer one in place, but Terri had let it slide. She had a new job and a new home. A new love. The groupie had faded from the scene until now, three months after their paths had last crossed. Was today's encounter intentional? How could it be? Terri's name had not been posted with the class schedule.

Tears pooled in Erin's big sapphire blue eyes. Her blonde-streaked hair was still in its dramatic up-swept style. "I promise, I won't bug you. I didn't know I was bugging you before. If you'd just told me."

"You took my dog!" She managed to keep her voice low, though she couldn't mask the intensity of her feelings.

"But I know you," she sobbed. "You hated leaving Zoë in a kennel. I just wanted to give her a little personal attention."

"You didn't have permission!"

"I'm sorry. It was a gift to you. I thought it should be anonymous."

In exasperation, Terri combed her fingers through her bangs. "And you never told me you were acquainted with that woman who died in the accident."

Erin wiped the corners of her eyes. "How could I admit that? I felt so horribly, horribly guilty! You've probably never felt so guilty you couldn't look yourself in the mirror."

She blew out a breath. Of course she had felt that guilty. Start with the incident of changing bus seats with Sunni at the age of 14 and just go from there. She had gained an inkling of Christ's forgiveness, but she still avoided digging too deeply into herself in spite of all that had happened in the past few months. Owning up to burnout and her refusal to recognize it in time was about all she could handle. There were emotional areas still rusted shut, covered with thick overgrowth of tendrils, hiding enough guilt and regrets to sink a ship. It was a Pandora's box best left untouched.

But… "Erin, I can't trust you."

The tears overflowed now. "But why won't you give me a second chance? You give Zoë second chances all the time."

"Zoë's a dog! She doesn't know any better!"

"Maybe I don't either."

The words impacted Terri like a hand pressed suddenly against her chest. Maybe the girl didn't know any better. She was an orphan with too much money. Perhaps she wasn't smart enough or didn't have the proper social skills to keep a job. No one had taught her. What was that Bible verse? A line referring to even dogs being allowed to eat the crumbs that fell from the master's table. The virtual hand released her, taking with it the steam from her voice.

"How's your arm?"

Erin wiggled her left arm around. "It's fine."

"No problems after they removed the cast?"

"No." She smiled and sniffed. "Thank you."

"One chance."

"I can take your class?"

Terri nodded. "I don't want to see you or hear from you outside of that classroom. If you have questions, they will have to wait until the next meeting. No phone calls. No visits. No so-called anonymous gifts. Do you understand?"

"Yes. Oh, yes, I understand. Thank you!"

Terri almost told her to go wash her face, but then she noticed the tears had left no tracks in her makeup. There really ought to be a law against perky women who cried with impunity, war paint intact, sleeves left dry.

~

While Erin returned to the classroom, no doubt to regale the group with her adventure of being extricated from a smashed-up car, Terri found the bathroom and splashed cold water on her own face. She needed a moment to regain her composure.

Giving Erin a second chance seemed the right thing to do. What harm could it bring? Terri had her guard up now. Cara, though, would have a fit. Maybe she wouldn't mention it to the policewoman. They talked occasionally. The investigation had hit a deadend. With no witnesses coming forth, there was no case. Cara dug more deeply into Erin's background, interviewing former coworkers. The general consensus was she was a flake, but no evidence was found of relationships paralleling that which Erin had with the dead woman. Except with Terri.

Yep, Cara would have a cow.

Holding a paper towel against her chin, Terri stared at herself in the mirror. The raccoon eyes were gone. Eliminating stresses like apartment hunting and talking to Lee worked wonders, but the addition of Gabe in her life clinched the renewal process.

Gabe.

She smiled. Her dating experiences had not prepared her for a relationship with Gabe Andrews. Subtle differences heightened her fascination with him. For starters, they hadn't exchanged a seriously cross word since those initial encounters. That had never been the case with any other guy after the first date. And then there was the physical aspect. Gabe never spent the night. He hadn't even come close to spending the night. She didn't doubt their attraction to each other, but he held back, even pulled back on occasion. He was taking it slow, and that was fine with her.

The only stresses she could identify between them were two perturbing thoughts. Actually, the thoughts had names. Jordan and Spencer. She hadn't spent much time with them, though she asked politely about them. Listening to Gabe speak of them did not disturb her. Of course he could read a list of sports scores and she would relish listening. His voice carried her to another place at times. But the kid thing...for now they remained distant, only perturbing if she thought about being with them. Out of sight, out of mind. Or was love just blind? She wasn't sure which cliché fit.

Terri pitched the paper towel into the trash can, turned back to the mirror, and pushed her hands through her short hair until it stood on end. Would Gabe like it that way? Maybe she'd take Erin up on her offer to style it.

She laughed. Nesting instincts and now concern about her appearance? Gabe Andrews was indeed impacting her life.

⌣

"Well, I want to become an EMT because...because..." A choke cut off Erin's voice. She smiled, fanned herself with one hand, and swallowed, her eyes glistening.

The girl did have a commanding presence and looked attractive even under harsh fluorescent light. Terri glanced around the roomful of men and women, all under the age of 30. They had the appearance of people waiting with bated breath while a tightrope walker danced on the high wire.

Inwardly she cringed. She knew what was coming.

"Because," Erin pointed at Terri, "this woman saved my life."

A collective sigh went round the room and everyone applauded. Someone even whistled. Terri resisted the strong urge to flutter her eyelids in a Jordan-like expression. Instead she smiled tightly, a far cry from the gracious demeanor of women she had met at church. At least she knew how to wait wordlessly until the group was finished.

The room contained actual student desks, the type with small writing surfaces that looked like right arms growing out from the chairs. She sat on the edge of a metal desk at the front of the room, thinking that it was time for The Speech, her own invention that had nothing to do with stabilizing a patient. After Erin's performance, she might have to especially emphasize it.

"Thank you, Erin. I appreciate your gratitude. Okay, everyone, this is where I tell you the good, the bad, and the ugly. It's your chance to get out now and not waste anymore of your time."

Gone was the circus audience, replaced by a mob whose faces indicated they had thoughts of lynching. They were earnestly attentive, which was right where she wanted them.

"You all gave valid reasons for wanting to become an EMT, things like a desire to help people or to work in the medical field. But beneath the altruism there may be a fundamental trait you all share. I think everyone in this room is, to some degree or other, an adrenaline junkie."

A few smiled, understanding immediately what she was talking about.

She went on. "When you were a kid, your teachers kept asking why your parents didn't give you some drug so you could focus on your navel like all those smart kids could. You videotape shows like *ER* and watch them over and over. You're fascinated by blood and gore. Your favorite part of biology class was dissecting the frogs and cats. Your most fun childhood memory was when Susie or Johnny broke an arm and you saw the bone poking through."

There were scattered chuckles and nodding heads. Somebody repeated his earlier assessment, "Cool."

"You may ask how I know this." She smiled and called on a young woman who was waving her hand. "Brianna?"

"You know this because you just described yourself."

"A-plus for you. Except I watched *M.A.S.H.* reruns and hung out at the hospital where my dad worked. My best friend was an older woman who worked in the emergency room. When I heard a shooting victim was en route, I'd beg her to let me go in the back. Oh, man! The more stuff hanging out, the better!"

They laughed.

She laughed with them. "Okay, you're all certifiably sick enough to continue with the program."

A couple of the guys hooted.

"But, there is one thing more you must have. Without it, you'll fizzle in a very short time and have to go through the whole process again of figuring out what you want to do with your life." She held up a finger. "The one thing you must have is compassion. I'm not talking about some vague desire to help or save humankind by stitching up every broken body. This is not a job for the fainthearted, nor is it a job for someone who doesn't like people. You'll be bored. Let me tell you what I did yesterday."

She described checking in with the paramedic going off duty, restocking the ambulance, roll call, how she and her partner started the detailed check of the rig when they were called out.

"It was a SIDS. The baby's body was stiff and blue. There wasn't a thing we could do except pretend we were doing something so the parents, who are living the worst nightmare moment of their lives, will remember that we tried everything possible. After that we finished checking the ambulance. Then we were called to an elderly woman's house. She had fallen and couldn't get up. We transported her to the hospital.

"The rest of the day included a fender-bender with the patient complaining of neck pain, a man with chest pain, another having trouble breathing, a temporarily unconscious kid who got knocked down in gym class, a drunk who vomited all over me, a drug overdose that wasn't pretty either, a cardiac arrest who made it to the ER in plenty of time, and, at three in the morning, a woman who was just plain lonely. I got off duty late because of an early morning fire where we treated two people for smoke inhalation."

She flashed a smile. "I didn't save one life during the entire twenty-four hours. Didn't even deliver a baby. Didn't get two straight hours of sleep. Spent an inordinate amount of time kneeling and not in prayer. Strained my back lifting and carrying people. Got blamed for not saving the baby, whose death I have to figure out how to mourn in a healthy way so it doesn't accumulate in here." She flattened a hand against her stomach.

"Now if that sounds like a day you don't ever want to have, you're free to go now. No hard feelings. I understand completely."

She looked around the room slowly, pausing to make eye contact with each student. Nobody flinched.

"Okay, then. Let's get to work."

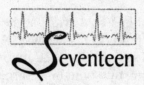

Seventeen

"Are you living with my dad?" Jordan Andrews asked the impertinent question during a lull in dinner, after the egg drop soup and before the Mongolian beef was served.

Terri glanced around the bustling restaurant. Eight-foot tall red dragons with gaping mouths and beady eyes glared back at her from wall-mounted tapestries. Gabe and Spencer were nowhere in sight. They'd gone to the men's room hours ago. She crossed her arms and squeezed her biceps, the equivalent of giving herself a good kick in the shins. The kid was 15 years old! Terri refused to be undone by a teenager.

"No, Jordan, we are not living together. We work together and occasionally have dinner together." *Or breakfast, or we go to a movie, museum, or ice skating rink. None of which is any of your business!*

The girl fluttered her pretty, heavily mascaraed and kohl-lined blue eyes and lifted the teapot. The ever-present pout was in place. "Would you like more tea?"

Terri thought she must be a miniature of the mother, polished and poisonous. "No, thank you."

Jordan poured some for herself. "'An occasional dinner.' Does that mean you're dating? Like a man and a woman do?"

Oh, yes indeed they were dating like a man and a woman. Dating as in the woman was infatuated with the man...as in she should have had a toothbrush and three changes of clothes at his house by now.

But Gabe was showing her a new way. He was light years ahead of her in the faith department. If the New Testament was to be followed to the best of their ability, they wouldn't be sharing a bed, let alone a house, without a marriage license.

Terri broke out in a cold sweat at the mere thought.

Yet, she knew it was the better way. While living with Lee, she had begun to suspect that their union was incomplete. It needed a defining by something larger than themselves, something abstract and mysterious. A blessing.

She answered Jordan. "Yes, we are dating. Like a man and a woman do."

"Thank goodness. He's such a dork. He never dates. And he *cleans* house."

Terri realized the girl was questioning Gabe's masculinity. The workings of a child's mind. Or... "Is that what your mother says?"

"She doesn't have to. I've got two eyes. He hasn't had a girlfriend since the divorce." She held the teacup, her little finger crooked just so. "Mother doesn't talk about him."

Two points for Mother. "Your dad is a dork, in the most positive sense of the phrase. He doesn't care what other people think. He answers only to God. He's honest, compassionate, and a hard worker who faithfully serves the community."

"I know he doesn't care what his kids think."

"And what do his kids think?"

The pout wavered briefly, as if some inner turmoil threatened to topple it. The struggle ended with a haughty expression winning. "Well, his daughter thinks he's still dork. But at least you're a *woman*."

"Not quite up to your standards though, right?" Terri bit her tongue. Obviously not in time.

"I'm not looking for a stepmother."

And I'm sure not looking for a snotty stepdaughter.

"As a matter of fact," the girl-woman went on, "when I turn sixteen in May I plan to talk to my attorney about this ridiculous schedule of visiting on weekends and holidays whenever he doesn't happen to be out 'serving the community.' I have my own life to live and it's not down here in this south suburb."

"Have you talked with your dad about how you feel?"

"Talked *with* him? Ha! That's a laugh—"

"Then *tell* him, Jordan." Terri used what Rachel called her cop tone, a firm command uttered in a low growl enhanced by an icy glare. "Tell him. He needs to hear it from you."

For once the teen's eyelids did not flutter.

⌇

The four of them walked through the darkened parking lot bordered by five-foot mounds of snow. They reached Gabe's pickup. The truck underscored the obvious. He did not own a vehicle able to accommodate more than three people. He was not in the habit of bringing women along on his outings with the children.

Gabe held the door as Spencer and Jordan climbed in.

Terri waved. "Hey, thanks for letting me tag along to dinner."

The boy grinned. "You're going to miss a good movie!"

Jordan stepped onto the running board and shoved her brother's arm. "Move over."

"Hold your horses. Bye, Terri!"

"Bye!"

Gabe handed his keys to his daughter. "Start the heater. I'll be right back." He closed the door behind her.

He swung an arm around Terri shoulders and pulled her close as they continued walking toward another row of parked cars. Their breath frosted the air.

He said, "Thanks for coming."

Sliding an arm across the back of his parka, she leaned her head against him and savored a moment of almost pure contentment. The knowledge that they were within Jordan's view hampered the impact.

"Terri, why did you change your mind about the movie?"

"Jordan and I had a talk."

"Uh-oh."

"No, it was fine, Gabe. It just made me realize she needs to have a serious conversation with you. Alone. And you need to listen."

"What'd she say?"

"That's not for me to tell."

"You're right. Sorry." He squeezed her shoulders. "Any hints are welcome though. We don't communicate well."

"Or at all."

"Ouch."

"I'm not giving you a hint except to say my dad still doesn't hear me. Not in a way that I need. Oh! I can't even put it into words! I've never gotten a sense of acceptance from him. It's left this hole deep inside of me. So I'm taking the advice I gave Jordan, and I'm going to talk to him tonight."

They reached her car and stopped. She dug into her pocket for the keys.

Gabe faced her, his hands on her arms. "Spence thinks you're awesome. And so do I. Your dad probably does too. He just doesn't know how to communicate it."

She shrugged and fiddled with the keys, avoiding eye contact. "Thanks. Spencer is a cute kid. Jordan is a hurting teenager."

"I'll listen. I'll try to hear her, I promise. Pray for me?"

She looked at him and nodded with a smile. "And you for me?"

"Yes." He studied her face as if memorizing its features.

"Jordan's probably watching us."

"A kiss will upset her? Her mother—"

"You're not her mother, Gabe. She needs to experience fatherly affection from you. I don't know if our kissing will upset her. I don't date men with kids. Remember?"

He didn't laugh.

"That was a joke."

"I know." He squeezed her arms. "But this is exactly why you've avoided men with kids. Things are getting complicated."

"True. There's a simple solution, though."

"What's that?"

"You owe me an extra kiss."

He laughed.

The man was so worth the complications.

⌁

Thank You, Lord.

"Schuman, you're talking to yourself again." Rick "Mac" Macauley's voice boomed in the small bedroom.

Standing across the king-size bed from him, Terri winced involuntarily. Her new partner had transferred into her district after Bill left at Christmastime. She would have given half a year's salary to have Kai in that room and Mac under whatever rock he'd crawled out from. To say he bore one of those neon forehead signs proclaiming "I'm obnoxious" scarcely began to describe the man.

Terri turned her attention to Mr. Johnson, all 350 pounds of him, and thanked God again—this time without moving her lips—that backup had radioed. They were downstairs. Calls happened that way sometimes. Dispatch would receive a garbled 911 and send out two medics and five firefighters to carry a 90-pound wisp of a woman. Or they'd send two medics to Mr. Johnson, three flights up an old apartment building with no elevator.

She patted his hand. "We'll have you out of here in just a few minutes, Mr. Johnson."

"I'm sorry I'm so fat." His voice was breathless and muffled behind the oxygen mask.

Mac said, "Hey, it's not your fault, man. She's sorry she's a woman. Not her fault, but she can't help me carry you down. Tell you what. Soon as the doc gets you patched up, I'll take you with me to the gym."

Terri double checked the IV line and reread the EKG strip, tuning out the body builder who imagined himself the ultimate specimen of mankind. Mr. Johnson's heart was in trouble, its rhythm in sinus tach, bounding along too fast for comfort.

Gabe walked through the door first, followed by two others. There wasn't space for all of them and the stair chair they would carry Mr. Johnson in down the steps. Somebody had to go.

"Flo?" Mac's Florence Nightingale nickname for her rankled, but not nearly as much as his tone, which revealed his unspoken question, *Why are you still here?*

She glared at him. *This is my patient and I am strong enough to help carry him!*

He glared back. *Give me a break.*

Gabe, standing beside her, gently and discretely pressed her elbow.

She turned and saw no condemnation in the raised brows and half smile. One dimple appeared. His look showered her with affirmation. She didn't have to prove herself to anyone in that room.

For the first time she could remember while on the job, she allowed the macho mask to slip away. With a graciousness beyond her natural ability, she left to wait in the hall.

⁓

An hour later Terri and Mac returned to the firehouse. They hadn't exchanged a word unrelated to the call.

Her partner was a large man, about 30, with bulging muscles, brown eyes, a head full of black hair, and a bushy mustache. Three or four caterpillars' worth of fuzz. His demeanor was argumentative, overbearing, and borderline intimidating.

They reached the entrance to the supply room, and she placed her hands on her hips.

"Mac, let's get one thing straight." In the month they'd worked together, she had said that phrase or its equivalent at least a dozen times.

"It's lecture time again, boys and girls."

"Maybe this will cover everything."

"Let's hope not! You're so cute when you're ticked at me, Flo."

"You do this stuff on purpose?"

He grinned. "I don't know. You didn't tell me what I did yet."

"You said something inappropriate."

"I try."

She refused to rise to the bait. "You said I'm sorry I'm a woman. For the record, I am *not* sorry I'm a woman."

"Me neither!" He roared with laughter.

Not wanting to raise her voice, she waited until he quieted. "Don't ever say it or imply it again. And don't ever insinuate to my patient he is not getting the best care because I'm a woman."

He chuckled. "Come on, Schuman. The guy could have died while we just shot the breeze waiting for backup."

Terri knew the cost of losing five minutes. Fortunately Mr. Johnson didn't have to pay it. "Then blame his wife for being so hysterical she couldn't completely explain the situation. Or blame dispatch for not clarifying with her. Or blame drivers for not moving out of our way fast enough. Or blame three flights of stairs. These things happen. But don't upset the patient by blaming my gender!"

He grinned.

Lasciviously. There was no mistaking it.

He hooted, "Whoo-oo! You are something else!"

"Macauley, get a grip." She twirled on her heel and collided with Gabe. "Excuse me," she said and walked away.

Mac's voice followed her. "Andrews, you can call me Tonto. I'll ride with our Lone Ranger anywhere."

Terri went outside. A blast of cold air washed over her, blowing away the remnants of frustration and mental grime that usually clung to her after a conversation with Mac.

"Lord," she whispered, "why him? Oh, I get it. Patience, right? This is Your idea of a training session."

The door opened and Gabe walked through it. He joined her on the sidewalk and smiled softly. "Tonto says don't worry, he's got a handle on the restocking."

She burst into laughter and shook her head. "Gabe, what am I going to do? He's driving me crazy."

"Well, if you want to get serious about things, you've probably got a case for sexual harassment."

"Oh, he's not the worst I've worked with in that department. And I don't want to come across as a whiny troublemaker. If I can't make it on my own, I may as well quit."

"You're not completely on your own, you know."

"I know. There's God. And there's you. And there's the genuine respect of the other guys. Have I told you how much I appreciate their acceptance of me?"

"Once or twice." He grinned. "It helped that we had other female medics working out of the station before you came along. I don't think Mac's ever seen one in person. You think he's harmless?"

"In general, yes. He knows his stuff well enough. It's his mouth that gets him in trouble."

He laughed.

Terri realized what he was thinking. She was the pot calling the kettle black, one loud mouth identifying another. "Don't you dare say a word."

"Wouldn't think of it." He reached over and brushed her hair from her eyes. "How did last night go with your dad?"

His touch and soft voice derailed her thoughts, spinning them off like a whirling top.

"Terri?"

"Uh, long story. How'd things go with Jordan?"

"Long story. Want to have breakfast?"

She smiled and glanced at her watch. "Meet you in the parking lot in twenty hours?"

"It's a date." His eyes twinkled.

Terri knew that as long as his eyes kept twinkling and his voice kept mesmerizing, she could handle anything.

∽

Twenty hours later, Terri sat in a darkened hospital room, holding the hand of a woman she first met shortly before dawn.

As the temperature dipped to its lowest point of the night, Terri and Mac arrived at Mrs. Lynn Singer's house. A few stars blinked in a navy blue sky. They'd disappeared by the time they wheeled the stretcher back out to the ambulance.

Mrs. Singer was 67 years old. She had suffered a massive stroke. She would be dead before most Chicagoans arrived at work. Long before her children flew into O'Hare from various parts of the country. Even longer before anyone would think to inform the ex-husband, who was scum according to the helpful neighbor who'd called 911. She had noticed Mrs. Singer's lights on half the night and, when her knock went unanswered, used her key to go inside. She even answered health history questions and retrieved the Do Not Resuscitate documentation.

The woman had drifted in and out of consciousness. She was out of it now, probably for the final time. They would pronounce her soon. Terri held her hand, talked, and prayed.

She had left Mrs. Singer's side only long enough to return to the station, check out, and drive back to the hospital in her own car. Protocol dictated she had to return in the ambulance with her partner. It also said she be available for the medic replacing her on the next shift, let her know what needed to be restocked. She performed the returning part, but ducked out a few minutes early, creating an indebted relationship with Mac by expecting him to cover for her.

"I don't get it, Flo. What's the big deal?"

"Mac, it's just something I've always done, okay? Nobody should die alone. The hospital staff is too busy to sit with her. I'm available. I'm going back."

Terri sensed it now. Another presence in the room. Briefly. And then...that silence. She was all alone. Life had exited.

Gabe was in the ER lobby, waiting. She knew he would be. It was what people falling in love did for each other.

She linked her arm with his. Wordlessly, they left the hospital and walked through the parking lot. He opened the passenger door of his truck for her. She slid across the bench seat and unlocked the driver's door. It was what people falling in love did for each other.

He started the engine and then turned and pulled her to himself. She laid her face against his soft, cold jacket. She had already shed tears for the stranger. What she felt now was an overwhelming sense of the reality of *life*. Her heart pounded with it. Her head spun. She wanted to crawl out of her skin.

Gabe's left arm moved. Her back felt an instant emptiness. She heard the heater fan go on.

He touched her cheek, slid his hand under her chin, and lifted her face. When he lowered his and their lips met, Terri knew it was the most natural thing in the world. It was what people did when they loved each other.

Eighteen

Noisy chatter filled the busy restaurant. Wait staff scurried about, dishes and silverware clanked. Sizzling bacon and coffee aromas dominated.

Terri and Gabe sat in a booth, not yet engaged in conversation. She felt as if her oxygen supply had been spent during the episode in his truck. Evidently he'd been holding back on previous occasions. Not today. The impact of his kisses blotted out the impact of the woman's death. Maybe if she kissed him at the end of every shift, she'd have less need to call her sister or Rachel and vent the heavy emotions. His arms around her sure beat snuggling with Zoë. On the whole, this was not a bad idea.

"Well." Gabe broke the comfortable silence and smiled over his coffee cup. "Happy Valentine's Day."

Terri choked on the sip she had just taken. The date hadn't registered beyond a number to fill in on run forms in the middle of the night. She pressed a napkin to her mouth and coughed.

"You okay?"

"No."

"Me neither." He smiled briefly. "Terri, I'm tired of being fearful."

"Of what?"

"Us."

"And now?"

"Life's too short to spend it living in fear of what might or might not happen. Jesus said we shouldn't fear. Do not fear, period. No ifs, ands, or buts in His economy. He's got things under control. He knows the beginning and the end."

"Whew. That was a mouthful." She thought over his words. "But trusting Him does not mean everything will be blissfully hunky-dory from this moment on."

"No, it doesn't."

"We're not perfect." She nervously tapped her fork against the plate. "The world is not a perfect place."

"Right." He reached over and stilled her hand. "Terri, what are you trying to say?"

"You've got kids." She frowned, not daring to meet his eyes.

"Yeah. Go on."

"I don't particularly like kids. I mean, they're fine and all that. I've treated every brand and haven't intentionally hurt one beyond poking them with the necessary needle or whatever." The pitch of her voice rose. "And I am kind to my nieces and nephews. But I never, ever wanted to be involved with a kid on a regular basis." She looked at him.

"Hmm. So you're afraid Jordan and Spencer might come between us?"

"They *will* come between us. They will *rightfully* come between us because they are such a huge part of your life. They require your time and energy. There will be situations when you have to choose between them and me. Or there will be activities we engage in when, again rightfully, you'll want them involved. Like weekends and holidays and trips."

He remained quiet for a moment, and then he grinned. "You kissed me back."

Her reply fell somewhere between a sigh and a groan.

"Then my kids are not a deal breaker?"

"No." Her voice almost squeaked now.

"I'm not asking you to be their stepmother."

"Yes, you are. In a sense."

"Aren't you jumping the gun here?"

"Gabe." She swallowed, pressing her voice down into its normal range. "You're a father. Besides being a genuinely nice guy and a fireman and a carpenter, you're a father. The man I kissed back is all of those things. You can't take one of them away, or you wouldn't be you."

He smiled. "Kissing isn't exactly being married."

"Granted. And I've said too much." She clamped her teeth together, squelching the urge to declare her steadfast love for him, which was the only explanation as to why she accepted, without kicking and screaming, the fact that she was about to become involved on a regular basis with two kids, one of whom was a bona fide pain in the neck.

He finally removed his hand from hers, picked up a knife, and began to spread jelly on a piece of toast. "Let me see if I understand this. The major holdbacks for you have been that you don't trust men and you don't want to hang out with kids. You're on the verge of reversing both of those positions because— Because why?"

"Because I've finally gone completely round the bend."

He laughed.

She'd scare both of them away if she verbalized her love for him, which was a ridiculous notion to begin with considering they hadn't known each other all that long. But there was nowhere to hide from his steady gaze. She owed him at least a glimpse of where she was. "You're the first thought I have when I wake up and the last one before I go to sleep."

His face relaxed. She hadn't noticed the tenseness around his mouth and eyes until now as it disintegrated. In spite of everything, he really hadn't been sure how she felt.

"Terri." Something beyond compassion warmed his expression and his voice. "It's the same with me. I have conversations with you all day long. You're in my dreams. I look for your face wherever I go. I'm always praying for you. You have no idea how many times I *haven't* called you just to hear your voice. Everything in my life is beginning to take a backseat to you."

As if cotton suddenly plugged her ears, nearby conversations were enveloped in a whooshing noise. The view behind Gabe grew wavy as if it had been plunged under water. No man had ever said such things to her. Red flags snapped in her imaginary peripheral vision. Was Gabe Andrews for real?

"Terri?"

"Huh?"

"You okay?"

"Uh-huh." She blinked and cleared her throat. Her senses readjusted themselves.

"You look a little dazed."

"I am." She chuckled, buying time while her heartbeat withdrew from the area of her throat where it certainly didn't belong during the course of a conversation over breakfast. Her trademark flippant tone finally found its way to her vocal cords. "Whew. You meant all of that?"

He winked and took a bite of scrambled egg.

"Okay." Bagel in hand, she tore off little pieces, not in the least bit hungry. "My turn. What were you afraid of? What were your holdbacks?"

He took another bite and chewed.

She crossed her legs and jiggled a foot.

At last he said, "Three things. First of all, the obvious. Is she like Paula? Why set myself up for failure? Where is this leading? I'm just her rebound guy. Talk about vulnerable."

"Oh." His answer surprised her. From what she knew, she wasn't anything like Paula. And she took issue with the rebound remark. She was way over Lee. "Why would you think rebound?"

"You moved out from Lee's because you thought it was the right thing to do. That choice did not mean you had stopped loving him. I didn't stop loving Paula overnight."

She nodded. "It took a while, but I really don't feel anything toward him. The memories have lost their fondness."

"I appreciate you saying that."

"It's true!"

"But it's okay if you have periods when it's not true. When emotions toward him just sort of pop up." He gave her his half smile. "I've been there."

She did a quick mental survey. The image of Lee remained, a shadow of his former self. For a time he had been hidden behind barbed wire; merely touching the thought of him hurt beyond measure. Now she saw his outline as a distant shadow walking away.

Terri noticed Gabe watching her, as if waiting for her to finish the imaginative exploration. His ability to tune in sent chills through her. "Why would I feel anything for him? He's not in my head or my life."

"It just happens."

"Okay." Not that she believed it true for herself. She picked up the other half of the bagel and began tearing it apart. "I'm not sure I want to know the second thing."

"Being open is good. In the long run."

She nodded. "I know. Go ahead."

"Kai called you a hot dog and a loose cannon. I saw glimpses and thought, I *really* don't have enough energy for this unpredictable woman."

Terri laughed. "Unpredictable? Now that's a compliment. Why not call me a flake, you tired old fogey?"

He grinned. "The flake and the fogey. It has a certain ring to it, don't you think?"

She watched him take another bite and sensed it was a delaying tactic. How could the man eat at such a time? They were breaking new ground! Plowing up emotional soil! For her, all regular activity had come to a halt. They might as well finish it.

"Gabe. Number three?"

He swallowed, set down his fork, wiped his mouth with the napkin, and cleared his throat. "The Lone Ranger."

As much as the nickname was bandied about, his mention of it inserted a serious note into the conversation.

He moved aside the syrup pitcher and salt shaker, and took her hand. "You know how he wears a mask? I see a mask on you, Terri. I'm still not exactly sure who you are. You allow people to get only so close."

Instinctively she tried to pull her hand away, but he held it fast.

"Sweetheart, only so close is close enough. Something inside of me says that exactly who you are is exactly what I'm looking for."

Tears stung and her arm tensed in her desire to yank her hand from his. A feeling akin to releasing bicycle brakes and sailing down a steep hill tore her breath away.

Terri nearly bolted after Gabe's wild declaration. He rubbed his thumb across the back of her hand in a calming motion while his words sank deeply into her heart.

She knew she wore a mask. With the precision of a surgeon wielding a scalpel, he sliced through the knot holding it in place. She hadn't even seen it coming. Was that what love was all about?

"Terri, I don't expect you to change. I'm not asking you to change. I guess it's like me being a combination of things. You're a combination too, and the Lone Ranger is included, his independent nature as well as his mask. The combination is who I want to spend time with. Okay?"

"O-okay."

"Are you going to eat that bagel?"

She shook her head.

"Egg?"

"No."

He released her hand and helped himself to food from her plate. True fireman. He ignored how cold the eggs were. "Thanks. I've been thinking about the guys. Some of them suspect 'us' already. May I have that cream cheese? Thanks. I'm getting flak whenever you and I happen to get three seconds alone at the station and someone walks in on us talking. It's a joke for now, but there will be others who will not want us working together, even if it is less than once a week. So what do you think? Unless we're directly asked, we won't advertise the fact that we're on..." He winked. "Serious kissing terms?"

"Like I'm going to confide in Mac." She tried to grin, but her mouth wouldn't cooperate. Full composure eluded her grasp.

Gabe laughed. "Mind if I tell you about Jordan?"

He was doing a superb job of allowing her time to regroup, of letting her align the mask with the new freedom he offered her. She understood that he'd given her the liberty to wear it or not. Except in rare instances, specifically with Rachel or Bryan when it subconsciously slid away, she had always worn it. To say that she was discombobulated was an understatement.

"No, I don't mind if you tell me about Jordan."

"I made a conscious effort to listen, like you suggested. I didn't dismiss her opinion. I didn't reprimand her when she rolled her eyes. There was definitely less tension between us."

"That's good. Why do you usually dismiss her opinion?"

He took a moment to reply. "She's disrespectful. And I imagine she doesn't respect me because she blames me for the divorce. Which is where the blame belongs."

"Maybe you can win her back and she can forgive you."

"You think so?"

"I don't disrespect my dad, but if he validated my opinion or showed me unconditional love, I'd forgive him in a heartbeat. I'd—" She stopped talking.

"You'd what?"

She shrugged a shoulder. "Stop wearing this mask?"

He stared at her. "Jordan's attitude is a mask, isn't it?"

"I think so."

"I need to apologize to her."

"That'd be a good start, Gabe. She'll be years ahead of the game." Terri gave him a thumbs-up.

"How'd it go with your dad the other night?"

"He was asleep. The chemo treatments are so hard on him, and now they've added radiation. They had wanted to avoid that. I sat with Mom for a while. She was watching television and was not much interested in conversation. I asked why it was Dad never accepts me for who I am. She said she didn't know what I was talking about, that with seven kids somebody's feelings were always going to be hurt. I argued against that and gave examples of how the other six get positive feedback from him. She said as usual I was the squeaky wheel, which was why I spent so much time at the hospital, and maybe *Lois* would know why. We always teased about Lois being my 'other mother.' This was the first time Mom sounded ticked mentioning her name."

She paused long enough to take a breath and realize she'd left herself wide open for scrutiny. "So how's that for mask-free communication?"

"Not bad."

They exchanged a smile. A waitress walked by, a whiff of perfume in her wake. A sweet scent...pungent...popular designer label. Nausea hit Terri like a fist to her stomach.

She glanced over her shoulder. In the booth behind her sat Erin Morgan, the back of her swept-up hair inches from Terri's head.

Gabe asked, "Terri, what's wrong?"

She pointed a thumb toward her shoulder and said sotto voce, "Erin."

The ever-present gentle expression disappeared from his face. The eyes narrowed, the jaw muscle tensed up.

She had told him about the girl attending her class. He strongly recommended she call Cara. She hadn't. Things were under control. No need to bring in the cavalry.

How long had Erin been sitting there? How much had she overheard? The restaurant was still a bustling place. People eating and talking and moving about. Terri hadn't heard any neighboring conversation. Not consciously. But then, she hadn't been trying to.

Erin chose that moment to make her presence known. "Terri! Is that you?"

She didn't turn.

The girl appeared beside their table, smiling. "Hi! I overheard someone say 'Terri' and I turned around and there you were." Enthusiasm bubbled in her voice. "You must be Gabe."

Terri started. How did she know his name? She must have overheard it. "Erin, this is one of those situations I talked about. It's absolutely, totally off limits."

"But we just *happened* to be in the same restaurant!"

The same restaurant which just happened to be midway between Terri's two frequent hangouts, the hospital and fire station. She had inadvertently mentioned the station number in the class, making it easy enough for Erin to track her down.

"I am not discussing it. You're done with the class. Do not show up again. If you want to take it, you'll have to wait until someone else teaches it."

There was a subtle shift in Erin's expression, almost as if the face closed in upon itself, transforming the perkiness into something indescribable. "Well, toodles then." She turned on her heel and sashayed away.

Terri shuddered. "Excuse me for not introducing you."

"I'm not offended. Good call about the class. She shouldn't be in it."

"But she looks fairly normal, doesn't she? I mean, until she got mad at the end there. She's friendly."

"She's neither normal nor friendly, Terri." He signaled the waitress. "I'll take you to the courthouse."

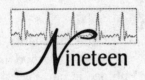

Nineteen

Only sheer adrenaline kept Terri from falling asleep in the chair beside Cara Fleming's desk. The nervous energy was fueled by a combustible mix of Gabe's attention and Erin's appearance. She didn't even need the styrofoam cup of mud the policewoman referred to as coffee.

Listening intently to the latest report of Erin Morgan's shenanigans, Cara drummed her fingertips on the desk. Between her icy stare and the image of quiet Gabe breathing fire as he insisted Terri meet with the cop now rather than later, Terri felt squeezed in from all sides. Who did they think they were, wresting control from her? Gabe even shot down her excuse about needing to get home to Zoë. As always, one of the neighbor teens would have already taken the dog out early for a short walk before school, but Zoë expected Terri home soon. Gabe said he'd keep Zoë company for a while before heading to his construction job. After all, unlike Terri, he had slept most of the night at the station.

Cara stopped the finger tapping. "So you and Gabe got things rolling for another emergency order of protection?"

She nodded.

"Ms. Schuman, repeat after me: 'I will not allow Erin Morgan into any situation whatsoever, such as a class, where I am involved.'"

"Cara, come on."

"Say it."

She said it.

"Now say, 'I will call the police if she comes near.'"

Terri complied.

"And, 'I will pursue getting an interim order before time runs out on the emergency one. And then I'll go for a plenary order.'"

"I get the picture, Cara!"

The woman leaned toward her. She wore a white blouse wrinkled more than usual by a shoulder holster that housed a gun. Her familiar nonchalant expression and semi-bumbling demeanor were gone. Terri sensed her own flippancy had gone too far.

"No, Terri, I don't think you get the picture at all. None of the rules of human decency apply to people like Erin Morgan. She is perfectly capable of murdering you. Of all people, I thought you would understand. Time and again you've seen up close the senseless horrors people commit against each other. It doesn't just happen to others. This woman is in your life and she is not going to go away."

"A piece of paper won't change that!"

"But it gives us legal leverage!"

"Like that will help after she kills me. What am I supposed to do? Change jobs again? Move again?"

"Maybe." Cara leaned back in her chair.

They sat quietly. Terri tilted her head from shoulder to shoulder, releasing tension. There had to be some way to fight back.

She said, "Why don't you devise some sting operation, where Erin comes after me but I'm wired. So at the last moment you and your friends barge in, rescue me, arrest her. You've got the tape recording; she's confessed to all sorts of misdeeds; you lock her away."

"I'll get right on it." Cara picked up a pen and fiddled with it. "I'm sorry." A new solemnity marked her tone.

"This is personal for you."

"Yeah. I consider you a friend." She glanced away, those wide set eyes seeing all and revealing zilch. Her gaze returned. "It's more than that. Years ago I was stalked. I moved two thousand miles away."

"Who was it?"

"My husband." She gave her head a slight shake. "You could say stalking is a pet peeve of mine."

"How awful."

"You'll take me seriously?"

"Okay."

"Thank you."

"Do you want to talk about—"

"No. Let's change the subject. How's Gabe?"

Terri had met Cara for dinner during the holidays; they had discussed the developing relationship. "Major kissing today."

"It's not even noon!"

"But it's Valentine's Day." She grinned. "Anyway, we seem infatuated with each other."

"Infatuated? That's a wishy-washy term."

"We're taking our time. I sensed red flags today."

"Warning you of what?"

"I don't know. I'm not crazy about kids and he has two. But it's not that. It's like he's almost too good to be true."

"There's got to be a few good ones out there."

"But infatuated with me?"

"Don't sell yourself short."

Terri shrugged. "Whatever. Have you permanently signed off on men?"

"The jury's still out."

"I thought I was wary with men, but you must have something like a triple dose of distrust."

She smiled. "That's why I carry a gun."

"I didn't mean to make light of it."

"I know. But laughing is healthier than crying all the time."

Terri's cell phone rang. She pulled it from her jacket pocket and checked the incoming number. "It's my sister. Excuse me?"

"Sure."

She pressed the talk key. "Shelley?"

"It's Dave, Terri."

Why would her sister's boyfriend be calling? "Yeah?"

"It's-it's your dad. They want you at the ER right away. Cutler-Barr."

"They who? What's going on?"

"Just-just go." Dave was an articulate prosecuting attorney. He did not stutter.

"Dave! You can't drop a bombshell like that and not tell me why it's blowing up."

"Yes, I can. Just go. *Now.*"

The dial tone hummed in her ear.

"Terri, what is it?"

"I don't know. My dad. He's at Cutler-Barr. I have to go there. Why would he be—"

"Come on." Cara stood, grabbed her jacket, and took hold of Terri's arm. "I'll drive you there. You're white as a sheet."

That squeezed feeling returned full force. What was going on?

∽

Like a homing pigeon, Terri wound her way through the emergency room, Cara following in her wake. She didn't seek out acquaintances from the staff to ask directions. Some sixth sense told her Bob Schuman was behind closed doors and Maria Delgado Schuman was in a private waiting room. Her mother would need to see her first.

As they hurried down the hallway, the sound of hysterical yelling in Spanish grew distinct. Familiar. Her mother? The woman who refused to speak her native tongue?

Terri reached the room and flung open the door. The scene before her imprinted itself on her mind. Pretty, white-haired, trim Lois stood to the left, arms holding shut a gray cardigan, tears streaming down her face. To the right stood her mom, not overweight but compact in stature, hair still thick and naturally black as ever, a curly halo encircling a face ravaged with unadulterated anguish, her fists raised.

She screamed at Lois, *"Fuera!"*

Her mother ordered their old family friend to get out. "Mom?"

"Teresa! Teresa! *Está muerto! Está muerto!"*

"He's dead? Who's— Oh dear God." Her *father?* "No!"

The impact of the news was like being slammed against the wall. Her entire being felt jolted and stunned. Confusion scattered her thoughts. Through the daze she saw her mother hold out her arms. She went to them.

Mother and daughter sank onto chairs beside each other, cried together and spoke in Spanish, shutting out the whole world. Maria had few answers to Terri's questions. When?

A shrug.

What happened?

He felt ill all night.

But he was getting better. Wasn't he?

The radiation... There were complications.

What complications?

Another shrug.

Her mother had called Bobby, the eldest, who notified the other siblings. Everyone was en route to the hospital. Bobby from his office. Shelley from downtown. Laurie from the suburban school where she taught. Kenny from his car repair shop. Missy would catch a flight from Cincinnati as soon as possible. Jimmy should fly too, from Champaign, and not drive the winter highway while upset.

Terri's name was conspicuously absent in the litany of where and how they'd heard. Indignation flashed through her. She interrupted. "Mom! They all know? *Shelley* knew? Why didn't Dave tell me?"

Maria stroked her daughter's cheek and whispered, "They wanted you here in one piece. You would have forgotten your car does not have flashing lights and sirens."

Terri's ire fizzled. Her family's anticipation of her actions rang true.

With a start, she remembered Lois. "Why were you yelling at her?"

"*She had an affair with him!*" Maria growled the words, still in Spanish.

"Mom, that's ridiculous. Dad wouldn't—" Her words stopped cold at the look on her mother's face.

Terri turned around. Lois still stood on the other side of the small room, crying softly.

"Is this true?" Lois did not speak Spanish; she would not know what they were talking about. Terri had to spell it out. "You had an affair with him?"

"Let me explain. Please."

"Is it true?" Ice crept into Terri's tone. She couldn't stop it. Wasn't sure she wanted to.

"Yes." Her friend's voice broke.

Terri stared at the woman who'd had as much a hand in her upbringing as did her own mother. The friend who loved her since childhood, who opened her eyes to emergency medicine, who fed her dream with wise and practical advice. She would never have achieved the status of paramedic without Lois Quayle.

But the choice was as clear as if Terri faced the decision whether or not to administer CPR to someone not breathing.

"Get out."

Lois drooped her head and left without a word.

Cara came forward and knelt before Terri and her mother, laying a hand on each of their arms. "I am so sorry for your loss." Surprisingly, she spoke in flawless Spanish. "Is there anything I can do right now? Anything you need?"

Turn back the clock.

Terri said, "No, thank you."

"Can I call anyone?"

"No." Numbness was setting in. She felt civility slipping through her fingers like water. There was only one thing to do: pull up the family drawbridge and wait out the storm. Anyone not biologically related was an unwelcome intrusion.

"Terri, your friends will want to know. I'll call Kai and the station. Okay?"

"Whatever."

∽

Terri felt as if she'd lost her father twice over. Once to death. Once to Lois. Three times over if she counted never having received from him words of affirmation. Death cleared away all dodging of the truth. She craved those words. Words she never would hear.

Rachel Koski sat at the opposite end of the couch. It was nearly midnight. The visitation had ended hours ago.

"Terri, it's okay to be angry."

"Angry? I'm beyond angry. There's no word for where I am."

"Sweetie."

Terri looked away. Rachel had driven from Iowa that morning to be with her during the funeral. Her friend's presence was acceptable. She was the only one besides her sister Shelley who knew Terri's dark side and loved her anyway. The present situation would put her friend to the test, though. That dark side was about to eclipse light altogether.

Rachel said, "This is a lame thing to say, but it will get better."

Terri slid to the floor to snuggle with Zoë and avoid eye contact. Rachel spoke from experience still fresh, still ongoing, not yet referred to in the past tense. Terri didn't want to see those depths in her friend's eyes. "It can't get better.

Things weren't finished between us!" She bit her lip. "What a stupid thing to say to you. I'm sorry."

"It's okay. I'm your 'ventee,' remember? Just like you've been mine. Don't worry about hurting my feelings. Vent away."

Terri buried her face in Zoë's neck. The thick golden fur was as good as any hankie.

After a bit, Rachel said, "I had a nice chat with Gabe tonight at the home."

She sniffed and raised her head. "He's a nice guy."

"He said he almost didn't recognize you in a dress."

"It belongs to Shelley."

"Sisters and their helpful dress codes and closets." Rachel smiled. "He also said you were beautiful."

"Men and their bunk at the sight of a pair of female legs."

She chuckled. "I think there was a healthy dose of love and respect mixed in with the bunk."

"He's out of my league."

"Don't talk that way. Don't even think that way. He cares about you and you are worthy of that care."

She remembered how at the visitation Gabe had kissed her cheek and whispered in her ear, "I'm here for you." No reproach for her not returning his calls. He'd left at least half a dozen voice mail messages in the past few days.

"Ter, don't go down that road again."

"What road?"

She took an audibly deep breath. "You didn't pull any punches with me. I guess I'll return the favor."

Terri suspected the brief smile on Rachel's face was meant to soften the coming blow. "Okay."

"You always used to hide your real self. You wouldn't let people in and were always trying to prove your worth. I realize to a certain extent you had to on the job because the guys wouldn't take you seriously. It goes beyond that, though. It's rooted in your dad not accepting you. But you've been down the *other* road, the one of grace and forgiveness. In

Christ you are good enough. You know your *heavenly* Father's boundless love and acceptance. You're free to receive it as well as give it away."

"I tried to give it to my dad. He didn't want any part of it." Her voice choked. "Where is he tonight, Rache? Where is he?"

Without a word, Rachel slipped to the floor and, reaching across Zoë, embraced Terri. They cried for a very long time.

⌇

Early morning sunlight streamed through the window of the kitchen door, giving a false sense of warmth. Audible through the closed door, the sound of snow crunching under Zoë's big paws told a different story. Terri's breath left moisture droplets against the cold pane.

At least the cemetery portion of the funeral would be held inside a mausoleum. Although unheated, it was preferable to standing in the raw force of a northwest wind.

Cara Fleming might appreciate that too. Ever since Bob Schuman's death, the policewoman and Kai had taken turns shadowing Terri, a tag team of self-appointed bodyguards. Today Cara was on the unofficial duty. Terri couldn't help but wonder what it mattered that an emotionally unstable girl followed her. How could Erin Morgan possibly cause any more grief than Terri had already experienced?

The coffeemaker grew silent. She turned from the window and pulled two mugs from the cupboard.

Rachel entered the kitchen, already dressed in a white blouse, black suit skirt and hose. The natural waves of her thick reddish brown hair were slightly damp. "Thanks." She accepted a cup from Terri and sat at the table. "Did you sleep at all?"

"A little." She joined her. "I think. Can I get you a bagel? There's an egg casserole too. A neighbor brought it over."

"I'll help myself."

They sipped coffee in silence. Her friend wore a wedding ring, a diamond tennis bracelet, and a worried expression.

Terri guessed at what she was thinking. "Rachel, I wouldn't have slept anyway. It didn't matter that I took the couch and not the bed."

"I wasn't going to say that again."

"Then what is it?"

"Nothing about your dad was your responsibility. Not his choices, not his death. I wish I could make you *believe* that, deep down inside."

"What does it matter?" Another thing that didn't matter at this point in time.

"It shouldn't matter, but I know you. The guilt is going to eat you alive."

"I can't just wish it away."

"No, but will you promise me one thing?"

"Don't ask me to do anything right now, Rachel, please."

"This is easy. Promise me you'll talk to God every time that guilt starts in on you and makes you want to hurt your-self—"

"What do you mean, hurt myself?"

"Pull away from people. Work too much. Not take the time to read those books still packed in that box in your room, all those Biblical expositions you couldn't get enough of last year. And last but not least, don't hurt yourself by telling Gabe you're not interested."

Terri crossed her arms. Those were the exact things that would protect her from wallowing in the guilt that bubbled even now just below the surface.

Rachel stretched across the table and touched her arm. Urgency underscored her tone. "I'm reading your mind, right? Just don't stop talking to God, even if it's to yell at Him or ask Him why."

"I have a why question. And I asked Him all night long. I said, why is it I sit with a stranger while she dies, and four hours later I don't sit with my own dad while he dies down the hall in the same stinking hospital? God let me down, Rache. He let me down, which is par for the course. I wasn't good enough for Dad. Why would I be good enough for God?"

Rachel stood, walked around the table, and gave Terri a brief hug. "That's your pain talking. Go on now and get ready. I'll unpack that box of books."

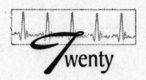

Twenty

The day after the funeral, Terri sat at the large rectangular dining room table in her parents' house. Her mother's house. Familiar scratches in the maple caught her eye. Some had been there as far back as she could remember. She glanced down at a table leg near her chair, at the 'T' she'd carved with a dinner knife when she was seven and beets were particularly disagreeable to her palate. Her dad used his belt for the first time, a sons-only discipline up to that point. Becoming a member of that exclusive club was a source of pride.

Maybe she should see a therapist.

Shelley, Missy, and Laurie sat with her and their mother, writing thank-you notes and tossing around ideas of what should be done next. Plans were going nowhere fast. Terri voted silently that they all get back to work as soon as possible and wondered why her brothers were exempt from this nonsense.

Her cell phone rang. She checked the incoming number to make sure it wasn't Gabe. His tender kiss on her cheek at the funeral home was all she could handle in the foreseeable future. Her dad's death, Lois's confession, and her mother's yo-yo swinging between anger and despair muddied Terri's emotional waters. To add to that was impossible, despite Rachel's stinging words. *Don't work too much. Don't pull away from people...from Gabe.* How could she sort through all the garbage without cloistering herself?

The caller ID read *Unavailable.* Some of her friends blocked their numbers. Gabe didn't. She needed a break. "Excuse me."

She carried the phone into the front room, Zoë padding at her heels. "Hello?"

"I'm sorry about your dad."

She hesitated. The female voice was familiar, but she couldn't place it. "Thanks."

"I would have come, but I thought you might still be mad."

"Erin?"

"The cops gave me another restraining order. Why did you have to do that again?"

"How did you get this number?"

"You're so *exclusive!*"

Terri figured someone at the station had inadvertently supplied it. One death in the family and sympathetic people tried to be helpful by sharing all kinds of information with others who sounded likewise.

"Melanie was never like that."

Terri sank onto the couch. Melanie Lareau was the woman killed in the car accident...the accident probably caused by Erin.

"Melanie always invited me to do things. I volunteered at her campaign stuff. Went to parties at her house. You have never invited me to your house. And you've got that nice new condo. What kind of rent does Gabe charge?"

A chill went through her. "Erin—"

"Probably not much since he's your boyfriend."

"He's not my boyfriend."

"Sure looked that way in his truck on Valentine's Day." She giggled. "Does he have a brother? Well, I gotta go, girl-friend. Talk to you later."

The line went dead. Terri shuddered, took a deep breath, and began reviewing her options. Supposedly this was a thing to report. Not that it would make a difference. "No contact by phone" was included in the restraining order, but what did that mean? Did someone have to dig through phone records to prove it happened? Would Erin, the poor little rich girl, be fined? Would Terri have to press charges or go to court?

Still Cara should be apprised. Terri would call her. Right after she called the paramedic scheduler. Life outside of work was way too complicated. She'd report for duty tomorrow morning...if not before.

Kneeling beside the cot, Terri placed her gloved hands on the teenager's shoulders and lowered her face to within centimeters of his. "Jeremy, have you taken any drugs recently?"

"No! I swear!" The boy moaned and hugged his knees to his chest. Beads of perspiration lined his forehead and upper lip. Obviously he wasn't lying about abdominal pain, but his dilated pupils, respiration, and heart rate suggested otherwise regarding her drug question. He had answered her earlier questions with great deliberation, his mouth forming the words in slow motion, as if his brain function wasn't quite up to par. Just pain or was he high on something?

"How about alcohol? Did you drink any last night? This morning?" The questions would sound preposterous in the normal scheme of things at 8:30 A.M. at Weis Academy, an exclusive parochial school. Emergency conditions, however, insisted she throw "normal" out the window and ask everything.

Between groans, Jeremy mumbled, "No."

"Jeremy." She spoke quietly so as not to be overheard by the principal. A few feet behind her the man breathed down the neck of Mac, who in turn breathed down her neck. The school nurse's quarters were, to say the least, cramped. "Listen to me. I am not with the police or the school. This stays between you and me. Have you ever done drugs or drank?"

"No!" He was a good-looking kid with neatly trimmed dark brown hair and an athletic build, a subtle air of wealth hovering around him.

"Never?"

He closed his eyes and swore under his breath.

Terri remembered that Gabe's attractive children attended Weis. Perhaps looks were a requirement. Wealth certainly was. How could he afford their tuition? The guy must be a whiz at finances. The school was an anomaly. Despite its excellent reputation, it was housed in an old public school building located in a rundown area and only a hop, skip, and a jump from the most undesirable neighborhood in her district.

She stifled a sigh. The Jeremy conversation was going nowhere fast. What were they dealing with? His blood pressure was high, his pulse racing, his skin feverish. He said the pain had started the previous night in his stomach; it was now in his lower right abdomen. He said his mother advised— long distance from New York before he left for school—that it could be appendicitis. The power of suggestion. Terri wasn't buying it. She wanted specific answers before transporting.

"All right, Jeremy. No dope, coke, speed, crack. No booze. Not even a beer. This is good to know because I have to give you a drug. And if you've done *any* of that stuff, *this* stuff will kill you by dinnertime."

"*Kill* me?"

"Yeah. That's why I gotta ask those questions. Mac." She snapped her fingers over her shoulder. "Let's start an IV."

"Flo, you are nuts! Certifiable. Kid, don't believe her. We're not going to give you anything that'll kill you."

Terri twisted around on her knees and glared up at him. Kai would have caught on to her subterfuge when he heard the stifled sigh. By the time she snapped her fingers, he would have had an intimidating needle ready to hand her. Mac was an idiot.

Movement behind the principal caught her attention. Jordan Andrews came into view.

"Terri?" All color was drained from her pretty face. "Mr. Jackson, may I come in? I know her."

The speechless principal quietly moved aside. Since ushering them into the school, the man had worn a stunned expression which was now colored with a sickly shade of green. Terri wondered again exactly what he had said to cause dispatch to send them, an advance life support team rather than a basic one. Probably something to do with the rich parents he answered to.

Jordan gracefully sidestepped Mac's hulking figure. "Jeremy." Her voice was on the verge of tears, and she sank to her knees. "Terri, is he all right?"

"No. But I don't know how to treat him until I know what's in his system. If he needs surgery, the presence of alcohol or drugs will affect the doctor's decisions."

For a moment the girl resembled her father. A replica of Gabe's compassion wiped away every snobbish nuance from her demeanor.

Terri's own pragmatic manner softened. "Jordan, please, can you get him to tell me? I'm not here to judge him."

She whispered, "Dad always says he doesn't represent the law. This will stay just between us and the doctor?"

Why was it she felt as though she were making a pact with the devil? "Yes. It stays between us and the doctor."

She looked back at the boy who was now writhing about on the small bed. "Jeremy, it's for your own good."

He closed his eyes again.

She blinked back tears and began to shake. "His parents are out of town. There was an all-night party. At his house. He drank vodka. And...he took some pills. And..."

"I need it all, hon."

"And...he did...some coke."

The girl spoke as from firsthand knowledge. Had she been at the party? Terri cursorily surveyed Jordan's eyes, skin color, and breathing. Other than the fact that fear eclipsed her usual disdainful tone and she hadn't batted her eyelids, she appeared normal.

"Jordan, you might want to move out of the way. Your friend's about to upchuck. I'm surprised he hasn't yet."

As if on cue, he did just that.

Scrambling to her feet, Jordan emitted a noise of disgust. "I *swear!* I don't know how you and Dad handle this!"

Terri grinned. Those words were the most complimentary she could expect from Gabe's daughter.

⌒

After leaving a very ill Jeremy at the hospital, Terri and Mac resumed their argument on the ride back to the station. It was still in full swing as they climbed out of the ambulance.

"Mac, the bottom line is that you did it again. You undermined my position in front of a patient."

"Yeah well, that was a stupid trick you tried to play on him. That we were going to kill him! Why couldn't you just talk straight to him?"

"Because he wasn't going to give me a straight answer. He was a rich kid lying his way out of trouble. I went on instinct, Mac."

"Instead of facts. The girl could have been lying." His face reddened. "The kid was coherent."

"He was higher than a kite but able to disguise it. They all react differently. You do realize he had enough junk in him to code before we got to the ER if we hadn't treated him for an overdose. Right? If we'd just assumed it was appendicitis?"

"You're nuts, Flo." He stomped off.

Terri clenched her fists. Things were not improving with her partner. The man really was impossible.

"Hey."

She turned and saw Gabe approaching. Guilt flushed through her, warming her face. She hadn't returned his calls, and now she was about to skip mentioning the fact she'd just seen his daughter, who had more or less confessed to attending a party last night where booze and drugs were readily available.

"Hey."

"You're back on the job already?" He stopped in front her.

"Two days of sitting with Mom was long enough."

"Terri, the department will give you time off to grieve, with or without your mom."

"Grieving isn't all it's cracked up to be." Eyes downcast, she polished the ambulance door handle with her jacket sleeve. She hadn't seen him at roll call. Not that she needed roll call to know whether or not he was on duty. Her imaginary referee who counted seconds had begun counting days, informing her when Gabe's shift coincided with hers and when it didn't. "What are you doing here?"

"I'm picking up some tools I left. May I take you out for dinner tomorrow night?" He jumped from one subject to another. No pause between to signal, to warn.

"I—I have plans." It sounded lame.

"Breakfast then."

Lame or not, repeating the three words was all she could handle. "I have plans."

"Terri, look at me."

Her stomach felt as though a belt had been cinched too tightly around it. First run of the day with Mac and her energy was nearly drained. But she had to hold firm. Getting entangled with Gabe could only lead to disaster. No guy would put up for any length of time with Terri Schuman and her dark side. Might as well nip things in the bud right now.

She bit her lip, steeling herself to remain firm in the warmth of his gaze. At last she looked up. "Honestly, I have plans."

"I believe you." The color of melting caramel darkened. He blinked twice, a mannerism indicating he was narrowing in on a resolution of his own. "Terri." His velvet voice softened to a faint whisper. "I just want to say this to you once. I will not give up."

He turned and walked away.

A sudden insight burst upon her like a spotlight piercing the night. That was why she loved him. *That.* That there. That double blink. That subtle tensing of his jaw muscle followed by the brief hint of a smile. That quietness emanating from somewhere deep inside of him. That firmness of character. That totally unwavering sense of integrity.

Get real, Schuman.

She wiped her hands across her face.

Okay. Real. Real was not being attracted to lean, under six-feet, California surfer clones. Receding hairlines were out. For that matter, so were blonds. Ash or strawberry, burnished gold or otherwise. And kids? *Give me a break.* She never would have looked at him twice.

Except for *that.*

~

Early the next morning after her shifted ended, Terri shuffled along the sidewalk, past dingy storefronts that were either boarded up or not yet open for the day's business. She had avoided as much as possible outgoing and incoming staff, thereby missing out on small talk. She wasn't up for small talk.

She headed toward her car, cell phone at her ear, listening to voice mail. She truly did have breakfast plans, but they fell through when she heard Missy's message. Her sister was taking their mother back home with her to Cincinnati for the time being. Terri breathed a sigh of relief, echoing what she heard in her sister's voice. Maria had been adamant about going through her husband's things already. The sisters thought it a bad idea. Three cheers for Missy for delaying one major ordeal.

She closed up the phone and shoved it into her pocket. The change of plans freed up time to have a good run with

Zoë. They were both long overdue for one. Temperatures had been on the rise. Maybe snow would melt and her breath become invisible again. Then there was the issue of a bare cupboard. She would have time to go to the market. And, at some point, nap. Maybe scrub the kitchen sink.

Melancholy nipped at her heels. She walked faster, as if physical movement could shake it. The emotion wasn't her style. Granted, she'd never lost a dad before. Nor an old friend with pearl-white curlicues. Nor a new friend. Was it just six days ago Gabe had kissed her at the end of a shift?

Neither had she worked with such a contentious fool before. One of last night's calls had been for a baby. A baby with a broken leg. A baby not old enough to stand. Not old enough to fall down. Mac had been clueless.

She had to talk to somebody about that baby.

Terri ran and ran. Ran until the cold air turned to fire in her lungs.

A police car screeched to a halt at a corner, going against traffic and blocking her path. The driver's window slid open, and a young officer poked his head out. "Ma'am, are you all right?"

Terri puffed and took a moment to catch her breath. This wasn't the first time she'd noticed a cruiser in her vicinity that week. She suspected Cara had put the word out. "Yeah." Her shoulders heaved. "Look, I don't care what Detective Fleming says, you guys don't have to keep an eye on me. You've got better things to do, like help people in real trouble."

"Well, we thought you might be in trouble. You passed up your car two blocks back."

She gazed to her right and left until the storefronts registered. The guy wasn't kidding. "Yeah. Okay." She pinched the bridge of her nose. *Oh, God.* This was how medics lost it. Bottle it all up. Keep going. Not take time out to grieve. *You'd think after one major collision with burnout I'd know better!* She had to get a grip.

"Ma'am, *are* you all right?"

"Sure," she lied and turned around. "Thanks."

Terri walked now, making a conscious effort to aim for her car and to get a grip. She could list every detail of the past week from her father's death to fear of loving Gabe Andrews to the battered baby and still not hit the main artery. Why open up that? Bleeding to death was something one avoided at all costs. Wasn't it?

Oh, God, she thought again, not sure if it was a prayer or a curse.

Rachel had urged her to keep talking to God, wanted her to promise to do so.

Rachel. Her nagging, trusted friend who always, but always, knew best.

God. I don't want to. It's like handing You a razor blade and sticking out my wrist. Cut here. She placed two fingers at her neck. *Or here. It's called the carotid artery. Works fast. But You know that.*

Didn't I bleed to death for you?

She stopped, fingers still at her neck.

It wasn't an audible voice. Just a thought as clear as that morning's sky.

She lowered her hand. *What do You want from me?*

No answer came. No voice or thought, no mental picture speaking a thousand words, no sense of connection with the unseen.

"Okay."

Terri went to her car, got in, and started the engine. "Scarlett and I will think about the main artery business tomorrow." She cupped her cold hands over her mouth and blew into them. "Tomorrow or the next day."

An ache gnawed at the back of her throat. She laid her forehead against the steering wheel and gritted her teeth, refusing to release the cry. Thoughts could not be so easily stopped, no matter how hard she fought against them. They would open that so-called main artery, that source of her emotional upheaval because it was all about right now. Today. February 20.

Earlier that morning, when Terri had checked her cell phone, the displayed date caught her attention. February 20.

Of course she was always well aware of dates. Up until midnight she had written February 19 on run sheets. After midnight, emergency dates changed to February 20. But as usual, work consumed her. The February 20 she wrote at the hospital was different from the digital February 20 on her phone.

February 20. Her birthday. Her thirty-sixth birthday.

As far back as she could remember, it was the one day out of the year on which her father genuinely smiled at her. As if he liked her. As if she met his expectations. As if she'd done something right. As if she'd done enough.

And all she had done was be born.

Sometimes a gift accompanied the smile, or a one-armed hug, or a breakfast out with no siblings.

Then UAD. He up and dies on me, six days—six days!— before bestowing his annual approval. Not even a week.

There is something wrong with this picture.

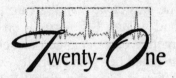

Twenty-One

Terri sat on the couch, legs curled beneath her, television remote in hand, and flipped channels. Zoë snored softly from the floor.

Old movies. Basketball game. Cooking show. The image of that baby with the broken leg crowded them from the screen.

Three o'clock, Saturday afternoon. February 20.

None of her siblings had called to wish her a happy birthday. Not that they usually called aside from Shelley. Sometimes Bobby or his wife called. One of the younger ones, now and then. Not that Terri kept score. They weren't a sentimental bunch, she least of all.

It wasn't that she minded. She didn't even mind that her mother had forgotten. After all, Maria was a brand-new widow being scuttled off to Cincinnati, probably against her wishes.

Still...

It hurt.

Like some virus she couldn't shake, introspection took hold of her again, forcing her to examine her emotions. At the moment she felt as though they trampled her common sense like a pack of wild horses across a neatly manicured lawn.

She missed her family.

She missed her dad. She had probably missed him her entire life, only now it was a debilitating emotion.

Overall she felt vulnerable. Exposed. In need of love. Desperately in need of a love that had no attached strings. There was a giant hole inside of her, a gaping vacant space that physically ached.

The doorbell rang. She jumped and Zoë bounded to her feet with a yelp.

Terri turned, separated the vertical blind slats, and peered through them. A figure stood at the front door. In profile she saw a black-coated woman with a headful of pearl-white curlicues. Lois Quayle.

Of all people.

I don't owe her a thing! Our relationship is over and done with. How could she do this to me? To my family? Terri waited for the flash of righteous indignation to roll through her. It was short-lived. That pathetic craving for love raced in hot pursuit, shooing it away.

She walked to the door and pulled it open. Through the glass of the storm door Lois stared back at her, the wintry wind blowing at the tails of the blue woolen scarf wrapped round her neck. Terri unlocked the latch and pushed open the door.

Lois came inside, carrying her purse and a white plastic grocery bag. "Happy birthday, punkin."

Terri shut the door behind Lois. "Whatever. I mean, thanks."

The older woman smiled in a gentle way. "Well. We made it through the first awkward moment." She held out the bag. "This was hanging on the door handle."

Terri accepted it from her, wondering how long it had hung out there. She seldom used the front entrance. "Have a seat."

Lois chose the nearest, an armchair. She sat on its edge, bundled in her woolen coat and scarf, clutching her purse on her lap. A hesitant visitor, unsure of her welcome. "Nice place."

"Of course it's nice. You wouldn't expect less from Gabriel the angel." She set the bag on the couch as if it contained a bomb.

"Aren't you going to open it?"

Terri sat down and crossed her legs. "No. I'm not up for another surprise."

"Maybe the angel himself left it."

All the more reason not to touch it.

"Terri, for goodness' sake. It's your birthday. Someone is expressing love for you. Open the silly bag."

Out of a long-ago deeply ingrained habit, she obeyed the compassionate general's voice. A strong scent of mint chocolate floated upward as she untied the sack's plastic handles. Inside was a rectangular box wrapped in green paper. In white fancy script across the center was imbedded the word *Frango.*

"No angel," she said, pulling out the box and a small unmarked envelope. "It's from Lee."

"Marshall Field's candy." Lois recognized the name of chocolate sold through Chicago's landmark department store. "How do you know it's from him?"

She shrugged to make light of it. "Our first Christmas together, we both gave each other a one-pound box." The memory of them laughing until their sides hurt came to mind. They admitted to craving the chocolate and proceeded to devour two pounds in two days. "It sort of became a thing between us."

In spite of the way he had hurt her, some Lee memories were sweet. They had cared for each other...for a time...in a way. Probably in the best way two human beings could manage.

She opened the envelope and slid out a card. Lee's nearly indecipherable scrawl filled it. *How about a birthday dinner next week? Love, Lee.*

Love? The word settled in that vacant space, oozing a warmth.

She tucked the card back in the envelope and set the box on the end table. "I wonder when he left it? Come to think of it, I wonder how he got my address? We haven't talked in months."

"You know how word gets around."

Terri looked at the older woman. Her cheeks were flushed. Lee would have to wait. "Why don't you take off your coat?"

⁓

Lois unbuttoned her coat and slipped her arms from it, letting it fall against the chair. She scooted back from the edge, her expression less distraught than initially. As usual, she was fashionably dressed, today in tailored gray slacks and a robin's egg blue cashmere sweater. Involuntarily an image of Maria Schuman jumped into Terri's mind. She winced, comparing her mother's matronly figure and wardrobe to the senior runway model sitting before her.

"Terri, I came to apologize. Your father loved your mother very much. I love my husband. But Bob and I loved each other too. We were intimate—"

"Honestly! Do I really have to listen to this?"

"Yes, you do."

"I don't want to!"

"I need your forgiveness." Lois blinked rapidly. "Above all, I need that. The details might help."

Terri squeezed her own eyes against tears forming.

"We were intimate for only a short period of time. You were seven years old. I ended things the day you walked in on us kissing in the supply room."

"I never—"

"We heard you in time to stop. That was the first time I really looked at you. I guess you could say I fell in love with a little girl." Lois had never been able to have her own children. Terri knew it was a heartache for her. "And I realized that no matter what I felt for Bob, there was no way on God's green earth I would be responsible for breaking up his family."

"What was your relationship then, all these years?"

"Just good friends."

"Did my mom know?"

"She suspected. Your dad finally admitted it to her when you were a firefighter down in Bloomington."

Talk about heartache!

"In retrospect, one of us should have left the hospital. That would have been the honorable thing to do. We weren't very honorable people."

"But you treated me like a daughter! You taught me so much about life! You helped me believe that I could do something worthwhile."

"Then one very good thing came from the situation."

Terri replayed childhood memories. New lights and shadows were cast over those times she spent at the hospital, adding nuances she could not have perceived before now. Disturbing nuances.

"Lois, was he angry about your decision to break things off?"

"Yes." She pressed her lips together. Fine wrinkles gathered about her mouth. "Not enough to give up on us, though. And I didn't really want him to. For years we talked now and then of what we would do if we were free to be together."

Terri imagined the two of them arguing quietly over her head, using subtle adult words that a youngster could not decipher. Suddenly the root cause of their argument pounced like a tiger finding its prey. She whispered, "Then I was responsible."

"What do you mean? For what?"

"For you two not being together. If it hadn't been for *me*, you wouldn't have broken things off with him and he wouldn't have blamed me and your dream would have come true."

"He didn't blame you."

"Of course he did, Lois. He might not have said it out loud, but he knew I was the one standing between you two. *I* was responsible. Don't you see that? *That's* why he never liked me!"

"Terri, that's nonsense! Calm down."

"It is not nonsense. He always treated me as if I weren't good enough to be his daughter."

"You're exaggerating."

"Not by a long shot. He resented me for *existing*. I guess the good news is that now, at the age of thirty-six, I finally understand it's not because I wasn't good enough!"

Lois hurried to her side and enveloped her in her arms. "Shh, punkin. It's okay. It's okay."

Terri shuddered. Her emotions felt like a swirling black mess. Zoë whined and laid her head in Terri's lap, nudging her hand.

"Lois, I'm fine." She straightened, away from her friend's arms, and rubbed Zoë's head. "This will take some getting used to, you know?"

"I hope you'll be able to forgive me."

"Yeah." *Whatever.* "I just…just don't want to talk anymore right now. Okay? I'm sorry." *Why am I apologizing?*

Lois stroked her cheek. "I understand. I only hope you'll…pray about it."

"Sure."

"He didn't mean to hurt you."

Terri stood, gesturing at her sweat pants. "I have to change. Kai invited me out for a birthday dinner."

"That was thoughtful of him."

It was. Her white lie wasn't. She didn't need to change clothes yet. What she needed was to call Lee. Lois would not approve. Neither would Kai. Nor Rachel. Nor Bryan. Nor Gabe.

A sense of weariness fell on her, suffocating the last ounce of emotional energy. She was so incredibly tired of feeling guilty. Her ex-boyfriend wasn't perfect, but neither was he her judge. Nor was he too good for the likes of Terri Schuman, who only wanted to feel loved.

⌣

Though he didn't speak a word or remove a hand from the steering wheel to gesture, Terri knew Kai seethed with frustration. They were on their way to Mario's, a popular Italian restaurant, a favorite of hers. She had just informed him that Lee was meeting her there after dinner.

"Look," she said, "I'm sure you don't approve of my choices, but it's my life."

"Welcome back."

"What do you mean by that?"

He blew out a noise of disdain. "The old Terri has returned. You haven't talked like that in a long, long time. Oh, Kai!" His voice rose into his falsetto imitation of hers. "Get over it. It's my life!"

Terri stared through the windshield.

"I just don't get it, Ter, this self-destructive bent of yours. You've got everything going for you. You're good-looking, fun to be around most of the time, smart. You love what you do and you're excellent at it. Why is it you do such dumb things like yell at a cop or get tangled up with the doofus not just once but now twice?"

"I'm not tangled—"

"You know who you remind me of? Those battered women we treat more than once. For crying out loud, we're on a first-name basis with some of them! I will never understand why on earth they don't move out."

"For starters, they totally lack a sense of self-worth. It was beaten out of them. Lee never abused me."

"Not if you don't count his running around on you."

"That's different."

"It is not."

"You don't understand."

"That's for sure!"

"You want to watch the road?"

"Ter, I thought you were getting the hang of it. You moved out and— I don't know. Something changed in you. I said it before. It was God. You didn't talk much about Him, but you said enough. Or else you didn't say things you used to say. What happened?"

My dad happened.

You have to forgive your dad. Bryan O'Shaugnessy's words.

Whatever.

She said, "Life got complicated. Can we drop it? Let's just have dinner, and then Lee will join us—or me—for coffee."

"Well, he won't be the only one," he muttered.

"What? Oh Kai, you didn't."

He grimaced.

"I don't like surprise parties! You know that!"

"It wasn't my idea! But I would have taken you out for dinner. If I'd remembered it was your birthday."

"Whose idea was it?"

"Hey, how about we drop this too?"

"Kai!"

"It's over and done with." His voice hardened. "Deal with it, Schuman. This one makes us even."

She knew he referred to their old battle of pulling jokes on each other. She knew she should have replied they weren't even, that he'd just signed up for a big payback. But for some reason she didn't have the heart.

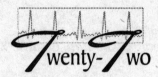

Twenty-Two

Terri didn't get out of Kai's truck at Mario's Italian Restaurant. Arms crossed, she sat, oblivious to the creeping cold, and pondered who would do such a thing. Halfway across the parking lot, he must have noticed she wasn't with him. He walked back and opened her door.

"Come on. It'll be fun. Pizza. Cake."

"Rachel wouldn't do this. Besides, she called from Iowa. I know it wasn't her cell phone. And she said she's having dinner with a *farmer*. She wouldn't make up something like that. Maybe Shelley? Nah. Shelley wouldn't do this either. Nor Bobby. Not Nan or Jill or Patti. Not *Lee*. Anybody who *knows* me knows— Oh!" She looked at Kai. "No! Not Gabe? Tell me it's not Gabe."

"I'm not saying anything."

"He asked me out for tonight! I suppose that was supposed to be a decoy. Like he didn't know anything about this."

Kai pulled on her arm. "The sooner you get in there, the sooner it'll be over."

"How did he know it was my birthday anyway?" She let Kai guide her from the truck and through the parking lot. "Probably read it in my file. Like he's got any business reading that. Who does he think he is planning a *surprise* party for me?" She grumbled all the way to the door.

Kai stopped and looked down at her. "Finished?"

212

Frowning, she clamped her mouth shut.

"If anybody shows up, it's only because they care about you. Okay?"

"I didn't ask Gabe Andrews to care about—"

"Okay?"

"Okay!"

"Now go in there and play nice. The guy's just doing the best he can."

"Then it is Gabe."

"Schuman!" His voice rose in exasperation. He shook his head and opened the door.

As usual, a large crowd waited in the entryway, content to bide 45 minutes until they could taste the best garlic bread in Chicago. Kai still had a grasp on her elbow and now towed her through the packed bodies. She could see no empty seats at the tables each lit by a votive candle in a clear jar. White twinkle lights were strung across the ceiling. The scent of garlic was overpowering.

Though she knew there were private back rooms, she'd never been in one. Kai steered her in that direction. They paused outside a set of closed double doors.

"Ter, act surprised," he whispered in her ear. "I'll never live it down if they know I ruined it for you."

"I am not an actress." She grinned in a not-so-nice way. "*Now* we're even, Rushman."

His eyes narrowed. "I have no idea what Gabe sees in you."

The words hit her like a slap in the face. She stopped grinning. Kai teased, of course, but he voiced a sentiment she'd been harboring since Christmas. What did he see in her?

The doors opened before them. "Surprise!" The shout came from a roomful of people. "Happy birthday!"

Terri didn't have to fake her response. Her jaw dropped. Those people were talking to her? All those people? At first glance she noticed balloons, streamers, and a host of familiar faces. Friends. Coworkers with spouses, some from her old station, a few from the new one. Bobby and his wife. Shelley...without Dave. No surprise there. Brother Kenny. Her sister Laurie.

As she walked into the crowd, she saw Gabe. He was watching her from the back of the room. That unsettled feeling came over her again, but she shook it off. No matter how attracted she might have thought she was to him, she knew better. It wouldn't last. They weren't right for each other. Why prolong the inevitable?

Eventually he approached, catching her in between groups. He smiled. "Happy birthday."

"Thanks."

"How's it going?"

"Fine." She glanced around the room. "I assume this party was your idea."

"Why would you assume that?"

"Process of elimination. My *friends* know I don't like this sort of thing."

"Hmm. It's funny then, how they all came."

"Free pizza." She met his eyes, daring him to be nice.

"Cutting off your nose to spite your face is not going to work with me, Lone Ranger." Before she could move, he leaned over and kissed her cheek. "You forget. I've seen behind the mask." He sauntered away. Whistling.

~

If her sister hadn't been present, Terri easily could have ducked out after the brief encounter with Gabe. She wasn't exactly in a party mood. Her confidante since childhood, Shelley was the recipient of her hissed complaints as they sat at a table beside each other.

"Well, yes, it is a strange time for a party so soon after the funeral." Shelley speared a forkful of green salad. Lettuce was not on the pizza buffet. Often preoccupied with her diet and figure, she must have ordered it à la carte. In her long black dress and with her long hair coiled around the back of her head, she could have passed for a model. Taller than Terri, she resembled their dad in stature, light brown hair, and a square-shaped face. Her eyes were their mother's though, like Terri's; the irises a brown so deep they sometimes masked the pupils.

"But," Shelley went on, "it is your birthday. Gabe is a doll to have organized things on such short notice."

"So it was Gabe?"

"You know it wasn't me. And Rachel couldn't make it."

"What do you mean 'short notice?'"

"Rachel mentioned the date to him on Tuesday, at the visitation. He said she was concerned about it being forgotten in the midst of everything else."

"Not Rachel!" Terri whined in a defeated tone.

"Gave him my phone number too. I called the others. We thought, why not? Life goes on."

"But you know I hate birthday parties."

"Terri." Her sister set down the fork and leaned toward her. In the process, Shelley's demeanor changed.

Terri knew she was looking at her sister's professional face. Shelley was a psychiatrist and worked mainly with children. In her field she had seen as much heartache, if not more, than Terri had as a medic. Hands down, her sister was ten times smarter and surpassed even Terri's battering-ram pragmatic approach.

Shelley touched her arm. "We lost Dad. I am going to relish any chance I get to be with you and Bobby, Jimmy, Laurie, Kenny, and Missy. This day is special. It's yours. And I will celebrate you on it. Heck, I might even eat pizza and not count the carbs." She squeezed Terri's arm. "I love you, sis." She stood and headed to the buffet line.

I love you, sis? Shelley had never said anything close to that in all of Terri's 36 years. Their parents and other siblings hadn't either. Terri herself had said it to Pete a few times. Peter Zahringer. Hockey player. Love of her life. He had come after Garret and before Lee. He was why she hadn't said it to Lee.

I love you. Rachel had said it to her. Other than for those occasions, it remained a foreign-sounding phrase.

"Happy birthday."

She looked up and saw Lee smiling down at her, a bouquet of red carnations in his hand.

Who needed words? She had red carnations and a football coach who used to make her feel really good.

Terri stood and accepted the bouquet and his bear hug. "Get me out of here."

~

They got as far as the doorway.

"Hi." Gabe stepped in front of them, blocking the exit, and stuck out his hand. "Gabe Andrews."

Lee accepted the handshake. "Lee Reynolds."

"Ah. The ex." That muscle in Gabe's jaw visibly twitched, the one that tensed when he and Jordan exchanged words. Incongruously, a strange little smile lifted his mouth. "It's good to meet you."

Lee's expression was wary. "You work with Terri?"

"Yeah." He cut his eyes toward her and then back to Lee. "Yeah. We work together. I'm her landlord too."

"No kidding? Then you're responsible for getting that hound out of my place. Thanks."

"Not a problem."

"Well." He placed a hand on Terri's shoulder. "The birthday girl here wants to get going. If you'll excuse us…"

"Sure. But before that, Terri, can we talk?" The grin he threw Lee fell somewhere between a sneer and an out-and-out dare to get in his way. "Drippy faucet."

Subtleties were lost on Lee. He clapped her shoulder. "I'll get—"

"I don't have a drip—"

"The car." The volume of Lee's voice drowned hers. "Meet you outside." He left.

Terri felt her teeth clench.

Gabe said, "Out in the hall? Just for a sec." He stepped aside to allow her to precede him.

She stomped through the doorway and a short distance down the narrow hall. Stopping near a back door covered with an emergency arm, she whirled on him.

"I did not ask for this party!"

"I know. It was a lame attempt to show you I care." Gone was his tensed jaw and snarling grin. His gentleness hit her full force, underscored by that voice of all voices.

Her shoulders slumped. "Oh, Gabe. I appreciate it. I do. It's just not me. *You're* just not me. You know what I mean?"

"No, I don't. Will you explain it?"

She waved an arm down the hall. "That's me. That lunkhead out there and everything he represents. Common and everyday and ordinary."

"Sweetheart, I'm a *fireman* and I hammer nails. I try to make ends meet. I'm divorced. There's nothing more common than—"

"Don't call me that."

He blinked.

And don't blink again. "I'm that verse I told you about. Unspiritual, ordinary, jealous, and wrangly. You're everything but. Don't you get it, Gabe? You have this depth, this integrity, this faith. I'll never live up to those standards. You deserve someone better."

He blinked again. "To quote an old friend of mine, horse-feathers."

"Whatever." She lowered her head and began to step around him. Her forehead bumped into his arm she hadn't seen him prop against the wall. She stood still and closed her eyes. "Please."

"I love you, Terri."

Like raindrops on a waxed car hood, his words sat on the surface of her heart.

"I love you. I love the woman who knows how to act macho when she has to take charge in an emergency or when some guy puts down her ability. And I love the woman behind the mask who's learning to walk by faith and sometimes doesn't quite *get* how much God loves her." He raised her chin with a finger.

She opened her eyes. That melting caramel swam before her.

"Sweetheart," he whispered, "if you go with him, I'll still love you." His lips brushed hers ever so lightly. And then he turned, walked down the hall, and went back into the party room.

An odd feeling of heat filled her, as if his words had hit their mark, as if something must have cracked that waxed surface.

Oh, horsefeathers. Who needed words? She marched down the hall to the main exit.

Twenty-Three

Terri stood with Mac and Jim, a firefighter taking a break from battling the nearby inferno. Alongside them, the command van was parked on a street chock-full of emergency vehicles. At a safe distance from them, flames shot skyward from a four-story warehouse, lighting the night sky. Glowing embers fell, untouched by whirling snow flurries. The noise was intense, causing them to practically yell at each other.

"She's chomping at the bit." Mac laughed, turned to Terri, and lightly cuffed her shoulder. "Aren't you, Flo?"

Jim chuckled. "That's our Flo." At least the new nickname had eliminated the use of Hot Dog. "She always wants to be smack-dab in the middle of things."

And the guy had only known her for three months.

Mac said, "Go ahead, Flo. Say what you say at every fire."

Terri unzipped her short blue jacket. With adrenaline pumping full force, she felt warm despite winter temperatures still lingering at the end of February. "Jim knows what I think, Mac."

"Oh, go on. Say it anyway."

"I don't say it at every fire."

"You have ever since we got hitched."

"We didn't get—" Why did she let him drag her into pointless discussions? "Okay. We'll make the record perfect just for you. Ready?"

"Ready."

"It's stupid we medics don't have turnout gear."

Mac roared. "Every time."

Laughing, Jim walked off into the night, the yellow stripes on his large black coat visible.

It is stupid, she thought. Since September 11, though, word was out that they would all eventually get them. Eventually didn't change the current situation. If she could don the coat, thigh-high boots, and helmet, she could join the action and *help* instead of waiting for someone to get hurt, all the while hoping no one would. Instead of listening to fuzzy radio reports and watching others orchestrate the battle on a dry erase board, she could see things with her own eyes.

Supposedly no one was inside the warehouse when the fire broke out. Now there were 48 emergency personnel within its burning walls, beside them, or on top of them. Gabe included.

The people inside the van knew where he was. They knew where all 48 were.

Lord, keep them safe. Keep Gabe safe. I know I haven't talked to You much lately. But I'm not asking for myself. Or maybe I am. He said he loves me. Please keep him safe.

"Flo, you're talking to yourself again."

"I am not." She might as well tell him. "I'm talking to God."

Mac didn't reply. Mac always replied.

She tore her eyes away from the burning warehouse to look at him.

He stroked his mustache. "You too?"

"Me too what?"

"I met this girl at the gym. Whew." He gave his head a quick shake. "Knockout. We had fruit smoothies the other day."

"You drink fruit smoothies?"

"Yeah. They sell them at the gym."

She smiled to herself. Who would have guessed?

"She tells me she's real involved in church. Says any first date with me has to include church."

Terri smiled. "Go for it."

"You're crazy."

"You keep telling me that. Meanwhile somebody else is going to get the girl."

He grunted.

"Just go to church with her. It won't hurt. All you do is smile, watch what the other people do, and if it doesn't totally weird you out, do it too. Then you can listen. God's talking to you. You just have to listen for it."

"He's talking to me." His tone was skeptical.

"I know you don't believe me. I've been there too. But I'm starting to recognize it. Like right now He's suggesting to you to go to church. The girl told you. I'm telling you."

"He talks through other people?"

"Sometimes."

"What's He saying to you—"

A whooshing noise drowned his voice. Terri turned in time to see a portion of the warehouse roof disappear.

Dear God.

Where was Gabe?

Commotion ruled momentarily as the command people determined where everyone was. Radio communications flew back and forth. Diagrams on the board were checked and rechecked. They knew immediately that no one was on the roof. Those who had been up there tearing holes in order to vent the fire assessed the battle as lost and hightailed it down the ladders three minutes ago.

Where was Gabe?

"Engine 89's not answering."

Terri's heart pounded in her throat. That was Gabe's group.

"They were here."

"Roof's gone there."

"If they…"

The scene blurred before her eyes. Her mind stopped distinguishing between sound and words. She bent at the waist and hung down her head, letting the blood rush into it.

"Andrews…"

Static. On the radio or in her brain?

"Rescue…"

"…medic…"

"Flo!"

She looked up. Mac was opening the back of the ambulance.

Fighting down nausea, she hurried over to grab her things, about 40 pounds worth of equipment. She'd let Mac go first. No. He wouldn't know where they were going either. They'd follow a firefighter. Yes. They couldn't get too near the building. They could if they had turnout gear. The searing heat wouldn't matter then.

She couldn't think straight.

Rushing through the shadows, she kept her eyes glued to yellow stripes.

Mac shouted at her elbow. "Two down. Least they got them out."

Dear God. Not Gabe, not Gabe, not Gabe.

One firefighter was prone, writhing in obvious pain on the cold, wet, rough concrete, snow falling on his face. His helmet was off. No golden hair caught her eye. Mac and others had him on the backboard while she gazed around.

She spotted Gabe between a couple of firefighters. They were removing his helmet and the self-contained breathing apparatus canister strapped to his back. In the near distance, the fire still roared.

She hurried to him. "Gabe."

"I'm." He struggled for a breath. "Fine."

A fireman beside him said, "We think a steel beam whacked him in the chest. He walked out."

Fumbling with the hooks on his turnout coat, she asked, "Are you dizzy? Ears ringing?"

He grabbed her wrist. "No." Another gasp for breath. His voice was a grating whisper. "Get Hinson. Leg." Gasp. "Broken."

She looked toward Mac. He was bent over Hinson. Two other firefighters were helping with him.

Gabe let go of her wrist and leaned toward her so only she could hear him. "Triage, Schuman."

Triage was paramount when facing more than one injury. He was telling her to take care of the most critical patient first. Order had to be established. Proper triage would have placed Sunni first in line to receive emergency care. Terri had always believed that, even more so as her knowledge of medicine deepened.

As if some ethereal finger flicked on a VCR, the old tape of that adolescent scene began to play yet again in her mind. She watched it, imagining what she as a paramedic would have done. Imagining how she would have whipped out a bag-valve-mask resuscitator, got her friend breathing. Wrapped a C-spine around her, immobilizing her head. Started an IV, pumped her full of solution to counteract the internal bleeding. Stuck on a pair of MAST pants, the inflatable antishock trousers to keep up her blood pressure, to keep the blood pumping to every organ. Intubated, kept her breathing on the ride, all set for surgery at the hospital where doctors would have *fixed* all that unseen damage.

"Terri!" Gabe was still in her face. She saw the warning in his eyes. *Hinson is in worse shape. Go to him! This is why they won't want us working together. You can't focus!*

At last her training kicked in, the second nature that shoved aside old tapes as well as new ones proclaiming she'd blown it with the angel, the genuinely nice guy.

She turned. Mac and the others already had Hinson packaged on the backboard. "Mac! You okay?"

"Yeah!" he shouted.

The radio lay at her side. Information had been relayed and stored in her unconscious mind. She knew help was on the way. "Go! We'll grab the next ride. It's three minutes out. I need a nonrebreather."

He gave her a thumbs-up and dug inside the bag for the mask she requested.

Reaching through Gabe's coat, she carefully felt along his chest. "There, Andrews. Triage all taken care of."

"Go."

"Shut up and sit down. Tripod."

Complacent at last, he sank onto the ground, put his elbows on his knees and his head in his hands.

She knelt before him. "I don't detect any bones out of place." Maybe only his breath had been knocked from him. Maybe there was no internal damage.

A fireman handed the mask to her, and she quickly put it on Gabe. "Do you hurt anywhere besides your chest?"

"No." He closed his eyes.

One hand on his shoulder, she grabbed her radio and checked on the status of the other ambulance, requesting they get a backboard to her stat. Gabe wasn't walking anywhere.

His eyes were open now, watching her closely. She glared at him, sending her own message. *I can focus where you're involved. And this is why we can work together. So I can take care of you.*

~

Terri stood outside the partially open hospital room door. Soft light glowed from within. The sound of deep, regular breathing reached her.

Gabe was probably asleep. The nurse said he insisted he was going home; the doctor ordered a little something extra. Not only would he feel no pain, he wouldn't be able to keep his eyes open until tomorrow afternoon.

Terri heard a gentle snort. Still, she hesitated entering the room. What right did she have to be there? Ten days ago he said he loved her. At one time she thought she loved him. A doomed relationship if she ever saw one. She'd always told herself he wasn't her type with his California golden hair, perpetual tan, his two kids, and house in the suburbs. It went deeper than that. His type was integrity and old-fashioned goodness. Definitely not her type because she lived at the opposite end of that spectrum.

She had no right to be there.

Except that they were coworkers.

Firefighters had stopped in before he fell asleep. She had chatted briefly with Hinson after his leg was set. It was a brotherhood thing, this wanting to see Gabe.

And I'm a blue-eyed blonde.

Should she call his kids? His ex-wife? No...that was someone else's job. But she hadn't seen them around. Wouldn't his children come? And what would Paula's reaction be? Didn't she care at all anymore?

Terri peered around the door. He was asleep, lying on his back. She tiptoed to the bedside.

Thank You, Lord.

His face was peaceful. The sweat and grime had been washed away. He wore a short-sleeved, sea green hospital gown. His bare arms were atop neatly tucked and folded covers, an IV line hanging from a bag and taped to his left one.

The ugly bruise was visible. In the ambulance, after his shirt had been removed, she watched it deepen in color and enlarge. It went from blood red to royal purple to nearly black, starting on the right side of his chest and spreading along his side, from his abdomen to his shoulder, neck, and arm.

Thank You, Lord.

They wanted to watch him overnight, but the X-rays showed—miraculously—no organ damage. Gabe's body was seriously bruised. He would be sore for a long time. But other than that...

Thank You, Lord.

The room was cold. She noticed a thin blanket on a chair, unfolded it, and covered him with it.

He would be fine. She'd make sure someone told his kids that he was all right.

Time to get back to work.

Twenty-Four

Terri and Mac cruised along in four lanes of rush hour traffic, making good time on their trip back to the firehouse after a run. Always her partner's second pair of eyes, she watched the road. Suddenly it turned into a sea of brake lights. Streets wet from melted snow reflected the bright reds. As the ambulance barreled swiftly toward them, she braced herself. Mac was good, but he habitually took more chances than Kai ever had.

Mac braked hard. There was a moment of silence, and then he cursed softly.

She let out a breath. "Brakes still work."

He slapped the steering wheel.

She said, "Hey, if you want to turn on the sirens, I won't tell. I mean, if you're so hungry that endangering innocent bystanders is no big deal, go ahead. Who am I to stop you? A man's gotta eat."

"It's ten till six. Rig's clean. Report's written. If we get back before another call, the food is hot."

"Cold mashed potatoes aren't all that bad. It's a taste you develop." She thought of Kai and wondered if he enjoyed cold potatoes yet.

She still missed him on the job. They'd only talked once in the more than three weeks that had passed since her birthday. Spring was in the air. He was dating someone new. Not that she had the time to see him. She was teaching more. And her mother needed attention; Terri spent many off-duty hours with her.

Not to mention the time she spent avoiding.

She avoided Rachel's calls. She would return her friend's messages by leaving messages of her own when she knew Rachel wasn't at home. She avoided church. She avoided going out after dark. She avoided driving the same route to work. She avoided calls from *Unavailable*. She avoided getting into discussions about *that* with Cara Fleming.

She avoided God except in emergencies when someone was in dire need and she had a split moment to think on that level. She'd finally removed the Bible from her backpack, putting distance between herself and the weight of guilt it added. The book sat on a shelf next to the study ones Rachel had neatly arranged.

And...she avoided Gabe. Which was a trick when she needed his help on a scene. Yet she managed. After all, she was a master at slipping on the mask, totally separating private and public faces. On the other hand, the simple act of writing and mailing the rent check to him was sheer torture.

Avoiding was exhausting work.

Mac impatiently drummed his fingertips on the steering wheel, probably considering her suggestion of lights and sirens.

"So how's the new girlfriend?"

He grimaced. "Still insisting on church."

"Why won't you go?"

He shrugged. "Your love life seems on hold too." He glanced at her and grinned. "You look surprised. Like no one noticed you and Andrews."

"Noticed what?"

"Noticed you were more hyper than usual the night he got hurt and now you don't talk to him."

She looked out the side window.

"I see him talk to you and you cut him off. You're friendlier to me these days. Oh, man!"

The dispatcher's voice crackled on the radio.

"Don't answer that."

Such perfect timing. There was no need to expend any more energy avoiding the conversation with her partner.

～

Lights and sirens parted the traffic like Moses at the Red Sea. Had that event been in slow motion too? Motorists had little space in which to maneuver. Understandable. But their delayed reaction time had Terri bouncing in her seat, shouting directions to them and Mac.

"Terri!"

She looked over at her partner. He never called her Terri.

"You're nicer but you're also harder to work with these days. It's like you're going to blow up. Can you calm down?"

It's been like a flash point...You're this combustible liquid...Kapow. Kai's words. Mac had just repeated them.

No. It wasn't true. She was nowhere near that condition of four months ago. She had a great home with Zoë, a new job she thrived on. Sure, her dad had died, and she was still angry at Lois. And yes, she was distant with God. But those effects would change. It would take a little time. She wasn't ready to explode.

And what about Gabe?

Pipe dream.

She studied the map. They were two blocks away. She'd been to the area before. It was heavily Spanish speaking. If the cops didn't speak Spanish—

The dispatcher's voice interrupted her thoughts. "Scene is not secure. Repeat, scene is *not* secure."

Terri acknowledged. The caller had hung up the phone, which of course she'd been told not to do. She'd sounded hysterical. Her husband was drunk, brandishing a handgun, and, she assumed from previous experience, was having a heart attack.

The address indicated a second floor. Knowing elevators were nonexistent, Terri called for backup.

Mac drove through a neighborhood of four-story, low-income apartments and stopped one building away from the address. A patrol car, its rooftop lights flashing, was parked on the street close to it. Terri got out.

"Flo, what do you think you're doing?"

"He's having a heart attack."

"So?"

"So we can get closer than this."

"He's got a gun."

"But the cops are here." She pointed at their car up ahead, as if he'd been unable to notice the lights. "They'll be calling dispatch any second. Come on."

She grabbed her box and left him to gather the radio and his equipment and lock up. Dusk had fallen. The air smelled of damp earth. She walked across mushy ground, the grass still short and brown from winter's sleep.

Strange. No neighbors were huddled near the entrance, but then sirens were probably common in the area and didn't draw much attention. She opened the front door and toed down its tiny support leg to prop it ajar. At the end of the hall she saw the narrow staircase. There was a landing. They would need the stair chair.

She stood still, tuning her senses into the world she'd entered. At least three separate television channels could be heard. Cooking smells overrode other scents of garbage and things she didn't want to decipher. A colorless, torn carpet covered the floor.

And then she heard it, a low wailing. A soul in the pit of hell.

"Flo!"

She jumped.

"Dispatch hasn't heard from the cops yet."

"They gotta be upstairs. Their car's right out front." She pulled on her latex gloves. "From the way these doors are numbered, I think we're down the hall, one door on the left."

"We're not going upstairs."

She pointed at the ceiling. "Hear that?"

"What?"

"That wail."

Mac shrugged.

"It's his wife."

He shook his head but followed her down the hall and up the steps. They went slowly, Mac calling dispatch again. Terri knew she was breaching protocol. Paramedics were not to enter a dangerous scene before the police had secured it. A guy with a gun, most especially a drunk guy with a gun, was considered a no go.

It was the woman's cry. Maybe it reminded Terri of her mother's.

They rounded the landing and continued. The wailing grew more distinct, though it still wasn't loud. At the top they paused. On the left, one apartment down, the door stood open. Terri could see a bright blue skirt.

"Ma'am?" she called.

The woman came into view, visibly trembling. Her face, wet with tears, reflected horror. Her arms clutched a dish towel. Terri guessed her to be around 60.

"Oh!" she cried. "*Socorro!*"

Terri knew she was looking at her mother, at her grand-mother. At all the courageous women who had sought life in a new world that sometimes frightened them to such a degree they could only think in one language.

Terri spoke in Spanish. "Are the police inside?"

"No. My husband is asleep. He is sweating. He hurts here." She touched her chest. "Please help!"

"Does he have a gun?"

"Yes. But he is asleep. He's not moving!"

"Flo?" Mac touched her elbow.

She explained the situation.

He said, "No way. A gun is a gun. And how can you trust her?"

"Intuition. I'm going to peek inside."

"Don't. I'm calling the cops."

She ignored him and joined the woman.

"My name is Terri, ma'am. What's your name?"

"Maria."

Naturally. "Where is your husband?"

"Come."

Heart pounding in her throat, Terri went inside a few feet. Behind the door, across a small living room, a small man sat in a recliner. Even at that distance she was fairly certain the wife's diagnosis was correct. Sweat poured from him. His complexion was ashen. Her only hesitation was the gun dangling from his hand.

"Maria," she whispered, "is the gun loaded?"

"Yes. But he never hurts me or anyone. It's for protection. The neighborhood is bad."

The struggle between Terri's heart and head was over in the blink of an eye. The heart won, hands down.

"Flo." Mac was behind her. "Don't. Five minutes, cops'll be here. The guys from that squad car are in another—"

"Shh. He doesn't have a spare five minutes." She continued walking softly toward the man. He reminded her of Grandpa Delgado. Thick black hair, a thin mustache, wrinkled white dress shirt, sleeves rolled above forearms, black slacks. Spare frame shrunken to an unhealthy degree. His heart muscle hadn't been in good shape for a long time.

Something clicked.

The man raised the gun...and pointed it directly at Terri.

Something clicked again.

Mac yelled and violently shoved Terri. She fell hard against Maria, and they tumbled to the floor. A deafening explosion filled the room.

Time stood still.

And then it rushed at her like an atomic explosion releasing wave after wave of chaos.

Mac was bleeding.

She had to bring order to the chaos!

But Mac was bleeding.

She was the chaos.

Someone else would have to bring the order this time.

Mac was bleeding.

She crawled to him.

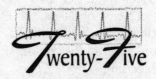

Twenty-Five

Sirens screamed and lights flashed as they had a short time ago, when Mac drove the ambulance through rush hour traffic and Terri sat beside him. Now Hank drove and Terri knelt in the back tending to her patient.

Her patient. Mac.

He was covered with a sheet and strapped to the stretcher, which was locked onto the floor. Terri held onto it with one hand as they rounded a corner, sirens wailing. With the other hand she continued applying pressure to his left knee. The wound still bled, though not profusely.

Dear Lord.

Mac lifted the oxygen mask and grinned. "I've been dreaming about this moment since we first met." His voice was husky with pain.

"Stop talking." She wiped away a tear. "Thank you. I'm sorry. I'm so sorry."

"I heard you the first ten times. Ask me what moment this is."

Right then she would have complied with almost any request of Mac's. He had saved her life, which needed saving only because she'd made the most idiotic choice possible. "Okay. What moment is this?"

"The moment you cut off my clothes." He winked.

She shoved the mask back into place.

"Terri." His voice was muffled. "I'm tough. Don't worry. I'll be back in no time."

She lifted the compress from his leg and stared at the spot his kneecap should have been.

∽

Terri knew how to push past every brand of pain. She knew how to work when her energy tank was on empty, when her nerves cried out *Enough!* She never ever gave in until things were finished.

Until now.

"Lois."

The old friend she'd blatantly avoided for weeks looked up from her desk. "What, punkin?"

"I can't do this." The report form fluttered in her trembling hand. Its printed words and lines blurred together. Her head still echoed with that explosion. The odor of burning gun powder coated her nostrils, so thick she still tasted it.

"Let me help."

Lois asked questions and filled in the blanks as Terri whispered fragmented answers.

Terri pushed over a notepad. "Will you write down Hennessy Gym on Ninety-one, please? And Lexi."

She wasn't trusting herself to remember the name of the gym Mac frequented or that of his not-quite girlfriend. Somebody should tell her.

∽

Mac was in surgery. The police needed to talk with Terri. A uniformed officer sat with her in a private room near the ER. It was the same one in which she learned of her father's death. The memories at Cutler-Barr Hospital accounted for way too much of her life.

A 40-something African-American, Officer Patone wasn't one of the two who had arrived at the apartment and helped her with Mac. Those two were probably being interviewed by Patone's partner.

"Ms. Schuman, what happened after the gun was fired?"

Chaos. Confusion. Mac screaming in pain. Maria wailing.

"Ms. Schuman?" His demeanor was polite and kind.

"The guy died."

"Just like that?"

"Yeah. Clutched his chest, slumped over, and stopped breathing. I went to Mac."

"How did you know without examining Mr. Lopez that he was dead?"

She didn't. At times death was obvious to her, even when she was nowhere near the body. At other times, even up close, she wasn't always sure. With cardiac arrests she kept going, kept pushing the drugs, kept defibrillating until the ER doctor took over.

Triage. Who should have been treated first? In that split moment, in the midst of the chaos, she experienced a flash of clarity. A glance at Mac told her an artery had not been hit; there wasn't that much blood. She knew full well if she'd tossed Mac a bandage, the tough guy was capable of administering first aid to himself at that point. But she chose to ignore jump-starting the heart of a man who fired a gun at her and hit Mac. Was that wrong? She didn't know.

"My partner was bleeding."

"Did you examine Mr. Lopez after you tended to Mr. Macauley?"

"No."

"You didn't try to revive him?"

"No. I stayed with Mac." She could go into the details of a gunshot wound, of how narrow the window of opportunity was to counteract the trauma it detonated on a body. Patone would know. His age and profession indicated a likely chance he had seen such effects.

"All right." He reviewed his notes. "The officers arrived. Then what?"

"One helped me. I assume the other one took the gun out of the guy's hand and checked for a pulse."

"Mr. Lopez still held the gun?"

She remembered seeing it, stark pewter against that white shirt. "Death grip?"

He smiled briefly.

She continued. It was their third time through the litany of events. With each repetition, new details made an appearance. "The firefighters from our station arrived." Gabe hadn't been one of them. He wasn't working the same shift. She missed him. "Then two more officers."

"The patrol car you saw outside?"

She nodded. Those were the two she assumed had entered the Lopez apartment. As Mac had tried to tell her, they were elsewhere, mediating a domestic dispute. "We got Mac downstairs. Another unit arrived as we drove away. I assume those medics worked on..." Her voice trailed off. She couldn't say the man's name. Where was Maria Lopez now? She would blame Terri.

Patone slid a box of tissues across the lamp table toward her.

For a woman who seldom cried, it seemed people had been shoving Kleenex at her an awful lot lately. She yanked one from the box.

"Ms. Schuman, did you think Mr. Lopez was dead when you entered and saw him sitting there, eyes closed, not moving?"

"Not a chance." She blew her nose. "He was breathing."

She knew he was alive. And she knew that while it seemed highly unlikely an inebriated man suffering a cardiac arrest could aim a gun and pull the trigger, it was always a possibility. She'd ignored the facts and went against regulations. Tomorrow morning she'd be at the EMS headquarters, explaining herself. There wasn't much to explain.

Officer Patone stood. "All right. That takes care of things for now. You should get some rest."

She smiled grimly. "It all sounds like a lawsuit in the making, doesn't it?"

He winced.

"That's okay," she said. "It'll give me something to do while I'm on suspension."

~

The initial order suspended Terri for three shifts. She assumed it would be lengthened indefinitely as all the concerned parties began to unravel their strings. Three shifts meant at least nine days off. She lived the first two at the hospital.

The doctor kept Mac heavily sedated. Recently appointed to the staff, he knew Terri only as the patient's partner, the one who entered the unsecure scene. He refused to share his prognosis with her and barred her from visiting. She wasn't family. Not that he had family in the area; his mother was en route.

Terri avoided coworkers. How could she face them? She didn't go home that night or the next day. She turned off her cell phone and kept a lone vigil closeted on the sixth floor in a windowless waiting room large enough to accommodate two people if one of them sat. Nobody knew about the place.

Except Kai.

He tried to hug her.

She pushed away his arms and paced the small area.

"Schuman, you can be such a porcupine."

"Just leave me alone."

"You need to quit feeling sorry for yourself. It could have happened to anyone." He crossed his arms and leaned back against the wall. "You took good care of Mac. Word is he has a long row to hoe, but they can probably fix his knee."

"Who told you?"

"The chief sent out a memo. If you'd talk to people, you would have known."

"I can't talk to anyone right now, Kai. This was all my fault. Totally my fault from the get-go."

"No one's denying that. You had no business sticking your head in that building, let alone *walking* into the apartment."

"Tell me something I don't know!"

"Gabe Andrews practically throttled a plainclothes cop."

"What?"

"That night. You and Mac were behind closed doors with cops standing guard. They wouldn't let anyone near you two. Apparently Gabe doesn't take 'no' well. He grabbed the guy's lapels. When that didn't get him what he wanted, he smacked a crash cart. Sent it sailing clear down the hall."

Gabe assaulting a cop and medical equipment? His composure snapping? "No way. Not Gabe. Not in a million years."

"Are you kidding? He's crazy about you and he couldn't get to you to make sure you were all right. Nobody really knew at that point who'd been shot. The staff wasn't even talking."

She puffed a noise of disbelief. "Hearsay."

"Hearsay my eye. I followed him into the hospital. Could hardly keep up with him."

"You were here?"

"I happened to be in the neighborhood."

She closed her eyes. He was joking.

"Ter." Kai's voice softened. "Everyone says they easily could have done the same thing under the circumstances."

"Mac didn't want to." She looked at her former partner. "Oh, Kai! If you'd been there, you would have stopped me. I would have listened to you. I never listen to Mac. I always dismiss his opinion like it was some annoying gnat. That's what's so wrong with this. I treat him disrespectfully and then he saves my life."

"Ter, you will get through this. You'll be a better person for it. Mac will be a better person."

She shook her head. "I don't think so, Kai. I really don't think so."

~

The second day Gabe opened the door. Silently she cursed at Kai for revealing her hideout.

He nearly throttled a cop...He's crazy about you.

Sweetheart, if you go with him, I'll still love you.

She said bluntly, "I don't want to talk to anyone."

"I figured as much." He stepped into the small room and set a white bag on the single end table. His complexion was pale, nothing like its usual healthy tan. "Latte and bagel."

She sat down, propped her elbows on her knees, and looked at the floor instead of him. "Thanks."

"I'll go."

She nodded.

"Just tell me— Are you all right?"

She jerked her head up, surprised at his inane question. She'd never been so not all right in her entire life.

"I mean, you didn't get hurt?" He wiped a hand across one side of his face, then the other, clearly disturbed.

"N-no. I didn't get hurt." The ache from being tackled didn't count. It wasn't a bullet.

"Okay." He pressed his lips together, turned on his heel, and left.

Oh, how she missed him!

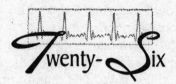

Twenty-Six

Terri tossed another log into the fireplace and stoked the blazing fire. It threw off enough heat to warm the rustic one-room cabin. The sweet scent of oak filled the place.

From the braided hearth rug, Zoë raised her head and watched Terri sit back down in the recliner. She picked up a book with one hand, a mugful of tea with the other. Zoë lowered her head. They'd spent the better part of four days doing little else.

"God, what do You want from me?"

She had spoken few words beyond those.

The cabin belonged to Shelley's boyfriend, Dave. Technically it belonged to his widowed mother, who never used it. Annually in August, he spent a week there, fishing at a nearby lake. Still, Shelley's requesting the key for Terri was tantamount to Queen Esther approaching King What's-His-Name. Dave had a short fuse when it came to sharing his toys with those he labeled losers, a category in which he placed most of the Schumans. Evidently Shelley thought her sister worth the risk. The getaway was her idea after she read about the incident in the newspaper.

By then, the walls of Terri's condo were closing in. The suspension was still in place; no word yet on it being continued. If and when the Lopez family's attorney, the CFD, the EMS, and the CPD ever finished investigating the matter, the Lone Ranger, a.k.a. Hot Dog, would be history. She was preoccupied with thoughts of paying Mac's hospital bill. Surely the insurance company could pass the buck to her. Their fine print probably read *we are not liable when a partner makes an unbelievably stupid decision which leads to the other partner's injury*. They would interview Kai, and he would say, "Yeah, she's good. A loose cannon, but good."

Before leaving town, she had dodged Mac's doctor and walked into the ICU as if she belonged there. He was groggy, but he recognized her, gave her a thumbs-up, and held out his arms. She hugged the man who 72 hours previously set her teeth on edge with a single word: Flo.

The next day she visited him briefly, ducking out before his mother returned, and promised to call.

She welcomed the chance to escape alone to the woods of Wisconsin. Two hours outside of the city she finally stopped watching the rearview mirror for a tail. An hour later, silence enveloped her. The handful of cabins she passed on the dirt road were unoccupied.

Twice a day she and Zoë hiked on a carpet of brown leaves, crunchy in places, soggy in others as the earth slowly defrosted itself. Southerly breezes carried hints of Tennessee, Arkansas, Mississippi, the Gulf. Canada geese honked overhead, their beaks pointed north. If she peered closely at the ground, tiny bright green shoots of vegetation were visible in the midst of brown. Life pushing aside death. Again and again. An unending cycle.

At the top of a rise, her cell phone picked up a signal. She called Mac daily. His knee prognosis was not good. Reconstructive surgery and a brace would allow him to walk again. But to continually bend, squat, and kneel beside a patient? Carry a 350-pound person in a stair chair? Forget it.

Miracle of miracles, he didn't blame Terri. He wasn't about to give in to the dire predictions. He asked her to pray for him, and he thanked her for leaving a message at the gym for Lexi. Apparently she was spending quite a bit of time at the hospital.

And, twice a day, she listened to Gabe's voice mail messages. At least one new encouragement arrived daily. *You'll get through this...I'm praying for you...I'm here for you...I love you*. No hint of distrust. No whiny tone of complaint about her actions.

Lord, is he for real?

She deleted two messages from *Unavailable* and ignored Rachel's for the time being as well as a few others left by concerned friends. There were no official calls. She assumed her status of pariah assigned her to no-man's land, which was fine with her. The status suited this season of soul-searching.

The first day at the cabin she opened a book that promised to answer her questions about prayer. She read a page, closed it, and then grabbed another from the gym bag packed with nothing but books. They all promised unheralded insight into the Christian life. They all contained margin notes written in her handwriting, question marks, exclamation points, "why" in capital letters, and yellow highlighted markings.

The promised insight had been delivered the previous year. A new horizon exploded into being on her landscape. Now...Terri suspected there was more, that there was a bottom line to all the rhetoric, some red ribbon for tying it together.

With prayer and trepidation and tears, she went back to the source. Unlike ever before, she immersed herself in God's Word. For three days, morning, noon, and night, she studied the gospel according to Matthew, to Mark, to Luke, and to John in six different translations and paraphrases. Like a beacon on that horizon, Jesus grew brighter and brighter.

"Come to me, all whose work is hard, whose load is heavy; and I will give you relief. Bend your necks to my yoke, and learn from me, for I am gentle and humble-hearted; and your souls will find relief. For my yoke is good to bear, my load is light."

"Are you tired? Worn out? Burned out on religion? Come to me. Get away with me and you'll recover your life. I'll show you how to take a real rest. Walk with me and work with me—watch how I do it. Learn the unforced rhythms of grace. I won't lay anything heavy or ill-fitting on you. Keep company with me and you'll learn to live freely and lightly."

Now, as shafts of the setting sun glimmered through the tree trunks and into that tiny cabin, Terri slipped to her knees on the braided rug and buried her face in the chair's scratchy worn cushion.

"Oh, God, I don't understand it. All I know is I can't carry this load of guilt anymore. I give up. I'm crying uncle. Or Jesus. I'm here, Jesus. I've come. Just like You said."

⌇

Terri parked her car, turned off the engine, and clutched the keys in her gloved hand. The night wind howled, rattling the Blazer. From the backseat Zoë continued to snore contentedly. Terri shivered and debated about running the heater. No. People might call the cops if they saw exhaust spouting from an unfamiliar, older vehicle on their street at two o'clock in the morning.

She introspected, no longer a wretched exercise. Either she had won the lottery or else she had been handed a red ribbon. There were no words to explain the sense of peace and freedom that enveloped her after praying the words "I give up."

She slept her first sound sleep since the shooting. She awoke laughing in the middle of a dream she couldn't recall. The giggles stayed with her throughout the day. Zoë gave her sidelong looks and stayed near her heels as they tromped through the woods. At sunset she knew in that mysterious way of knowing, when no rhyme or reason accompanies the knowledge, that it was time to talk to Gabe. In person.

She cooked up a storm and cleaned the cabin in a whirlwind. Her plans to sleep there one more night evaporated.

She drove three hours and now sat on Gabe's street while he slept.

She looked around. The suburban neighborhood was fairly new. Attached double and triple garages. Only a handful of cars were parked outdoors. Evergreens, leafless trees, and other vegetation were short, young. No potholes. No burned-out streetlamps. It wasn't a gated community with enormous houses she'd spied along the freeway, but it was pleasant. Contemporary and yet homey.

She stared at the darkened house across the street and wondered if Erin Morgan had parked outside her apartment and condo in just such a way. She shook her head. She wasn't stalking Gabe...she just needed to be near him.

He had built an attractive place, a modest ranch-style home with a reddish brick front. She noticed white shutters had been added since he had shown it to her. His truck would be parked in the double garage. To the right of the front door were three bedrooms. To the left the living room. Behind that the kitchen-family room area and screened-in porch. He wanted to add an old-fashioned porch across the front complete with railing, pillars, and a bench swing.

Face it, Schuman. This is about as close to Leave It to Beaver *as you could get.*

Gag me with a spoon. I never liked that sappy show. What am I doing here anyway?

I love you. If you go with him, I will still love you. I'm here for you. Sweetheart.

Sweetheart...

"Well, we'll see, Mr. Andrews. We'll see."

Terri climbed out of her car, opened the back door, hooked Zoë's leash onto her collar, and nudged the dog awake. They crossed the street and strode up the sidewalk leading to Gabe's front door. She aimed for the lighted doorbell and, after a slight hesitation, pressed her finger against it.

She paused briefly and pushed it one more time. The window blinds brightened. Then the porch light went on.

Gabe the fireman, up and at 'em, raring to go in four seconds flat.

The interior door opened. Through the glass storm door she saw him, dressed in long pajama pants and a short-sleeved white T-shirt.

He pushed open the door. "Terri! Come inside. Hey, Zoë!" He held the door for them, his arm above her.

Just like that.

I so do not deserve this.

"What?" he asked.

She stood rooted in place. Tears flowed down her face as her mind replayed Bryan's voice. *"Not weighing our merits, but pardoning our offenses, through Jesus Christ our Lord."*

He prayed that phrase every single service. It must have buried itself in her subconscious. Did God really answer it? Did He really work that way? Instead of weighing her good behavior, did He really forgive the bad? Was it true?

Gabe pulled her inside and shut the doors behind her and Zoë. "You're going to have icicles on your cheeks." He began unbuttoning her coat. "Why don't you have your parka on tonight?"

She wiped at her tears and dropped the leash. "It's spring."

"Only on the calendar." He smiled.

She noticed a greenish-yellow bruise covering his right bicep. "Oh, Gabe! Are you all right? It's still there!"

"Huh? Oh, you mean this. It's almost gone. I'm fine. No complications." He knelt and unhooked Zoë's leash. "There you go, girl."

The dog's nose went straight to the floor, and she scurried around the room, sniffing. Gabe laughed and straightened.

She blinked against the tears that wouldn't slow. "Lee and I—" She swallowed, determined to get the words around the sob that threatened to cut them off. "We—we didn't do anything."

He slipped the coat from her shoulders and threw it onto a chair.

"We didn't do anything!"

He pulled her to himself and wrapped his arms around her. "It doesn't matter. I told you it doesn't matter."

His soft cotton shirt smelled of a fresh-scented detergent. She slid her arms around him, basking in the incredible comfort of Gabe Andrews. "How can it not matter?" Her voice was muffled against him.

"Shh." He whispered something indecipherable into her hair. It sounded like *thank You, Jesus.* And then, in her ear, "I love you no matter what."

"But I wanted to! I wanted to spend the night with him! I wanted—"

"I love you." He rocked her back and forth. "It doesn't matter."

"He wasn't the first, Gabe. He wasn't even the second!"

"It doesn't matter. 'There is no condemnation for those who are in Christ Jesus.'"

At the sound of the Scripture words, Terri's breath caught. She felt as though she were watching fireworks explode silently all around her, as though she stood in the center of a waterfall of sparkles bursting into every color of the rainbow.

"Oh, Gabe." She looked up at him, at those caramel eyes bright as the fireworks in her mind. God loved her in the way that Gabe loved her. And Gabe loved her in the way that God did. Unconditionally. With no condemnation. "It's true, isn't it? There is no condemnation."

He grinned. "Sweetheart, I've been trying to tell you that for a long time."

∽

Terri clutched a warm mug with both hands. Sweet cocoa-scented steam rose from it. Her legs were folded up on the couch and covered with a plaid stadium blanket. Zoë slept on the floor. "Last time you didn't give me chocolate and marsh-mallows with my milk."

Gabe chuckled. His arm lay stretched along the back of the couch, his hand close enough to touch her arm or hair which he did now and then, as if to make sure she was really there. "You were lucky to get milk that night. The cupboard was bare."

The dark liquid rolled too near the edge of the cup. Her hands wouldn't stop trembling. She bent her head and carefully took a sip. "The kitchen looks great. Neat as a pin. You even have window coverings."

"Just call me Mr. Homemaker."

They sat in his combination kitchen and family room, a rectangular shape with a breakfast bar as divider. A low-watt light glowed from under the stovetop's hood, as did a lamp in a corner. At the far opposite end from the kitchen was a wall of vertical blinds. She remembered a sliding door there which opened onto the screened-in porch. A fire snapped and popped from a wood-burning stove to one side, throwing off enough heat so that Gabe still wore short sleeves.

He smoothed her bangs aside. "I can't see your eyes. Are you warm enough?"

"N-not yet." Her attempt to smile failed. She was chilled to the bone. "We didn't do anything."

"Terri—"

"Let me say it."

He nodded.

"He took me to his house and... He kissed me. And I couldn't. I just couldn't. He called me a few choice names."

"Did he hurt you?"

"No. I deserved to be called—" She bit her lip.

He smiled.

"No condemnation." She tried another smile. "I'm starting to get the hang of it. Gabe, I haven't...I haven't slept with anyone since I left him over a year ago."

"It doesn't matter."

"Before that... Lee wasn't faithful to me. But I've had tests done. I'm...okay."

Gabe touched her cheek. "I'm glad for your sake. It wouldn't have changed anything though."

She stared at him. He would have forgiven her even that. *Oh, Lord.* "Sometimes I'm afraid you're too good to be true, Gabriel. That you're an angel whose going to poof out of sight any second."

"No." He shook his head. "I'm no angel, just forgiven. How can I not extend His forgiveness to others? Not that I always want to. I've been arguing with Him since you showed up at the soccer field to apologize. I told Him I would never have chosen you. You weren't my type. I mean, the air around you crackles with energy, the kind that complicates things. Besides that, I knew you had more baggage than I wanted to handle. You're so attractive, there had to be a string of guys in your past."

He had the string right, but *attractive?*

"But God planted a seed of love for you that day, and it just won't stop growing. So I've stopped arguing." He grinned.

A warmth began to seep into her bones.

He said, "For the record, I wanted to rip Lee's head off at the restaurant. Until I checked out his biceps. How did you get away from the Neanderthal?"

"Tsk, tsk."

He shrugged a shoulder.

"I called a cab. He made me wait outside. I went home and threw out the chocolate mints he'd given me for my birthday. Sat up most of the night trying to figure it all out." She took a drink of chocolate.

"And what did you figure out?"

She inhaled deeply, gathering breath to give life to words that had lain dormant far too long. "That I love you."

A slow smile spread across his face. He leaned over and kissed her temple. "Then what took you four weeks and five days to get here?"

"You've been counting?"

"No." His dimples indicated that was not the truth.

Her smile took hold this time. "I've been arguing with Him too. Surfer clone with kids, a *Leave It to Beaver* house, and a gorgeous ex-wife? Give me a break."

He laughed. "What makes you think Paula is gorgeous?"

"Jordan is, and she doesn't look like you."

"Terri." He took the mug from her hands, set it on the coffee table, and drew her to himself.

She snuggled against him.

He kissed the top of her head. "She's pretty in a plastic sort of way. You're the beautiful one because you have a heart that radiates compassion. It lights up your whole face, especially your eyes."

Sheer contentment flooded through her. "Gabe, why is it your words make my insides turn to mush? All I could think about that night at Lee's was your words. They made me lose interest in everything about him. All I wanted to do was go bask in your words."

"It's how I see you love others, sweetheart. Do you realize how much you talk when you're treating a patient? Nonstop cajoling and comforting, whether they're conscious or not. You call them 'hon.' You talk with their families. And the whole time you're encouraging us guys working with you."

"I'm that loudmouthed EMT."

He chuckled. "Sometimes. You're just being honest, if brutally so. Which indicates that all those other times, when the words are positive, you're being honest too."

His arms around her, she listened to his heartbeat for a long moment. "I didn't have words from my dad."

"I know. Paula never had them from me either. The male species is a slow learner."

She pushed herself up to look at him. There was such an incredible goodness written all over his kind, boyish face. She touched his receding hairline, the other thing she'd argued about with God. But now, up close like this, she knew he was going to be handsome as a bald man.

He said, "I have so many words for you."

"Thank you." She kissed him.

~

Gabe didn't share too many more words with her that night. Kissing interfered.

"Mmm," he said. "I should take a long bike ride to get Terri Schuman out of my system."

She bolted upright, surprised by a new thought. "Gabe! I've never been in a relationship like this!"

His eyes widened. "Hmm. Come to think of it, me neither."

"What do we do? I should go home!"

He glanced toward the kitchen. "It's four-thirty. I have to get up in an hour."

"You work today!"

"Do you always speak in exclamations at four-thirty in the morning?"

"Probably!"

He laughed. "Well, you're not going anywhere. You're exhausted."

"But the neighbors!"

"Their opinion can't be helped at this point. I'll pray no one gets the wrong impression."

"Do you pray about *everything?*"

"I try." He kissed her cheek, stood up, and stretched. "I'm going to make some coffee and tell myself it's five-thirty. But you should sleep."

"I'm fine." She scrambled to her feet.

"Hey, Lone Ranger. It's me."

Yesterday's giggles bubbled again. Gabe didn't care if she was exhausted. She sank back onto the couch, laid down, and pulled the blanket up to her shoulders. "Mask-free communication could be marketed as a muscle relaxant."

He laughed. "Go find a bed. The kids both have two in their rooms."

"How about I stay here?"

He sat beside her and straightened the blanket. "How come?"

"Down the hall is too far away." She yawned. "From you."

"I'm grinding coffee beans," he warned. "Fixing breakfast. Taking a cold shower."

Her eyes closed. "I can sleep through anything but the firehouse alarm."

"I'll get you a pillow."

She fell asleep, his lips against her ear as he whispered sweet nothings that meant everything.

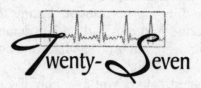

Twenty-Seven

"That's Terri."

Terri heard the voice. It sounded close, but she couldn't locate the source.

"She works with Dad."

Terri opened her eyes.

Jordan Andrews and her older twin gazed at her from across the family room.

"Oh my gosh!" She threw aside the blanket and swung her legs to the floor.

From the foot of the couch Zoë lifted her head and growled softly.

The woman shook her head and crossed her arms. "Unbelievable." Her tone was solid disdain.

"You can say that again." Terri rubbed sleep from her eyes and attempted to gather her bearings. What an awkward way to wake up! Sunlight poured through the kitchen window above the sink and outlined the family room's vertical blinds. What time was it? She refocused her eyes at the kitchen and found the clock on the microwave. Ten-sixteen. Ten-sixteen!

"May I ask what you're doing in my husband's house?"

Husband? Terri almost laughed out loud. "Sure."

The woman tapped her foot. She was as gorgeous as Terri had imagined. Blonde hair pulled back in a sporty ponytail. Makeup just so. Lipstick in place. Flawless skin. High cheek bones. Perfectly arched brows. The blue of her eyes evident even across the room. Small gold hoop earrings. Real gold. Tailored gray slacks, a thick white turtleneck showing above a short, black wool coat. Not wool. Cashmere. A subtle scent of expensive perfume drifted across the room.

Terri waited, biting her tongue. Funny the effect a few kisses from Gabe Andrews had on her demeanor. Not even Paula could unnerve her. And she hadn't even had her coffee yet!

Jordan pouted. "Mom, you *asked* her if you could *ask*. So ask." She flounced from the room.

Paula said, "Oh, honestly! You know what I meant."

"I believe you meant ex-husband. And it's a long story as to what I'm doing here, which is none of your business."

"Sassy sluts in the presence of my children are always my business."

Zoë jumped off the couch and stretched.

Terri stood. "Sorry to disappoint you, but I'm only a sassy *friend*. Excuse me. Come on, Zoë."

She went to the sliding door, pushed back the blinds, and opened the door. Through the attached screened-in porch she noted the yard was completely fenced in. She let the dog out and returned.

Paula was in the kitchen area, inspecting things. At Terri's approach she turned and swept her gaze over her head to toe, taking in her unbrushed hair and wrinkled sweatshirt and jeans. It was obvious from Paula's sneer that Terri did not meet whatever standard she had in mind for her ex-husband.

Paula made a ladylike harrumphing noise. "He's not allowed to have women overnight when the children are here."

"The children weren't here, and I didn't stay overnight. What are *you* doing here?"

She turned her back to her and faced the window above the sink.

Terri saw it then, the sticky note on the coffeemaker next to the sink. He'd made coffee for her again. The words were indecipherable from her vantage point. What effect were they having on his ex-wife?

Jordan entered the room. "Play nice, girls. Remember, you are the grown-ups here."

Talk about sassy.

She held an armful of clothes. "I have my own key, and Mom hadn't seen the house yet. I needed this sweater for a party tonight."

A party. Like that other one? Terri shot her a knowing glance.

"So here we are." Jordan tripped over her words. Her voice rose a notch, making it sound forced and insincerely friendly. "And here you are! You and Dad must still be dating?"

Still or again? Or what would she call it? This relationship that felt as though she were standing on the verge of a cliff and had just been handed the most beautiful, colorful hang gliding canopy imaginable? To experience the ultimate joy of her life, all she had to do was jump. Her stomach tickled in anticipation.

She said, "Um, yes. We're dating." Her voice belied a calmness she did not feel. She wanted to whirl around in cartwheels. "And this." She gestured to the couch with its rumpled pillow and blanket. "Is not what it looks like."

Paula brushed past her daughter toward the living room. "What that looks like is you spent the night on the couch and not in his bed." There was a hint of triumph in her voice. "Let's go, Jordan."

"Be right there. I think I left some shoes here too." She didn't move except to tilt her head as if listening to her mother's retreating footsteps.

Terri walked around the breakfast bar, intent now on pushing that coffeemaker switch. Caffeine! She flicked it and removed the note taped to the carafe. *Morning, Terri. Coffee's ready to go. Call me. Love you. G.* Whew. A flush crept up her neck. His ex-wife had read that.

She heard the front door open and then close.

"Terri."

She turned.

Jordan was hugging the clothes to her chest. "Thank you for not telling Dad about Jeremy."

"How do you know I didn't?"

"He would have fussed at me if he knew."

"Does your mother know?"

The girl shook her head.

"They need to know, Jordan."

"No, they don't. They wouldn't understand."

"Where's the party tonight?"

She shrugged and glanced away. "I don't do drugs."

Translation: but she drank alcohol. "Jordan, listen. Even if you don't, things get out of control. You can get arrested or hurt being in the same place. I've treated innocent bystanders, you know, and it wasn't just to clean off their friend's puke."

She grimaced. "I'll be fine. Jeremy's a little mixed up right now. That's all. He needs a friend."

And the girl wasn't mixed up? "Tell your parents."

"You don't understand either. Mom would need drugs to cope, and there's no way I can talk to Dad. He'll freak. He is so out of touch with reality. Doesn't have a clue about the real world. You promised not to tell!"

If Gabe's daughter got hurt, Terri would not forgive herself. But she had promised. And she wanted to keep the girl's trust. Without revealing details, she would insist he talk with her. In the meantime... "I need a promise from you."

Jordan chewed her bottom lip. "What?"

"When things get out of hand—and they will get out of hand—don't hesitate to call 911 immediately. That's why people like me and your dad go to work."

The girl nodded. "I know. Dad taught me that when I was three. I would call for a *hangnail*, but nothing's going to happen. It never has before."

"Just promise to take care of yourself. He does care, Jordan. He just doesn't know how to communicate that to you."

"Whatever."

The resemblance of the girl to Terri at that age was growing bizarre. Maybe they did have something in common after all.

Terri grinned. "Hey, thanks for stopping by!"

A corner of Jordan's mouth twitched. Could it be a smile?

〜

Terri drank coffee from a large mug. "What on earth am I signing up for?"

A good-looking guy in the 'burbs...a bratty teenage girl sliding in way over her head...a boy who didn't like to hammer nails with his carpenter dad...a jealous ex-wife— *Jealous?* No way! That couldn't be! But the note had obviously disturbed Paula, and she acted downright glad to believe that the disheveled coworker had not slept with her ex-husband.

Now why would she feel that way? Hadn't Paula been the one to leave Gabe in the first place?

There are two sides to every story. Lois had often reiterated that truth to her.

Paula found someone else because... Gabe told Terri why. Because he didn't love his wife the way she needed to be loved. He gave her no words. He made the decision on his own to become a firefighter, reversing their financial progression, nixing her dreams in the process.

But that was the old Gabe. He freely owned up to his mistakes and had been trying to change. By God's grace he had changed.

And was that woman who chose money over her husband the old Paula? Had she too changed? Did she now see what she had let slip through her fingers eight years ago because she couldn't imagine the man's potential?

Terri shuddered. She wouldn't want to get in a contest with the gorgeous mother of his children. There would be three strikes against her before she even stepped to the plate. Gabe had once loved Paula. They had children together. And the woman was a knockout. What man wouldn't—

"Oh!" The word burst from her. "Stupid rabbit trail. You *are* good enough for him. He loves you. So just shut up."

She poured herself another cup of coffee. Paula, Jordan, and Spencer, three strangers in apparent pain, intruded upon her mind and settled in, getting all cozy as if they were *staying.*

Now what was she supposed to do?

Pray.

"Oh, Lord. Get real. I mean...really?"

With a loud sigh she closed her eyes, and began to pray haltingly for them. This was something new, praying for one's—what were they? Enemies? Opponents? Competitors? Pains in the neck?

She sighed again. This was going to take some time. She set the mug on the counter, went to the family room, pulled a pillow from the couch, and tossed it onto the floor.

Eventually the words came, words for the healing and peace of others, of those she wished were of no concern to her. Her own family crept into the conversation. And then Lois. And finally, Gabe.

Gabe. A man she hadn't asked for, hadn't looked for. A man totally unlike any she'd ever known or even imagined. And he loved her.

Thank You, Lord.

The giggles sneaked up on her again. Such joy was a foreign feeling. She didn't know what to do with it except laugh.

Or...spin cartwheels.

She got up from her knees and joined Zoë in the backyard.

"Hi." Terri sat in her car at a stoplight, grinning into her cell phone.

"Hi, sweetheart." Gabe's smooth voice carried his own smile.

"Whoops. You're going to have some explaining to do talking like that at the station."

He laughed. "No one's listening. How are you?"

"Great. I met Paula."

Dead silence.

"Jordan wanted some clothes she left at your house, so they—"

"She came into my house?"

"As a matter of fact, they woke me up." The light turned green and she drove through the intersection.

"I'm sorry."

"No, it's okay. It was almost noon."

"I mean I'm sorry you had to meet her like that."

"Well, it's over and done with now. And just think, you didn't even have to be there. We bared our claws and fangs until Jordan reminded us we were the grown-ups."

He chuckled. "Terri, trust me. There's no contest going on here. You don't have to fight for my affections. You've already won."

She smiled. Her entire being felt mushy again. "Really?"

"Really."

"That's what I told myself later, but Paula may sees things differently."

"Then that's her problem. You're not driving, are you?"

"Uh, yeah, I am."

"Terri!"

"I know, I know. But I swear, I'm paying close attention. I had to get going, and I couldn't wait until I got home to hear your voice."

"Really?"

"Really." She felt her smile stretch from ear to ear.

"I'm hanging up now. Talk to you later."

"Gabe!"

"Bye." The line was disconnected.

Frustrated, Terri closed up her phone and tossed it onto the other seat. And she thought she was a stickler for safety!

Jordan's hesitancy to open up with her dad began to make some sense. The guy knew what was best and acted accordingly. Certain things were taboo, such as talking on the cell while driving. It simply wasn't done. Beginning and end of discussion. He wouldn't take well the fact that his daughter hung with the fast and loose crowd.

She and Gabe had to do some serious talking.

⁓

Terri unlocked her kitchen door and pushed it open, letting Zoë enter ahead of her. The dog got as far as the refrigerator and stopped in her tracks. A low growl rumbled from her.

"What's wrong, girl?" Terri dropped her gym bag on the floor and skimmed through the handful of mail she'd picked up from her box out on the complex's driveway. She spotted a square, white envelope from an out-of-town acquaintance. Probably a sympathy card. Why didn't people just let it go by now?

Zoë barked.

"What is wrong with you, dog? You're home!"

And then something tugged at her subconscious. Something vague… All senses alert, she studied her kitchen. The fridge hummed and the clock's second hand swept around its face. The basement door stood ajar. She might leave dishes in the sink, newspapers on the table, and clothes everywhere, but she always, always closed that door—

There were no dishes in the sink.

No newspapers on the table.

No stray shirt in sight.

Her mind replayed the morning she left for the cabin. She'd thrown a robe and all those books in a bag. Tucked jeans, T-shirts, underwear, and socks into her backpack. Thrown an extra sweatshirt over her arm. Downed a glass of orange juice and rinsed it with water while gobbling a few spoonfuls of cereal. Rinsed that, left it in the sink with the glass and a mug. Dumped the rest of the coffee into a thermos. She left, planning to buy food for herself and Zoë along the way. She had been in a hurry.

No dishes were in the sink. The stainless surface shone as if it had been scrubbed.

Gabe? He would have told her.

The neighbor kids? They only walked Zoë and filled her bowl with water.

The smell registered itself then. Perfume. Sweet. Yet pungent. Department store smell. Something designer.

Terri backed toward the door. "Zoë!"

Her dog recognized the commanding voice and followed Terri outside. A moment later they sat in the car with the doors locked.

A heart attack victim with a gun couldn't stop her from entering a home. Not so the possibility of a disturbed young woman lying in wait.

She pulled the cell from her pocket and dialed Cara's number.

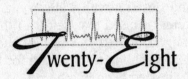

$\mathcal{T}$wenty-$\mathcal{E}$ight

Three hours later Cara tapped her pencil against the kitchen table. "I think Erin Morgan saw you pack up your car. She followed you, maybe all the way to the Wisconsin border, and concluded you were leaving town for a time. Then she stayed here."

Terri stared at her. "But there's no evidence."

"Not even a shred."

Oh, they found plenty of evidence proving someone had been in the condo. Subtle things. Things like clean dishes, basement door left ajar, CDs rearranged, magazines stacked neatly, a cockeyed dresser drawer, white athletic socks paired instead of lumped together, a slightly damp bath towel. One dark blue work shirt and pair of slacks missing.

Cara had called in a host of helpers to investigate the scene with her. They'd interviewed neighbors, some Terri hadn't even met. Those on either side of her supposed she was home. She hadn't informed them she was leaving town. The teens knew she was off work for a while, that they didn't need to take care of Zoë before and after school. Someone noticed "her" black Blazer in its usual spot. The walls were fairly soundproof, but someone else thought she heard a television late one night. Another heard the back door open and shut.

A sliver of broken glass was discovered in the downstairs bedroom beneath the window that faced the enclosed back patio. After closely inspecting the window, the policeman concluded the glass was brand new. Someone could have broken the original, climbed in, and taken the window to a glass company for repair. If the police found time that didn't exist, they could visit those shops and hunt for a needle in a haystack. Terri checked a kitchen drawer. Her duplicate house keys were gone.

The guy from forensics could find no fingerprints. None, except on the back door handle, which turned out to be Terri's. Whoever had been in the place had left it spotless. Literally.

Terri blew out a breath. "Just like there's no evidence to prove she ran Melanie Lareau off the road."

"Just like."

"Cara, what does it mean?"

The policewoman laid down her pencil, her wide-set eyes studying Terri closely. Gauging her response? "I think it means she's moving in. Excuse the pun. She's getting bold. It concerns me that she has your uniform."

"She didn't take the shoes."

"She'll know you always wear black oxfords on duty."

"How do you know that?"

Cara touched her temple as if that explained everything. "Terri, we're at a dangerous place. Something has clicked in the woman's head, urging her to confront you, to challenge you. I don't know how she cornered Melanie. I imagine Erin tailed her, sped up to drive alongside her in the other lane and lowered her window to— I don't know. Threaten. Admonish. Beg. Melanie's rejection finally pushed her over the edge. Erin was suicidal, but she wasn't going alone. She was taking her alter ego with her."

Terri stared at her for a long moment. "So now what?"

Cara only raised her brows.

"I know. Move again. Don't drive alone. Don't go to work. No problem with *that* one! Cara, you can't prove any of this. If you catch her in the act of breaking the restraining

order— Catch her in the act! That's it. We can arrange a
meeting. You arrest her because of the order— No. That
won't work. She gets out on bail. We go to court. She gets
fined. Big deal. I told you before, we need a sting operation. I'm ready now. I'll let her get close, let her try to kill
me." Terri closed her mouth.

"I don't think so."

"But what else can you do?"

Cara stood. "That's my job to figure out. Your job is to stay
safe. Can you sleep at the station?"

Terri ignored the question. "Listen, this can work. If I see
her, I'm going to let her get close. She's not like a big guy who
could overpower me. She doesn't even look strong. And I
can drive better than she can. She forgets I know how to drive
an ambulance at full speed through traffic. I doubt she carries
a gun or a knife—"

"Terri!"

The steel in Cara's tone startled her. She stopped talking.

"If we bring her in for questioning, it may push her over
the edge. She'll slip up and we'll catch her. You stay out of her
way. Now answer my question."

"I'll go to my mother's."

"She knows where she lives." Her pitch softened. "The
announcement in the newspaper about your dad."

"Oh." She looked up at Cara and saw the eyes of a friend
looking back. Time to remove the macho mask again. "I can't
go to the station. I can't face the guys."

"Word is that guy Lopez still had the gun in his hand. No
way you should have approached him after he shot your
partner."

"But I entered in the first place."

"And Mac made his own decision to go in. Everyone
makes mistakes. This was a biggy, but it could have happened
to anybody. By the way, his wife praised your bravery in the
Trib."

"She did?"

"Sunday's edition. Mac's a hero for saving you. Of course you'll both be teased for doing such a dumb thing."

"I don't think I'm ready."

"Okay. How about my place?"

"I can't ask— How about Gabe's house?"

A slow smile spread across Cara's face. "Oh?"

"That's where I was last night. I was only there one other time, when Erin didn't seem to be around. And you can wipe that smirk off your face. It's not physical. Well. Yes. It is. But not in that way!"

Cara laughed.

The tips of her ears felt warm. "I mean, it's not like we're— Anyway, I'll call him at work. Right now I'm desperate for a shower. And I've got to go to the hospital to see Mac."

"Okay, okay." Cara glanced at her watch. "It's almost six. I'll go off duty and wait while you get ready. You're not going anywhere without an escort."

Terri stood. "I think my appetite's back. Are you hungry?"

"Yeah. That bagel I ate twelve hours ago seems to have run its course."

Terri smiled. "I know how that goes. You want to check the fridge? I have eggs if you want to cook. Peanut butter and jelly if you don't." She headed toward the living room, muttering to herself, "At least I did have eggs, peanut butter, and jelly a few days ago."

"Terri."

Something in Cara's voice pulled her back to the kitchen. Her friend stood before the open refrigerator door.

"I think you'd better look at this."

"What?"

"You've got a little more than eggs in here."

Terri went over and peered inside. The refrigerator shelves were filled with all kinds of food. Her stomach tightened. Maybe she wasn't hungry.

"Some of it hasn't been opened. Guess we might as well help ourselves. Look at this. Fresh crabmeat all sealed up. Wow. It's not even the fake stuff. Date's still good."

Terri sank onto a chair.

"What do you think? Seafood omelet?" She eyed her over the refrigerator door. "What's wrong?"

"I'm— I'm allergic to shellfish."

Cara's eyes widened. "As in anaphylactic shock?"

"Mm-hmm."

"Did you ever tell Erin?"

She shook her head.

"Something tells me she knows."

Terri lay curled on her bed wearing her terry cloth robe, glad she had taken it with her to the cabin because now she could rest assured it had not been worn by anyone else. Her freshly shampooed hair was wrapped in a towel. The phone lay snug between her ear and the pillow, the case of which she had changed. She felt as though she were in the middle of a grown-up version of a cooties game.

Gabe's voice soothed. "I'll come home and stay with you."

"No, I'll be fine on your couch with cops patrolling the neighborhood." She amazed herself by chuckling. The man had more than a mediocre influence on her sense of well-being. "I'll be fine as long as Paula doesn't drop in unannounced."

"We'll get through this, sweetheart, both Erin and Paula."

"Thank you for saying 'we.'"

"Thank you for accepting the word."

Terri changed her tone to one of self-mockery. "He said without a hint of condescension to the Lone Ranger, who had lost track of any Tonto sidekick by the time she reached age six."

Gabe laughed.

"You have the most wonderful laugh."

"You keep sweet-talking and I am coming home."

She smiled. "Thank you. Bye."

"Call me when you get to the house."

"Okay."

"Bye."

She disconnected and lay still in the dimly lit room, seriously considering not moving for the remainder of the night. Her mind cried out to shut down. Cara had offered to stay, but Terri knew her friend wasn't finished working for the night. And, deadbolts aside, the thought of Erin out there somewhere with the door keys unnerved her.

Downstairs one of Cara's team members had returned and was bagging the contents of Terri's refrigerator. More nonevidence. Pizza was on its way.

She'd give herself ten minutes. Close her eyes. Replay that voice. Let the velvet pitch and words engulf her. Let them sink deep into those places that still hurt. *We'll get through this, sweetheart.*

～

"Flo!" Mac boomed. His injury hadn't diminished his boisterous personality one iota. "Hi! How's the wilderness girl?"

He rested against the back of his raised hospital bed, not quite sitting up straight. His thick black hair was in stark contrast to the white sheet. His left leg was slightly elevated, held in place by wires hanging from some contraption overhead. His bulk left little mattress showing, but he patted it anyway, inviting her to sit. He pointed the remote at the television. The volume of a hockey game decreased.

Terri smiled, walked over to him, and planted a kiss on his cheek. "Blackhawks winning?"

"Yeah." He gazed intently at her. "If I'd known you were going to kiss me and bring me flowers, I would've put myself in the line of a speeding bullet a long time ago."

"Yeah, right." She set the vase of flowers on his window sill alongside the ones she'd brought last week. "How are you?"

"Have a seat." He patted the bed again and smiled. "I'm good. Aw, Terri, you're going white as a sheet on me again. Uh-oh. Here comes the green now. You sure you're a paramedic?"

A woozy feeling hit her as it had the other times she visited him. She sank onto a nearby chair rather than the bed and, leaning forward, pressed an arm against her stomach. After all the years she'd spent around hospitals and working on injured bodies in every imaginable and unimaginable shape, she couldn't handle seeing Mac in such a state. No mystery as to why that was. His suffering was a direct result of her idiotic decision.

"Here, Flo. Have a glass of water." He upended a plastic cup from a stack on the table beside the bed and poured from a stainless steel pitcher.

"Thanks. I'm sorry." She took a sip. "For everything."

"I told you. You're not allowed to say that anymore. Somebody might overhear and they'll think I'm a wimp. I did not walk into that room because you made me, you know. You think I'd jump off a bridge just because you did?"

"I know. You only walked in to save me." Of course they'd already had this discussion daily on the phone.

"Right. You can kiss my feet now and feed me grapes."

She smiled, admitting to herself that PEA was having its effect. Not that she wanted to fawn all over Mac, but she knew she would kiss his cheek the rest of her life. He would, without a doubt, always have a soft spot in her heart.

"Oh my gosh!" she cried. "Your mustache is gone!"

He grinned and stroked his clean-shaven upper lip. "You're a little slow tonight, Flo."

"You look totally different!"

"Lexi doesn't like facial hair."

"Then by all means you needed to shave it off. Can't have the girl wondering what kind of lips you're hiding."

"So what do you think?"

She drank more water. Her stomach settled. "I think you're fishing for a compliment and you think I'll give it because I owe you my life."

"You got it."

Tilting her head sideways, she made a point of studying his heretofore unseen lips, suitably full on the large man. "You have a great mouth, Macauley." She'd probably always outrageously praise him too.

He beamed like a kid who made the winning touchdown.

"I suppose you'll even go to church with her."

"Soon as the cast is on. Hey, did you hear about the autopsy?"

"What autopsy?"

"On Lopez."

"I didn't think they would do—"

"Oh yeah, they had to. Part of the investigation. Rushed it even. They gotta get you back on the job."

"What's it got to do with my job?"

"It makes everybody happy knowing you couldn't have saved the guy."

"Huh?"

"Between the cops, the other medics, and our guys calling dispatch every step of the way, times got recorded like crazy. When everybody showed up, when everybody left. When the other medics got there for Lopez. The medical examiner pinpointed the time of death, more or less but close enough. This wasn't the guy's first cardiac arrest. His heart was oatmeal. The report says nothing could have saved it. Nobody can officially blame you for not trying."

The details of that night hadn't lost their brutal clarity. She wondered if they would ever grow fuzzy. Hank had been there, the grandfather-type fireman who had directed her to Gabe's soccer field. The first time they worked together, she suspected he had one of those tiny referees in his head too. He wouldn't have lost track of a second. She remembered him quietly taking charge while she focused on Mac. Hank played the game by the book with unparalleled efficiency. He was the one who had driven the ambulance to the hospital, called in departure and arrival times. She trusted him, but...

"But we always try, Mac!"

"The guy didn't deserve a try."

"I don't work like that."

He sobered. "Yeah. I know you don't."

"It's not right for people to look the other way, thinking they should let it slide just because they're rooting for me, glad I worked on you instead of him."

"Some of them will, Flo. We're a tight bunch who look after our own."

"He was a human being!" *Just like Sunni.*

"We're all going to die. Some of us even do it on your shift. Let it go."

She frowned.

"Anyway, you can trust Hank and the coroner with his squeaky clean reputation. He doesn't allow anything to slide by. So." He grinned. "His report will satisfy John Q. Public that you did your job. EMS can be proud; they didn't license a wacko when they let you in. Our crew will be swinging from the rafters. Yippee, the Spanish-speaking Hot Dog is reinstated! We can stop talking with our hands!" He waved his arms around in exaggerated spirals. "And I get a vacation. See? Everybody's happy."

"Oh, Mac." She laughed and dabbed her eyes with the sleeve of her sweatshirt.

He shrugged. "You gotta roll with the punches, kid. You know, if you were a *man*, you'd understand that. None of this ooey-gooey stuff just because I'm laid up for awhile. And besides, I told you he took out my bad knee." His chin lifted as he looked over Terri's shoulder. "Lexi!"

She turned, eager to meet the girl who— "Erin?"

⌒

The scene unfolded as if behind a veil of smoke. Terri thought she even smelled something charred.

Erin Morgan and Mac engaged in a long, passionate kiss. When at last they broke apart, he grinned. "Surprised?"

His voice sounded tinny and far away.

"Oh yeah. She's green again. Pour her some more water, Lex."

Terri felt a dampness on her thigh seeping through her jeans. She must have spilled the cup when she jerked to her feet. "No. I'm fine." The smoke was clearing. She had to get out of there. Call Cara. Dial 911? No! There was a patrolman downstairs, just outside in the parking lot, waiting to follow her to Gabe's house.

Her knees gave way. She had no choice but to sink back onto the chair.

Mac chuckled again. "I sure was surprised. Lexi told me all about you rescuing her."

The girl with two names smiled. She sat on the edge of the bed, her hands entwined with Mac's. As usual, she appeared covered in spandex from v-necked black sweater to black pants. Her hairstyle had changed, though. No longer upswept, the highlighted brown hair was short, casual, tucked behind her ears. Long bangs sweeping her forehead.

Terri's cut.

Mac said, "I can tell this ain't sinking in. Lexi, you better explain the name thing to her."

"Oh, Mac. It'll make me cry."

"So what? That's all Flo does when she's here anyway." He shook his head. "Women. All peas in a pod."

"Oh, you!" They kissed again. "Well, okay." She turned to Terri. "Erin is my middle name. I was named after my mom, Alexandria. She was Alex and I was Lexi. After she died..." Her face crumpled. "My life fell apart. I was only seventeen.

Oh, I was so angry, Terri, so lost. I didn't even want her name anymore."

A chill began to spread slowly through Terri. Had Melanie Lareau been a mother figure? Another one who let Erin down? Was that how she saw Terri too?

Erin reached over Mac and pulled a tissue from its box. "But I found the Lord. He loves me." She dabbed at the corners of her eyes. "I can be Lexi again. My real self."

Terri felt numb, frozen in place. A bitter taste rose in her throat. She imagined Erin-Lexi in the condominium, touching her things, going through her closets and drawers, studying photo albums, reading her address book, her grocery list. Stocking her refrigerator with shellfish products.

She found her voice but not emotion to express it. Her tone remained flat. "Mac says you go to church."

"Yes, I found the most wonderful place—"

"St. James on Ashland."

Erin's mouth formed an oval, her eyes grew large, her brows rose. To anyone else, genuine astonishment. "How did you know?"

"Lucky guess." She stood, wishing Mac wouldn't look at Erin with such adoration. Breaking his heart was next on Terri's agenda. She wasn't about to say anything in front of him, but as soon as the cops showed up and the truth came out, their relationship would— Their relationship?

Terri almost fell back into the chair. Their relationship wasn't an issue. Mac's *life* was the issue. The brawny, sometimes intimidating man lay there like a helpless fish out of water. Would Erin literally hurt him in order to hurt Terri?

She squeezed the foot of his good leg through the covers. "Take care."

Ignoring their farewells, she hurried from the room, wondering what it cost to hire a bodyguard to live at the hospital.

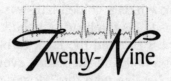

Twenty-Nine

Terri stood on Gabe's screened porch. Shivering in the cool spring morning air, she watched Zoë run laps around the backyard. Was it less than 24 hours ago Terri had spun cartwheels out there? A lifetime had passed since then. She couldn't imagine the feel of such a carefree moment.

"Hi, honey! I'm home!" Gabe's shout came from the family room-kitchen area.

Well...maybe she could imagine it. The mere sound of his voice triggered a flood of—there was no other way to put it—a flood of *wifely* thoughts. He was home. The man she loved had come home to her. He would kiss her, and she would feel his strong arms around her. She would cook. She knew how to fix scrambled eggs and toast. Then, if he had slept last night and if they hurried, they would go to church. They would sit beside each other. Kneel beside each other. Worship God together. Later he would tell her anecdotes about the guys. When she told him about Erin and Mac, he would hold her again. Together they would come up with a plan... Such comfortable thoughts. Such an overwhelming sense of safety accompanied them. The kind that annihilated her macho mask and offered a sweet contentment in its place. She was loved. And she loved. Oh, how she loved!

In happy anticipation she turned and entered the house. He stood near the breakfast bar, just inside the door that led to the attached garage.

"Hi." He grinned and knelt to untie his shoes.

Her happy anticipation pooled at her feet. She slid the door shut, watching him.

He was late. Smudges streaked his face, darkening the 24-hour stubble growth. His golden hair was matted down. An indentation creased his forehead. A helmet's indentation, not a cap's. Dampness covered the back of his navy blue shirt.

He'd been at a fire! And she hadn't even known it!

How did Rachel live with this? How did *any* spouse live with this? No wonder Paula had walked out!

He straightened, still grinning, and sauntered toward her. "I could get used to coming home to— What's wrong?" His smile faded.

"You-you!" She sputtered and raised her arms in a helpless gesture. "You've been fighting a fire!"

He stopped before her. "Yeah. And?"

"I didn't even know! What if you'd been hurt?"

He shrugged. "We'd, uh, deal with it."

"*We?* What's this *we* business? You could have been killed!"

He reached out, enfolded her in his arms, and held her tightly.

Burying her face against his neck, she wrapped her arms around him. He smelled of smoke and perspiration. The everyday hero, fresh from the fight.

"Terri, I love you."

"Like that's going to solve everything." Her voice was muffled.

"It does."

"You're just an adrenaline junkie."

His chest rumbled as he laughed. "Who loves another one."

She groaned. "Love shouldn't hurt like this, should it? Or be this complicated? Oh, Gabe. Where did you come from? You're the surprise event of my life, and I wasn't ready. I'm still not. Maybe you should go back from wherever you came from until I figure out how to handle all this."

He loosened his hold and looked down at her, that little half smile crinkling the dimple and crow's feet. The melting caramel of his eyes conveyed warmth. "I came straight home after the fire. Didn't bother to shower. You probably noticed."

Distracted by the nearness of his mouth, she didn't reply.

"I did that because I couldn't wait to be with you. Remember telling me about the nanoseconds? How you've learned to savor them at the station? You savor every scrap of time you're given there because it's limited."

"Mm-hmm."

"Life's nanoseconds are limited. They're numbered. You know that." He kissed her forehead. "The secret is in savoring them. We make the most of however many or few have been given to us. And we don't fear the ones that won't be ours. Because fearing wastes time. It subtracts from the ones that do belong to us." He kissed her again. Seriously. On the mouth.

Nanoseconds passed. Time multiplied itself. Infinity stretched before her. Fear disintegrated.

Breakfast was going to be late.

～

They held hands on the table, empty plates stacked and pushed to one side. Church too was pushed aside. That decision had been made when he walked through the door at 10 A.M. instead of 8:30. Maybe it had been made before that, when some homeless men lit a fire too near a garage. No one was injured, but a house burned and a neighborhood had been threatened. Gabe hadn't slept a wink.

He said, "So Erin split before the cops got to Mac's room. I'm not surprised. You have such a poker face," he teased. "I bet she knew you weren't buying her story."

"How could she talk about God like that? To look at her sincere expression and hear that God loves her— Oh!" Terri shuddered. "It's true. He does. But how twisted!"

He squeezed her hand. "What's next?"

"Cara planned to interview Mac this morning. I'd better go see him, let him wring my neck in person. They'll keep a policeman outside his room until Erin's brought in."

"They must have enough circumstantial evidence to at least question her. Maybe she'll crack and confess to trespassing at least. Breaking and entering."

"Or ask for help. Gabe, you're eyes are at half-mast. Why don't you go sleep?"

He gave her a lazy smile. "I'm savoring nanoseconds."

"Okay." She stood, leaned over the corner of the table that separated them, and kissed his clean but scratchy cheek. "Then there's something else I want to talk about." She sat back down.

"Uh-oh. Paula told you my deep dark secret."

"Hmm. And what would that be?"

"I snore. And crack my knuckles. *And* forget anniversaries."

"That's three deep dark secrets."

"There's plenty more where those came from."

Maybe he wasn't ready for a serious discussion. But it couldn't wait any longer. "No, she didn't say anything against you. Jordan told me she never does."

"Jordan told you that?"

She nodded. "Gabe, will you talk with your daughter?"

"I did after the last time you and I had this discussion. Things are…better."

"In my opinion, there's more to be learned. Do you know what makes her tick? What scares her? What makes her happy?"

His fingers tensed around hers.

She ignored the signal. They were going to slosh through this whether he wanted to or not. "How does she feel about herself? What kinds of kids does she hang out with? Who's her best friend? Does she have a boyfriend? Do you know answers to any of these questions?"

He blinked once. Then again. "No."

She waited a beat, allowing him time to make excuses. He didn't. It was one of the things she loved about him. "Gabe, I understand the situation. That you haven't been with her on a day-to-day basis for years. But you're her *father*. She told me some things in confidence. I—"

"What things?"

"I said in confidence. I won't betray that. I strongly suggested she tell you. She said you'll freak. That you're out of touch with reality. I take that to mean her reality, what's important to her."

Gabe stood abruptly and circled the family room, one hand on a hip, the other raking through his hair. "She said I'd freak, huh? Well, *numerous* subjects qualify to push old dad into the freaking category." He spun around to face her. "She's not *pregnant*, is she? You'd tell me that much at least, wouldn't you?"

A hollow feeling sank slowly through her. "Is that a dad's worst nightmare?"

"You know, an answer to *one* of my questions would be nice here." He began circling again. "Women. Unbelievable."

"You're freaking."

"Yeah! What of it?"

"You could try listening for a change!"

He halted in the middle of the room, both hands on hips now, and blew out a breath. "Okay. I'm listening."

"You're glaring and you're still freaking. If I were fifteen and your daughter, I'd run the other direction as far as I could go. And as fast."

"And I'd ground you. If we lived in the same house and I had any say in the matter!"

"Wouldn't work." She pushed herself from the chair and glared back at him. "Ask me how I know."

His jaw muscle twitched.

"Ask me how I know!"

"Consider yourself asked."

"I know it wouldn't work because it didn't work with me! And he lived in the same house and had the *only* say in the place. He didn't have a clue about my reality either. All that mattered to him was whether or not I was *pregnant.* Which is exactly the first thing you're concerned about with Jordan." Her hands were on her hips now, and she stood within three feet of him. "Come to think of it, you and my dad are a lot alike. Not a thing was allowed out of place in our house, and he never bothered to ask me who my friends were or what made me tick. Oh!" She clamped a hand over her mouth and turned away from him. *Oh, Lord. Oh, Lord. No.*

She heard Gabe's footsteps, as if he circled the room again. Where were her things? A bag in Spencer's room. She'd slept on the couch but, in deference to Gabe's spic-and-span tendency, had cleared the family room. Toothbrush in the hall bathroom. How quickly could she gather it up? She had to get out of there. Slip in to see Mac. Hide out at Cara's. Rearrange her life once more. Disentangle from what could become a decidedly untidy emotional mess. She walked toward the hall.

"Terri. Help me out here. Please. I don't know how to ask Jordan those things."

"I have to go."

"You don't fight fair, sweetheart."

His words stopped her before she reached the hallway.

"This is our second argument, and just like the first one, you're going to split before anything is settled. Fuss and fume and walk out the door. Is that what he did? Your dad?"

She swallowed, calming her voice, and turned. "This is a wake-up call. It's a fact that women from highly dysfunctional homes keep falling for guys who are exact replicas of their own dads. The stupid cycle keeps repeating itself."

"Until the woman falls for God and begins to let Him heal her soul."

She lowered her eyes and stared at the tweedy dark beige carpet. It was a good color. Neutral. Wouldn't show dirt dragged in by Spencer and his friends.

"I think I'm the only guy you've fallen for who isn't like your dad. Granted, I haven't connected with my daughter. That's not exactly a rare disease these days. But, hey, Spencer's room is a pit and you don't see me breathing threats down his neck."

True enough. She looked up at him.

"And." He smiled tentatively. "I pray about everything."

She was hooked. "Now that's a rare disease."

"I'm sorry I freaked." He reeled her in.

She wrestled against the pull. "Gabe, I'm scared. I'm confused. I don't know."

"That makes two of us. Why go it alone?"

The man was so gentle. She shrugged. "It's less complicated alone."

"But totally boring."

She smiled. How she had missed him! She didn't want to go back to the ache. "I'm sorry *I* freaked. You're not like him. Not really."

"Oh, I don't know. All men are alike in many ways. I told you for one, we're slow learners. He didn't have the chances I've had. I mean, I've spent eight years alone figuring out how I screwed up. One thing I learned was I don't want to do it alone anymore." He held his hand out toward her. "Help me win my daughter back?"

"I thought I only signed up for an occasional dinner with the girl. And that was a major concession on my part. Now I have to help you win her back? This is going to cost you a lot, mister."

"Mind if I pay in kisses?"

She took his hand. "I wouldn't mind a home-cooked meal now and then."

Both his dimples appeared.

"What did you mean when you said this was our second argument?" Terri sat on the couch, Gabe stretched out with his stockinged feet in her lap. She kneaded one of them.

"Mmm, that feels good." He rearranged the pillow underneath his head. "Our first one was the day we met at the ER."

"Or rather didn't meet."

"Yeah, but you get my drift. If someone would have told me at that moment that I'd fall in love with the loudmouthed EMT, I would have laughed my head off."

"If someone said to me Mr. Cool Surfer Dude was really an angel capable of making my head turn, I never would have believed it."

"I made your head turn?"

She swatted his foot. "Like you don't know."

"By the way, when I was a kid, anyone who teased me about my angel name got punched."

"I didn't call you Gabriel the angel. Lois did." *Lois.* Would things ever right themselves with her? "Sometimes you act like one."

He laughed. "Is that good or bad?"

"It's intimidating."

"No, *Mac's* intimidating."

"An angel can be that way too." She began kneading his other foot, her eyes averted from his. "Angels are— No I've never seen an angel. But angelic people are good and merciful and handsome. That intimidates us loudmouthed, everyday, guilt-ridden folk. We—*I* don't measure up."

He whisked his feet off her lap, sat upright, placed a finger under her chin, and turned her face toward him. His eyes bore into hers. "Seriously, please tell me you don't feel that way anymore."

"Yeah. I do. But only at times."

"It drives a wedge between us. I am not better than you."

"Well, I know you're not *perfect*." She kissed him softly. "I've met your daughter and ex-wife."

He wrinkled his nose.

"But you are good and merciful and so handsome. Women who like surfer types think you're handsome anyway." She batted her eyelashes.

Laughing, he fell back against the pillow. "Isn't it amazing how a split moment in time can so drastically change life? Like that moment Neva was fussing at me and you intervened. If you hadn't been within earshot, we never would have met."

"Not to mention Neva would have given birth in the back of a taxi, *much* to the surprise of the driver who picked her up at the ER." She pulled his feet back onto her lap and massaged one. "Then there's the Erin mess. Nothing's been the same since I met her! I can't believe I look over my shoulder all the time and I'm too scared to go home."

"But you get to stay at my house."

She frowned. "Temporary fix."

He grinned, his eyes closed a fraction beyond half-mast. "Look on the bright side."

"Then there's poor Mac, his life totally in pieces because a dying man shot a gun at me."

"I'll be forever grateful to Mac."

"My career is up in the air."

"You'll be back in no time."

"That's what you and Mac say. The chief says 'don't come back this week.'"

"Ouch!" His eyes reopened.

She loosened her grip on his foot. "Sorry. You should sleep."

"Not while there are nanoseconds to be savored. Have I mentioned I love you?"

"Once or twice in the last *five* minutes." She smiled. "I'm proud of you for leaving those dirty dishes on the table."

"And how about that other?"

"That other doesn't count until you see it. You've kept your head turned away." As an endurance test, she had scattered a few things about the room. Her shoes and a sweatshirt lay on the floor amongst Spencer's books and games.

He glanced out of the corner of his eye. "There. I see it. No freaking has occurred. Proud of me?"

"Yes, very."

"What does it mean to freak, anyway? Is that the vocabulary Jordan learns at that expensive school?"

Terri laughed. "You know what she meant."

"No, I don't."

"Let me see if I can help." She moved his legs from her lap and stood. With one hand on a hip and the other combing through her hair, she circled the room.

"Careful," he said. "You're going to trip over all that junk."

She stopped in front of him and contorted her face into an exaggerated frown. "Would you want to talk to a face like this? Confess your innermost thoughts?"

He reached out and grasped her wrist, pulling her toward him. "I get the picture. So what do I do instead?"

She sat on the edge of the couch. "Oh, Gabe. Talk to her like you talk to me. You love her. Tell her. Tell her you do *no matter what.* And then let her talk without trying to fix things for her. Don't offer solutions unless she asks." She stroked his cheek. "Your eyes are so warm. Let her see them, let her feel them on her face. Stop taking your frustrations with Paula out on Jordan."

"I don't."

"I think maybe you do. Not intentionally. It's just there. She's another woman who frustrates you."

His eyes lost their focus, as if his thoughts turned inward, considering her words.

"Pray about it."

"Yes, ma'am." He kissed her palm and fixed his gaze on her. "Tell me what I'm up against?"

"I can't, Gabe."

"Not even a hint?"

She sighed. Saying no to Gabe was becoming the hardest thing in her life. "You suspect she's doing something you don't approve of. If that's your first concern, you're missing the point."

"Which is?"

"She's trying to fill an emptiness, a void that's there because she doesn't *feel* like her daddy loves her."

"How did you fill your emptiness?"

A flush of shame warmed her, heating even the tips of her ears. *I am a new creation. I am. Old things have passed away.* Not totally. They stung. Tapes still played, old feelings, old reactions. *But I am forgiven. My sins forgotten by Him, flung as far as the east from the west.*

"Sweetheart, I'm sorry. You don't have to tell me."

"I don't mind confessing to you, Gabe. Honestly I don't. But you'll imagine Jordan in my shoes and you'll freak."

He smiled softly. "Test me?"

She steeled herself, fearing the impact of her words on both of them. "I drank. The alcohol eased the pain. I slept around. I needed hugs from a male. I got them."

Gabe flinched.

She took a deep breath and released it. "I barely graduated from high school. I was a snob. I was mean. I was a loser. I hung with losers. My best friends drove fast, were alcoholics by eighteen, addicted to coke or heroin by twenty. Two were dead before they turned thirty." She inhaled again. "That about covers it."

Tears pooled in his eyes. "Thank you."

"Still love me?"

"Always. No matter what." He sat up. "I want to call my daughter."

Thirty

Mac's laughter nearly shook the hospital's rafters.

Terri winced. "It's not that funny."

He only roared more loudly.

The door thumped open and a red-faced nurse rushed through it past Terri to his bedside. "What's wrong?" she asked breathlessly.

Terri said to the tall, middle-aged woman's back, "Nothing."

"Mr. Macauley, you're not allowed to get so excited." Her voice rose, competing with the volume of his guffaws. "Your blood pressure! Calm down!"

Wiping tears from his eyes, he totally ignored her advice.

She snapped her fingers. "Right this instant!" She turned to Terri. "Miss, this is not appropriate behavior for him."

Terri doubted Mac had ever behaved appropriately. She tried not to smile. "I'll do what I can."

"I may have to ask you to leave."

Mac closed his mouth, but his shoulders jiggled. "She stays."

"Then behave yourself."

"Yes, darlin'." He snickered.

The nurse shook her head and left.

Terri and Mac looked at each other and burst into quiet laughter.

He said, "She wouldn't know excited from a hole in the head." At last he sobered. "Of course I wouldn't know true love if it knocked me flat on my face."

284

"You'll find it someday, Mac. Maybe you could change your choice in women?"

"Nope. I'm an airheads kind of guy, through and through. Can't have them smarter than me." He winked. "That's why I never got serious about you."

She looked at the ceiling and ignored his chuckling. When she first arrived, Mac spoke tearfully of Lexi's betrayal, covering his face with both hands. His unabashed expression of heartache drove Terri to tears. She hugged him tightly and apologized profusely. That was when he burst into laughter, confessing between breaths that "Lexis" were a dime a dozen.

"Flo, to tell you the truth, I figured she would have bolted long before now. She was a groupie, more interested in the job than me. Come to think of it, she asked a lot about you."

"Did you tell her I was out of town?"

"Yeah."

"That I'm allergic to shellfish?"

He thought a moment. "Could have. You know how I thought you were too persnickety at that restaurant one time. It probably came up somehow when she asked something about you."

That's how Erin knew so much.

"I can smell a phony a mile away. She was using me. No problem. We had some laughs. And she is something to watch in the gym. I am a little ticked, though, to think how it was all a show. That she picked me because of you." He grinned. " 'Course I was using her too. Days can get kind of long in here. She did make me feel good, if you get my drift."

Terri didn't want to get his drift. "Has she phoned you today?"

"No. I tried calling her. No answer. Last night she hightailed it out of here right after you left. Five minutes after that a cop shows up and tells me she's wanted for questioning. Next thing I know he's setting up shop outside my door. They hope she'll show up tonight. That lady detective talked to me this morning. What's her name? Carrie?"

"Cara Fleming."

"Yeah. She's a looker. Like you. A face you don't mind staring at, even for a twenty-four-hour stretch." He winked again. "In shape, strong, smart written all over her face. Not my type." He shifted in the bed, not a quick movement. "Anyway, she told me Lexi, I mean Erin— Oh, let's call her Morgan. The cops watched Morgan's place. She didn't go there last night. Cara said she's been stalking you."

She shared the whole story with him, details Cara hadn't mentioned.

"No lie?" He whistled. "Weird. I just don't get why the uniformed cop's got to sit out there. Waste of manpower. It's not like she's going to waltz in with him in the vicinity. She's not that dumb."

"Mac, it's for your protection. Of course with a partner like me, you've needed protection for some time. Cara's concerned if Erin can't get at me, she'll hurt someone close to me. Like you."

A lineup raced through her mind. Zoë was safe at Gabe's. His new address wasn't in the phone book yet; there had been no evidence that Erin had knowledge of its location. He'd been watching his rearview mirror as Terri had. Gabe was safe. Her mother was in Cincinnati again. Safe. Terri's siblings were scattered; she wasn't in daily contact with them; it would be hard to trace them. They were safe. Kai was far enough removed. And besides, he knew Erin. Lois... Lois? She hadn't talked—

"Flo, what do you mean? He's out there like a *bodyguard?*"

"Yes."

"I'm six-four and weigh two hundred fifty pounds! I can take care of myself."

Terri glanced at his leg still tied up to that contraption. She met his eyes. An understanding registered. Her throat constricted.

He said, "I told you Lopez shot out my bad knee. That I needed a new one anyway."

She nodded. He just wanted to make her feel better. The guy really did have a medic's compassion, something she should have recognized a long time ago.

"It was a football injury. Knocked me out of the Northwestern lineup my second year."

"You played for Northwestern?"

"Not for long." He gave her a thumbs-up. "I can live with disappointment, Flo. I've been there. Not sure I can live without an airhead though. You got any more friends?"

She sniffed quietly. "You know that church Erin mentioned? The one you said you'd go to?"

"Yeah?"

"I go there." Now she was inviting him to church? Well, why not? She knew there was little else of true significance to offer a friend except an introduction to God.

"Hmm. Any other good-looking single women go there?"

Okay. Maybe an introduction to godly women would do for starters. "In numerous supply."

Mac grinned.

~

Terri's cell phone rang as she walked through the familiar hospital corridors. She recognized the number. "Cara?"

"Hi. How's it going?"

She described her visit with Mac.

"And how's Gabe?"

"Gabe is..." She smiled. "Great."

"Terri, I can see your head tilting."

"You cannot."

Cara laughed. "I just wanted to bring you up to date. We haven't found Erin yet. I had somebody in your church at both services. He showed her picture to various people and your— What's he called? Pastor?"

Terri imagined her flipping through her notebook. "Rector."

"Rector. Yeah. Bryan O'Shaugnessy."

Bryan! Her stomach twisted. "Is Bryan okay?"

"As far as I know. Why?"

"He's...a good friend. He's helped me out a few times. He's a chaplain with the department."

"Would Erin know that?"

"Not necessarily."

"Terri, you can't worry about everyone you've ever come in contact with."

Lee! "What about old boyfriends?"

"You still have something going with one?"

"No!"

"Then I'd say it's unlikely. Let's concentrate on current relationships."

"I want to go home, Cara. I want to wash the bedding she probably used. I want to scrub and wipe off everything she touched. I want to open the windows and replace the air she breathed. I want to sleep in my own bed! But I'm too scared. I've never been scared in my life."

"Where's a good hero when you need him?"

"He has houseguests. His kids." She sighed. "They're overdue for some quality time alone with him."

"I see. Well, how about a slumber party with your favorite cop?"

"You really don't have a life, do you?"

"Hey, this is the fun stuff. I'll bring the hair rollers and my Elvis tapes."

∽

Terri sipped coffee at a table in the hospital cafeteria. Across from her Lois ate a salad. She had aged since the last time Terri had seen her. Though dressed fashionably as always, she appeared haggard.

"Punkin, mark my words. You'll be back on duty next week. It's just paperwork holding things up, I'm sure. The review board will have to meet. Your actions have been cleared with the police and unofficially with the fire department."

"I hope you're right. I'm going a little bit stir-crazy."

"I imagine so. Weren't you scheduled to teach last week?"

"And this week. It all got canceled, but they said I can attend a training session tomorrow. At least it's something."

"You keep glancing around, like you're expecting someone."

She shook her head. "Remember Erin Morgan?" Terri relayed the entire saga to Lois. "I feel like I shouldn't spend time with my closest friends. Who knows? I might be endangering you."

Lois smiled broadly.

"That's supposed to concern you."

"Oh, it does. But you said 'closest friends.' As if I'm included on that list."

"Of course you are. Promise me you won't fall for some perky young blonde-streaked thing who, out of the blue, wants to be your best friend?"

"I promise."

"Thank you." Terri glanced around again at the busy area, avoiding eye contact with Lois. *Oh, Lord. I need the words. Help me with the words.*

"How is Gabe?"

As if an unseen hand had flipped some switch connected to tear ducts, Terri's eyes filled. "He's an angel, just like you said. And he loves me."

Lois set down her fork and reached over the table to squeeze Terri's hand.

"I can't hold this grudge against you any longer. God has forgiven me so much, Lois. And now He's given me this intense love for Gabe and vice versa. There's no space left in my heart for such an ugly feeling. I forgive you."

"Punkin, that means the world to me," she whispered, dabbing her wet cheeks with the paper napkin. "I don't mean to pressure you, but you know me."

Terri wiped her own tears and drew in a silent, unsteady breath. "Yeah, yeah, all right. What have I forgotten?"

"Your dad. Can you forgive him too?"

"He's dead."

The careworn expression returned to her friend's face. "It's not for his sake."

Terri's emotions were like a wobbling stack of toy blocks. *Can you forgive him too?* To take on the weight of Lois's request would be to place the final block on the top, the one that would bring them all crashing down.

Not today. No, sirree. It's not going to happen.

⌒

With the phone gripped between her shoulder and ear, Terri spread the freshly laundered comforter over her bed, listening to Gabe's rendition of his evening with the kids.

"And Jordan actually giggled." His voice sounded on the verge of a giggle itself. "I haven't heard her giggle since she was ten."

"Way to go, Pop!"

"I had to bite my tongue a few times to keep from giving her the third degree, but I didn't come out and charge her with anything. Which means I didn't get any of those questions answered."

"That's okay. It takes time. You made a great start. She's spending a school night at your house, and she giggled. You couldn't ask for more. How did you get her to giggle?"

"We played board games." He lowered his voice. "And I let her win a couple of times."

"Aww. Did you do that when she was little?"

"Yeah."

"What about Spencer?"

"We both let him win some." He chuckled. "It was good, Terri. Incredibly good. Thank you for giving me a push in the right direction."

She sat on the bed and pulled off her socks. "More like a shove."

"Told you I'm slow."

"You sure were slow in asking me out."

He groaned.

"Somebody could've given you a shove back in October." She climbed into the bed, pulled up the covers, and sniffed the pillow case. Summer rain? Spring bouquet? Something like that.

"In October you would have said no. You're breathing funny."

"Mmm. It's a new fabric softener. Smells fantastic, like a warm, fresh air, flowery kind of day." She inhaled another deep, noisy breath. "I'm trying to take my mind off the fact that Erin Morgan laid her head on this exact pillow just the other night."

"That's too weird."

"Tell me about it."

"Do you think you'll be able to sleep?"

Her eyelids felt heavy with exhaustion. "I think so. There's a comfort in knowing a cop is asleep on my couch downstairs and under her pillow is a gun."

"Okay, now I won't be able to sleep."

"We'll be fine. The no-key entry deadbolts are fastened. Erin's keys won't help. Cara says she hears a pin drop in her sleep, so she's not worried about loud noises like windows breaking."

"I'll come over tomorrow afternoon and put new locks on the doors."

"Thanks, Mr. Landlord."

"You're welcome. Of course, I may have to raise the rent. Probably in the form of dinner dates. Kissing."

Smiling, she closed her eyes as he continued teasing her in that vein. His late-night, easy-listening radio voice lulled her mind, siphoning off its excess of concerns.

"Terri?" His tone changed. "About Jordan?"

She rolled onto her other side, tucking his voice between her ear and the pillow. "What?"

"Is what she's involved in…" His voice trailed off.

Don't ask me to tell you. Please don't ask. "I don't know details." *Only that she attends teen parties without chaperones. That drugs and alcohol are available. What she does while there is pure conjecture.*

"I'm not asking for details. I'm asking… Do I have the *time* to build a relationship with her, to earn her trust? Or am I going to be out on a call and have to watch a medic work on my daughter because she OD'd?"

His heart was breaking. She could hear it. Her own began to ache. *Love shouldn't hurt like this.* "Gabe, she told me she doesn't do drugs."

He sighed audibly.

"The way I see it…" Why did the hurt keep turning her thoughts toward her own childhood? She swallowed. "Gabe, I don't have the board game memories. The giggling, the knowing my dad let me win a game, the sharing of just-for-fun time. Jordan does. She has all that, and you rekindled the memories in her tonight. If some major trouble came up, she would turn to you in a heartbeat."

When he finally replied, there was a tightness in his voice. "You know one thing I love about you?"

She smiled. "What?"

"You wouldn't feed me a line just to make me feel better."

"Loudmouths like to give it straight."

He chuckled. "Well, thank you."

"Thank God. We're both praying about this, right?"

"Right. So anyway." He paused again. The odd pitch of his voice suggested he was still regaining composure. "The kids want to do this again Saturday night."

"That's great."

"With you. They both made a big deal insisting I invite you."

"Really? Why would they think of me?"

"I'm guessing it had something to do with Jordan finding you asleep on my couch."

"Oh. That." She felt uncomfortable remembering how she met Paula.

"Will you join us?"

Join them. It sounded like a date. With kids. Swell. *Welcome to your future.* "Sure."

"I hear a slight hesitation in the lady's voice. She thinks all of her Saturday nights are going to be spent with the rugrats."

"And Fridays. Sundays. Mondays."

"Terri, married couples spend time together without their children. I won't always include them."

"I-I know."

Silence filled the phone line for a long moment.

"Sweetheart, I don't mean to get the cart before the horse. We can take our time. You don't have to come Saturday. The kids are my responsibility, not yours."

"That makes them sound like a problem. They're not a problem. I don't think of them that way. I think of them like...like Martians. I just need to get to know them. Maybe we'll like each other."

"Are you sure this isn't a deal breaker?"

"Let's see. My choice is Gabe Andrews in my life with kids, or Gabe Andrews not in my life. Easy decision. I'm sold on you being in my life."

"I wasn't so sure this morning. I thought you might split. Maybe for good."

"As someone once said to me, I cut off my nose to spite my face. And Rachel warned me that to hurt myself, I would pull away from you." She paused. "I guess I still have the tendency."

Again a long silence.

Gabe exhaled loudly. "Anything I can do to convince you that you are worth all the love I can give you?"

She smiled. *Gabe's voice. Gabe's words.* "That should do it, you smooth-talking angel."

Thirty-One

A mindless, late-night sitcom flickered on the television screen. The muted volume prevented the show from interfering with Terri's stream of thoughts. Still, its presence served the purpose of giving the illusion that friendly company lingered in her home.

She sat curled up on the couch, remote clutched in one hand, cell phone clutched in the other. Zoë snuggled against her. They had dispensed with the dog rule against climbing on the furniture. Like a 100-pound breathing, furry security blanket, she warded off chills.

All sorts of chills threatened to overwhelm Terri. The room was cool because she didn't want the furnace running. Its noise would interfere with her ability to hear strange sounds. Then there was fear itself, chilling her to the bone.

As she had told Cara, she'd never been afraid of anything in her life. Her dad and his wrath never scared her. She always held her own against neighborhood bullies, boy or girl. Consequences, real and imagined, never interfered with her self-destructive activities as a teenager or as a young adult. Downhill skiing? No problem. The steeper and more moguls the better. Skydiving? Pure fun. Emergency situations only energized her adrenaline in a positive sense. She simply did what needed to be done, whether it was go inside a smoke-filled building as flames shot from it or administer medical aid to a victim whose body scarcely appeared human because of the damage that had been inflicted upon it.

But...Erin Morgan scared her. The girl had worn her down to a state of extreme weariness unlike anything she'd ever known before.

Earlier that morning, Cara had said on her way out the door, "I don't think she really wants to kill you. You're her mother figure. She's angry because her mom died. She feels this love-hate ambivalence toward you. You aren't giving her the attention she craves. She tries every which way to get close to you, through Kai or Mac. She admires you, wants to be like you, so she takes an EMT training class, drives a car like yours, moves into your house."

"What about the shellfish?"

"It was wrapped and clearly marked. She knew you wouldn't eat it. Nothing else was contaminated."

"What about Melanie Lareau?"

Cara zipped up her backpack that had served as her overnight bag for two nights. Like Terri, she traveled light. Only after she put on her wrinkled khaki suit jacket did she answer. Finally she met her eyes. "Something triggered that episode, something that convinced her that Melanie, the mother figure, totally rejected her. It pushed Erin to suicidal thoughts. She wasn't good enough. She confronted Melanie, not necessarily to kill her. You've had restraining orders, you've kicked her out of your class, and still she hasn't approached you in a way to harm you. She hasn't threatened to kill herself because you've rejected her. I don't know." She winced. "Just keep your doors locked."

"Maybe I should be her friend if that's what she needs. Then I could convince her to get help."

"Terri, I didn't say she's not potentially dangerous to you and herself. As soon as we find her, we'll bring her in and go from there. I'm sorry we can't make it a priority."

"I know. Thanks for everything."

Cara hitched the bag over a shoulder. "Well, dear, I don't know how to say this, but I'm not coming home tonight."

Terri smiled. The detective had already informed her she couldn't stay a third night. She walked with her to the door. "Mind if I ask what you're doing instead?"

"There's another slumber party."

"You're guarding someone else?"

"Terri, I don't do this with other people." Cara's grin was crooked. "I consider you a friend. No, tonight the party is at a homeless shelter." She brushed her jacket front with exaggerated motions. "This suit fits the image, don't you think?" Her rare laugh was like a girl's, a distinct lilting, carefree note.

Terri had to admit to herself that the suit was as wrinkled as if Cara had slept in it, but then so were her other outfits. "You're going undercover?"

She winked and opened the door. "I won't have my phone with me. Promise to call 911 if you get spooked. The police don't mind checking things out. Okay?"

Her words echoed the advice Terri had given Jordan. Strange to hear them directed at herself.

Now Terri shifted in her seat, closer to Zoë. Was she spooked? Yes, but where did one draw the line? She hadn't heard any strange noises. "Spooked" was an imaginary state, something she brought on herself. Calling 911 wasn't for "spooked."

Gabe had called twice from the station to check on her. She was determined to spend the night in her own home. It would be the first step toward getting back to living her normal life. Day after tomorrow would be step two: She was going back to work. Of course, things wouldn't be exactly as they were before. Gabe was part of her life now. Gabe and, like never before, God. It was time to turn cartwheels, not feel spooked.

The phone rang in her hand, the effect of its trill like a thousand volts of electricity shooting through her. She jumped. Her heart hammered in her throat.

She checked the incoming call number. It wasn't familiar. Again the trilling. She hesitated. It wasn't familiar, but it wasn't tagged *Unavailable* either. Another ring. Zoë whined.

If she answered and heard Erin's voice, she could simply hang up. Or...

Or she could try talking to her. After all, she was in the business of patching people up, getting them to a doctor.

A fourth ring.

Talking to Erin could be step three toward getting on with her own life.

"Hello?"

"Terri? It's J-Jordan. C-can you help m-me?"

~

Terri flew across town, driving as if strobes and sirens were attached to her car. She wished a policeman would catch her in the act of cruising through a red light. Backup would be good at this point.

She couldn't call for it. She needed to keep the line open with Jordan. The girl sobbed quietly and directed her to an all-night restaurant called Clipper's, but offered no other real information.

Terri entered the brightly lit place, phone still at her ear, and paused near the cash register.

Jordan's voice came through the line. "I'm in the next room, n-not by the w-windows."

"Okay." She slid the cell into her pocket and proceeded toward the back.

Close to midnight, the place wasn't overly crowded. The usual scents of coffee, syrup, and hot oil permeated. As she stepped into a separate dining area, she spotted Jordan in the furthest corner booth, her arms crossed over the front of a white denim jacket, her head turned sideways. Her disheveled blonde hair obscured her profile.

"Excuse me!" A rather hefty waitress cut into Terri's narrow path between tables and nearly collided with her. "Can I help you?"

"No, thanks. I'm meeting my friend."

The woman, a head taller than Terri, gazed around the room and shrugged. "Not here."

"The girl."

"Kind of old to be hanging out with high school kids, aren't you?

Gabe's daughter sat 20 feet away. Her need must be desperate indeed for her to have called Terri, of all people. Evidently the woman had appointed herself bodyguard, but there was no time to dither. Mentally Terri dug in her heels and paused until her professional demeanor settled upon her like second skin.

"Ma'am, I'm a paramedic and a friend of the family. Excuse me, please."

Taken aback, the woman gave Terri a head-to-toe sweeping glance, but moved slightly. "You don't look like a paramedic, but she said she was calling one."

Terri pushed past her. "Off duty."

Jordan was staring at her now, visibly trembling.

Oh, dear Lord.

The girl's left eye was swollen shut. A bloody gash sliced across the cheekbone below it. Her lips were puffy.

"Jordan!" Terri whispered. She gritted her teeth and fought back a crushing wave of compassion. The emotion had to go to the back burner.

At the table, she slid onto the bench seat. "Let me see, hon." Gently she brushed aside Jordan's long hair and inspected the wounds.

Behind her the waitress said, "I gave her ice. She wouldn't let me call the cops."

Jordan whimpered.

"Shh," Terri soothed. "What happened?"

"Don't c-call the police."

"I just want to know what happened. I need to figure out how badly you're hurt." The cheek needed attention, probably a few stitches.

"H-hit me."

"What?"

"He didn't mean to!"

"Jeremy did this?"

Jordan winced.

"Hon, did he hit you anywhere else?"

She clutched the jacket more tightly at her neck. Blood streaks marred the white fabric.

"Hey, it's just me and your bodyguard here. Let me take a peek?" She lightly touched the girl's fingers. "I'm like a doctor, you know? You've seen one body, you've seen them all. I want to make sure you're not bleeding anywhere."

Jordan blinked and let go.

Terri unfastened the buttons, partially opened the jacket, and peered inside. She bit back a gasp. *Seeing a stranger's body was not seeing a loved one's.* By extension through Gabe, Jordan had leapt into the "loved one" category. Terri knew it the moment she glimpsed the girl's torn shirt. Bright, ugly red marks covered her exposed chest.

Rage mounted in Terri. She spoke softly, her voice almost obliterated in the furious thump-thumping of her heart. "Where do you hurt, hon?"

"M-my left side."

Terri watched the uneven movement of her chest as she breathed and gently felt her bones. She guessed at least one rib was broken and tried not to think of the amount of force inflicted upon Jordan to cause such damage. Buttoning the coat, she noted the jeans were snapped and zipped.

"Jordan, do you hurt anywhere else?"

She shook her head violently.

Terri removed her own fleece-lined windbreaker and helped Jordan slide her arms into it. She snapped it up and then let her gaze rest on the girl's face, still pretty despite its battered condition. The anger she felt almost choked her throat shut. "Did he rape you?"

"No!" Her face crumpled and fresh tears poured.

"Did he try?"

Jordan only cried harder.

Terri gathered Gabe's daughter into her arms and held her fast. For the moment there was nothing else to be done.

⌇

Della the bodyguard-slash-waitress brought coffee for Terri, more hot tea for Jordan, and another bag of ice wrapped in a towel. Terri put money on the table, enough for a large tip, anxious to leave as soon as possible.

The girl was coherent, though not the most cooperative of patients.

"Okay, hon." Terri interrupted her protests as she held the ice pack against Jordan's brow. "Here are the options. You need stitches and X-rays. They only do these things this time of night at the ER. I am going with you. We will either go in an ambulance or, if I talk to one of your parents, we'll go in my car. I can't transport you without their permission. There are absolutely no other choices and no more discussion. Understand?"

Put that succinctly in that tone, Jordan changed her answer from an adamant "No way" to a weak "Mom."

As Jordan recited numbers, Terri pressed the keypad. She handed the phone to her. "Where does she think you are?"

"At Dad's."

Terri tried not to flutter her eyelids, the girl's trademark response in happier times.

"Mom?" Jordan said into the phone and started crying again. "I'm okay. Daddy's girlfriend has to talk to you. She's a paramedic... Nothing! I'm okay!"

Terri accepted the phone with a deep breath and told herself the news she was about to impart could be much worse.

"Paula, this is Terri Schuman." Not wasting words, she briefly explained the situation. "We'll meet you at Cutler-Barr..."

Paula's reaction was understandably anxious. She kept interrupting, wanting more details, arguing about the hospital choice.

"Sorry, we're closer to Cutler-Barr. If I call an ambulance, that's where they would take her from here."

And finally, the ex-wife asked about Gabe.

"He's on duty." *Which you should have known!* "See you there." She disconnected and looked at Jordan. "Okay, we've got the go-ahead from Mom. Ready?"

She leaned against Terri's shoulder, clearly in need of another hug.

Terri held her again and rested her cheek against the girl's soft hair. "You're going to be just fine. Have you ever been to the ER?"

She shook her head.

"Really? My dad used to work at the hospital, so I hung out there a lot. I especially loved the ER. It's always been one of my favorite places. I realize that makes me sound really weird."

Jordan's faint chuckle was muffled.

"Listen, I promise I'll stay with you the whole time. Everything will be all right. You don't have to be afraid. Tonight Dr. Karen should be on duty. Karen is her first name. She's a sweetheart. Smart as a whip. It's always good when they're smart as whips. You'll like her, though she won't take any nonsense from you. None of that fluttering your eyelids. You know how you do sometimes when you think we grown-ups are clueless..."

Terri let her voice drift off as she sensed someone else nearby. She lifted her head and turned.

Erin Morgan stood beside the table, watching.

Terri froze.

Anger distorted Erin's face. Not a hint of her usual perky friendliness was evident. It was a Jekyll-and-Hyde switch, as if a totally different personality had erased the spunky one who gushed adoration and gratitude. Her eyes narrowed, her mouth twisted. "You never hold me like that. You never tell me everything's going to be all right."

Call 911. This is when you call the police. Now!

"You never mothered *me!*"

By now Jordan was sitting up straight, staring at the stranger.

Terri found her voice. "Erin, I'm calling the police unless you leave this instant."

"Oh, I'm leaving all right. I'm leaving for good. You'll be sorry!" With that she turned and rushed through the dining room.

Terri picked up her phone. "Jordan, I have to call the police."

"Don't. Please don't!" She was shaking again.

"That woman—"

"You said we could talk about the police later! Not now!"

Terri could see she was losing Jordan again. The girl didn't want Jeremy to get into trouble. They could deal with that later, so Terri had promised no cops, knowing full well the doctor would have them called after one look at Jordan. Pressing charges was another matter.

For now they had to get to the hospital. Cara wasn't available. If Terri waited for the police to show up and then explained the whole Erin situation to them, precious time would be lost. They'd take one look at Jordan and want *her* story. She'd go hysterical again.

"Okay, okay. But I have to let your dad know."

"Why?" she cried.

"Hon, listen. He's going to freak one way or another at you and now at me because of— oh, never mind. If I call, he can freak on the phone and we don't have to watch him act like a bear at the hospital." She tried to smile.

Jordan held onto her arm, panic creeping into her expression again. Terri laid one hand atop hers, held the phone with the other, and pressed the phone pad with her thumb. The fireman who answered told her Gabe's unit was out on a run.

"Tell him I called. Tell him I'm taking his daughter to Cutler-Barr. It's not life-threatening, but he should meet us there as soon as possible."

"Got it. She's okay?"

"Yeah."

"I'll radio, see if I can find out what's going on. If the ambulance is headed that way, maybe he can hitch a ride." He grunted. "Thanks a lot, Schuman. I hate relaying this kind of stuff. Even cool, calm, collected Andrews will flip out."

Tell me about it. She decided against adding news of Erin's visit to the message.

Thirty-Two

Abruptly halting their exit from the restaurant, Terri stopped just inside the door, one hand on its push bar and one arm around Jordan's shoulders. She scanned the parking lot for look-alike Blazers and drivers sitting in any make of car with its engine running. Nothing caught her attention except the glaring fact that Jordan's well-being rested solely on her shoulders.

An unfamiliar impression stirred within her, rapidly growing into a fierce determination almost primal in its urgency. She wanted to roar like a bear. She knew she would do whatever it took to fight off anything or anyone that threatened this child. Nothing would hurt Jordan Andrews.

But she knew her limitations.

Lord, I can't do this alone. Please. Keep Erin out of the way and get us safely to the hospital.

Jordan slipped an arm behind Terri's waist. "You sound just like Dad," she murmured. "Praying."

She'd spoken aloud? "You're discovering all sorts of weird things about me. Come on. Let's go."

Terri drove quickly but cautiously, obeying red stoplights. Traffic was sparse but steady on the midnight streets. Every time she felt her gaze drift to the rearview mirror, she jerked her sight forward and thought to herself, *Yours.* The one-word prayer reminded her that worrying about Erin was God's department.

With a little prodding from Terri, Jordan opened up. The initial terror had receded. "He didn't mean to. It was the coke or something. He was high. Not himself."

Out of control. "How did you get away?"

A long pause. "His friends. They...pulled him off. I ran."

"How did you get to Clipper's?"

"I...ran. I...guess. I don't remember too much."

"How far away were you?"

She shrugged and grimaced. The slight movement must have hurt. "We were at Bree's." She gave a street name. Terri placed it at a minimum of two and a half miles from the restaurant.

She wondered why the girl had called her, but for the moment she didn't want to pry. It was easy to guess. A torn blouse. Her friends. The girl's parents not home. Drugs. An amorous evening spun horribly out of control. Jordan could have been just plain too embarrassed to call police or Gabe or her mother. She saw Terri as trustworthy because she had protected her secret friendship with Jeremy. She knew she needed medical attention, something Terri could offer.

"Jordan, how did you get my number?"

She didn't answer.

"I don't care, hon. I'm just curious."

"I found it listed in Dad's cell. I thought if Jeremy ever... You know, if something happened, and we didn't want the police involved, I could call you to take care of him again."

Oh, how she regretted promising not to tell Gabe that first time! If he and Paula didn't send the cops after Jeremy now, Terri would hit the roof. The boy couldn't be allowed to get away with it! And even more importantly, Jordan couldn't be allowed to continue a relationship with a first-class loser who abused her! Had he hurt her on other occasions?

Kai's voice intruded upon her thoughts. *You know who you remind me of? Those battered women...* Although Terri's loser boyfriends had never physically abused her, there were other forms of abuse she had accepted and even expected as her due. Kai recognized that about her before she did. She saw the tendency in Jordan.

No, she wasn't about to let this innocent child walk that path. She would get in her parents' faces and harangue until something was done! Until charges were pressed and a counselor called!

She glanced at the girl huddled in the other seat and a pang shot through her. Jordan Andrews had somehow wormed her way into Terri's heart, whether via their similarities or via Gabe. The means didn't matter. What mattered was: Would Terri's opinion count? More than likely it would not. What place did she have haranguing and getting in their face, trying to convince them to see things her way? Jordan was Gabe and Paula's daughter, not hers.

Something else to give up.

Yours, Lord.

~

Neither Gabe nor Paula were present in the ER when Terri arrived with Jordan.

Terri the paramedic made herself at home and ushered Jordan straight into an examining area as if she were her ambulance patient. She answered the nurse's questions before they were asked, swished shut the curtains, and helped Jordan change into a hospital gown.

And then, momentarily, Terri the friend overwhelmed Terri the medic. Beneath the harsh lights, the severity of the contusions intensified. She grasped the side of the bed.

Jordan's whimper had the effect of dousing the friend's face with cold water and reviving the medic.

"Jordan, hon." She helped her settle onto the bed and pulled a sheet over her. "The doctor will be here in a few minutes. She'll look you over, kind of like I did. Then, before they wash your face and take X-rays—" She bit her lip. *Get a grip, Schuman.* She brushed Jordan's hair back. "They have to take pictures of the bruises."

Fear filled the girl's eyes.

"Just in case somebody needs it for evidence. Don't worry. There's a nice lady who does it. I'll make sure we get her. Your mom can stay with you." She continued soothing, assuring Jordan of the simplicity of it all, as if it were a matter-of-fact, everyday event.

It was neither of course. It was a complex humiliation and as far removed from Jordan's everyday life as bad hair days and zits. But the anxiety eased from her expression.

Dr. Karen Underwood stepped inside. Word must have spread rapidly: A firefighter's daughter was in the ER. Any non-life-threatening emergencies took a backseat to her.

She exchanged a glance of recognition with Terri and introduced herself to Jordan. A tall, 50-something mom and grandmother, she wore her graying hair in a bun at the neck and colorful rather than plain white lab coats. Tonight's was a neon fuchsia. Compassion oozed from her pores.

Terri held Jordan's hand as the doctor examined her, chatting the whole time. "You know what we call your dad around here?"

"What?"

"Gabriel the angel."

Jordan didn't respond. Terri thought of how she didn't respond either when people praised her dad. Jordan hadn't seen the angelic side of Gabe. To her he was just an absent father.

"Jordan, I have to talk with Ms. Schuman for a moment. Will you excuse us?" Her wide smile crinkled the eyes behind black-rimmed glasses. Worn laugh tracks folded into creases around her mouth. "Be right back."

Terri followed her through the curtain. They walked a short distance away.

Karen removed her glasses and pressed her fingertips against her eyes. "Police and photographs." Her statement was a sigh.

"Yes."

"Where are her parents?"

"On their way."

"Terri, she trusts you. Will you hang around for the ugly part?"

"Her mom will want to. I'd be in the way."

Karen replaced her glasses and smiled again. "I hear you and the angel are an item."

Terri's mouth fell open. "That Lois—"

"Uh-uh. The angel himself mentioned it." She held out her arms in a helpless gesture. "He's grinning like a Cheshire cat. I ask about his love life. So sue me."

Terri clamped her jaw shut.

"Anyway, I know things can get complicated, but stay if you can." She patted her arm. "I have to check on someone else."

As she walked away, a nurse approached with Paula on her heels. Distraught, but...wearing a nice pair of black slacks and the cashmere coat. Hair brushed back into a ponytail, diamond studded earlobes all a twinkle. Skin a smooth, even tone. Eyes lined. Lips a polished pink. She had applied makeup? At one o'clock in the morning? While her daughter lay in the hospital?

They passed Terri without a glance. Sweet perfume swept away the hospital aroma. The nurse indicated Jordan's cubicle and Paula entered it alone.

Gabe's ex did her own version of freaking.

Understandable. Terri stood like a statue, oblivious to the hubbub around her, and listened to the agonizing cries as Paula saw Jordan's face, a sight that had turned Terri's own stomach.

A hand touched her elbow.

She turned and saw Gabe. He wore his large black turnout coat with the yellow stripes. Her message had gotten through. Someone had brought him straight to the hospital.

"Jordan?" His eyes asked a hundred questions.

"She's okay, but her face is bruised. Her boyfriend hit her."

"Boyfriend?" Another hundred questions tumbled into play. She had a boyfriend? Since when? Who? Why didn't he know?

"Go." She steered him toward the cubicle.

He looked back at her, his forehead creased, those hundreds of questions unanswered. Then his jaw clenched and he turned, pulling open the curtain.

Terri felt a literal ache in her arms. She wanted to hold him, to offer comfort. She wanted his comfort in return, to release the emotions she'd been repressing since Jordan's phone call. He could absorb them. But not now. His daughter needed him first.

And, evidently, his ex-wife.

Through the parted curtains Terri glimpsed them now. Gabe held Paula. She was shorter than Terri. She was petite She didn't even come up to his shoulder. He leaned over her, his chin resting on top of her head, his eyes closed, his lips moving. His words would be soothing, his voice the manifestation of what velvet would sound like if it could whisper.

Terri turned. The Andrews were a family again. For now anyway. And she wasn't part of it.

～

Rushing through the parking lot, Terri shivered in the cool April night and told herself the long-sleeved polo would be sufficient once she got the car heater going. Her jacket was back on the chair next to Jordan's bed. It would have to stay there.

Waiting for the heater to warm up and the tears to finish spilling, Terri sat in her car and assessed the situation.

First of all, there was work to consider. Her shift started in less than five hours. Therefore, she had to go home and sleep. Calling in sick after two weeks off would not be the smartest thing to do. Secondly, if she went back inside, she would only be in the way. Jordan was in the good hands of parents, doctors, nurses, police. As with every run, it was the appropriate time for the paramedic to step aside.

Thirdly, Gabe and Paula might resent her because Jordan had chosen to call her rather than them. Jordan would have to explain that one when she was able. It was a family issue. They needed time to work through it.

Lastly…Gabe. She loved him. He loved her. He would not blame her for not preventing Jordan from getting hurt tonight. Though she knew Jordan was possibly headed for trouble, the situation was in the making long before Terri entered his life. He and his daughter had a ways to go. The incident might serve as a jumpstart to speed them along their path to healing.

Was it a jumpstart for something else? Something between Gabe and Paula?

She didn't want to go there. The hug was a natural reaction.

Wasn't it?

Welcome to your future, she reminded herself again. Paula was always going to be in the picture. Gabe's past with Paula was always going to be in the picture. The evidence was in two children, living and breathing proof of a one-time love. Kids celebrated main events, like graduations, birthdays, weddings. Both parents were invited. Paula wasn't going away.

"So, Schuman, get used to this." She spoke aloud to herself. "If you want to be in his life, you have to deal with this here and now."

She sniffed and hiccuped. "Okay. Lord, this one's Yours too."

She shifted into drive and pulled away from the hospital.

The world came to a standstill at precisely 2:27 A.M. that morning.

Terri noticed the time because she was doing math to keep her mind occupied on anything but the Andrews family. She calculated she would be home in 13 minutes, in bed five minutes after that, and asleep in ten more. If she set the alarm for the last possible minute, she could conceivably sleep for three hours and five minutes. Not the best way to start a 24-hour shift, though she knew from experience it could be done.

She drove on a wide, flat four-lane highway at 55 miles per hour. Chicagoland, like any large city, never slept. Lights from restaurants and discount mega-stores glowed from each side, beckoning passersby to eat and shop 24 hours a day. She never wondered why her 911 runs to public arenas continued around the clock.

She wiped away an occasional tear. For Jordan. For Spencer, who wouldn't understand and was probably home alone with his stepdad. For Gabe. For herself.

Okay. For Paula too. I suppose now I'm supposed to love her as well as pray for her? Because she is, after all, the mother of his children and not some ogre to be avoided? Even if she did take the time to apply makeup.

"Lord, this isn't me talking at all. What have you done with Terri Schuman anyway?" She smiled. Tired. Confused. In love. In awe of what God was capable of doing. That He would bother to fill her heart with love for a snotty teenage girl and her little brother.

"And Paula." She said it aloud and rubbed her nose. The scent of woman's perfume wouldn't go away.

That was when the world came to a standstill.

A black shadow filled her rearview mirror. An inhuman screech assaulted her eardrums. Automatically her foot went to the brake. The shadow took shape, lunging between the front seats, crushing Terri, blocking her view. Hands wrenched the steering wheel, twisting it violently from her grasp. The car whipped into a squealing spin.

There was a thud. The car jerked sideways, its speed increasing. Someone screamed. Another thud, metal crunching against metal. Up became down, down became up. Glass exploded. Then, like some bull yanked at the end of a lasso, the car stopped.

The scream had been Erin Morgan's.

Terri recognized it a split second before everything turned black.

Thirty-Three

Sirens wailed.

Terri listened to the volume. It was loud. The whoo-whooing, as Kai always referred to it, came from more than one ambulance, more than one fire engine. That meant the emergency was major. Anytime more than one ambulance went, multiple injuries were expected. Was it a fire? She hadn't seen smoke.

With a jolt, she opened her eyes. The night was eerily silent. No wailing sirens. Had she been dreaming? She wondered whose car she was in. Its moon roof gave her a wide view of the stars. Panic grabbed hold, bubbling in her chest even before she fully realized she sat in her own car looking through what used to be the windshield.

Erin. Where was Erin?

Fighting off a wave of nausea, she unhooked her seat belt and looked around. The air bag hadn't detonated. Everything was crooked. Off balance. She felt for the door handle. It wasn't in its usual place.

"Ma'am! Ma'am! Are you all right?"

A face peered at her through the opening.

"Yeah." *I think I am.* She could breathe, see, hear, move, and think. *My name is Terri Schuman. Today is Wednesday. No, it's Thursday morning. I'm in Chicago, not far from home.* She was oriented, her level of consciousness alert. "I'm fine. I can't get the door open."

"Just wait. It's all smashed in. Some guy's on the phone with 911. Help is on the way."

There was a shadow in the passenger seat. She groped at it, ran both hands through it. Only a shadow. Where was Erin? In the back? No. An impact would throw her forward. Through the windshield.

Terri pulled up her legs and braced her knees on the console. "Give me a hand?"

"Ma'am, maybe you should wait."

"Or don't give me a hand," she muttered and boosted herself onto her knees. Her head cleared the wide opening of the windshield. She scrambled onto the dashboard. Something cut into her shins. She ignored it.

As she crawled out onto the hood, the stranger took hold of her arm. He helped her slide onto the pavement, which wasn't as far down as it should have been from that height. "Maybe you should sit."

She twirled around. Vague impressions of the scene implanted themselves in her mind. Too many vehicles littered the road and shoulders. There were people everywhere. Walking, standing. Shouting, crying. Still no sound of sirens.

Chaos. *Bring order to the chaos.*

She looked at her helper in the obscure light. He was young, younger than Kai, shorter than Kai. "I'm Terri and I'm a paramedic. I need your help. What's your name?"

"Uh, Michael. Your head's bleeding."

"Someone was in the car with me, Michael." She turned in a slow circle, gaining no sense of direction whatsoever. Which way was west? She was traveling west. How many times was the car hit? Which way did it spin? At what point would Erin have—

"There's somebody hurt over here."

The lights and shadows coagulated into a blur. She grabbed hold of Michael's arm, and he led her to a pickup truck. It sat sideways across two lanes, its front end dented. The driver's side door was open.

The person in there would not be Erin.

Triage, Schuman! Figure it out. Who comes first? Check everyone!

Michael spoke to a handful of people. "Move. She's a paramedic. Excuse me." He cleared a path for her to the door and informed the man in the truck who she was. Then he backed away.

Focus, Schuman! She stepped up onto the running board.

A middle-aged man smiled at her. "Oo-whee! That airbag was no fun, let me tell you."

"Sure beats the alternative though, huh?" She touched his shoulder, looking him over.

"Don't even want to think about that."

The man appeared fine. She wasn't about to linger over details and build a rapport. "Do you know your name, where you are, and today's date?"

"Last I checked, yeah." He laughed. "Want my rank and serial number too?"

"Do you hurt anywhere?"

"My arms feel on fire. Otherwise I don't think so."

She didn't detect any bleeding. "Why don't you just stay put until the medics get here? Sit real still. Don't move your head around a lot."

"Miss, I don't think I could stand up if I wanted to. That was the scariest thing I've ever seen. That Blazer doing a one-eighty in front of me? Whew! Nowhere I could go except straight into it."

She patted his shoulder. "I'm glad you had your seat belt on."

"You and me both. Maybe you ought to do something about your head there."

She stepped down from the truck. *Where was Erin?*

"Uh, Terri." Her young helper appeared beside her again. "There's another car—"

"I have to find—"

"It's right here." He pulled her along. "Two women. They're hysterical."

She let him lead her. They jogged a distance along the pavement. Veering off onto the shoulder, they scrambled down into a shallow ditch.

Dear Lord.

The car was a good sized SUV. In a colliding duel, it would have the advantage against her Blazer. It sat wedged between the two embankments, a space much too narrow for the huge vehicle. From the direction she approached, no structural damage was evident.

Once again Michael walked ahead, announcing her presence and asking people to move aside. What were all those people doing out at 2:30 in the morning?

Terri did her best rendition of paramedic in charge while her own anxiety mounted and her legs trembled. Totally gone, though, was her knack for instilling calm. The two young women in the front seat sobbed loudly. She quickly determined they were in no immediate danger and left them to their weeping. She asked bystanders to round up some blankets to keep them warm.

"Michael." She turned to find her helper at her elbow.

"This way." He hurried her along. "I saw your car spin and roll."

She didn't even have to ask. The young man was tuned in to her thoughts.

"It's not far."

And then she heard it. The silence. The eerie quiet. The absence of breath. Life exiting—

"No!" she cried.

And then she saw it. A shadowy bump in the short grass.

She ran, shouting orders to Michael, who ran beside her. "Get in my car. Backseat. First aid kit. Flashlight. Blankets."

"Got it."

She reached Erin. Enough light from a distant parking lot shone to reveal the blood. Erin lay on her side, deathly still.

The silence assaulted Terri now, like a roar of white noise. Life making its exit.

"No!" she screamed at the top of her lungs. "No!"

She fell to her knees in the grass and leaned forward until her head rested in it, the scent of black earth and new grass rich in her nostrils. Spring. New life.

She whispered, "Father, author and finisher of life, spare this one. Please spare this one."

A peace settled within her. "Amen. So be it."

She went to work, quietly talking as she always did, the timbre of her voice reassuring yet commanding. "You will not die on me, Erin Morgan. You will not die. Do you hear me?"

She gently rolled Erin onto her back and located the source of the bleeding, in a thigh. From the looks of things, an artery had been severed. Her life poured out onto the earth...

"But you will not die." She pressed on the wound. "No, sirree. Not today. Not on my shift."

Erin's face, dimly illuminated, remained expressionless. Terri thought she detected a slight rise in her chest.

"At least you had the good sense to land in the grass. Now that was a smart plan. And sideways instead of face first through the windshield? Brilliant. Your makeup isn't even smudged. The hair could use a little work, though."

A wavy light skimmed over the area. A flashlight. She turned to see Michael rushing her direction. Already? He *couldn't* be back— Yes, he could. In chaos, the paradoxical had become the familiar. *Thank You, Lord.*

"Terri, what can I do?"

"Lay the flashlight next to me. Latex gloves are in the box. Put them on."

"Don't you want—?"

"No." She glanced over to make sure he was following orders. "Okay, see those big packets there? Yeah. Open them up. You'll need all of them. Hey, Erin, don't you love this? I got a good-looking young guy to save your life. Name's Michael. Michael, meet Erin."

"Hey, Erin. How you doing? Guess you've had better days. Terri, I hear sirens now."

"Two minutes out. Another two to find us. Four more to check vitals, start IV, load, decide about a tourniquet, yada, yada, yada— Okay. Hold the dressings and slide your hands under mine. Here. That a boy." She placed her hands on top of his and pressed firmly. "Just like this. Okay? Don't let up."

She scooted nearer Erin's head, giving her bloodied hands a quick wipe across her jeans. "Michael, keep talking to her."

Waste of time to check her pulse and breathing. There would be none. Terri knew.

She opened Erin's mouth and made sure the airway was clear. Placing her mouth over Erin's, she gave her two breaths.

No response.

With Michael's soft voice soothing, Terri unzipped Erin's sweater, located the midpoint of her chest and began compressions, counting to herself. At 15 she again gave her another two breaths, and then she began to repeat the process.

As the sirens grew louder, Terri focused solely on one thing: sharing her life's breath with a dying Erin Morgan.

⌒

"Over here!" Michael shouted. "This way!"

At last lights grew brighter at the scene and a group of people surrounded Terri, Michael, and Erin. Terri, still breathing for the girl, saw equipment lowered onto the ground. She counted legs. Three sets were partially covered with turnout coats. Two sets wore dark blue slacks. One pair now bent at the knees beside Michael. They belonged to a woman.

"How long you been at this?" a male voice said.

Michael answered. "Six minutes."

Terri gave him a thumbs-up. She wondered if he was interested in emergency medicine. He seemed to have the whistle-toting referee in his head. He wasn't guessing at the passage of time based on her earlier prediction. He knew it had taken the group longer than she anticipated to find them off in the shadows away from the other vehicles.

The woman moved aside Michael's hands. "I'll take over."

"Don't let up," he said.

Terri wanted to hug him.

The male paramedic was kneeling beside her now. "I'm not getting a pulse."

What's your point?

"BP is in the basement—"

"Give me the bag," Terri gasped out the order, referring to the resuscitator. "Start a line."

The guy stared at her.

Michael said, "She's a paramedic."

"Patient's gone. They could use us over—"

"No!" Terri replied fiercely. Images of Sunni flashed through her mind. "No! You will not quit on this one until I say so!"

With no further disagreement, he complied.

∽

A split moment before the ambulance doors were pushed shut, Terri caught a glimpse of Michael standing just outside them. He grinned and held up two thumbs, his hands still gloved, bright red darkening against powder blue. Lights shone behind him like a backdrop, outlining his frame and throwing his face into shadow. She hoped she would see him again and have the opportunity to better express her appreciation. *They had a pulse!* Without the young man's help, that never would have happened.

The female medic drove. In the back, Terri entered into the familiar blur of overlapping procedures and dialogue with the other paramedic and a fireman. She remained in the center, fully engaged. The scene was hers. Erin was hers. *They had a pulse!*

"Ma'am." The fireman spoke. "You're hurt."

"What?"

"Your brow's split."

"Somebody throw me a bandage?"

They returned her brief smile. No hands were available to throw anything.

～

Cutler-Barr Hospital was too far under the circumstances. They arrived at Trinity South's ER, and a surgery team met them. Only then did Terri remove her hands from Erin Morgan. Only then did she stop talking. She watched them wheel her away.

Her hands felt damp. She looked down and noticed she hadn't gloved them. Erin Morgan's blood was on her hands. In how many ways was that true?

Lord, I should have helped her sooner. I should have—

"You're Terri Schuman, aren't you?"

She looked up to see the male paramedic standing before her. He resembled her brothers, dark complexion and stocky build, medium height.

"I was in one of your classes."

"I'm sorry, I don't remember—"

"Chris Herreras."

"Chris. Well, Chris, I'm sorry I yelled at you back there."

"You yelled at me in class too." He smiled. "You always said— Can I take look at your head? That gash is bleeding again."

"I'm fine. What'd I always say?"

"You said we had to have compassion. I never really understood that. I mean, I care about people or I wouldn't be doing this. But, man, I would've given up on that girl tonight.

And now she might make it, all because you had this wild compassion. You made us feel it too."

She let his words sink in. "Did I pass you?"

"No." His smile was a full-fledged grin now. "I avoided you after that, but you were the best instructor I ever had."

She smiled, trying to focus her eyes on his face. It had begun to wiggle.

"Terri, I think you should sit down. I'm guessing you'll need eight stitches. Your eyebrow's about gone."

"You any good at guessing stitches? I'm fine. I'll just…" Words failed to fill in the blank. She watched the room shift from left to right.

"You were in the accident. The Blazer?"

"Yeah." Now it shifted from right to left.

"The car looked totaled. You must hurt somewhere. Everyone's kind of busy around here. Come on, let's go sit—"

As the room spun her into oblivion, Terri wondered if Chris Herreras spoke Spanish.

Thirty-Four

Morning sunlight filtered through semi-closed blinds. Terri dangled her bare legs over the side of the hospital bed. "And here, ladies and gentlemen, we have the world-famous gown in a lovely blue floral print. One-size-fits all. That is, if you're three feet tall and five feet wide."

Lois didn't even crack a smile. "Lie down." It was the third time she'd repeated the order.

"I'm fine."

The tip of her friend's nose almost touched hers. "Nine stitches, a concussion, four cracked ribs, cuts everywhere from crawling through a windshield, and a bruised kidney. You are not fine."

"The hospital needs this bed for sick people."

Lois glared.

Terri lay back down because Lois said so and because the room was teetering out of focus again. A prone position with her head completely immobile seemed to work best.

Evidently the police had found her identification in the Blazer. Lois's name was still listed as an emergency contact person after her parents. With her mother back in Cincinnati, Lois was tagged with hospital duty. She'd been there when a nurse woke Terri up the first time.

Lois arranged the sheet over her and rubbed her arm. "The doctor said you can go home tomorrow morning. Are you still dizzy?"

"No." A sense of queasiness disagreed. She turned onto her side and curled her legs up to her stomach. "Not as bad."

"Sleep, punkin. It'll get better. It'll all get better. I'll keep trying Gabe's number."

Terri closed her eyes and hoped Lois would leave before the tears slid sideways onto the pillow.

Lois had called Shelley, who in turn called their mother. According to a nurse, Maria phoned and talked with the doctor. Shelley left a message, promising to bring dinner. Lois also contacted the neighbors and asked them to care for Zoë. She left word for Kai in the ER, knowing that if he were on duty, he'd show up at Trinity sooner or later. He showed up. Terri didn't remember much about his visit to her room except he announced to anyone within shouting distance that she should be awakened more often.

The attention tugged at her heartstrings. The fact that Erin might not make it yanked at them.

But she knew the tears threatened for another reason. *Love shouldn't hurt like this.* Gabe didn't answer either his cell or house phones. Lois left messages on each. Terri saw no reason to try calling. He was preoccupied. His daughter had been horribly hurt, emotionally and physically. His family needed his attention.

All of it.

⌒

The doctor released Terri from the hospital with strict orders to return if symptoms intensified. She wasn't sure if she would recognize that. Her head felt three times its normal size, and her body couldn't have hurt worse if she'd bailed out of an airplane without a parachute.

As promised, Shelley brought her dinner that evening. Miniature white cartons littered the kitchen table where they sat. Chopsticks poked through the open lids.

Terri smiled. "That was great. Thank you for not bringing chicken soup."

Her sister laughed. "Mom would be appalled."

"We didn't exactly inherit her culinary skills, did we?"

"Nor passion. Who cares as long as there's takeout?" She folded her arms on the table. Though still wearing her business attire of black skirt and white blouse, she seemed much younger than her 39 years with her light brown hair tied back in a pony tail. "Not that I mind if Dave wants to cook."

"I'd eat his cooking any time. Or Gabe's. He makes these garlic mashed potatoes, better than Teague's..."

Their eyes met briefly.

"Terri, why don't you call him?"

"Lois left messages. He'll call when he gets a chance. Jordan needs him now. They've got *years* of catching up to do."

Shelley gave her head a slight shake. "His, hers, ours, theirs."

Terri blew out a noisy breath. "I didn't choose him."

"It happens. I like him a lot."

"Me too."

"Blended families can work. Though why he'd bother with you, I don't know, after the way you bailed out of your own birthday party that he arranged."

Terri shoved back her chair.

"Sit." Shelley stood up and began clearing the table. "You know, you are the world's worst patient. What if all of your patients behaved like you do? You'd have to tie them down. I'll clean up." She laughed. "I wouldn't want you to wear yourself out putting all this stuff in a trash bag. It's hard work. How about some tea?"

"No thanks."

"Can Zoë have this last potsticker?"

The phone rang. Shelley gasped dramatically and paused, bent over the table, her arms in midair, fingers holding cartons, her eyes wide. She whispered, "It's him!"

Her sister's antics didn't help matters. Terri's anticipation mushroomed, throwing her ambivalence all out of proportion. She had wanted—no, she had *needed*—to talk to Gabe since 2:27 A.M. She was shaken to the core by the night's events. There was only one respite. That was in Gabe's arms. But now? Now, after 16 hours of surviving without his comfort, she knew life would go on. And besides, he needed her to be strong, not weak, not dragging his attention away from—

"Hey!" Her sister was waving the ringing cordless in front of her face.

She took it. "Hello?"

"Terri! Are you all right?"

She closed her eyes. That voice of all voices. "Gabe. Hi."

"Hi yourself. Are you all right? What happened?"

Slowly she stood. "I'm fine."

Her sister watched her and frowned. "You are not fine."

Terri waved a shooing hand at her and shuffled stocking-footed into the living room.

Gabe was talking. "Lois left a message. I just got home. Didn't have my cell—"

"How's Jordan?"

"She's good. Better than I expected. She's here at my house now."

"I'm glad." She sat on the couch, wincing at the movement.

"We are so grateful to you. If you hadn't been there when— Howard. Terri, excuse me." His voice grew faint. "Try this one. Yeah. That's good. Sorry." He addressed her again. "The grandparents are here too."

The grandparents? They would be Paula's parents. Gabe's were dead. Add one more to the list. *His, hers, ours, theirs,* and *them,* the ex-in-laws.

"Sweetheart, when I say we're all grateful, I mean we're *all* grateful. The entire family. Thank you."

"You're welcome."

"What about you? Tell me what happened. Lois only said you were in a car accident and your injuries weren't life threatening."

No one knew yet what went on inside that car. No one knew Erin Morgan had been involved. Wisely, Lois had given Terri the space she needed and not demanded details from her. Terri didn't know where or how to begin to describe the horror of Erin hiding in the back of her car, of the crashes, the spinning and flipping, of how she worked in the dark with a stranger named Michael, of Erin's present comatose state.

Her throat constricted. Gabe was the only one she thought she could talk to. But it wasn't going to happen, not now. Not on the phone while he was surrounded by family, his thoughts rightfully occupied with them.

She put a lilt in her tone. "That's about it. The details can wait. I just wanted to make sure Jordan's all right."

"In that cupboard." Gabe's voice was faint again. "Excuse me, Terri. How did it happen? Did someone hit you?"

Not now. No way was she going into it. "I'm really tired."

He expelled a frustrated breath. "Okay, I understand. You don't want to talk right now. But at least tell me how hurt you are."

"It's not bad. I'm sore. My head must have banged into the side window. I got a few stitches."

"Where— Paula, next shelf over. Sorry again. Things are kind of crazy here."

Paula? "Sounds like you have a houseful."

"Yeah. Jordan's getting the royal treatment. Hey, the kids are still planning on you coming over tomorrow night. Are you up for it? Jordan wants to thank you. Say around seven?"

I don't have a car. I don't ever want to drive again. Paula is in your house. Evidently by invitation this time. "I-I don't know, Gabe. I-I'll see."

"Terri, are you sure you're all right?"

She gathered every ounce of strength and poured it into her voice. "Yes, I'm fine. I just need to sleep."

"Then I'll let you go. Take care, and we'll see you tomorrow. Bye."

"Bye."

Terri held the phone to her chest and closed her eyes. They were a family, pulling together in the middle of a crisis. Just like the Schumans had done when her dad died. It was hard to let others into the circle. As a matter of fact, it was almost impossible.

He needed plenty of slack. She owed him plenty of slack after that birthday party fiasco. Not to mention the Lee business and all those times she ignored Gabe's overtures of kindness.

Welcome to your future. He has a family. Deal with it.

⌒

First thing the next morning, Cara Fleming called. Her agitated voice nearly shrieked through the phone. "Terri! What happened?"

She burst into tears at the sound of her friend's voice.

"I'll be there in fifteen minutes."

The coffee wasn't even finished dripping into the carafe before she saw Cara walk into the patio, a uniformed officer in tow. Terri pulled a third mug from the cupboard and opened the door.

Cara stepped inside and wrapped her arms around her, murmuring. "Thank God you're all right. Thank God. Thank You, God. Oh, Terri." She grasped her shoulders and studied her face. "I am so sorry."

"What could you have done? You can't protect the whole world."

"And you can't save it."

They exchanged sad smiles.

"Terri, this is Officer Patone."

He grinned. "We've met."

Oh, no. He was the policeman she'd talked with after Mac's shooting. Like the fire department, he probably had a file going on her, one with new nicknames like "Trouble" or "Schuman the Schmuck."

Terri looked at both of them. "You know about Erin."

Cara nodded. "We know she was in an accident involving three vehicles, one of which was yours. That's it. Do you feel like talking?"

Gabe wouldn't be the first to learn the story. The police needed to know. And Terri needed to talk. Now.

"Have a seat."

~

The session with Cara and Officer Patone felt like a combination critical incident stress debriefing and police investigation. They asked questions and took notes. Terri emoted. Everyone left satisfied.

Almost. Terri knew it was only the first of her personal CISDs. In the past she would have said one was enough, that she would think about things *tomorrow* and then indefinitely postpone doing so. But since fussing at Gabe Andrews outside the emergency room those many months ago, she had learned a thing or two about dealing with life and about dealing with it now, today, not tomorrow. Talking with Gabe might have to wait, but he was not the ultimate source of her comfort and wisdom.

That was God's role.

Late that afternoon she made her way stiffly to the back pew in the vacant sanctuary of St. James on Ashland. She sat, gazed at the stained-glass windows, and waited for her breath to return to normal. Coping with the physical pain was a piece of cake. A few ibuprofen and moving in slow motion did the trick. The fear, however, nearly crippled her.

Her brother Kenny's lifelong fascination with cars meant he always had a spare one sitting around. Glad not to have to bother with a rental, she accepted his offer. He even delivered it to her door. The fear hit her after he drove off with a friend.

While lying in the hospital she knew she would be reluctant to drive. She imagined the first time would unnerve her. She had no idea that simply standing beside the car would cause such dread, such bowling-ball-slung-to-the-stomach kind of fear.

Terri pulled down the kneeling bench and slid onto it. "Lord, thank You for getting me here."

She had never driven *under* the speed limit in her life. At every movement in her peripheral vision she braked. At every red light she sat until someone honked. At every moment she prayed.

Terri closed her eyes.

So much more to pray about than being able to drive again. Mac's knee. Erin's life. Jordan's healing. Gabe.

Gabe.

Love shouldn't hurt like this, should it?

Not knowing where or how to begin, she opened her eyes in frustration. Directly in front of her on the far wall hung a wooden cross no more than 12 inches tall. The wooden Jesus nailed to it was not post-resurrection. There was no beatific expression. No halo, no flowing robes, no soft locks. The small body sagged, straining against the spikes driven through hands and feet. It was covered with a loin cloth. His head, crowned with thorns, fell forward. The agony of Jesus was carved in minute detail.

The small crucifix was hardly noticeable at first glance in the large room, but it drew her attention now.

Because it said everything.

"Yeah, Schuman, love *should* hurt like this."

Thirty-Five

Terri managed to drive to Gabe's street. In the deepening shadows of dusk, she braked even more often. The image of a darkness emerging from the far back of the Blazer replayed in her imagination. She knew now that Erin had hidden behind the backseat, waiting for the right moment. At least her brother's small car had a completely visible backseat and a trunk with a lid.

There were two drawbacks to the car. Its size didn't accommodate Zoë, and its manual transmission was no picnic to drive in her condition. Her entire body protested every time she depressed the clutch and manhandled the stick.

She parked in front of Gabe's *Leave It to Beaver* house, pulled on the emergency brake, and winced. As she had done earlier in the church, she sat still and waited for her breathing to return to a normal cadence. She lowered the visor mirror and watched pain register on her face with each inhalation. Most of the injuries were internal and only hurt when she did something like breathe or shift. Not a big deal. She fluffed her bangs. Their length helped cover the laceration. Nine black-threaded stitches had replaced most of an eyebrow. At least the swelling had gone down some. She wondered if her head had broken the side door window.

What a sight she was! If it hadn't been for the flowers, she would have postponed the reunion with Gabe and his kids. The flowers arrived that morning, a huge bouquet of fresh spring blossoms with a note profusely thanking her. It was signed from "Jordan's grandparents." Their gesture broke down her defenses.

She picked up a shiny purple foil gift bag by its petite handle. Puffy bunches of delicate lighter purple tissue paper overflowed at the top and hid an outrageously expensive bottle of bubble bath. It was a frilly wrapping job, but then Jordan was the frilly type. Terri had told the salesclerk to go for it and tried not to think of the wasted paper.

Grimacing, she opened the car door and hoisted herself out. A fine mist fell. She wondered if it would be enough to wash the blood from the grass along the highway.

Terri rang the doorbell. As soon as she saw the warm twinkle in Gabe's eyes and heard his mesmerizing voice, she knew everything would be fine. They had become a mainstay in her life, a touchstone.

Jordan opened the door. The previously red bruises and swellings had darkened. Stitches closed the cut on her cheekbone.

Terri shifted her thinking. "Hi." She stepped inside and pushed the door shut behind her.

The girl's tentative smile kept slipping away. "You look worse than I do." The flippant tone didn't quite take hold. She quit trying to smile.

Terri held her arms wide and Jordan went into them, letting go a very unladylike sob. Her hug would have brought tears to Terri's eyes if they hadn't already been there.

"Shh." Terri smoothed back the long blonde hair. "It's all over, hon. It's all over."

They embraced for a long time until at last Jordan calmed and Terri wiped her own eyes. She heard voices coming from the back of the house, probably from the family room behind the kitchen. Gabe's voice wasn't distinguishable. A feminine laugh tinkled like a small bell.

She handed Jordan the frilly bag. "I brought something for you."

"You didn't have to do that!" She sat on the couch and pulled out the tissue paper, a genuine smile emerging. "Bubble bath! Thank you!" She opened the lid and smelled the contents. "Mmm."

Terri sat beside her. "It's got lavender and a bunch of other herbs. They're supposed to totally soak away all your stress."

"What makes you think I have stress?" She smiled again. "Did you get some for yourself?"

Terri laughed. "Yeah, actually I did."

"It was a car accident?"

"Fender bender. No big deal."

"It looks like a big deal. How many stitches?"

"Nine."

"You win. I got four."

Terri smiled. "I hear you're getting the royal treatment."

She nodded. "They're going overboard. Even Grandma and Grandpa— Oh, you just missed them! They wanted to meet you."

"They sent me flowers."

"They would. They're sweet." A faraway look had crept into her eyes. Terri knew it would come and go for some time, that haunted sense of something gone terribly wrong.

"Jordan, how are you?"

She looked down at the bottle. "They arrested Jeremy."

Terri tilted her head to make eye contact. "And?"

"It's so hard! But he needs help, and I can't give it."

Terri sighed to herself, glad the girl was not taking responsibility for the abuse inflicted upon her.

"The lawyer told Daddy that if Jeremy goes to a rehab clinic, maybe his sentence won't be so bad."

"Rehab would be a good place to start." She reached over and touched her hand. "And how goes it with the 'rents?"

Jordan giggled. "Terri, don't get me wrong. I love my mom, but I wish she could be more like you. You are so cool. You don't ever freak. I remember you with Jeremy at school..." The faraway look crossed her face again. "Mom's still freaking over the whole thing. She keeps clinging to all of us."

"Totally understandable. I'd probably ground you for the next five years. So, how's your dad doing?"

"He's the only one who can calm her down. Kind of weird. Or sad. I get hurt and the family gets back together. I don't mean *together* together, but the four of us sat at the table and had homecooked dinners two nights in a row. Now we're playing board games. Unreal."

Yeah. Unreal. "Your dad's not freaking then?"

"No. He keeps...apologizing to me." She looked down again.

"For what?"

Jordan shrugged a shoulder. "For not paying closer attention to me. Stuff like that."

"Can you accept his apology?"

She shook her head. "I don't know."

"Well, he doesn't deserve it. He doesn't deserve your forgiveness."

Jordan raised her head and stared at her.

"He doesn't." She pictured her dad and felt an overwhelming sense of gross unfairness. Bryan's voice played in her mind. *Your dad let you down simply by being imperfectly human. That left a wound within you.* "Jordan, you need to forgive him for your own sake. Not his."

"What do you mean?"

"When you don't forgive, something ugly begins to grow inside of you. Eventually you feel so ugly about yourself you don't think you deserve any love or any good thing."

"Why is it up to me? It's his fault."

"Yes, it is. Your forgiving him will not change that. And he will regret his actions for the rest of his life. But you don't have to regret anything or let his wrong dictate who you are. If you decide you want to forgive him, God will help you do that. Forgiveness is a powerful weapon, hon."

Bryan's voice continued to weave itself around the thoughts of her father. *Only God can heal that wound and give you the ability to forgive.* She had fought against it. She didn't want it.

Jordan said, "I don't get it."

"It's heavy. Just think about it?"

Jordan blinked once, slowly. Then she did it again.

Terri smiled. "Your dad does that, blinks twice when he's reached a decision."

"I know. It drives me crazy. Tell me I didn't really do it."

"I'm afraid so."

"Oh, brother!" Her swollen eye interfered with the fluttering of her lids.

"So what did you decide?"

"I'll think about it."

"Good." Terri stood. "Well, I just wanted to see how you're doing. I'd better go now."

"You're not staying? Dad's making popcorn. He makes the best, from scratch, the old-fashioned way. And we're starting Monopoly."

"I have some things to do." *Like figure out how to forgive my dad. Like not be in the way here.*

"Hold on." Jordan rose gingerly and walked to the kitchen doorway. "I told him I wanted some time alone with you, but we thought you were staying." She disappeared. "Daddy!"

Terri missed her chance to slip out. She stood in the center of the room and fiddled with her bangs, listening to muted voices, smelling fresh popcorn, wishing she were almost anywhere else on the face of the earth.

~

Gabe strode into the room. Paula was on his heels.

"Terri!" she cried and pushed her way around Gabe. "Oh my goodness!" She grasped Terri's forearms. "Are you all right?

Oh, this would never have happened if you hadn't been out in the middle of the night with Jordan!"

The woman didn't pause long enough to take a breath as she continued to fuss about Terri's stitches and everything being their fault.

Terri protested. "I'm fine. And it's not your fault." *It would have happened sooner or later with Erin.*

"How can we ever thank you?" Tears pooled in her gorgeous blue eyes. Suddenly she threw her arms around Terri's neck. "Thank you for saving my daughter. Thank you for being her friend!"

In that instant Paula became a hurting, grateful mother. She wasn't the snobby ex-wife Terri wanted to keep at arm's length. "You're welcome." She returned the hug.

Paula released Terri's neck, squeezed her forearms again, and gave her a probing gaze. "If there's ever anything we can do for you, please don't hesitate to let us know. All right?"

Terri nodded. "Thank your parents for me. The flowers they sent are beautiful."

"Of course." She gave her arms a final squeeze and let go. "Are you sure you won't stay?"

"I'm sure. Thank you. I have…things to do."

"Of course," she said again. "Thank you for coming by. Well, I better go keep an eye on Gabe's popcorn. He's very particular about it." She smiled and turned. As she walked past Gabe, she pressed his arm. "Aren't you?" She left the room.

Terri looked at Gabe and stretched her mouth into a brave smile.

He stared at her, wordless for a long moment, anguish written all over his wrinkled forehead. "Sweetheart." His voice was a raw whisper. "You said you were fine."

"I am." She kept smiling.

"Oh, drop the macho mask." He went to her and grabbed her into a fierce hug.

Pain shot through her body and she gasped.

"What?" He loosened his hold and put his hands on her shoulders. "It hurts?"

"A little."

"Where?"

"Mostly my ribs."

"What *happened?*"

"A fender bender. I spun. Rolled. Once. I think."

"You *think?* Does that mean maybe you didn't roll at all or maybe you rolled *more* than once?"

"Gabe, I'm fine. Stop with the third degree."

"You're not fine and the third degree is because you're not talking in complete sentences! Why don't you just tell me what happened?"

"This isn't an appropriate time. It's a long story."

"And I've got all night to listen."

His voice was hoarse, as if he'd talked for days on end, which he probably had. The caramel color in his eyes was hard, like the candies all wrapped up in cellophane.

"Gabe, you don't have all night to listen to me. Your family needs you. We'll sort us out later."

"What does that mean?"

She whispered, "I think you know. I see the four of you pulling together, for Jordan's sake. Evidently Paula's husband isn't part of this picture?"

There was a subtle shift in his breathing.

Oh, no. It was the worst she imagined. "He's *out* of the picture?"

Gabe hesitated. "They're seeing a marriage counselor. Terri, I know what you're thinking, what this looks like, but there's nothing between us."

"Except two children who will always need you both." She kissed his cheek. "Gabriel, I love you no matter what you do."

"No matter what?" The cellophane peeled away.

"No matter what." She smiled softly. "There. You try being on the receiving end of that for a change."

He laid his forehead against hers. "It feels like an awful lot of freedom."

"Oh, there's scads of freedom, but absolutely no condemnation." She felt lightheaded, as though she had accomplished a great feat with a courage not entirely her own. Going against every fiber of her being, she had just let Gabe Andrews go.

"Terri." He kissed her stitches. "Does your mouth hurt?"

She grinned. "No."

"So it's okay if I kiss it?"

"I suppose."

"Dad!" Spencer yelled from the other end of the house.

He groaned and put his chin atop her head. "What?" he shouted.

"Mom's ruining the popcorn!"

"I am not!"

Gabe looked at her, the cellophane encased the caramel again, shutting off the warmth. "No matter what?"

"No matter what." She kissed him quickly, not sure now how long that shot of courage would last.

He followed her to the door and opened it for her. "Let's talk soon. I'm taking some time off work."

"Me too." She went outside. "At least it's not a suspension anymore. Bye."

He waved, his smile not quite strong enough to attract a dimple.

Terri walked to her car, a new sense of freedom on her mind. She had survived everything from Lee to her dad's death to Erin Morgan to Jordan to Paula—all without leaning on Gabe. But she wasn't the Lone Ranger anymore. Rather, she had found the true source of strength. It was in her faith, in that figure on the cross.

Still, she desperately wanted Gabe in her life. She loved him. But there were no guarantees. He faced a new struggle. Should he reunite his family under one roof? That dilemma caused the hardness in his eyes. It came from the guilt, the wanting to fix what he had helped break.

They would both survive his battle. One way or another.

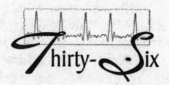

Thirty-Six

For the next three days, Terri kept vigil at Erin's bedside in the ICU. As if working a nine-hour shift, she arrived at eight in the morning and left at five in the evening. The young woman had no other visitors. Comatose, she was breathing on her own, a surprising development to the doctor. *The paradoxical had become familiar.* With her makeup washed off, her pale skin matched the white sheets.

Hours of sitting gave Terri's body the rest it needed to heal. As always with unconscious patients, she talked out loud. No feedback from the hearer gave her mind time to untangle. It gave her soul time to catch up.

She told Erin about the paradoxical in the accidents. About how Erin should not have been able to walk away from her car last summer. About how a tourniquet should have been needed the other night but wasn't. About how she could have lost her leg but didn't.

She read to her from the Bible, all the things she had underlined in the last year and a half, her favorite words that spoke to her heart.

She told Erin about Bob Schuman Sr. She listed all the hurts she could remember that her dad had caused in her lifetime. She imagined Jesus at her side as she experienced each one again in the telling. After a while she began to imagine Him absorbing them, taking on the burden of them. And so, she was learning how to forgive her dad.

She told Erin about Gabe, about how loving him hurt because she had to let him go when she wanted nothing more than to *marry* him. "For real, Erin. Marry him! I thought that about Lee once, but I made it up. I didn't really want to. This— oh! This is totally something else."

She told her about Mac, how he wasn't walking yet but he would as soon as things healed. In the meantime, he was getting around in a wheelchair and teaching EMT classes. "He even says he's coming to church next week."

She told her about Michael, the young man who never showed up again after helping her work on Erin. "I thought he might drop in at the hospital to see how you're doing. But he hasn't. You know there's an angel in the Bible named Michael. What do you think? I still don't know how this kid got to my car, got into it, found all that stuff, and got back to us in less than ten minutes. Less than ten? He made it in *three*. Not possible. Not in the human realm." She smiled at the possibility.

She told her about Cara, about how much she liked the offbeat policewoman even if she did say Erin would be arrested. "Obviously you need help, hon. And it's not the kind I can give. I can forgive—I do forgive you—but that alone is not going to heal. Maybe we can talk about God's healing power. We'll talk about how it works through love and forgiveness."

It was the fourth day. Erin opened her eyes and said in a crystal clear voice, "That's all you've been talking about." And then she slept again.

Terri went home early.

~

She parked in one of the two covered spaces allotted to her condominium. An unfamiliar minivan sat in the other space. Odd. The neighbor usually asked her permission before letting his visitors use it.

Not that it mattered. She grinned as she shut her car door. Who cared about parking spaces? Erin Morgan woke up! Terri felt as though she'd spent the past four days scaling a mountainside. The instant she heard Erin's voice, she knew she'd reached the summit. What an extraordinary sensation! It encompassed all the wonder and beauty of free-falling from an airplane. No, it went beyond anything like that, beyond anything she'd ever experienced. It was free-falling through rainbows. Soaring through them, her ears ringing with great peals of laughter.

She wanted to set up camp and stay a while.

Still grinning, she walked to the privacy fence that enclosed her patio and stretched over the gate to unhook the latch. She pushed open the gate and saw Gabe sitting on the stoop outside the back door.

Umpf! The sight of him felt like a blow between her shoulder blades that sent her tumbling, jolting down the mountainside.

A slow smile spread across his face. "Hi."

She pushed the gate shut and leaned back against it, rooted to the spot and clutching her backpack with crossed arms.

The April afternoon was balmy, an early taste of spring. Slanting sun rays shone on the back of the condo and on Gabe, highlighting the gold in his hair and causing him to squint. He wore jeans, a white T-shirt, and an unzipped navy blue hooded sweatshirt. He sat on the top of the low stoop, his elbows on his knees, his hands dangling, fingers loosely entwined. A casual pose.

That was her future. She was looking straight at it. If Gabe's eyes were still wrapped up in cellophane, she didn't want to see it.

She finally found her voice. "Hi."

"How's Erin?"

She started. He knew? "She, uh, woke up for a minute this afternoon. It's a good sign."

"It's a great sign."

"How did you know?"

"I stopped by the station and heard the story." As always, there was no accusation in his tone. His voice was low, soft. The songs-through-the-night radio announcer voice. "It should have been me who told the story."

"It should have." She gazed off to the side. A grouping of tiny green shoots poked through brown leaves, crocuses making their first appearance. They were promises of spring. Of life after death. "I wanted to tell you. I wanted to tell you first. But with Jordan and everything..."

"Sweetheart."

She glanced at him, not letting her sight linger on his face, and then she averted her eyes again to the crocuses.

"I understand why you didn't tell me, but I should have been there for you. I am so sorry. Will you forgive me for not being with you through it all?"

"It wasn't your fault."

"But the fact is, I let you down. Will you forgive me?"

"Of course I forgive you."

"Then why are you standing over there like a porcupine and not looking at me?"

Surprised at his slightly exasperated tone, she looked at him.

"Why?" he repeated.

"I have my reasons. Why are you sitting over there like a bump on a log?"

"Because between you standing there and Saturday night's kiss, I figure you're not so sure about me."

Her mouth fell open. *He* thought *she* was wavering?

"Don't look so surprised. Any other woman would have been a basket case after someone attempted to murder her. Not to mention spinning and rolling in her car. Or administering CPR while suffering from a concussion. Even the Lone Ranger would have told me that story. But not the love of my life. Nope. She just kisses me goodbye. *Hasta luego!*"

She pressed her lips together to keep from smiling at his accent and convoluted reasoning.

"Slow learner that I am, it takes me a while to figure out why she is not a basket case. She can handle a crisis without me. She's strong and her faith is growing. She'll even forgive me just like that." He snapped his fingers. "This is all great. But add in the facts that she never was too sure about kids and that she's certainly not going to sign up for ex-wives hanging around and flirting. That leaves no question about that kiss. It meant see you around, bucko."

She resisted giving in to him. "So why are you even here?"

"Like I said, she's the love of my life. It's not as though I had a choice."

"Then what took you three and a half days?"

Gabe rubbed his forehead. "This is the tough part." His voice had lost its bantering tone.

The sensation of a downward slide accelerated. Her heart raced. Love of his life—sure. But he wasn't finished.

He lowered his hand and still squinted in the bright light. Melting caramel or cellophane? She couldn't tell.

"Terri, I considered getting back together with Paula."

She squeezed the backpack more tightly against her midsection.

"Because of Jordan." He paused. "I thought if we were a family again, I could make up for all my mistakes. Jordan's problems would be healed. Maybe she could forgive me and my guilt would go away. However, there is no condemnation in Christ. I can't make Jordan forgive me. All I can do is try to love her better than I have in the past. Pretending that I want to be married to her mother is not the way to do it. And besides, Paula is married. Encouraging her to consider divorce again, even if they are having problems, isn't right. She's chosen her road." He blew out a breath. "Terri, I'm not attracted to her in any way whatsoever. I want you to know that when she flirts, it means nothing to me."

She tilted her head, still not sure where he was going with all this confession.

"But I had to think it through, figure it out. Thank you for giving me the freedom to do that."

Thank You, Lord.

"Sweetheart, you said you love me no matter what."

She nodded.

"Then why are you still standing over there?" He smiled.

Time for her own confession. "I thought if you came to tell me goodbye, I didn't want to see it in your eyes. I couldn't handle that."

He shook his head.

"Are you absolutely, positively sure?"

In three long strides, he stood before her, took the backpack, set it on the ground, and gently cupped her face in his hands. "Terri, I love you. I've never been so sure of anything else in my life."

Both dimples showed up as his smile widened. His voice settled like soft velvet against her ears and tickled all the way down to her toes. The caramel melted into liquid, intense heat that warmed her face.

She smiled. "It took you three and a half days to figure this out?"

"No. I had to go shopping. Did you notice the van out there? Spence and I picked that out. Kind of silly not to own a vehicle that accommodates at least four people. Then I took Jordan out. She loves baubles, but I've never given her any. Another example of my learning speed. Anyway. While she was looking at bracelets, I was looking at—" He reached into his sweatshirt pocket and pulled out a tiny gold box topped with a miniature gold bow. "At these."

Terri stared at the box.

"And Jordan comes over and says, which one do you think she'd like? And I said, I'm not sure. Which one do you think she'd like? Just like that. I hope you don't mind that my daughter helped me choose an engagement ring?"

Terri blinked away tears, speechless.

Gabe dropped to one knee and took her hands in his. "But I thought I'd propose all by myself."

She smiled.

"Terri Schuman, I want to spend the rest of my life with you. Will you marry me?"

Two kids and a *Leave It to Beaver* house? What else was there?

"Yes, Gabriel Andrews, I will marry you. *If.*"

"If?" He grinned. "If what?"

"The kids don't come on the honeymoon."

With a laugh he stood and drew her into his arms. "I don't know why they think you're going to make such a great stepmom."

And then he kissed her.

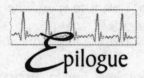

$\mathcal{E}$pilogue

In the absolute middle of nowhere in Iowa, a light southerly breeze wafted across the patio, delivering the sweet scent of clover from some distant field. Under a cloudless July sky, Rachel and Terri sat in white wicker chairs padded with yellow-and-green floral print cushions. Large orange tumblers of iced tea sat on a round, glass-topped table between them.

Eighteen-month-old Victoria Koski Gallagher toddled about, pulling toys from a bright red plastic tub and chattering to herself in some undecipherable language. She was a chubby bundle with a head full of wavy, deep brown hair and blue eyes that matched the department's navy blue shirts. Every so often she stopped to look at the women and pronounce with great solemnity, "Bubbie. Auntie."

Terri whispered to Rachel, "She's got all that hair, but you can still see her ears. Maybe her head will grow into them someday."

"Hush! She's adorable just the way she is." Rachel held out her hand. "Let me see the ring again. It is so gorgeous and so you."

Grinning, she put her left hand in Rachel's and watched the band of diamonds dance in the sunlight. "I think he knows me pretty well. It's not a typical engagement ring, but then I probably wouldn't have wanted to wear a raised stone to work."

Rachel released her hand and smiled. "You haven't stopped grinning since you got here."

She sighed dramatically. "Gabe Andrews."

"He's adorable too."

Terri laughed. "Yeah, he is, isn't he? Could you ever have imagined me with an *adorable* guy?"

"Never!" She laughed with her. "But he's perfect for you."

"I'm finding that to be more true every day. It's been hard to wait, though. I mean, I would have married the guy in April a week after he proposed. But I am glad we're taking things slow and really getting to know each other."

"I've never seen you happier. So contented and at peace."

"It shows then?" She smiled.

"It shows. Are you still thinking a fall wedding?"

"Yeah. We don't want to make a big deal of it. Just family, close friends, two attendants." She paused. "Rache, will you be mine?"

Her eyes filled with tears. "It would be an honor."

"It'd be mine. Thank you." She picked up her glass of iced tea. "You're looking pretty great yourself."

"The absolute middle of nowhere still agrees with me. I loved subbing all year, and I love being a grandma with my grandbaby just down the street."

"Well, there is all that, *and*..." She tilted her head toward the patio wall. "There's that." Her reference to a man in the distance was not lost on Rachel. "You're blushing, girl."

"The sun is hot."

Terri laughed and turned to gaze out over the low stone wall. Beyond it was a stretch of grass that ended in a row of maple trees. Behind those, field after field of soybeans rolled as far as the eye could see. They all belonged to Philip Rockwell, the cause of Rachel's blush. He stood alongside the short, bright green plants, talking with Gabe, their backs to the women.

"Terri," Rachel said.

"Huh?" She turned to her friend. "What's wrong?"

"It's been two years next week."

Wordlessly, Terri reached across the table and grasped her hand.

"I don't know if I can love any other man in the same way."

She nodded. "There's a but in your voice."

"Something's growing soft in my heart."

"It's okay, hon."

"Is it?"

"Yes."

"Philip is extraordinarily kind and considerate. He's my age. He *isn't* a volunteer with our fire department. He makes me feel comfortable."

"And he makes you smile."

"Yes."

"I'm glad."

Rachel nodded. "Okay."

"Okay." For now, nothing else needed to be said.

Terri let go of Rachel's hand and looked back out toward the fields. The men strolled up through the grass. She couldn't help but smile. Gabe's golden hair reflected the sunlight. At the sight of his bronzed arms and strong shoulders in the jade green polo shirt, she wanted to giggle like a schoolgirl.

He caught her gaze and flashed a two-dimple grin. What else was there?

As they reached the low wall, he stooped over and held out his arms to Victoria. "Hey, munchkin. Uncle Gabe needs a hug."

The girl squealed and toddled over to him. "Unc!"

He scooped her up and twirled in a slow circle.

Rachel said, "He's so good with her. A natural."

She heard the implication in her friend's voice. "No way."

Rachel laughed. Gabe danced with the baby. Philip, the kind and considerate farmer, smiled.

The last vestiges of Terri's macho mask slipped away. Over Victoria's little head, Gabe winked at her. She smiled back, certain she wouldn't miss the Lone Ranger at all. Not one bit.

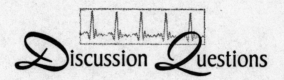

Discussion Questions

Discussion Questions

Little by little Terri discovers the reality of Romans 8:1: "There is therefore no condemnation for those who are in Christ Jesus," which is the theme of the book.

1. What are some of the events, situations, and people that help make this truth a reality to her?

2. In what ways has the truth of Romans 8:1 been revealed in your own life?

3. Terri feels unloved and unaccepted by her father. Can you identify with her feelings?

4. How do you think your relationship with your father has affected your relationship with God, our heavenly Father?

5. Though Terri's emotional wounds were unintentionally inflicted by her father, she must ultimately forgive him for her own sake. They are at the root cause of her self-condemnation and her inability to completely grasp God's unconditional love. She calls forgiveness a powerful weapon. What are some examples of how she forgives others? What were the results?

6. How have you been changed through the process of forgiving someone else?

7. Does the fact that God unconditionally loves you make a difference in your life? If so, how?

8. Not feeling loved by her father contributed to her perceived need to wear a "macho mask." Do you feel you have mask-free communication with anyone?

9. Terri and Gabe say there is a freedom in being loved by someone "no matter what." What do you think they mean by a freedom?

10. Do you love someone "no matter what"? Does someone love you in that way?

Books by Sally John

The Other Way Home Series

A Journey by Chance
After All These Years
Just to See You Smile
The Winding Road Home

In a Heartbeat Series

In a Heartbeat
Flash Point
Moment of Truth

The author invites you to contact her at:
sallyjohnbook@aol.com

Or visit her website and chat with other readers at:
www.sally-john.com

Sally John is a former teacher and the author of several books, including the popular books of The Other Way Home series (*A Journey by Chance, After All These Years, Just to See You Smile,* and *The Winding Road Home*). *Flash Point* is the second book in Sally's new In a Heartbeat series. Sally and her husband, Tim, live in the country surrounded by woods and cornfields. The Johns have two grown children, a daughter-in-law, and a granddaughter.